LOVECRAFTIAN PROCEEDINGS 5

HIPPOCAMPUS PRESS LIBRARY OF CRITICISM

S. T. Joshi, *Primal Sources: Essays on H. P. Lovecraft* (2003)
———, *The Evolution of the Weird Tale* (2004)
———, *Lovecraft and a World in Transition: Collected Essays on H. P. Lovecraft* (2014)
———, *The Recognition of H. P. Lovecraft: His Rise from Obscurity to World Renown* (2021)
Robert W. Waugh, *The Monster in the Mirror: Looking for H. P. Lovecraft* (2006)
———, *A Monster of Voices: Speaking for H. P. Lovecraft* (2011)
———, *The Tragic Thread in Science Fiction* (2019)
———, *A Monster for Many: Talking with H. P. Lovecraft* (2021)
Scott Connors, ed., *The Freedom of Fantastic Things: Selected Criticism on Clark Ashton Smith* (2006)
Ben Szumskyj, ed., *Two-Gun Bob: A Centennial Study of Robert E. Howard* (2006)
S. T. Joshi and Rosemary Pardoe, ed., *Warnings to the Curious: A Sheaf of Criticism on M. R. James* (2007)
Massimo Berruti, *Dim-Remembered Stories: A Critical Study of R. H. Barlow* (2011)
Gary William Crawford, Jim Rockhill, and Brian J. Showers, ed., *Reflections in a Glass Darkly: Essays on J. Sheridan Le Fanu* (2011)
Steven J. Mariconda, *H. P. Lovecraft: Art, Artifact, and Reality* (2013)
Massimo Berruti, S. T. Joshi, and Sam Gafford, ed., *William Hope Hodgson: Voices from the Borderland: Seven Decades of Criticism on the Master of Cosmic Horror* (2014)
Donald R. Burleson, *Lovecraft: An American Allegory—Selected Essays on H. P. Lovecraft* (2015)
Mark Valentine and Timothy J. Jarvis, ed., *The Secret Ceremonies Critical Essays on Arthur Machen* (2019)

Lovecraft Annual
Dead Reckonings
Lovecraftian Proceedings
Penumbra

Lovecraftian Proceedings 5

Select Papers from the Dr. Henry Armitage Memorial Scholarship Symposium, NecronomiCon Providence: 2022

Edited by Elena Tchougounova-Paulson

Hippocampus Press

New York

Copyright © 2024 by Hippocampus Press. The terms "NecronomiCon Providence" and "Dr. Henry Armitage Memorial Scholarship Symposium" are trademarks of the Lovecraft Arts & Sciences Council, Inc., and used by permission. All works are © 2024 by their respective authors.

Published by Hippocampus Press
P.O. Box 641, New York, NY 10156
www.hippocampuspress.com

All rights reserved.
No part of this work may be reproduced in any form or by any means without the written permission of the publisher.

Cover illustration "The Shadow of His Smile" by Pete Von Sholly.
Cover design by Barbara Briggs Silbert.
Hippocampus Press logo designed by Anastasia Damianakos.

First Edition
1 3 5 7 9 8 6 4 2

ISBN 978-1-61498-450-4 (paperback)
ISBN 978-1-61498-456-6 (ebook)

Contents

Preface 7
    NIELS-VIGGO S. HOBBS

Foreword 9
    DENNIS P. QUINN

Introduction "Lovecraftian myth in the making: acquiring the path" 13
    ELENA TCHOUGOUNOVA-PAULSON

"Relatively Obscure Men": Continental Drift Theory and the Sociology of Science in *At the Mountains of Madness* 21
    BENJAMIN BREYER

Charting Ecologies of Violence through Algernon Blackwood's "The Willows" 36
    MATTHEW HOLDER

Inappropriate Death and the Body as Object in "The Hound" and "Herbert West—Reanimator" 56
    NICOLETTE A. WILLIAMS

"The Call of Cthulhu" and the Rhetoric of Things 71
    MICHELLE SAAVEDRA

Lovecraftian Elements in the Philosophy of Nick Land and the Cybernetic Culture Research Unit 96
    ROBERT LANDAU AMES

Firearms in the Life and Works of H. P. Lovecraft 116
    N. R. JENZEN-JONES, GEORGE COLCLOUGH, AND HANS-CHRISTIAN VORTISCH

Transdimensional Voices in Weird Fiction: Reverb, Echo, and Delay in Sound-Related Texts 145
    NATHANIEL R. WALLACE

Digital Dream-Quests: A Collaborative Project in Lovecraftian Game Studies 165
    DANIEL J. HOLMES

Hereditary Memories of Fright: The Gaming Industry's Response to Lovecraft's Xenophobia as Viewed through Most Recent Major Releases 187
    JOSHUA E. SHOCKLEY IV

Asexual Possibility in the Life and Fiction of H. P. Lovecraft 201
    RILEY CHIRRICK

Toward a Definition of Lovecraft Punk 216
    HEATHER MILLER

The Window to Madness: Creativity in Lovecraftian Fiction 227
    KYLE GAMACHE

Lovecraftian Elements in Cormac McCarthy's *Blood Meridian* 247
    ZACHARY K. RUTLEDGE

Gnosticism, Epicureanism, and Deism in H. P. Lovecraft's Fictive
   Cosmology 266
    LORIN GEITNER

Naked Sailors in a Swamp: Sea Men and Homoerotic Initiations in
   Three Lovecraft Tales 276
    PETER MUISE

Appendix: Abstracts from The Fifth Biennial Dr. Henry Armitage
   Memorial Scholarship Symposium of New Weird Fiction and Lovecraft-
   Related Research Providence, RI, 19–21 August 2022 293

Contributors 307

Index 313

Preface

The fifth iteration of the Dr. Henry Armitage Memorial Scholarship Symposium, concurrent with NecronomiCon Providence, 22–25 August 2022, came in the wake of a global pandemic that reminded us of just how indifferent the universe really is to our collective feeble existence. Yet, despite the real losses, lingering fears, warranted cautions, and heightened challenges, we managed to reunite for another remarkable gathering of Lovecraftian and weird academics, both professional and amateur, and showcase some superb scholarship.

As the overall director for all the swirling madness that is NecronomiCon Providence, and after five runs and hurtling toward a sixth, I have always strongly felt that the Armitage Symposium is the heart and soul of the convention. The symposium is a curated grassroots platform for any researcher who has something to contribute to a vibrant and expanding discourse on all things related to weird fiction, especially on topics related to Lovecraftiana or adjacent. Over the past decade-plus, we have hosted more than a hundred and thirty presentations, expanding our understanding and appreciation of the field, and opening the doors for new, diverse voices in weird academia. I couldn't be prouder.

Given the unmitigated success of the Armitage Symposium, I must extend credit and heartfelt appreciation to those who most helped make it a reality: Professor Dennis Quinn, who chaired the symposium from 2015 to 2022; Dr. John Sefel, who was the first chair in 2013; and Dr. Elena Tchougounova-Paulson, who has assisted in previous years and is now coming on as chair for 2024. Elena is also editing the 2022 proceedings embodied in this present work, a major task equally deserving of praise. I'm also grateful for the unwavering support, both material and metaphysical, of Ken Birdwell, who has kept this symposium going since the very first year. As for the published proceedings, I must also warmly thank Derrick Hussey and Hippocampus Press for providing the needed and welcome print home for this work over the years, and to the various editors and reviewers who have so ably made the series the important contribution to weird academia that it has become.

And, thank you, dear reader and researcher, for delving into this work. For my part, this whole effort is for you. I have the honor to be,
    Your servant,

Niels-Viggo S. Hobbs, Ph.D.
Executive Director, Lovecraft Arts & Sciences Council /
NecronomiCon Providence

Foreword

Dennis P. Quinn
Past editor of the *Lovecraftian Proceedings*
Chair of the Armitage Symposium, NecronomiCon Providence

I first encountered the works of H. P. Lovecraft on a blazing hot Sacramento, California, afternoon in July 1988. I had moved from there a few years earlier with my family to the eastern suburb of Los Angeles called Glendora after finishing high school. During a break in the overindulgent activities, I went to a Tower Books to catch up with a friend who was still in high school and find something to read during my down time when I knew friends would be working. It was *The Tomb and Other Tales* with the classic Del Rey cover. I carried that book with me throughout the summer, reading the short stories during my spare time. And even though I was enjoying myself with good friends, when I snuck off to read such stories in the anthology as "The Tomb," "The Festival," "In the Walls of Eryx," along with Lovecraft's early tale, "The Beast in the Cave," I was captivated by the settings, prose, and feeling of dread that was just below the surface during the joyful Northern California summer.

I returned to that little Del Rey book often and was especially drawn to a list of Lovecraft's stories that was included in the book's appendix. I did not know it at the time, but the stories included in that volume paled in comparison to many of those books, which were just titles to me at the time.

It wasn't until I was in graduate school at Claremont Graduate University studying the history of Christianity when I began researching modern religions based on contemporary fiction, particularly LaVeyan Satanism. I discovered that Lovecraft's so-called Cthulhu Mythos formed the basis for a chapter in *The Satanic Rituals* largely written by Michael Aquino before founding the Temple of Set. I decided to store this information away for future reference.

The opportunity came a few years later when a colleague who was a practicing Wiccan was organizing a conference at Claremont Graduate University on chaos and modern paganism. That conference allowed me the opportunity to explore the topic in more depth. I also became interested in the influence of Roman literature on Lovecraft's literature and discovered that chapter "The Tale of Inspector Legrasse" in "The Call of Cthulhu" had some parallels with Livy's account of the Bacchanalia and the Roman persecution of that cult. The original presentation was an amalgamation of the two topics, which I would detangle into two publications, as noted below.

It was not too long after the paganism conference that I discovered that a conference on H. P. Lovecraft was happening in Phoenix, AZ (of all places!) in January 2011. I attended with a copy of a paper in hand I had written, entitled "Endless Bacchanal."[1] Other than attending the conference to see what the Lovecraft community was like, I had a rather ambitious goal: to deliver the paper to S. T. Joshi directly and ask him to read it. Once I discovered who he was, I walked up to him, clumsily shook his hand, thanked him for his work on Lovecraft and other small talk, and then, which hands shaking, I handed him the printed essay and somehow asked him if he would be willing to give it a read and tell me what he thought. To be honest, I thought he might just put it away somewhere in his room and fly home without it. But the next day he saw me and said he would like to publish it in *Lovecraft Annual* No. 5. I was elated! I realized at that time that S. T. Joshi was and always will be very generous to young scholars delving into scholarship on Lovecraft and weird fiction.

A few years later in 2013 witnessed the first NecronomiCon Providence. I eagerly signed up and submitted a proposal based on my work on esoteric practitioners and religionists influenced by Lovecraft's Cthulhu Mythos. My paper was accepted, I attended, and I was hooked![2] NecronomiCon is an amazing hybrid of academic talks, author readings, gaming, and good fun with eclectic (and sometimes eccentric) colleagues. While working with the editor of the first *Lovecraftian Proceedings*, the very smart and generous Dr. John Michael Sefel, he asked me to take over du-

---

1. Dennis P. Quinn, "Endless Bacchanal: Rome, Livy, and Lovecraft's Cthulhu Cult," *Lovecraft Annual* 5 (2011): 188-15.

2. Dennis P. Quinn, "Genuine Pagans: A Foray into Lovecraftian Religions," *Lovecraftian Proceedings* 1. New York: Hippocampus Press, (2015): 215-33.

ties as editor of the second volume, since he had landed a professor position and was regretfully too busy to take on the task again. So that is how I got involved as editor. Now it is time for me to pass the baton to the excellent scholar and editor, Dr. Elena Tchougounova-Paulson.

It has been a tremendously rewarding experience editing *Lovecraftian Proceedings* 2 and 3 and coediting 4. I am indebted to Derrick Hussey, who, like the captain in silken robes from *The Dream Quest of Unknown Kadath*, has steered Hippocampus Press through calm and stormy waters. He has championed the *Lovecraftian Proceedings* into much of the success and respect the peer-reviewed publication has received over the years. In the editing process, the greatest thanks go to David E. Schultz who, like the venerable Henry Armitage himself, with use of his proverbial magic powder helped unveil to me editorial phantoms I was unable to see on my own.

I am excited to see *Lovecraftian Proceedings* 5, edited by Dr. Elena Tchougounova-Paulson, continuing the tradition of bringing high-quality new scholarship on Lovecraft and weird fiction in general to academia and interested fans and readers. Dr. Tchougounova-Paulson's work in this volume represents the best in academic editing and organization. I look forward to watching the *Lovecraftian Proceedings* grow in popularity and usefulness in furthering high-quality scholarship by the amazing group of scholars who present their original work at NecronomiCon Providence to ensure continued vital research and future revelations.

Introduction: "Lovecraftian Myth in the Making: Acquiring the Path"

Elena Tchougounova-Paulson
Editor of Lovecraftian Proceedings
Chair of the Dr. Henry Armitage
Memorial Scholarship Symposium
(Cambridge, UK)

The collection of works in this volume comprises the papers that emerged from the conference talks delivered at the Henry Armitage Symposium, NecronomiCon Providence, RI, on 19-21 August 2022. What makes this volume so special? To answer this question, let us look at the premise of the Symposium—its purposes, its significance, its location and, what is the most important matter, its people.

In this day and age, interest in academic Lovecraftiana and weird/horror studies is as strong as ever: starting as a niche literary commemoration to an obscure New England based pulp fiction author who died in dismal precarity in 1937, and subsequently a celebration of his works, which gained more and more prominence in the late 1960s/early 1970s (at such events as the World Science Fiction Conventions, or Worldcons),[1] it eventually grew into a colossal stream of studies, fandom, cinema and gaming, forming the *weird canon*. It feels at times as if some of those who love and treasure Lovecraft's universe would like to turn the clock back to assure the author that he will be appreciated and valued—things

---

1. One of the Worldcons, the 26th Baycon, took place at UC Berkeley and neighbouring Oakland in 1968, and brought together a few of HPL's most legendary contemporaries, some of whom were his friends (or, at least, good acquaintances), pen pals and colleagues—E. Hoffmann Price, Robert Bloch, Fritz Leiber, and others. There is an audio recording of one of the panels they were participating in, uploaded on YouTube (In: Baycon (1968) Worldcon–Remembrance of Things Past: H. P. Lovecraft and the Pulps panel).

that Lovecraft himself was quite skeptical about, considering his fiction.[2] Many of his friends and correspondents who knew him well were still alive until the early 2000s, and a new generation of researchers could see the progression of Lovecraftian studies to its full scale.

And this is critical—and, surely, would have been extremely meaningful to Lovecraft, too: it is common knowledge that due to financial instability (a result of a chain of crucial family misfortunes), his dream to obtain a degree at Brown University was crushed, and his somewhat frustrated urge to make scientific discoveries that could be dangerous, mysterious and macabre was released in his fiction, with a cursed grimoire-like encyclopaedia of phantasmal realms (*Necronomicon*) and a variety of scholarly types of protagonists—Prof. Emeritus George Angell ("The Call of Cthulhu"), Prof. Ferdinand C. Ashley ("The Shadow out of Time"), folklorist Eli Davenport ("The Whisperer in Darkness") and, among many others, Dr. Henry Armitage, chief librarian at Miskatonic University ("The Dunwich Horror"), whose name was given to the Symposium, which resulted in creating the current *Proceedings*.

That is why from the very beginning the chronicles of academic events dedicated to Lovecraft's life, his legacy, and publishing his works had that unmistakable feeling of discovering forbidden treasure, hidden in sacred volumes—a *Mysterium Conjunctionis* of sorts. Most of the time it took place in Providence, the birthplace of Lovecraft and his main source of inspiration, as he directly associated himself with the city, becoming its familial spirit[3]. And so did the people who fearlessly started the entire "Lovecraft's impact on the outward world" movement—Arkham House/Senior Lovecraftians,[4] and young enthusiasts from the 1970s and 1980s launched the first ever academic journal, *Lovecraft Studies* (starting in 1979/80 at Necro-

---

2. Look, for example, at his well-known and widely quoted statement about the negative critical appraisal of *At the Mountains of Madness* that did "more than anything to end my effective fictional career" (Joshi 236).

3. Of course, his most famous motto about himself as an embodiment of Providence, featured in his letter to James F. Morton, from 16 May 1926 (the first line was later carved on his gravestone, erected in 1977): "I am Providence, and Providence is myself—together, indissolubly as one, we stand thro' the ages; a fixt monument set aeternally in the shadow of Durfee's ice-clad peak!" (JFM 93)

4. We are using this term loosely here, mostly as an analogue of the chronological frameworks of the movement, as in case with *Senior/Junior Symbolists*, for example.

nomicon Press), and S. T. Joshi, the leading figure in Lovecraftiana, established the field of research—historical, philosophical, sociological, psychological, to name a few more angles—as we all know it: as an inexhaustive source of intellectual inspiration.

And then, there was another milestone in the theoretical history of the weird, The H. P. Lovecraft Centennial Conference, which was held at Brown University in Providence in 1990 (and was followed by unveiling of the Commemorative Plaque): it defined what we now consider as the primary standard of the Lovecraftian workshop—meticulous and engaging without being rigidly scholastic, sensibly challenging without being sanctimonious, and truly entertaining, too: after speaking about the macabre, mortido and the *Unheimlich* in connection with the omnipotent Great Old Ones, one eventually needs a bit of a distraction during the conference panels' breaks. This last part, which involves the art exhibition and the tour around the city of Providence, including all the key landmarks (the addresses where the Old Gent lived; the University and John Hay Library, where the extensive collection of Lovecraft's manuscripts and letters is held, Ladd Observatory, where he spent long hours studying astronomy, and Swan Point Cemetery, his burial place), has evolved into a tradition of its own: now, at the time of the new iteration of Lovecraftian scholarship—NecronomiCon Providence, the biennial August event that hosts the Armitage Symposium, everyone who has been lucky enough to participate in those, simultaneously adds to the creation of the new phase of Lovecraftian mythology, when one's perception of the canonical Mythos has been enriched with acquiring *Dasein* of the inseparable bond between the author and the place, as Lovecraft's delight regarding Providence had always been constant. We can see it everywhere in Lovecraft's immense correspondence; for example, in his letter to Rheinhart Kleiner from 16 April, Lovecraft says in particular:

> It is with the utmost delight that I hear of your proposed New-England trip, during which you certainly must not fail to give Providence's "hidden ways & quaint old places"[5] a liberal share of your time. [...] This time we can inspect wonders untasted last year. [...] we can next time behold some typical Georgian *interiors* by visiting the "Pendleton House" on Benefit Street. This house is a typical Colonial edifice, furnished magnificently with the richest

---

5. From Kleiner's poem "At Providence in 1918."

Georgian furniture, as if the owner were still in possession & the calendar indeed turned back to my beloved XVIIIth century. (RK 133)

And so, all of those who can share this infatuation—with the Zeitgeist of the city and the Old Gent himself—are presented in the current issue of *Lovecraftian Proceedings* 5: each of their papers is an excellent exercise in approaching the different facets of the Lovecraftian/weird canon. In his paper "'Relatively Obscure Men': Continental Drift Theory and the Sociology of Science in *At the Mountains of Madness*" Benjamin Breyer is exploring ideas from geology (more precisely, the continental drift hypothesis that was popularized in the early twentieth century by the German climatologist and geodesist Alfred Wegener) in connection with Lovecraft's magnum opus, *At the Mountains of Madness*, whereas Matthew Holder in his work "Charting Ecologies of Violence through Algernon Blackwood's '"The Willows'" is raising awareness of the ecological issues in weird fiction that are shown in forms of environmental degradation and the *revenge of nature* in one of the most famous of Lovecraft's stories, "The Colour out of Space," and Algernon Blackwood's "The Willows."

In her detailed essay, "Inappropriate Death and the Body as Object in 'The Hound' and 'Herbert West–Reanimator'," Nicolette A. Williams analyses two of Lovecraft's stories, "Herbert West–Reanimator" and "The Hound," to demonstrate how the ominous and problematic Gothic figure of a *necrophile* is connected with the entire discourse of characters' interactions with death and the dead, and Michelle Saavedra in her article "'The Call of Cthulhu' and the Rhetoric of Things" takes an epistemological approach and looks at Lovecraft's legacy ("The Call of Cthulhu" in particular) through the lens of *occultic rhetoric*. Robert Landau Ames's take on Lovecraft might look unexpected, but only at the first glance: in his paper "Lovecraftian Elements in the Philosophy of Nick Land and the Cybernetic Culture Research Unit" he demonstrates how the concept of Lovecraft's *nonhuman forces* among others impacted the works of English philosopher Nick Land and the Cybernetic Culture Research Unit (which Land was a member of) on the basis of techno-science, i.e. Accelerationism.

In the paper "Firearms in the Life and Works of H. P. Lovecraft" N. R. Jenzen-Jones, in collaboration with his colleagues, George Colclough and Hans-Christian Vortisch, establishes a thorough archival and historical study of the presence of firearms in the life of Lovecraft, as well as the portrayal of different types of guns in HPL's works; meanwhile, in his piece "Transdimensional Voices in Weird Fiction: Reverb, Echo and Delay in Sound-Related Texts" Nathaniel R. Wallace is researching the topic of *transdimensional voices and sounds* (echoes and reverberations) and their transfer from the works of weird fiction, including Lovecraft, Algernon Blackwood, Ambrose Bierce and others, to the world of television and cinema (*The Twilight Zone* in particular). Daniel J. Holmes's paper "Digital Dream-Quests: A Collaborative Project in Lovecraftian Game Studies" explores the exact intersection of Lovecraftiana and game studies and examining how Lovecraftian themes were incorporated into video games and put Lovecraft's name into the core of game design; Joshua E. Shockley's article "Hereditary Memories of Fright: The Gaming Industry's Response to Lovecraft's Xenophobia as Viewed Through Most Recent Major Releases," on the other hand, also examines the game industry, but this time from the perspective of acknowledging Lovecraft's xenophobic views and dealing with these complex issues, addressing them in the newly released role-playing games, such as *Call of Cthulhu* (2018) and *The Sinking City* (2019).

In "Asexual Possibility in the Life and Fiction of H. P. Lovecraft" Riley Chirrick considers another intersection of gender studies/queer studies/Lovecraftiana, focusing on the introspective question of Lovecraft's asexuality and its manifestations in his legacy; in her work "Toward a Definition of Lovecraft Punk" Heather Miller studies the subject of the pervasiveness of Lovecraftian lore in a variety of pop-cultural angles of modernity—especially in its punk (i.e., rioting and socially inconvenient) phase. Kyle Gamache takes another approach—a clinical and psychological one—in "The Window to Madness: Creativity in Lovecraftian Fiction," wherein he touches upon the subject of madness/insanity and creativity (including established archetypes, such as *the mad genius* and *the doomed artist*) in retrospect, analysing the works of Lovecraft and, specifically, the impact of Edgar Allan Poe on them. Zachary Rutledge's article "Lovecraftian Elements in Cormac McCarthy's *Blood Meridian*" is dedicated to a comparative study, juxtaposing Lovecraft's texts with Cormac McCarthy's *Blood Meridian*, highlighting certain identifiable commonalities—a grotesque aesthetics, a parodic evocation of religious symbology, and others.

In his paper "Gnosticism, Epicureanism and Deism in H. P. Lovecraft's Fictive Cosmology" Lorin Geitner explores Lovecraft's religious outlook and his personal view of *deity* in regard of the different systems of religious/mythological beliefs and seeking the answers to which of those systems is applicable to Lovecraft's Great Old Ones cosmology, whereas Peter Muise's piece, "Naked Sailors in a Swamp: Sea Men and Homoerotic Initiations in Three Lovecraft Tales," is another essay on gender studies/Lovecraftian discourse interconnectedness, considering queer topics in Lovecraft's renowned story "The Call of Cthulhu."

The body of research that has been done by the contributors for this volume is incredibly versatile and innovative, and it is indisputable that there is much more to come.

As a new editor of *Lovecraftian Proceedings*, I want to express my enormous gratitude to my incredible predecessor, Professor Dennis P. Quinn, who is the prime example of a remarkable scholar and a truly amazing friend: his mentorship was essential and irreplaceable. From my side, I promise to do my very best to continue all the fantastic work he has done for the *Proceedings* and the Armitage Symposium. Another huge "thank you" goes to our fabulous and highly professional reviewers, whom I cannot name, but who undoubtedly did their best to prepare the papers for publication.

My warmest thanks to the organizer of the NecronomiCon Providence, Niels Hobbs: without him, the Armitage Symposium with all its wonderful attendees and variety of panels would not be possible. I also want to wholeheartedly thank the legendary S. T. Joshi, who is a true pillar of the whole academic Lovecraftian community and to whom we must all be forever grateful for launching the field of Lovecraftian/weird fiction studies; and my thanks to the fantastic David E. Schultz, too, whose expertise in publishing Lovecraftian works is tremendous, and extraordinary Derrick Hussey, the head of Hippocampus Press, one of the best publishing houses in the field, thanks to whom all the works of Lovecraftian/horror/weird fiction and nonfiction can be introduced to the widest circles of readers and researchers.

I am looking forward to meeting all our colleagues and friends for new—weird and wonderful—explorations of the Lovecraftian world.

Works Cited

Joshi, S. T. *A Subtler Magick: The Writings and Philosophy of H. P. Lovecraft.* Mercer Island, WA: Starmont House, 1996.

Abbreviations

HPL	H. P. Lovecraft
AT	*The Ancient Track: Complete Poetical Works*, ed. S. T. Joshi (Hippocampus Press, 2013)
CE	*Collected Essays*, ed. S. T. Joshi (Hippocampus Press, 2004–06; 5 vols.)
CF	*Collected Fiction: A Variorum Edition*, ed. S. T. Joshi (Hippocampus Press, 2015–17; 4 vols. [citations to vol. 4 are taken from the revised edition of 2022])
DS	*Dawnward Spire, Lonely Hill: The Letters of H. P. Lovecraft and Clark Ashton Smith*, ed. David E. Schultz and S. T. Joshi (Hippocampus Press, 2017)
ES	*Essential Solitude: The Letters of H. P. Lovecraft and August Derleth*, ed. David E. Schultz and S. T. Joshi (Hippocampus Press, 2013)
ET	*Letters to Elizabeth Toldridge and Anne Tillery Renshaw*, ed. David E. Schultz and S. T. Joshi (Hippocampus Press, 2014)
IAP	S. T. Joshi, *I Am Providence: The Life and Times of H. P. Lovecraft* (Hippocampus Press, 2010)
JVS	*Letters to J. Vernon Shea, Carl F. Strauch, and Lee McBride White*, ed. S. T. Joshi and David E. Schultz (Hippocampus Press, 2016)
LL	S. T. Joshi and David E. Schultz, *Lovecraft's Library: A Catalogue*, 5th ed. (Hippocampus Press, 2024)
MWM	*Letters to Maurice W. Moe and Others*, ed. David E. Schultz and S. T. Joshi (Hippocampus Press, 2018)
OED	*Oxford English Dictionary*
RK	*Letters to Rheinhart Kleiner and Others*, ed. S. T. Joshi and David E. Schultz. New York: Hippocampus Press, 2020.
SP	*A Sense of Proportion: The Letters of H. P. Lovecraft and Frank Belknap Long*, ed. David E. Schultz and S. T. Joshi (Hippocampus Press, 2024)
WBT	*Letters to Wilfred B. Talman and Helen V. and Genevieve Sully*, ed. David E. Schultz and S. T. Joshi (New York: Hippocampus Press, 2019)

"Relatively Obscure Men": Continental Drift Theory and the Sociology of Science in *At the Mountains of Madness*

Benjamin Breyer
Lecturer, Department of English, First Year Foundation, Barnard College

H. P. Lovecraft's lifelong interest in modern science is well evidenced in his public writings and private correspondence. His incorporation of modern science into his stories of cosmic horror, especially in his later work, is one of his defining contributions to the genre of weird fiction. Especially notable in this regard among his late works is *At the Mountains of Madness*, which Lovecraft took pains to make as scientifically accurate as possible. For example, S. T. Joshi ("Introduction" to *Thing on the Doorstep* 420) notes that, when the story was finally accepted for publication, Lovecraft made changes to delete a hypothesis about Antarctica that had been disproven by aerial explorers after he had originally drafted the work. Beyond the scientific facts that he refers to, Lovecraft's use of some of the conventions of scientific writing in his novel reflects the broader influence of modern science on his writing. Even though his use of scientific writing genres such as the reports and research articles common in scientific journals is noted by Fritz Leiber in his essay "A Literary Copernicus" (55), the subject has not received in-depth attention from scholars in the case of individual works such as *At the Mountains of Madness*. More recently, S. T. Joshi ("Time, Space") has examined the role of science in Lovecraft's literary work, but he mainly focuses only on scientific principles in the stories, which he tends to interpret as providing an intellectual foundation in some cases.

This paper analyzes Lovecraft's use of the conventions of scientific writing in *At the Mountains of Madness* as they pertain to the reporting of new observations and explanatory theories. I will argue that the inclusion of theories of continental drift into the natural history presented in the story is more than simply Lovecraft's efforts at writing scientifiction. The then-contemporary debate over continental drift in the American academy offered Lovecraft a model for the promotion of and resistance to revolutionary scientific ideas, and the leading proponent of continental drift theory, Alfred Wegener, presented a model of a scientist who sought to revolutionize what was known about the earth's history. This historical context provides a better basis for understanding Lovecraft's unnamed narrator's use of scientific rhetoric and its sociological basis. More broadly, focusing on the probable influence of the continental drift debate's rhetoric and sociology of science leads to a fuller understanding of the range of ways through which Lovecraft sought to achieve a level of scientific realism. Additionally, the narrator's use of scientific rhetoric to support his claims to new knowledge draws attention to the mechanism by which Lovecraft connected epistemology with supernatural horror.

Lovecraft's correspondence includes several references to *At the Mountains of Madness* as a "scientifiction" (cf. JVS 53; *Lord of a Visible World* 271). Hugo Gernsback introduced this term in his *Amazing Stories* magazine, where he defined it as "a charming romance intermingled with scientific fact and prophetic vision" (3). Writing to J. Vernon Shea, Lovecraft expressed his belief that "there is a region on the border betwixt weirdness & 'scientifiction' [and that] the 'Mountains of Madness' belongs largely to this type" (JVS 30). He made this statement at about the same time that he was also beginning to envision how cosmic horror could be built upon elements of the known universe:

> The time has come when the normal revolt against time, space, & matter must assume a form not overtly incompatible with what is known of reality—when it must be gratified by images forming *supplements* rather than *contradictions* of the visible and measurable universe. And what, if not a form of *non-supernatural cosmic art*, is to pacify this sense of revolt—as well as gratify the cognate sense of curiosity. (SP 663)

The above statement is often quoted and makes clear that Lovecraft sought to integrate elements of current science into his writing of cosmic horror; however, his interest in geology in this respect remains unexamined. In separate letters to different correspondents, Lovecraft identified geology as of special interest to him in this regard, maintaining that "[t]here is material for ineffable phantasy in the rocks and inner abysses of Mother Earth" (DS 307) and that "[t]he science of *geology* . . . is directly concern'd with that main stream of cosmick pageantry which begins in blank aether and free electrons & ends in the perfection of Nordick man & Georgian architecture. [Geology] . . . appeals to the cosmic curiosity or interest-sense of the incurable layman" (*Letters to James F. Morton* 236). Focusing on Lovecraft's incorporation of geological science into *At the Mountains of Madness* deepens our understanding of how he sought to build his tale of cosmic horror upon the bedrock of an established scientific discipline and its claims to knowledge.

Lovecraft's use of Wegener's theory and those of other earth scientists is, however, more than simply the inclusion of contemporary science. This becomes apparent when we consider the aims of Wegener's theory and those of the other earth scientists who are referenced in the novel. Lovecraft's narrator in *At the Mountains of Madness* cites by name Wegener, Frank Bursley Taylor, and John Joly. These three advanced theories to account for the apparent match of continental margins, for biotic and geologic disjuncts across continents, and for the origin of mountain ranges during the Tertiary Period. Among leading North American scientists in particular, there was strong resistance to continental drift as an explanatory theory for these geological features. Consequently, Taylor, Joly, and Wegener's theories failed to find general acceptance during the 1920s and 1930s. This is especially true for Wegener's revolutionary theory of continental drift, which sought to reinterpret what some of the fundamental contemporary assumptions about earth's history were. Wegener's efforts to gain acceptance has parallels with Lovecraft's narrator's struggle to get the leaders of his scientific community both to heed his warning against further exploration of the Antarctic and to accept the findings of the Miskatonic Expedition. The influence of the continental drift debate is found in the rhetorical strategies that Lovecraft's narrator calls upon as he seeks to mount a persuasive argument.

Before turning to the evidence of the influence of the debate on Lovecraft, it is first necessary to identify the sources of his knowledge of continental drift theory. S. T. Joshi and David E. Schultz's catalogue of Lovecraft's library includes works of geology and natural history, but none could have provided Lovecraft with his knowledge of continental drift theory. All were published before the theory appeared. The most likely explanation for his knowledge of the theories is that he had read in translation the 1922 edition of Wegener's *Die Entstehung der Kontinente und Ozeane*, translated into English in 1924 as *The Origin of Continents and Oceans*. Evidence for this is found in Lovecraft's notes for *At the Mountains of Madness*, which Joshi dates to late 1930 or early 1931 (CE 5.249). These notes include "designs like Maps—Wegener—cont." and "diagrams—Wegener's theory proved" (CE 5.247). The 1922 third edition of Wegener's book was the first to include his maps and reconstructions of the supercontinent that was later named Pangea by others.

Moreover, in this edition Wegener cites the work of Taylor and Joly multiple times. Based on this, I believe that the 1924 English translation of Wegener's book was the chief source of Lovecraft's knowledge of continental drift theory. The maps the narrator found in the city of the Old Ones in *At the Mountains of Madness* all correspond closely to the maps printed in the 1924 English-language edition of Wegener's *The Origin of Continents and Oceans* (Wegener 6–7; CF 3.105–6).

While the chief source of Lovecraft's knowledge of continental drift theory is identifiable, his reasons for including it in his scientifiction are unstated and require contextualization and ultimately interpretation. The only reference to his inclusion of continental drift theory appears in a letter to August Derleth, in which Lovecraft notes in passing that "[i]ncidentally—a propos of my dragging in the Taylor-Wegener-Joly-theory of continental cleavage & drift—it gives me quite a definite pang to see by the papers that Wegener himself has virtually been pronounced lost on the Greenland ice-cap" (ES 337). The progress and eventual fate of Wegener's final polar expedition was reported in the *New York Times* in a series of articles beginning in 2 May 1930 announcing his departure for Greenland and confirming Wegener's death in the 5 May 1931 edition of the paper. Notably, during the series of articles covering Wegener's Greenland expedition, the *New York Times* also ran an article on 7 September 1930 on continental drift theory that set out Wegener's main argument as well as the contributions of Taylor and Jolly to the theory. While Edward Guimont has shown that the discovery of the remains of Andrée's Arctic balloon expedition of 1897 in 1930 was quite probably the inspiration for the 1930 Miskatonic Antarctic expedition in Lovecraft's novel (Guimont 149–51), we should also regard Wegener's final polar expedition and his defense of his theory of continental drift in *The Origin of Continents and Oceans* as another significant source of inspiration.

That Lovecraft accepted the theory of continental drift is evidenced in a letter to Frederic Jay Pabody in 1936, in which he addressed the possibility that continent of Atlantis existed during human history: "In past geologic ages, of course, land & water area were constantly shifting; but a comparison of the fauna & flora of America, of the West Indies, of the Canaries & Madeira, & of Europe & Africa, proves almost conclusively that they have been widely separated throughout the age of mammalian dominance" (*Letters to C. L. Moore* 333). Lovecraft's statements concerning his belief in the importance of corroborating evidence from across scientific disciplines provides a basis for understanding his acceptance of continental drift theory. Writing to Frank

Belknap Long in late 1930, Lovecraft explained that determining the truth of something requires teamwork in which professionals in different disciplines work together to analyze "concrete data." He maintained that "[t]he only thing the layman can do amidst this complex situation is to check one expert's statements and conclusions against those of another—correlating all the current data with a mind kept free of preconceived myths, traditions, and other biases and subjecting his own tentative conclusions to a round of searching criticisms from experts in the various intellectual fields involved" (SP 641). Wegener's *The Origin of Continents and Oceans* is notable for its use of correlating data from across the areas of disciplinary specialization in the earth sciences. The book is divided into different arguments in favor of continental drift, each from a different disciplinary or sub-disciplinary perspective. Given this, the organization and defense of Wegener's theory in *The Origin of Continents and Oceans* would probably have appealed to Lovecraft's belief in the importance of corroborating cross-disciplinary data in the establishment of facts.

The narrator of *At the Mountains of Madness* references continental drift theory at two points late in the story. In the city of the Old Ones, the narrator finds confirmation of the theories of Taylor, Wegener, and Joly when he observes:

> The persistence with which the Old Ones survived various geologic changes and convulsions of the earth's crust was little short of miraculous. Though few or none of their first cities seem to have remained beyond the archaean age, there was no interruption in their civilization or in the transmission of their records. Their original place of advent to the planet was Antarctic Ocean, and it is likely that they came not long after the matter forming the moon was wrenched from the neighbouring South Pacific. According to one of the sculptured maps, the whole globe was then under water, with stone cities scattered farther and farther from the antarctic as aeons passed. Another map shews a vast bulk of dry land around the south pole, where it is evident that some of the beings made experimental settlements though their main centres were transferred to the nearest sea-bottom. Later maps, which display this land mass as cracking and drifting, and sending certain detached parts northward, uphold in a striking way the theories of continental drift lately advanced by Taylor, Wegener, and Joly. (CF 3.100–101)

This is a remarkable moment in which the maps of the Old Ones independently corroborate the findings and explanatory theories of the three named earth scientists. However, it is not Taylor's, Wegener's, and Joly's theories alone that are confirmed in this map. Lovecraft's reference to the moon forming out of material drawn the South Pacific region is drawn from the fission theory of the moon's formation advanced by George Darwin in *The Tides and Other Phenomena in the Solar System* (1898). By the time Lovecraft wrote *At the Mountains of Madness*, the theory faced significant challenges, though at one time it had found general acceptance. Lovecraft may have found the theory compelling because of Darwin's efforts to ground it scientifically. In 1881 Osmond Fisher had identified the South Pacific as the specific region in which the material that would become the moon broke away from the earth. Interestingly, Fisher contributed important work on continental drift decades before Wegener, and, like Wegener's, his theories were strongly opposed by the leaders of the geoscience community, which led to their rejection (Frankel 43-44). By alluding to the theories of Darwin and Osmond, and through direct reference to Taylor, Wegener, and Joly, Lovecraft associates his unnamed narrator's struggle to gain acceptance for his findings with those of other earth scientists whose claims encountered resistance.

Shortly after this first reference to Taylor, Wegener, and Joly, the narrator reiterates the impact of the Old Ones' carvings on his understanding of the earth's geological history, again mentioning how the three earth scientists' findings were corroborated:

> The changing state of the world through long geologic ages appeared with startling vividness in many of the sculptured maps and scenes. In certain cases existing science will require revision, while in other cases its bold deductions are magnificently confirmed. As I have said, the hypothesis of Taylor, Wegener, and Joly that all the continents are fragments of an original antarctic land mass which cracked from centrifugal force and drifted apart over a technically viscous lower surface—an hypothesis suggested by such things as the complimentary outlines of Africa and South America, and the way the great mountain chains are rolled and shoved up—receives striking support from this uncanny source. (CF 3.105)

This passage from the novel and the one quoted previously show that Lovecraft not only invokes the names of the scientists associated with continental drift theory, but he also directly incorporates their ideas into his fiction. For example, the reference to the northward drift in the first passage is possibly an allusion to Taylor's theory that, during the Tertiary Period, Australia and South America broke away from Antarctica and drifted northward (Taylor 209). Lovecraft's use of controversial geological theories in such detail allows us to read his "scientifiction" as a realistic commentary on the reception of revolutionary theories.

Taylor, Wegener, and Joly all struggled to find acceptance for their theories, although for somewhat different reasons. In 1910 Taylor argued that continental creep, eventually leading to continental drift, was the cause of folded Tertiary mountain belts. He also sought to explain the similarities of the continental margins between Europe and North America by pointing to pre-Tertiary geological disjuncts. Taylor's theory, as Henry Frankel has shown in his history of the continental drift debate, attracted little attention because of its principal focus on the origin of the Tertiary mountain ranges in Europe and Asia (73). Overall, Taylor's lack of professional specialization and standing in the scientific community led to his words falling on deaf ears (Frankel 74). Joly's contribution to the debate was his theory of radioactively generated thermal cycles advanced in his book *The Surface History of the Earth* (1925). This was intended to explain the origins of mountains and other geological features. Joly's theory found little support even among scientists favoring drift, partly due to his own wavering commitment to drift and opponents' attacks on his theory. The latter found Joly's global theories insufficiently grounded in disciplines such as mathematical physics, and they could not believe in a force powerful enough to cause continents to drift (Frankel 196; Newman 205).

Of the three theorists named in the two passages from *At the Mountains of Madness* quoted above, Wegener's theory was the most ambitious in scope and rhetorical exposition. In *The Origin of Continents and Oceans*, he had proposed a revolutionary new explanation to account for the similarities in continental margins and the distribution of biotic and geologic disjuncts based on his reading of geology, paleontology, paleoclimatology, and tectonics research. This was in response to his belief that permanentism, the idea that the Earth's continents are largely unchanging, could not account satisfactorily for these realities. The reasons for Wegener's struggle to find general acceptance for his theory in America were more complex than the rejections faced by Taylor and Joly. Robert P. Newman (183) argues that, in addition to Wegener's unconvincing explanation of the mechanism behind continental drift, his theory was widely opposed by the permanentist mandarins of American earth science at the time for its lack of conformity with accepted beliefs. Newman asserts that "[p]ermanentism was clearly orthodoxy in early twentieth-century American geology" and that "the most virulent attacks on Wegener and drift came from opinion leaders" who could have otherwise helped gain acceptance for his theory (183, 197). Another reason for the resistance to Wegener's theory in America was that pre-eminent geologists in the academy believed in local diastrophism or the process of deformation that causes the folding and faulting of the earth's crusts, which seemed to support permanentism (Newman 203). Wegener's lack of professional training in geology was also an issue for some earth scientists.

The scientific and sociological reasons for the rejection of continental drift theory in North America serve as useful context for understanding how Lovecraft can be interpreted as drawing upon this controversy. There are clear parallels between the way that the North American scientific community received the respective drift theories of Joly, Taylor, and especially Wegener and the response that the leaders of the narrator's own scientific community give to his initial warning and to how the narrator uses the rhetoric of science in his argument. Examining these parallels allows us to see how Lovecraft can be interpreted as using the debate over continental drift and the type of rhetoric found within it as a model to comment upon resistance to revolutionary ideas.

Lovecraft's novel begins with his unnamed narrator's plea to the scientific leaders of his community who, he hopes, will accept his findings and his warning against further exploration of the Antarctic. We can understand Lovecraft's narrator's use of the rhetoric of science to speak about the reality of what he has found in Antarctica as a way to substantiate his claims to knowledge about that reality. This manner of speaking about the discoveries that the Miskatonic University Expedition has made is a strategy for discouraging the upcoming Starkweather-Moore Expedition He hopes to do this by convincing fellow scientists of what he has witnessed during his participation in the earlier Miskatonic expedition. In "A Warning to the World: The Deliberative Argument of *At the Mountains of Madness*," David A. Oakes interprets the argumentative structure of the narrator's text as based in Aristotelian rhetoric. He claims that:

> The tale, at its heart, takes the form of a deliberative argument. [The narrator's] carefully constructed plea for the abandonment of plans for new expeditions shows Lovecraft's ability to utilize classical models of Greek rhetoric in twentieth-century Gothic literature.... The deliberative argument as Lovecraft constructs it serves as far more than a simple warning against future exploration. It becomes a vehicle for the presentation to readers of a new reality and a new understanding of the nature of the world the human species seeks to dominate and control. (21)

While I agree that the text has an argument-driven structure and that it seeks to present knowledge of a new reality, I believe that, instead of interpreting it in terms of ancient Greek rhetoric, we should use the context of twentieth-century norms of scientific writing and its attendant social structure. This provides a better context for understanding the argumentative situation in which the narrator finds himself caught. While the narrator states, "Here I shall sketch only the salient high lights in a formless, rambling way" (CF 3.94), his narration, overall, exhibits conformity to modern communication conventions of scientific writing and can be analyzed according to his use of its rhetorical techniques.

The opening of the novel immediately establishes the expectations of the scientific community for the presentation and explanation of events in a particular way, which the narrator has apparently failed to do in his initial warning:

> I am forced into speech because men of science have refused to follow my advice without knowing why. It is altogether against my will that I tell my reasons for opposing this contemplated invasion of the antarctic-with its vast fossil-hunt and its wholesale boring and melting of the ancient ice-cap-and I am the more reluctant because my warning may be in vain. Doubt of the real facts, as I must reveal them, is inevitable; yet if I suppressed what will seem extravagant and incredible there would be nothing left. The hitherto withheld photographs, both ordinary and aerial, will count in my favour; for they are damnably vivid and graphic. Still, they will be doubted because of the great lengths to which clever fakery can be carried. The ink drawings, of course, will be jeered at as obvious impostures; not withstanding a strangeness of technique which art experts ought to remark and puzzle over. (CF 3.11-12)

Oakes reads the narrator's opening statements as an attempt to establish his ethos as a "rational and coherent scientist" (21). The goal of this rhetorical strategy, according to Oakes, is that the narrator "through this admission ... hopes to discredit any counter-arguments against his warning based solely on the conclusion that his tale is so strange that it cannot be real" (21). However, as Charles Bazerman points out in his analysis of the rhetoric of written scientific communications (140-41), while ethos was at one time used to establish an author as a reliable witness, in the context of the social structure of twentieth-century scientific communication, this was an insufficient means for validating research findings. In place of appeals to ethos, authors sought to persuade their audiences to accept their findings by offering detailed explanations of experimental research procedures and explaining how the procedures refute any possible objections. The initial rejection by men of science that the narrator experienced lies in the failure of his findings to address objections. As he himself admits, he has previously withheld photographic evidence that might otherwise have helped persuade his intended audience to accept his claims.

In framing this second written appeal specifically to "scientific leaders," the narrator is acknowledging their gatekeeping role in the acceptance and promotion of new knowledge:

> In the end I must rely on the judgment and standing of the few scientific leaders who have, on the one hand, sufficient independence of thought to weigh my data on its own hideously convincing merits or in light of certain primordial and highly baffling myth-cycles; and on the other hand, sufficient influence to deter the exploring world in general from any rash and overambitious programme in the region of those mountains of madness. It is an unfortunate fact that relatively obscure men like myself and my associates, connected only with a small university, have little chance of making an impression where matters of a wildly bizarre or highly controversial nature are concerned. (CF 3.12-13)

It is not difficult to find parallels between the narrator's appeal to the leaders of his scientific community and the resistance to the attempts of Taylor, Wegener, and Joly to gain acceptance for their theories. Lovecraft's narrator's struggle to gain acceptance of his claims is the most obvious parallel with the initial fate of the three real-world scientists. Another parallel is observable in the narrator's hope for the scientific leaders to show "independence of thought," which calls to mind the pernicious effects of the leading American geologists' commitment to the doctrines of permanentism and uniformitarianism. In fact, the influence of these doctrines is challenged by Wegener in the second chapter of *The Origin of Continents and Oceans* and offered a direct rhetorical model to Lovecraft. We can see how this might have appealed to Lovecraft when we consider how Frank Belknap Long recalled that, in regards to the sciences, "HPL maintained a critically rational approach to the observable aspects of reality. He thought that only minds capable of discarding every instilled traditional belief concerning man's place in the universe were worthy of respect as investigators of the unknown" (70). A third similarity shows up in the narrator's humbling reference to himself and his colleagues as "relatively obscure men" within the scientific establishment, ones lacking association with a prestigious research institution. Their lack of standing in the community is reminiscent of both the attacks against Wegener for his lack of formal training in geology and the criticisms of Joly over his insufficient background in mathematics.

Summarizing the problems of stifling scientific authority in the debate over continental drift during its early decades, historian of science Naomi Oreskes asserts:

> In science ... we hold those most knowledgeable about matters to be the ones most qualified to judge. In doing so, we recognize the importance of scientific expertise and the experience in judging matters of evidence and plausibility. . . .

And we are placing responsibility for making new knowledge in the hands of those who have the most old knowledge to unmake. The recognition of scientific expertise—the very stuff that enables scientists to build on prior results—that enables science to progress—at the same time makes scientific judgements inescapably personal and historical, undermining our deepest wishes for knowledge that might somehow be transcendent. (317-18)

Despite the urgency of Lovecraft's narrator's message, he must persuade the scientific authorities to change what they think they know about the Earth's history and humanity's place within it. This means they must accept what the narrator admittedly terms "alien natural law" (CF 3.94) and let go of "accustomed conception[s] of external Nature and Nature's laws" (CF 3.49).

Lovecraft's narrator proceeds after his opening statements to detail the expedition's research aims, method of organization, and general scientific procedures, emphasizing detailed explanations over appeals to ethos, as Bazerman found in his analysis of the rhetoric of scientific articles. This emphasis is observable in the description of the Miskatonic Expedition's research aims:

> [W]e expected to unearth a quite unprecedented amount of material; especially in the pre-Cambrian strata of which so narrow a range of Antarctic specimens had previously been secured. We wished also to obtain as great as possible a variety of the upper fossiliferous rocks, since the primal life-history of this bleak realm of ice and death is of the highest importance to our knowledge of the earth's past. That the antarctic continent was once temperate and even tropical, with a teeming vegetable and animal life of which the lichens, marine fauna, arachnida, and penguins of the northern edge are the only survivals, is a matter of common information; and we hoped to expand that information in variety, accuracy, and detail. (CF 3.14)

The importance of explaining methodological procedures is also acknowledged by the narrator when he concedes that his narration is incomplete: "It is of course impossible for me to relate in proper order the stages by which we picked up what we know of that monstrous chapter of pre-human life. After that first shock of the certain revelation we had to pause a while to recuperate, and it was fully three o'clock before we got started on our actual tour of systematic research" (CF 3.92). Even though his narration is admittedly incomplete, he nevertheless refers to their investigation of the city of the Old Ones as "systematic research," a term that implies logic and rigor. Similarly, he will go on to establish the basis of the dates that he assigns the objects observed by cross-correlating them with accepted facts in other scientific disciplines. The narrator is attempting to respond to disbelieving scientists by putting forth a written argument that conforms to evidential and methodological conventions, disciplinary standards, and epistemological practices of accepted science. Nonetheless, he acknowledges the deficiencies of his reporting when he points out that "[t]he full story, so far as deciphered, will eventually appear in an official bulletin of Miskatonic University" (CF 3.94). The bulletin, carrying the imprimatur of the university, will not only carry the weight of authority but presumably also meet the standards of the scientific community for a research publication.

As the narrator describes his discoveries in the city of the Old Ones, he seeks to support his interpretation of them through correlation with previously established theories. This is part of his effort at persuasion. Bazerman observes, "As findings and theory develop, consistency of results with other results aides in persuasion" (141). There is a particularly notable correspondence in this regard between the way that Wegener built his argument in *The Origin of Continents and Oceans*, in which he uses a range of correlating disciplinary data to support his claims, and the narrator's efforts in *At the Mountains of Madness* to support his own interpretive claims about his findings. The narrator explains that, in interpreting the depictions found in the artwork of the Old Ones:

> [T]he infinitely early parts of the patchwork tale–representing the pre-terrestrial life of the star-headed beings on other planets, and in other galaxies, and in other universes–can readily be interpreted as the fantastic mythology of those beings themselves; yet such parts sometimes involved designs and diagrams so uncannily close to the latest findings of mathematics and astrophysics that I scarcely know what to think. Let others judge when they see the photographs I shall publish. (CF 3.92-93)

In this appeal to the findings of other disciplines as a means for confirmation, there is also a clear avoidance of an appeal to ethos. The reader of the narrator's report is focused on the findings of science and the supposed objectivity of the photographic evidence.

In their history of the scientific article, Alan Gross, Joseph Harmon, and Michael Reidy assert that twentieth-century journal articles reflect an "increasing concern with mounting an argument that not only establishes new facts but also offers theory-based mechanical or mathematical explanations for them" (231). This emphasis on relating observed facts to established, theory-based mechanical explanations is used repeatedly as a strategy for persuasion by the narrator. For example, when he initially reacts to Lake's discovery of the fossil prints, he is repeatedly unmoved by Lake's claims. First stating that "[s]ince slate is no more than a metamorphic formation into which a sedimentary stratum is pressed, and since the pressure itself produces odd distorting effects on any markings which may exist, I saw no reason for extreme wonder over the striated depression" (CF 3.22). He later asserts, "These markings, however, were of very primitive life-forms involving no great paradox except that any life-forms should occur in rock as definitely pre-Cambrian as this seemed to be; hence, I still failed to see the good sense of Lake's demand for an interlude in our time-saving programme" (CF 3.25). These quotations show how Lovecraft's narrator depicts himself as an interpreter of evidence according to accepted facts and theories in his professional discipline of geology.

According to Bazerman's analysis of the rhetoric of modern science, to persuade the gatekeepers of the scientific establishment, as Lovecraft's narrator seeks to do, the author of a written communication must "establish ... authority on communally accepted grounds beyond himself" and "although [something] may be a fact to the person who first locates it, it is not a fact until other researchers have been satisfied that the event has occurred" (140). Even though he expresses his desire not to reveal what he has witnessed, when he states, "I am constantly tempted to shirk the details and to let hints stand for actual facts and ineluctable deductions" (CF 3.60), the narrator understands that the leaders in the scientific community will not accept his discoveries and the warning that he bases upon them. The demand to prove and to demonstrate requires that the facts and events be represented in a particular way in a scientific text. It is not hard to see how Lovecraft absorbed this from his reading of contemporary scientific literature, such as *The Origin of Continents and Oceans*, and used it in his narrator's argumentative plea, his methodological descriptions, and use of corroborating theory and disciplinary knowledge.

When read in the context of the then-contemporary debate over continental drift, *At the Mountains of Madness* is interpretable as a representation of the resistance to revolutionary ideas in the scientific community and the kind of arrogant human naïveté behind it. Lovecraft's narrator and his struggle to find acceptance for his findings were inspired by the polar explorer Wegener and his struggle to gain acceptance for his theory of continental drift. Comparison of the contemporary fate of Wegener's theory and those of his fellow scientists, Taylor and Joly, with those of the narrator and the rhetorical strategies he uses to gain the acceptance of his scientific community reveal a number of parallels, such that we can see the probable influence of this debate on Lovecraft. Previous research into Lovecraft's influences in *At the Mountains of Madness* has established the novel's relationship with the history of Antarctic exploration and Edgar Allan Poe's *The Narrative of Arthur Gordon Pym* among others. To this list of influential intertexts should be added Alfred Wegener's *The Origin of Continents and Oceans* and the attendant debate over the theory of continental drift.

Works Cited

Bazerman, Charles. *Shaping Written Knowledge*. Madison: University of Wisconsin Press, 1988.

Frankel, Henry R. *The Continental Drift Controversy: Wegener and the Early Debate*. New York: Cambridge University Press, 2017.

Gernsback, Hugo. "A New Sort of Magazine." *Amazing Stories* (April 1926): 3.

Gross, Alan G., Joseph E. Harmon, and Michael S. Reidy. *Communicating Science*. West Lafayette, IN: Parlor Press. 2009.

Guimont, Edward. "An Artic Mystery: The Lovecraftian North Pole." *Lovecraft Annual* 14 (2020): 138–65.

Joly, John. *The Surface History of the Earth*. Oxford: Clarendon Press, 1925.

Joshi, S. T. "Introduction" to Lovecraft's *The Thing on the Doorstep and Other Weird Stories*. New York: Penguin, 2001. vii–xvi.

———. "Time, Space, and Natural Law: Science and Pseudo-Science in Lovecraft." *Lovecraft Annual* 4 (2010): 171–201.

———, and David E. Schultz. *Lovecraft's Library: A Catalogue*. 5th rev. ed. New York: Hippocampus Press, 2024.

Lieber, Fritz. "A Literary Copernicus." 1949. In S. T. Joshi, ed. *H. P. Lovecraft: Four Decades of Criticism*. Athens: Ohio University Press, 1980. 50–62.

Long, Frank Belknap. *Howard Phillips Lovecraft: Dreamer on the Nightside*. 1975. Cabin John, MD: Wildside Press, 2022.

Lovecraft, H. P. *Letters to C. L. Moore and Others*. Ed. David E. Schultz and S. T. Joshi. New York: Hippocampus Press, 2017.

———. *Letters to James F. Morton*. Ed. David E. Schultz and S. T. Joshi. New York: Hippocampus Press, 2011.

———. *Lord of a Visible World: An Autobiography in Letters*. 2000. Ed. S. T. Joshi and David E. Schultz. New York: Hippocampus Press, 2019.

Newman, Robert P. "American Intransigence: The Rejection of Continental Drift in the Great Debates of the 1920s." *Earth Sciences History* 14 (1995): 62-83.

Oakes, David A. "A Warning to the World: The Deliberative Argument of *At the Mountains of Madness*." *Lovecraft Studies* No. 39 (Spring 1996): 21-25.

Oreskes, Naomi. *The Rejection of Continental Drift: Theory and Method in American Earth Science*. New York: Oxford University Press, 1999.

Taylor, Frank Bursey. "Bearing of the Tertiary Mountain Belt on the Origin of the Earth's Plan." *Geological Society American Bulletin* 21 (1910): 179-226.

Wegener, Alfred. *The Origin of Continents and Oceans*. Tr. J. G. A. Skerl. New York: E. P. Dutton, 1924.

Charting Ecologies of Violence through Algernon Blackwood's "The Willows"

Matthew Holder
College of Arts and Sciences, Saint Louis University

Contemporary genre fiction invested in the environment finds roots in the early twentieth-century weird tale. Anchored in the inexplicable and uncanny, weird fiction traffics in the unsettling and insurmountable. To capture this sense of estrangement, many early practitioners turned toward the natural world as a catch-all motif for cosmic horror. Several of the best-known weird tales are as much about the landscape as they are about alien entities or unnamable ancient evil, such that the environment itself becomes the locus of unearthly dread. Whether filtered through pagan forests (Arthur Machen's "The Great God Pan" [1894]), the barren wastelands of Antarctica (H. P. Lovecraft's *At the Mountains of Madness* [1931]), the nightmare of rural farm life (Lovecraft's "The Colour out of Space" [1927]), or the unpredictable Danube River (Algernon Blackwood's "The Willows" [1907]), the weird tale has been from the start preoccupied by and attuned to the strangeness of the nonhuman world. By casting characters into a world that displaces their significance, writers such as Lovecraft, Machen, and Blackwood created tales in which the human subject is dethroned from its position as an autonomous agent. This shift in subjecthood is accomplished less through these tales' emphasis on outright cosmicism than through their byzantine formal properties that suggest the intimate horrors of ecological entanglement more than existential obsolescence.[1] Weird fiction's prevailing (and ongoing) crises of ontology, I argue, is as invested in environmental dread as it is in cosmic notions of humanity's insignificance. It works toward this affect by: 1) developing a deep-

---

1. See Newell's argument for "aesthetic disgust," an effect which imagines how "absolute differences of essence are obliterated by the enmonstered reality that the affects of weird fiction convey . . . weird revulsion . . . creates aesthetic encounters which help us to think about the unthinkable" (3, 4).

ly descriptive prose style that blurs the lines between the human and the nonhuman; and 2) introducing an element of nonhuman vengeance. This argument departs from conventional scholarship on the weird tale, which often positions this ontological collapse as metaphysical and, importantly, dispassionate. In reading weird fiction along vectors of ecology and environmental revenge, I demonstrate the genre's utility as a mode of inquiry not only oriented toward more accurately representing environmental degradation but also reckoning with its effects and affects.

For better and worse, Lovecraft remains the premier figure for the weird genre, both in terms of his influence and the attention he demands in scholarship. His essay "Supernatural Horror in Literature" (1927) continues to provide fruitful ground for analyzing the genre's development and its conventions. For Lovecraft, weird fiction understands "atmosphere is the all-important thing," while conventional narrative elements such as character and plot are minimized greatly or eschewed altogether (CE 2.84). The intended effect is "the creation of a given sensation . . . a profound sense of dread," such that the reader experiences a "subtle attitude of awed listening" (CE 2.84). Weird fiction, then, evokes a reorientation of the human subject accomplished through a heightened form of reader-awareness toward notions of geographical (and cosmological) presence—this "subtle attitude of awed listening," a phrase that reads as much as a contemporary ecocritical slogan as it describes Lovecraft's melodramatic prose. But while writers such as Lovecraft are more explicitly concerned with the existential and cosmological challenges posed by emerging strains of materialist thought—one of the primary sources of Lovecraft's anxieties—we also find in weird fiction an equally compelling ecological thought, one that productively foregrounds a more contemporary focus on ambiguity, animosity, and intimacy.

In the wake of our own contemporary and continuing environmental collapse, reading weird fiction of the early twentieth century acts as a prophetic precursor to contemporary ecofiction's ongoing process of ecological reorientation of the human/nonhuman relationship. It does so not by turning toward the infinitude of the cosmos but by tethering itself to the Earth, only to find that the ground itself is seething, frothing, annihilating.[2] Such dread is

---

2. My emphasis on a language of orientation and topography borrows from Frederic Jameson's notion of cognitive mapping, as well as Bruno Latour's more recent work in ecocriticism. In the wake of collapsing ecospheres under late-stage capitalism, Latour writes, "we shall have to learn how to get our bearings, how to orient ourselves. And to do this we need something like a map of the positions imposed by the new landscape within which

not pointed toward solutions or to provoke guilt; indeed, one of weird fiction's generic strengths is its treatment of dread/horror/terror as the subject itself, the emotional disorientation of the reader. In what follows I will identify and analyze how this manipulation of the reader is necessarily and productively tied with the narrative's environment. This will, in turn, allow me to trace the development of the human/nonhuman relationship at the center of weird fiction, from its xenophobic origins to its current iteration as one of the premier genres of contemporary climate fiction.

For the remainder of this piece, I focus on the work of Algernon Blackwood (specifically the short story "The Willows"). His work introduces a useful tension between malevolence and indifference into conceptions of the natural/nonhuman world, complicating contemporary conversations around humanity's interaction with the environment. My goal is not to argue that "The Willows" assumes the position of nature's vengeance, but its suggestion of environmental revenge and blurred distinctions between the human and the nonhuman stand out as critical elements in the development of the eventual wild justice novel. Blackwood was not explicitly concerned with writing a polemic against humanity's exploitation of the Earth, but he does cast his characters into a world of natural hostility, which, I argue, frames them as victims of the Earth's retribution for humanity's trespassing and hubris. Ultimately, Blackwood's story introduces a productive intersection between the natural environment, the human subject, and violence, and his marriage of these elements through the affordances of his given genre provides a useful starting point in mapping out the ensuing topography of natural revenge, environmental justice, and contemporary genre fiction.

Toward a Moveable Background

Before turning directly to Blackwood's work, I will briefly sketch the literary environment of nature writing from which his fiction emerged. When set beside other fiction writers imagining the natural world, Blackwood's own ecological sensibilities become distinguished from those of his peers. I consider two areas of generic diversion: realism and the weird. Though written after "The Willows," the classic realist tale "Big Two-Hearted River" by Ernest Hemingway establishes the anthropocentrism that weird fiction works to challenge, notably in Lovecraft's own nature-gone-wrong staple of the weird can-

---

not only the affects of public life but also its stakes are being redefined" (2).

on, "The Colour out of Space." Blackwood anticipates each of these approaches while rejecting the boundaries of realism on the one hand and the extraterrestrial pull of weird fiction on the other. As we shall see, each story's approach to the landscape and its relationship to the human clarifies not only their various generic affordances and limits, but also the ways in which Blackwood's work imagines alternatives.

Blackwood's affinity for outdoorsmanship and adventuring puts him into an intriguing dialogue with Hemingway, another outdoorsman and a man who relished the primacy of experience. "Big Two-Hearted River" serves as a productive foil for Blackwood's story, which is also set in and around a river. Against Hemingway's realism, Blackwood's fantasy is thrown into sharp relief. But also revealed is weird fiction's opportunity for ecological engagement and its investment in a vast network of oppositional actors, as opposed to the singularity of human agency in Hemingway's work. Although Hemingway and Blackwood both experienced nature repeatedly and at first hand, Blackwood's approach always leaves open the possibility of human corruption and ontological rupture, while Hemingway imagines a much more benign nonhuman landscape, the borders of which function less as portals into the unknown than they do entrances into green hospitals. In "Big Two-Hearted River," Hemingway intends to disclose elements of the psyche, but it is a distinctly *human* consciousness. Hemingway's natural topography in this short story is one that inspires wistful melancholy—a landscape radically altered, perhaps, damaged, burnt, abused, yet still recognizable.

While perhaps emotionally lost, Nick, Hemingway's protagonist, becomes defined and anchored through his ritualistic actions: hiking through the woods, setting up camp, preparing and eating food, gathering grasshoppers for bait, catching the fish, cleaning the fish, etc. In typical Hemingway fashion, each of these actions is slowed down and metastasized into its component parts until the action itself becomes the subject, but through it all every motion and consideration remains tied to a human agent. For all Nick's listless, seemingly directionless motion, he treks, cuts, casts, and kills unimpeded within and through the natural world.[3] In this way Hemingway imagines the natural world as a kind of salve to Nick's wounded psyche, a nonhuman healing ground where Nick can wander and sport and play while the catastrophe of

---

3. In addition to the grisly grasshopper death, Nick also kills several trout by snapping their necks against a log. As he cleans his catch in the river, he notices that "they looked like live fish. Their color was not gone yet" (155).

war recedes into the background, its sounds and sights swallowed by the balm of the river and wind. Rejuvenation is mediated through the natural world: Hemingway sketches a beneficial relationship between the human and the nonhuman. Yufeng Wang notes that "it is the trivial camping and fishing experience that vividly reflect Nick's harmonious relationship with the natural environment, taking mental recovery and relaxation without destroying the ecological balance" (799).[4] But this relationship is decidedly one-sided and, again, privileges the human actor as the singular beneficiary. Nick's return to nature is a humbling and healing experience for him, but the nonhuman world remains bound by realist modes of expression, incapable of receiving any reciprocal healing process or conciliatory gestures. Rendered through this realist lens, Hemingway's natural world, for all its symbolic weight, remains a static backdrop, a landscape to be acted upon and acted through.

Published two years after *In Our Time*, "The Colour out of Space" brings the full force of weird fiction's speculative conventions to bear on the natural world, introducing an environment tinged with threatening malignancies. Lovecraft's tale represents a sharp stylistic shift away from Hemingway's realism, but the sustained attention to an altered landscape remains, even down to the description of the tainted environment as a "blasted heath" covered with "only a fine grey dust or ash which no wind seemed ever to blow about" (CF 2.368, 369). The story takes the form of an investigative report from an unnamed narrator recounting the strange events following a meteorite's crash onto a farmer's land. After initial studies of the meteor from Miskatonic University determine "it was nothing of this earth, but a piece of the great outside" (CF 2.374), the narrator shifts to describing their encounter with local testimonies related to subtle changes in the environment. Nahum Gardner, the owner of the farm, "declared that the meteorite had poisoned the soil" (CF 2.375), and from there Lovecraft relates a series of increasingly grotesque and bizarre distortions of the natural world. A local woodchuck had its body "slightly altered in a queer way impossible to describe," while cabbages took on a "monstrous" appearance; the "bloodroots grew insolent in their chromatic perversion" as the natural world writ large succumbed to an inexplicable "strangeness" (CF 2.376, 378). The invasive and infectious nature of the meteorite's influence even carries over into the human characters, and it is here

---

4. This reading is a common one among Hemingway scholars, that the function of the river is a cleansing one, and Nick's experience in the natural landscape helps to facilitate the healing process wrought by post-traumatic stress.

that Lovecraft's choice of genre allows him to not only distort the nonhuman but also to collapse the distinction between the human and the environment itself, a dichotomy to which realism remains tethered. As the surrounding countryside continues to undergo radical genetic transformations, Mrs. Gardner, Nahum's wife, undergoes her own form of annihilation: "Something was taken away—she was being drained of something—something was fastening itself on her that ought not to be" (CF 2.380).

Not only has Mrs. Gardner taken on the animal aspect of moving "on all fours" (CF 2.380), but she begins to radiate with the same bioluminescent glow of the landscape. While this humanimal degeneracy is a trope dating from antiquity, Lovecraft imagines the transformation not as a form of divine punishment but merely a side-effect of an extraterrestrial encounter. In other words, the human becomes compromised by way of geographical coincidence; as the environment experiences alterations, Lovecraft removes the human characters from the dominant foreground and blends them into this shifting background that he later reveals is conscious and active and penetrating.

"Colour" climaxes with an explosive moment of environmental rupture as the alien presence seems to extricate itself from all the organisms it has infected and escape into the atmosphere. The narrator recounts how a group of locals decides to investigate Nahum's farm in the wake of the entire family perishing from the alien anomaly, and as they approach they begin to experience a series of increasingly violent encounters. The trees themselves began to move without the aid of wind "as if jerked by some alien and bodiless line of linkage with subterrene horrors writhing and struggling below the black roots," and those few observers left witnessed "a monstrous constellation of unnatural light" erupt from the earth and drain into the sky (CF 2.392). As they explore the farmer's abandoned home the strange color returns, and Lovecraft's descriptions are telling in their continued suggestion of nonhuman agency:

> It glowed on the broad-planked floor . . . and shimmered over the sashes of the small-paned windows. It ran up and down the exposed corner-posts . . . and infected the very doors and furniture. Each minute saw it strengthen, and at last it was very plain that healthy living things must leave that house . . . it shrieked and howled, and lashed the fields and distorted woods in a mad cosmic frenzy, till soon the trembling party realised it would be no use waiting for the moon to shew what was left down there at Nahum's. (CF 2.395-96)

The passage is emblematic of Lovecraft's tendency not only for melodrama but also his assignment of agency; the narrative pulse, in other words, is generated through the movement of the landscape, the human characters often simply left to flail against it. Even amidst the generic trappings of weird fiction, this divestment of human agency is perhaps the most notable departure from realist works such as Hemingway's, and it allows for an environmental imagination that includes notions of a hostile landscape and human collapse.

But for all the generic innovation that Lovecraft's work with "Colour" represents—the challenge to human hierarchy and autonomy, the formal emphasis on an extended network of environmental actors, the realization of a conscious landscape—his threat remains cosmic in nature. "It was just a colour out of space," the narrator records, "a frightful messenger from unformed realms of infinity beyond Nature as we know it; from realms whose mere existence stuns the brain and numbs us with the black extra-cosmic gulfs it throws open before our frenzied eyes" (CF 2.399). Though animated and conscious, Lovecraft's environment is not itself wholly earthbound; it is instead a proxy for an alien presence. This distinction is important because it points up the innovation of Blackwood's work two decades earlier in "The Willows," an early weird fiction effort that resisted a purely cosmic pull for its source of dread and instead embedded the terror in the natural world of our planet. In this way contemporary ecofiction—which uses the speculative affordances of genre to render a nonhuman Earth that is threatening, conscious, and intentional—owes a greater debt of influence to Blackwood than Lovecraft.

Mapping Blackwood's Terrain

For Blackwood, the idea of natural strangeness and horror was bound together with his upbringing and personal experience of nature. Blackwood was born in England in 1869 to a life of gentility, a source of benefit as well as discomfort for him. From an early age he was enraptured with nature and pushed against the tenets of the traditional Christianity of his family, preferring instead the more esoteric subjects of Theosophy and spiritualism he encountered in his time at Edinburgh University. He moved to New York and courted poverty in 1892, though his meager earnings from steadier newspaper and translation jobs provided stability, and his growing friendships granted opportunities for continued exploration of the natural world.

One of these opportunities came in October 1898, when Blackwood accompanied John Dyneley Prince on an expedition into the Canadian wilderness to study Indigenous cultures and hunt moose. The experience was profound for Blackwood and inspired several classic stories, including "The Wendigo." According to his biographer, Mike Ashley, this initial trek into the northern Canadian forest was transformative, noting that Blackwood "had sold his soul to nature" (98). Blackwood returned to Liverpool in 1899, continuing to write fiction and nonfiction, with his premier collection of short stories published in 1906 under the title *The Empty House and Other Ghost Stories*, followed a year later by *The Listener and Other Stories*, containing "The Willows." Along with his weird fiction, he also wrote philosophical novels, children's stories, and dramas, and he was acquainted with several of his writing peers, including W. B. Yeats and H. G. Wells. He died in 1951 at the age of eighty-two, leaving behind a significant literary legacy that remains underexplored, as his contribution to the weird genre is often overshadowed by figures such as Lovecraft and Machen.

Blackwood's oft-anthologized "The Willows" is paradigmatic of the conventional weird tale, but it also anticipates an ecology that encompasses both the human and the nonhuman that Lovecraft's "Colour" only gestures toward. Consisting of only two characters—the narrator and his companion, "the Swede"—Blackwood's plot, as with most early weird tales, is a straightforward exercise in linearity, going so far as to frame the unfolding events around a river. But once our characters stop at an island located off a particularly choppy and uncharted meander of the Danube, Blackwood starts to introduce the now generic staples of the weird: an uncanny sense of being observed, inexplicable phenomena, and the simmering approach of madness that boils beneath the surface, threatening to destroy every rational explanation the characters struggle to conjure to account for the strange world into which they have stumbled.

Even before our human characters are introduced and subsequently land on the eerie island, Blackwood's nature is dynamic and controlling. From the opening sentence he connects the Danube with strangeness and hostility as it "enters a region of singular loneliness and desolation," where its "willow-grown islands . . . somehow give the impression that the entire plain is moving and *alive*" (17). Far from static, Blackwood's nature is rendered with a novelist's eye toward human characterization. The Danube is "happy" and "wanders about at will . . . making whirlpools . . . tearing at the sandy banks; carrying away . . . forming new islands," always active and caught in processes of creation and destruction, existing in a state of "impermanent life" (17). Blackwood continues:

> ... but the Danube, more than any other river I knew, impressed us from the very beginning with its *aliveness* ... it had seemed to us like following the growth of some living creature. Sleepy at first, but later developing violent desires as it became conscious of its deep soul, it rolled, like some huge fluid being, through all the countries we had passed ... (19)

Coupled with the tale's title, the initial sequences of "The Willows" frame it as a tale of natural wonder that just happens to feature human characters whose own agency/autonomy is questioned at the outset, their subjectivity cast against the violent, propulsive, and strange river. The narrator and the Swede are simply one more piece of flotsam subjected to the Danube's force, their own plans of discovery and leisure soon subjected and lost to Blackwood's narrative precision and thick description of the nonhuman landscape.

Once on the island and forced to make camp, the two men are overwhelmed by "the eeriness of this lonely island" (28), as Blackwood seems to transfer the animus of the Danube into the willow trees. "For ever they went on chattering," the narrator remarks about the trees, "and talking among themselves, laughing a little, shrilly crying out, sometimes sighing" (29). From the outset Blackwood frames the intrusion onto the island as a form of invasion, of human trespass into nonhuman environments, one that the landscape itself reacts against: "we were the first human influences upon this island, and we were not wanted. *The willows were against us*" (29). Importantly, this agency embedded in the environment is endemic to the Earth itself, not a result of external tampering. And though Blackwood does imbue the story with cosmic (read, extraterrestrial) potential, he is pointed in keeping his strangeness grounded. During the first night on the island, the narrator awakens to violent winds tossing the branches about into "a series of monstrous outlines" that, instead of fleeing or awakening the Swede, prompts him to observe what he only refers to as "these huge figures" (32). The encounter comes early in the story, but its affect haunts the entire tale:

> ... these huge figures, just within the tops of the bushes—immense, bronze-coloured ... they were very much larger than human, and indeed that something in their appearance proclaimed them to be *not human* at all ... they rose upwards in a continuous stream from earth to sky, vanishing utterly as soon as they reached the dark of the sky. They were interlaced with another, making a great column, and I saw their limbs and huge bodies melting in and out of each other, forming this serpentine line that bent and swayed and twisted spirally with the contortions of the wind-tossed trees. They were nude, fluid shapes, passing up the bushes, *within* the leaves almost—rising up in a living column into the heavens. (32; Blackwood's emphases)

Here Blackwood presents us with the closest possibility of extraterrestrial beings, but his narration entangles these beings with the landscape to such an extent that reading them as disparate feels inappropriate. Instead they emerge as "the personified elemental forces of this haunted and primeval region," extensions of the environment that the narrator feels their presence has awakened: "our intrusion had stirred the *powers of the place* into activity" (32; my emphasis). The narrator is only assured of two things: that these creatures are nonhuman and that they emerge from and move within the environment, to the point that their motions resemble the trees themselves. Blackwood's landscape is a far cry from the cosmic puppetry of Lovecraft's "Colour" and instead emerges as a force unto itself, carried along by his characters' vivid imaginations and his own literary approach to entanglement.

John MacNeill Miller draws attention to Blackwood's specific style of narrative description in "The Willows," noting that, traditionally, scenic description is often treated as background noise both for the reader and the author, but weird fiction exploits this seeming moment of narrative disarming by sustaining the focus on the scenic to such an extent that it becomes its own subject. Once disarmed, the reader encounters an environment in which every actor enjoys equal play. "Weird fiction," Miller argues, "resists description by pointing up the ideological function of description as a kind of cloaking device that hides potentially significant, agentic beings. In doing so, weird fiction offers a portal that opens out onto a fuller, richer, and more ecological conception of reality" (249).[5] In effect, Blackwood's positioning of his characters as yet another background element anticipates some of our own contemporary understandings of permeable ecologies and non-human environments; in adopting a formal ecology, Miller notes, Blackwood "reveals a world without background" (250).[6] In this "world without background," Blackwood invites the reader to approach and appreciate the nonhuman world as distinctly and radically strange. Importantly, Blackwood's disorienting ecology and his use of moveable backgrounds is a distinct feature of the generic register of weird fiction, and it is one he deploys to great effect in "The Willows." A writer such as Hemingway can project human psychoses onto a nonhuman setting, but he cannot animate the river beyond its perceptible course and

---

5. Blackwood's narrator and the Swede refer to the Danube as both "a Great Personage" and "the great creature" (19, 21).

6. See Morton: "Since everything is interconnected, there is no definite background and therefore no definite foreground" (28).

subsume his human characters into the background without sacrificing his subject. To make Nick disappear into the environment would collapse the story's thematic weight, even if Nick himself wishes to fade into the landscape. Blackwood's proto-ecological storytelling not only activates the natural world but also compromises the human subject itself by diffusing that anthro-agency onto the Danube and its islands and willow trees—"with everywhere unwritten warnings to trespassers for those who had the imagination to discover them" (18). The natural world, in Blackwood's hands, steps into the foreground to take center stage.

However, S. T. Joshi argues that "to say that 'nature' is at the core of Blackwood's thought does not get us very far, given the imprecision of the term—or, rather, its multiplicity of connotations" (91). What's more, to approach Blackwood's work solely against "nature" is ultimately flattening and plays into the danger of reifying the Nature that contemporary ecocritics and environmentalists warn against.[7] Joshi reads Blackwood's nature as an almost entirely symbolic cypher for what he argues is the writer's larger goal: "the expansion of consciousness—that is what Blackwood is after. The terms vary from work to work—expansion, extension, intensification, sometimes merely change—but at its heart is some mystical awareness of a broader vista than science and rationalism provide" (93). Joshi leans into Blackwood's occasional preoccupation with occultism and Eastern religions to ground his claim, later writing that "awe is perhaps the dominant motif" in Blackwood's entire bibliography (xii). In contrast to Lovecraft's detached and intellectual approach to weird fiction, "Blackwood seeks some mystical merging with the cosmos . . . [and] feels that these limitations can in reality be overcome, whereas Lovecraft felt they could be only imaginatively or psychologically" (Joshi 93). For Joshi, then, Blackwood's weird aesthetic—and by extension his treatment of the natural world—is pointed upwards toward the metaphysical, and his ultimate goal is to "have some sort of direct communion with a larger sphere of entity, one

---

7. In many ways "The Willows" is a story that relies on the capital "N" nature that both Joshi and Timothy Morton warn against, a pseudo-utopia that feels so detached and distinctly unnatural that its representation is ultimately harmful. Morton: "Ecology equals living minus Nature, plus consciousness," a sentiment that Blackwood could have written himself (19). See also: "To have ecology, we must give up Nature. But since we have been addicted to Nature for so long, giving up will be painful" (95). Morton's attention to pain is noteworthy here, as it echoes Blackwood's own insistence on hostile, sometimes painful relationships, which pushes against the idealist impulse of Nature.

where the distinctions between terrestrial—or, for that matter, cosmic—objects are seen to be illusory or nugatory" (94).

While Blackwood's work does interrogate the realms and pull of the nonhuman, Joshi's broad characterization of his oeuvre as one ultimately concerned with expanding consciousness is overstated; by projecting Blackwood's philosophy into the metaphysical cosmos, his transformative approach to the terrestrial—and humanity's interaction within it—becomes diminished.[8] Filtering the entirety of Blackwood through the lens of "nature" is only flattening if we consider nature as some hegemonic pseudo-utopia that is objectively distant and never attainable. But Joshi's reading of Blackwood remains productive because its emphasis on expanding perceptions and consciousness often aligns with ecological philosophers such as Timothy Morton and Gregory Bateson's ecology of mind, and it forces a useful reconsideration. While Joshi is invested in Blackwood's spiritualism, I want to shift the emphasis from Blackwood the New Age Priest to Blackwood the Ecological Philosopher; while both schools of thought push against the boundaries of traditional consciousness, the latter maintains a material investment in the natural world—the difference between a transcendence from the environment (and one's own mind) and an encounter within it. And if we approach Blackwood's narrative with an eye toward ecology—both of intersecting biospheres and agencies—his work rings remarkably similar in tone and intent to contemporary ecocriticism and its attention to strangeness (Morton), violence (Nixon), intra-action (Barad and Bennet), and Latour ([dis]orientation).

In developing his own proto-ecology, Blackwood drew on both his personal studies in mysticism and his penchant for adventuring outdoors.[9] In this way, the visceral, lived-through quality of his settings is always already entangled with notions of expanded consciousness and a specific attention to nonhuman forms of meaning and communication. Writing in his memoirs in

---

8. Joshi is not alone in foregrounding Blackwood's efforts to expand human consciousness, and, with Blackwood having been a member of the Hermetic Order of the Golden Dawn, the draw to extricate those mystical elements is not unfounded. Cosmicism and metaphysics do occupy significant attention in his writings. See Graf's chapter on Blackwood.

9. Through his familiarity with W. B. Yeats, Blackwood joined the infamous Hermetic Order of the Golden Dawn shortly after returning from a trip to Hungary in 1900, a trip in which he and friend Wilfred Wilson canoed down the Danube, the setting and inspiration for "The Willows." See Ashley 109-19.

1923, Blackwood admits the natural world's profound impact on him, as well as the extrasensory, almost alien-like quality he finds in it:

> By far the strongest influence in my life ... was Nature ... Always immense and potent, the years have strengthened it. The early feeling that everything was alive, a dim sense that some kind of consciousness struggled through every form, even that a sort of inarticulate communication with this "other life" was possible, could I but discover the way—these moods coloured its opening wonder. (*Episodes Before Thirty* 36-37)

Blackwood's language here is certainly tinged with the pseudo-science language suggestive of magic and hallucinatory incantations common with the late nineteenth and early twentieth century's obsession with occultism and magic,[10] but it also gestures toward contemporary ecology's own indebtedness to occultism writ large in its emphasis on remapping existing cosmologies and ways of being. Blackwood's natural spiritualism, then, anticipates the ecological philosophy that all life (or nonlife), all states of matter and instances of mattering, are interconnected, entangled, mutually constitutive and destructive, bound up in processes of knowing, unknowing, disclosure, and recognition, animated through strange intimacies and radical gulfs.

This recognition of nonhuman consciousness risks reifying anthropocentric notions of perception and states of being, but Blackwood maintained that such an encounter with nonhuman existence is anything but familiar, and his intuition regarding the human and nonhuman interconnection extended beyond the dichotomy of capital "N" nature and industrialized life.[11] And if there is a familiarity present in projecting human-oriented affects onto the nonhuman, it is a strange one that produces disorientation, an effect called for in Morton's ecological manifesto, *The Ecological Thought*, in which he argues that the art that operates in an ecological mode will stage an encounter with what he calls "the strange stranger." "The more we know about life forms," he writes, "the more we recognize our connection with them and the

---

10. See also: "As the darkness of the night slowly merges into the first streaks of the sunrise lights, the beholding spirit seems to leave its own plane of consciousness and to enter that of the surrounding nature-life, to commune, indeed, with the potencies which, above and behind all natural phenomena, render them beautiful, mysterious or weird" (in Ashley 53).

11. Though, admittedly, Blackwood also maintained this distinction. Ashley notes, "Blackwood held the view that by withdrawing from this oppression of civilization and by refocusing on the harmony in Nature you could become aware of the earth spirit and of the true spirit of Nature" (52-53).

stranger they become. The strange stranger isn't just a blank at the end of a long list of life forms we know . . . the strange stranger lives within (and without) each and every being" (17). Such encounters produce moods of anxiety and hostility, "ugliness and horror," predicated on an intimate understanding—a continual process of "opening," to use Blackwood's language—with not only nonhuman existence but also the human's own vulnerable instability, pivoting on the collapsed notion that there was ever any distinction between the human and the nonhuman.

An Ecology of Hostile Intent

While "The Willows" grounds the weird genre in notions of biological interpenetration—folding the subjectivities of human and nonhuman into each other until the distinction between the two blurs or disappears entirely—it also casts a net of malign intent over this relationship. The topography Blackwood sketches in "The Willows" is chaotic and resistant, lending itself to labyrinthine, enmeshed ecologies over clean paths and signposts. "For a change," the narrator thinks, "had somehow come about in the arrangement of the landscape," shortly after surprising himself into thinking that "the winds were about and walking" (36). There is an environmental orientation present, but it is born of confusion and a feeling of helplessness. "Our insignificance perhaps may save us," the Swede says to the narrator, "in the tone of a doctor diagnosing some grave disease" (51). As Blackwood's characters attempt to reconcile the seemingly shifting landscape, the haunting atmosphere of the willow trees, the discordant harmonies surrounding them, they fail "to localise it correctly," for all their expertise and experience (46). Left without a clear conception of their changing environment—and the control such knowledge could bring—the narrator and the Swede slowly succumb to emotional extremes, such that the lines between supernatural imaginings and the reality of an unknown cosmic presence collapse entirely. "These bushes," the narrator says, "assumed for me in the darkness a bizarre *grotesquerie* of appearance that lent to them somehow the aspect of purposeful and living creatures. Their very ordinariness, I felt, masked what was malignant and hostile to us" (44). And in a particularly evocative passage, Blackwood continues to render the natural world as an agential subject, only now, as the narrator and the reader begin to experience the ensuing horror of the environment, elements of vengeful purpose enter into this thickening web of human and nonhuman subjectivities:

> Creeping with silent feet over the shifting sands, drawing imperceptibly nearer by soft, unhurried movements, the willows had come closer during the night. But had the wind moved them, or had they moved themselves? I recalled the sound of infinite small patterings and the pressure upon the tent and upon my own heart that caused me to wake in terror. I swayed for a moment in the wind like a tree, finding it hard to keep my upright position on the sandy hillock. There was a suggestion here of personal agency, of deliberate intention, of aggressive hostility, and it terrified me into a sort of rigidity. (36)

Ultimately, the horror of "The Willows" is fueled by this liminality breaking through perceived boundaries. Whether human or nonhuman, supernatural or real, earthly or alien, imagination or materiality, Blackwood's work creates an ecological orientation of disorientation that holds these dichotomies in simultaneous and unresolved tensions. Questions of agency, cause and effect, and even morality fail to account for the actual environmental investment that Blackwood brings to "The Willows." By returning attention to his terrestrial concerns, his originating source of dread becomes better oriented around questions of biological (or material) interpenetration and human annihilation and transformation. Blackwood's fiction anticipates the anxieties around "posthuman subjects of knowledge—embedded, embodied and yet flowing in a web of relations with human and non-human others" (Braidotti 34). And as Miller writes, "what really creeps the narrator out is arguably just an accurate view of nonhuman life that suddenly breaks through his anthropocentric perspective" (249). This destabilization of the human, while the source of much critical invention and insight, is the source of horror and madness for early weird fiction and Blackwood in particular, who taps into his own fascination with the environmental landscape, a fascination that is equally tinged with intimacy and helplessness, strangeness and hostility.[12]

Blackwood's innovation is indeed this distinctly natural hostility that belies a sense of nonhuman purpose and agency.[13] The narrator in "The Willows" thinks as much as he and the Swede consider their vulnerability among

---

12. As the Swede and the narrator delve deeper along the Danube, they "entered the land of desolation on wings," a passage that "woke in [the narrator] the curious and unwelcome suggestion that we had trespassed here . . . a world where we were intruders, a world where we were not wanted or invited to remain—where we ran grave risks perhaps!" (18, 24).

13. Blackwood's forests, Kokot notes, "seem to be endowed with life themselves, or even consciousness . . . the sense of loneliness . . . is accompanied by a sense that the nature follows the actions of the intruders, ready to absorb or destroy them" (135).

the willows and struggle to rein in their imaginations, which had been "investing them [the willows] with the horror of a deliberate and malefic purpose, resentful of our audacious intrusion into their breeding-place" (50). Here, not only does Blackwood clearly articulate the nonhuman agency at play, but he also imbues it with potential motives: retaliation against the human for their intrusion.[14] This threat of force produces an anxiety not unlike the emotions elicited in Gothic fiction, Joanna Kokot argues, where violation of a sacred space leads to forms of annihilation. "Man becomes gradually absorbed by natural forces," Kokot writes, "experiences a change in personality, sometimes acquiring unity with nature—but it is a unity which deprives him of the very essence of his humanity" (137). This notion of a compromised humanity is a recurring theme in Blackwood's work.[15] To become something other than the human, to be always in the process of becoming, either consciously or physically, ultimately subsumes all other concerns, up to and including death. As the Swede slowly begins to unravel and speculate about their fate, he worries their encounter with this threatening nonhuman entity "means a radical alteration, a complete change, a horrible loss of oneself by substitution—far worse than death, and not even annihilation" (52). Blackwood's topography becomes entirely composed of porous boundaries; the lack of fixed definitions for nature, the human, motives and moralities, and so on, finds a resounding resonance for our own ontological crises in the wake of environmental collapse. Blackwood's work neither offers solutions nor stakes out a position, other than one of ambiguity and quiet dread, embracing precarity over stability, dynamism over stasis.

To speak again in language of affordances, Blackwood engaged the generic contrivances of the supernatural as a tool for this greater environmental imagination and (re)orientation. "For Blackwood," Camara writes, "the natural and the supernatural already overlap, not so much in a 'natural supernaturalism,' but more so in the sense that nature is always already a cosmic 'supernature' that reserves an infinite amount of hidden powers and creativity,

---

14. "... the willows connected themselves subtly with my malaise, attacking the mind insidiously somehow by reason of their vast numbers, and contriving in some way or other to represent to the imagination a new and mighty power, a power, moreover, not altogether friendly to us" (23).

15. See "The Man Whom the Trees Loved," a story in which a husband is slowly lured away from his wife by the trees that surround their home. At the story's end, the wife discovers her husband has been absorbed by the trees.

which only appears to us as supernatural when nature does something unprecedented" (59-60). The natural world of "The Willows" remains tethered to the earth and forces new ontologies regarding the relationship between the human and the nonhuman, and Blackwood's work begins to sketch out these new topographies, which, tellingly, become the source of horror and anxiety. What the characters read as extraordinary is a revelation of irreconcilable experience between conventional wisdom and "some region or some set of conditions where the risks were great yet unintelligible to us; where the frontiers of some unknown world lay close about us," a revelation that is so fundamentally disorienting that the only recourse is to imagine something "*unearthly*" as the source of their dread (Blackwood 49, 50). But for all the supernatural and cosmic gestures, Camara argues, the strangeness of the environment originates *from* the earth, not externally. Even while the narrator and the Swede struggle to map this new terrain—either materially or mentally—Blackwood works behind the scenes to render a nonhuman world that, though read as alien, is ultimately terrestrial and, disturbingly, *acting*.

But to label the terrestrial as an actor still carries the suggestion of purpose, whether benign or malignant or indifferent. Actors *act*, and their presence exerts a material force. Bruno Latour labels this nonhuman actor the Terrestrial agent, "with a capital T to emphasize that we are referring to a concept, and even specifying in advance where we are headed: the Terrestrial as a *new political actor*" (40). Latour argues that contemporary politics are entirely organized around the ongoing climate crisis; as such, the Earth has asserted itself onto the political stage with a totalizing effect not unlike the specter of late-stage capitalism: all around us, controlling every aspect of our lives and futures, but difficult to articulate and nail down. But unlike capitalism, which, though knotted and globalized into ubiquity, has distinctly human motives, the Terrestrial actor presents a challenge. How to account for ourselves, Latour wonders, if the landscape itself in "which we are located begins to react to our actions, turns against us, encloses us, dominates us, demands something of us and carries us along in its path?" (41). As climate fallout continues, as environments are destroyed and human beings displaced, the myth that the Earth was ever itself a stable concept—either discursively or materially—falls apart. In its wake are dynamism and political will: the Terrestrial actor now negotiating for itself and forcing the human subject to consider why it ever felt it had a right to occupation. The question remains, however:

> But how are we to act if the territory itself begins to participate in history, to fight back, in short, to concern itself with us—how do we occupy a land if it is the land itself that is occupying us? . . .
>   If the Terrestrial is no longer the framework for human action, it is because it *participates* in that action. Space is no longer that of the cartographers, with their latitudinal and longitudinal grids. Space has become an agitated history in which we are participants among others, reacting to other reactions. It seems that we are landing in the thick of *geohistory*." (41–42)

I turn to Latour because his work maintains a political urgency that I find more productive and encouraging than the new materialism of theorists such as Morton. Latour shares with these critics the concept of a borderless world of interacting networks, but his understanding of agency is not diffused into an oblivion so infinitesimal that direct action and questions of motives disappear. In mapping this new territory, Latour calls for "alternative descriptions" that "refine the representation of the landscapes" (94, 95). The task is difficult, "because the agents, the animate beings, the actors that compose it all have their own trajectories and interests" (95). Latour is ultimately concerned with political reorientations, but his work keeps open the possibility of an angry and hostile nonhuman actor, one that "fight[s] back" and exerts itself. Encountering alternative actors does indeed carry the possibility of fear, and part of that fear, that loss of control, is connected to the material reality of competing agencies. Weird fiction discloses Latour's Terrestrial actor and begins the messy process of drawing up these new topographies.

In "The Willows," the narrator and the Swede sense the Terrestrial actor's presence all around them, and as their terror grows, so grows their conviction of natural motives related to vendettas and vengeance for their invasion of the island. As their time on the island extends, they begin to reveal their nightmare imaginations to each other, the Swede now fully convinced of a nonhuman and hostile actor: "'There are things about us, I'm sure, that make for disorder, disintegration, destruction, *our* destruction'" (48). Blackwood himself never moralizes the natural force, but his characters and his eerie scenic description more than suggest ill intent. Greg Conley argues that the sinister quality in Blackwood's fiction is related to his intimate portrayal of the other, the nonhuman actor, such that the mere encounter itself causes unintentional harm due to the human's unfamiliarity with anything outside of itself (427). In other words, the willows did not go out of their way to menace Blackwood's characters, instead simply reacting to an outside stimulus, a reaction interpreted by the human characters (and the reader) to be hostile. But ecosystems are not hermetically sealed, static locations simply waiting for humans to wander into to trigger reactions. Ecosystems react, expand, and change; they choke out organisms to accommodate others, and when invasive species appear, they attempt to eradicate them or face their own extinction. While reading that eradication as malevolence or vengeance for trespass does anthropomorphize, such readings also point us toward the reality of competing agencies. Blackwood's fiction complicates notions of ecology that refuse to acknowledge the violence of cohabitation and coexistence.

Works Cited

Ashley, Mike. *Algernon Blackwood: An Extraordinary Life*. New York: Carroll & Graf, 2001.

Barad, Karen. *Meeting the Universe Halfway: Quantum Physics and the Entanglement of Matter and Meaning*. Durham, NC: Duke University Press, 2007.

Bennet, Jane. *The Enchantment of Modern Life: Attachments, Crossings, and Ethics*. Princeton, NJ: Princeton University Press, 2001.

Blackwood, Algernon. *Ancient Sorceries and Other Weird Stories*. Ed. S. T. Joshi. New York: Penguin, 2002.

———. *Episodes Before Thirty*. New York: E. P. Dutton, 1923.

Braidotti, Rosi. "A Theoretical Framework for the Critical Posthumanities." *Theory, Culture and Society* 36, No. 6 (2019): 31-61.

Camara, Anthony. "Nature Unbound: Cosmic Horror in Algernon Blackwood's 'The Willows.'" *Horror Studies* 4, No. 1 (2013): 43-62.

Conley, Greg. "The Uncrossable Evolutionary Gulfs of Algernon Blackwood." *Journal of the Fantastic in the Arts* 24 (2013): 426-45.

Estok, Simon C. "Painful Material Realities, Tragedy, Ecophobia." In Serenella Iovino and Serpil Oppermann, ed. *Material Ecocriticism*. Bloomington: Indiana University Press, 2014. 130-40.

Graf, Susan Johnston. *Talking to the Gods: Occultism in the Work of W. B. Yeats, Arthur Machen, Algernon Blackwood, and Dion Fortune*. Albany: State university of New York Press, 2015.

Hemingway, Ernest. *In Our Time*. New York: Scribner, 1925.

Joshi, S. T. *The Weird Tale*. Austin: University of Texas Press, 1990.

Kirksey, Eben. *Emergent Ecologies*. Durham, NC: Duke University Press, 2015.

Kokot, Joanna. "Dangerous Beauty: 'Gothic' Landscapes in Algernon Blackwood's Short Fiction." In *Exploring Space: Spatial Notions in Cultural, Literary and Language Studies*. Newcastle upon Tyne: Cambridge Scholars, 2010. 131-40.

Latour, Bruno. *Down to Earth: Politics in the New Climatic Regime*. Cambridge: Polity, 2018.

Miller, John MacNeill. "Weird Beyond Description: Weird Fiction and the Suspicion of Scenery." *Victorian Studies* 62 (2020): 244-52.

Morton, Timothy. *The Ecological Thought*. Cambridge, MA: Harvard University Press, 2010.

Newell, Jonathan. *A Century of Weird Fiction, 1832-1937: Disgust, Metaphysics and the Aesthetics of Cosmic Horror*. Cardiff: University of Wales Press, 2020.

Poland, Michelle. "Walking with the Goat-God: Gothic Ecology in Algernon Blackwood's *Pan's Garden: A Volume of Nature Stories*." *Critical Survey* 29 (2017): 53-69.

Wang, Yufeng. "Returning to Nature: An Eco-critical Study of 'Big Two-Hearted River.'" *Journal of Language Teaching and Research* 10 (2019): 796-99.

Inappropriate Death and the Body as Object in "The Hound" and "Herbert West—Reanimator"

Nicolette A. Williams
University of Stirling

Dangerous, unstable, and unruly bodies have always been of concern in American Gothic literature, and the American Gothic is saturated with stories of individuals treading the line between life and death, including tales of immurement, the resurrected undead and spectralized unalive, and murder most foul, which both enforce and trouble the boundaries of life and death. The Gothic's insistence on destabilizing boundaries, identities, and binaries, the work of abjection, and its preoccupation with violent death make it ideal for critiquing the societal practices that also enact violence on the dead and dying. This article is a variation of a chapter of my forthcoming doctoral thesis, "'A Jubilee of Rot': Degradations of Mourning and the Dead in American Gothic Literature," which focuses on close readings of representations of death, dying, and the violence enacted upon the corpse in American Gothic literature from 1917 to 2017. The chapter from which this article is adapted reads patterns of inappropriate death, mourning, grief, and treatment of the corpse in "Herbert West—Reanimator" as well as in C. M. Eddy Jr.'s "The Loved Dead" and William Faulkner's "A Rose for Emily," complemented by an analysis of contemporaneous cultural shifts in the medical and funeral industries and in the social acceptability of grief and mourning practices, which manifest a rejection of death through the possession of the corpse-as-object. While there are the many Lovecraft stories and collaborations that center around death and inappropriate treatment of the corpse, this article takes as its focus two of Lovecraft's short stories, "Herbert West—Reanimator" and "The Hound," which deal most closely with themes of the inappropriate treatment of the dead by the living. Through a close reading of inappropriate death and the treatment of the corpse in these two works, drawing on the

Gothic figure of the necrophile, I will show that the increasing distance between the living and the dead, reflected in the professionalization of death care, established a disruptive social pattern of rejecting death that resulted in the objectification of the dead, a rejection that is made problematic by the characters' obsessive interactions with the dead.

While death was something that nineteenth-century American society was beginning to believe should be preventable in certain circumstances, such as in children and from certain conditions, by the early twentieth century this belief had transformed into something more severe that regarded death not as a natural aspect of life but as a failure. During this period, America's "faith in science" (Stearns 39) to explain and prevent death, an attitude that had gained traction after the Civil War, took on its modern shape. This transition can be best seen in the growth of a mechanistic view of the body and the shift from family home-based to professional and institutional-based care for the dying/dead. Herbert West can be read as representative of the medical attitudes that characterized the early twentieth century for both his mechanistic approach to medicine and the extreme extents to which he is willing to go to return life to the dead. As medical technology advanced and specialization grew, the human body was increasingly viewed in a mechanistic light. Osherson and Amarasingham note that "Machines could be maintained, repaired, developed and replaced through [. . .] scientific knowledge and technology," (quoted in Uttley 28), an approach that was applied to the medical treatment of the human body, and which holds "a perception of disease and illness [. . .] as evidence of a defect in the mechanical world of the body which has to be identified and repaired" (quoted in Uttley 29). West, whose "wild theories on the nature of death and the possibility of overcoming it artificially [. . .] hinged on the essentially mechanistic nature of life" (CF 1.292), quite literally assumes what Laderman calls "the power to define death" (4-5) through his experiments with reanimating the dead.

Prior to the early twentieth century, care of the dying and the dead in the U.S. still occurred primarily in the home, provided by the family, but as medical and funerary technologies advanced, higher levels of skill and specialization in these industries gradually worked to separate the living from the dying and the dead, imperiling the idea of "appropriate" death and treatment of the corpse. It was during the early twentieth century that "medical professionals rapidly assumed the power to define death" and "a new perspective began to take hold in the United States: Life must be sustained at all costs, with death viewed as a devastating defeat" (Laderman 4-5). The imperative to preserve life at all costs prioritizes the continuance of life above any harms done to the patient to achieve that goal and, as Gilbert notes, many common medical procedures "associated with the saving of lives" such as CPR, chemotherapy, and defibrillators, can also "prolong misery" and "threaten to destroy lives" (171) even as they save them. In a medical sense, then, all death was unacceptable, and the medical imperative to 'sustain life at all costs' explicitly exposes a structure that prioritizes the prevention of death until such time as further treatment is ineffective, and sometimes at the cost of enacting violence on the dying individual. One effect of this was that death as the experience of dying became increasingly dissociated from the domestic sphere and more associated with the medical. Advances in medicine may have made death increasingly preventable, but it also inserted physical and emotional distance between the dying and their survivors as the process of dying was relocated to the hospital and the obligation of providing care for the dying was increasingly removed from the family.

Lovecraft's choice to ascribe neither reason, motivation, nor emotional drive to Herbert West's experiments underscores both the mania of his obsession and how little his motivations, whatever they might be, matter in the face of the horrors he commits. Indeed, West's companion notes that "his once normal scientific zeal for prolonging life had subtly degenerated into a mere morbid and ghoulish curiosity and secret sense of charnel picturesqueness" (CF 1.315). West's "normal" scientific insistence on preserving life at all costs[1] is a clear mediation on the attitude that death was not an integral, natural part of life but a failure, an attitude that was developing strength throughout American society. West's actions expose the fallacy that there can ever truly be a justification for the preservation of life 'at all costs' on two counts: firstly, by utilizing West's unemotional and immoral carrying of the imperative to preserve life 'at all costs' to its ultimate extreme, as when he commits murder for the express purpose of returning life, and secondly by his degeneration into "mere morbid and ghoulish curiosity," in which his heinous experimentation no longer makes even a pretense of scientific justification. This depiction of West also serves to distance him from humanity; any actualization of West's desire

---

1. The scientific zeal for preserving life, which West takes to horrific extremes, is reflected in a letter, written by HPL regarding his mother's illness to Rheinhart Kleiner in 1919, and collected in *Lord of a Visible World*, in which he displays a similar bargaining approach toward quality of life vs. prevention of death: "I shall be thankful if any procedure, *however protracted*, can restore my mother to normal or nearly normal health" (103; my emphasis).

to eliminate death through his reanimation experiments would foreclose his desire. With no interest in living bodies except as objects for experimentation, a successful reanimation of life would simultaneously render the corpse once more a subject and erase both its purpose and desirability in West's eyes.

Schneidman conceptualizes "appropriate" death as the death "'which a person might choose for himself had he an option'" (quoted in Langer 6), in opposition to which is Langer's "inappropriate" death: the death a person would not choose for himself (6). Langer's understanding of inappropriate death, however, reveals only half of a larger picture. While he focuses on death from an experiential perspective of the dying and their survivors that is typically based on a medicalized understanding of the individual's transition from a healthy to a dead body, he does not take into account the sociocultural pressures that prescribe and impose judgment on the practices that follow the event of death and dictate the appropriateness of everything from the disposition of the body to the performance of grief. For the purposes of this study, I have expanded upon this narrower, more medically conceptualized understanding of inappropriate death to include the treatment of the corpse, as inappropriate death and inappropriate treatment of the corpse often go hand in hand in the genres of the weird and the Gothic. By distancing Americans from the experience of death, the medical and funeral industries gradually divested the general public of the ability to make choices concerning the experience of dying and the treatment of the dead, resulting in an increasing number of "inappropriate" deaths and the objectification of the corpse.

Particularly illustrative of the ways in which West represents the medical attitudes of his time is the episode titled "The Scream of the Dead," in which West reanimates a traveler named Robert Leavitt. Leavitt has purportedly "suddenly dropped dead" (CF 1.311), and West preserves Leavitt's body using a "new and highly unusual embalming compound" (CF 1.310) for a period of "two weeks" until the narrator's return, so that "both might share the spectacle" (CF 1.311) of his reanimation. The horror here arises from the discovery of the inappropriate death that Leavitt suffers and the extent to which West will go in order to reject death. Following an injection intended to "neutralize" the embalming compound, as "a gentle tremor seemed to affect the dead limbs, West stuffed a pillow-like object violently over the twitching face, not withdrawing it until the corpse appeared quiet and ready for our attempt at reanimation" (CF 1.312). Clearly, West is willing to commit murder, smothering Leavitt in front of the narrator, in the interest of preserving life. It is quite a contradictory action to take and reveals that to West, all bodies, whether dead or living, are depersonalized objects on which he might experiment.

West's power to define death is emphasized in this episode by the narrator's acceptance of West's "assurance" that "the thing really was dead" (CF 1.311), despite the fact that Leavitt's state of existence could be more accurately described as a state of suspended animation, and his ability to watch, apparently untroubled and without concern, as West smothers Leavitt. Yet West's actions are still in keeping with the medical imperative to preserve life "at all costs," albeit taken to an extreme, and thereby West becomes what Mandal and Waddington call a "destabilizing" figure, an indictment of the medical industry, who "disclos[es] continuities in how doctors were viewed as objects of fear or scorn, almost vampiric in their avarice and characterized by a sham professionalism that concealed darker motives" (47). Lovecraft's emphasis on the preservative used by West as an "embalming" compound similarly indicts the funeral industry, which is further condemned in his collaboration with Eddy on "The Loved Dead." Where "Herbert West" focuses, as Mandal and Waddington do, on a medical doctor, "The Loved Dead" provides a similar account of "sham professionalism" and "darker motives" not from a doctor but from an undertaker. In counterpoint to West's mania for reviving the dead, which reveals West as a medically unethical and morally bankrupt figure, the narrator of "The Loved Dead," who finds employment as an undertaker with the express and explicit purpose of sexually assaulting dead bodies, situates the growing funeral industry as equally sinister to the medical profession. The disruptive effect that Mandal and Waddington recognize in the question of the (potentially malevolent) motivations of medical and funerary practitioners is magnified by the concurrent changes in both industries, specifically the objectification of the dying/dead body that results from the transition from informal yet unskilled to skilled yet impersonal care. It manifests itself in a rising prevalence of what Langer calls "inappropriate" death, which only serves to exacerbate the increasing distance between the living and the dead that is introduced by removal of the dying/dead from everyday life.

Furthermore, this episode suggests a high level of engagement with the medical question of when death occurs. As Andy Troy's work on radiation sickness and "The Colour out of Space" demonstrates, Lovecraft was scientifically aware and

> purposefully syncretized various scientific disciplines—chiefly chemistry, biology, and anatomy—into a fictional study of radiation poisoning that preceded formal recognition by several months, and widespread admission of its danger by years. (36)

Though "The Colour out of Space" was published more than five years after "Herbert West" went into serialization, I believe that Lovecraft utilized a similar approach to the one that Troy identifies as a basis for the medical components of West's practices.

In addition to reflecting the growing emphasis on preserving life no matter what its negative outcomes may be, Lovecraft utilizes the gaps in time between death and the administration of West's solution to suggest a progression of brain damage from a healthy, living brain to one with significant brain damage and finally to brain death, "the irreversible cessation of all functions of the entire brain" (Ngyuen), that is ahead of its time. At the time Lovecraft wrote "Herbert West," rather than the modern criteria of brain death, "'medical definitions of death [. . .] emphasiz[ed] the total stoppage of all vital bodily functions'" (Arnet, quoted in Nguyen) and were "not centered on any organ (or organ system)" (Nguyen). In spite of this, Lovecraft essentially conceives of the condition of brain death nearly fifty years prior to its introduction in 1968 by the Harvard Ad Hoc Committee as "a new standard for the determination of death" (Nguyen). This can be seen in the "freshness" required of the bodies that West reanimates with varying degrees of success. As West's companion (the story's narrator) observes, "reanimation [. . .] depend[s] only on the condition of the tissues" and "psychic or intellectual life might be impaired by the slight deterioration of sensitive brain-cells which even a short period of death would be apt to cause" (CF 1.292). This is made even more explicit in Stuart Gordon's *Re-Animator* (1985), in which the "six to twelve" minute survival period of the brain following death is a point of grave contention between Jeffrey Combs's Herbert West and David Gale's Dr. Carl Hill. The reanimations of Leavitt and Clapham-Lee are successful because West has immediate and unrestricted access to his subject's bodies at the moment of their deaths, and both are capable of intelligible speech. In contrast to the successful reanimation of Leavitt and Clapham-Lee are the more animalistic reanimates: the drowned workman obtained through grave robbing, Dr. Allan Halsey, and Buck Robinson. While West's solution is successful in reanimating them, they are not true successes. While all other organ systems are apparently functional and life has been returned to their once-dead bodies, there is impairment of their brain function that reduces them to something less than human, as seen in the inhuman "inconceivable cacophony" (CF 1.296) of their cries, their "nauseous eyes, the voiceless simianism, and the daemoniac savagery" (302), and their cannibalistic tendencies.

As a further exploration of the question of inappropriate death, I will turn here to the Gothic figure of the necrophile. Finbow writes that the necrophile "plays a significant role in the Gothic tradition" (11–12) and "embodies our worst fears and our most base desires" (9) as the sexual violator of the corpse. The nature of this violation, however, relies on granting to the deceased the rights of humanity that have been legally and socially stripped from them, turning the corpse from a person into an "inanimate, non-living possession" (25). As such, necrophilia provides an excellent vantage point for interrogating how death and the treatment of the body are determined to be in/appropriate and how the corpse can be positioned as subject or object. Finbow recognizes that the corpse cannot be cleanly designated as either object or subject when he asks why necrophilia is considered to be "so abhorrent" (25). Much of the horror generated by necrophilia lies, then, in the blurred situation of corpse: as both subject, the cast-off embodiment of an idealized individual, and as object, which Aggrawal and Rosman and Resnick argue is incapable of refusing or resisting the desires and actions of the living (Aggrawal 316; Rosman and Resnick 158). In other words, the necrophile desires a surrogate partner, the embodiment of the ideal of a subject without its actuality which they are free to treat as an object specifically because of its imitation of subjectivity.

While there is no explicit sexual violation of the corpse in either "Reanimator" or "The Hound," I contend that they are both necrophilic stories. Classificatory systems of necrophiliac behavior, such as Mellor's and Aggrawal's, which narrowly focus on the sexual aspect of necrophilia and on the "erotics" of the sexual desire for the dead, can be helpful in understanding patterns of behavior, but they also severely restrict our reading of necrophilia strictly to its sexual aspects when, as Spoerri and Rauch contend, "coitus is not an essential component of necrophilia" (paraphrased in Rosman and Resnick 160). Instead of "Reducing necrophilia to a single, highly taboo act," that of sexual intercourse with a corpse, which Downing finds "serves to distance us from its complexities" (3), "Herbert West" and "The Hound" broaden its definition to include any obsessive desire for a socially unacceptable level of closeness or interaction with the dead. In place of the traditional emphasis on its sexual aspect, the necrophilia included in these stories embraces the Gothic trope of decay, which Douglas argues foregrounds an "intense sensual experience" in the presence of "human bodily remains" (184). As the necrophilia in "Herbert West" and "The Hound" is implied but is never made explicitly sexual, we are prevented from teasing out which of the characters' behaviors are sexually motivated and which are not. In addition to this, the sense of scientific, emotional, and spiritual fulfillment or disquietude that the characters feel when they have or do not have access to the dead is prioritized over the physical. While the implications of necrophilia focus on scientific/emotional/spiritual satisfaction rather than sexual intercourse, they still provide an opportunity to develop a more nuanced interpretation of the spectrum of necrophilic practices. A wider spectrum of necrophiliac behavior also seems to be implied by Lovecraft through the description of West, St. John, and the narrators as "ghouls" (CF 1.294, 315, 341, 342). Though this term is used to describe their grave-robbing activities and is associated with cannibalistic cults, at a more fundamental level these characters also exhibit a desire to obsessively "pre[y] on corpses or lur[e] humans to death" in order to "indulge in their "appetite for human flesh" (*OED*) in ways that are experienced as sensual, if not sexual or cannibalistic. The ghoulish attributes associated with these characters will be discussed further below.

Though West is described as "Always an ice-cold intellectual machine" (CF 1.314) whose purpose in conducting his experiments is presented as wholly scientific, his obsession with reanimating the dead is implied to have a necrophilic dimension: he is also called "a fastidious Baudelaire of physical experiment—a languid Elagabalus of the tombs" (CF 1.316). Although Baudelaire's writing, especially *Les Fleurs de mal*, features heavy overtones of romanticized necrophilia, Callaghan notes that it is particularly "the sadistic emperor Elagabalus whose perversity Lovecraft associates with necrophilia" (49). I was unable to find any historical evidence to support Elagabalus' necrophilia, but there is evidence to show that he engaged in sexual practices that were considered abhorrent during his rule, notably having "married a male slave" and "dressed as a woman"[2] (Wasson). Even if the reference to Elagabalus is not intended to evoke necrophilia, as the reference to Baudelaire surely does; and together they are able to conjure up a tantalizing hint of sexual desires, desires for not only the dead, but the possibility of homosexuality. For Baudelaire, "murder is idealized and prioritized in such a way that it wholly replaces sex" (Downing 84), and as a central aspect of Lovecraft's story of reanimation, murder *is* prioritized over sex; yet Lovecraft's reference to Elagaba-

---

2. Whether Elagabalus was what we consider today to be transgender is a matter of debate. His condemnation by his contemporaries appears to be a result of his disruption of traditional gender roles and sexual practices. HPL's description of West includes feminized characteristics, he is "slight" and "soft voic[ed]," traits that serve to accentuate "the supernormal—almost diabolical—power of the cold brain within" (CF 1.298).

lus also suggests that, however denied and disdained sexuality is in "Herbert West," it does at least exist. Aside from these allusions, West's obsession reveals other details that support a necrophilic reading of this text, specifically in the aesthetic qualities he finds most desirable in his experimental subjects.

It is noted that West "looked half-covetously at any very healthy living physique" (CF 1.310) and with "hideous and calculating appraisal at men of especially sensitive brain" (320), but the scientific reasoning for his selection of experimental subjects is complicated by additional, purely aesthetic qualities. A "real dead man of the ideal kind," "what West had always longed for," is one that is both "sturdy" and "probably having vital processes of the simplest and healthiest sort" but also "grey-eyed and brown-haired" (295), details that hardly seem necessary if the true ideal body is simply one in appropriate condition for his experiments. Though West would be expected to have an interest in a variety of 'healthy' living bodies, his potential pool of subjects can be reduced significantly by two factors. West conducts not one experiment on a female body. Similarly, the overwhelming majority of West's subjects are implied to be white by the means of their race not being mentioned, in distinction to the racist depiction of Buck Robinson, the only Black individual to be included in the story. Though the ultimate success of West's solution in reanimating Robinson is treated by Joshi as "counter[ing]" the "suggestion of biological racism" (Joshi 377n16), it is noted that "it was wholly unresponsive to *every solution* we injected in its black arm; *solutions prepared from experience with white specimens only*" (CF 1.306, emphasis mine), which does indeed mark Robinson out as fundamentally different from the white specimens that West has treated. This passage implies that multiple solutions of presumably different formulations or strengths were administered that were not required for white specimens. For West, Black bodies are not desirable bodies but may still be used for his purposes with apparent impunity, and female bodies are not even worthy of experimentation. West desires the objectified bodies of men who meet specific aesthetic criteria, for purposes that, while they are shrouded in the pretext of science, are truly centered on possessing and controlling the passive corpse in a way that may not be overtly sexual but is certainly a sensual experience for West.

It must be noted that the "subjects" of Herbert West's experiments are subjects predominantly in the scientific sense, particularly as the narrator's unreliability requires that we be skeptical about the truth of whether the reanimates are, in fact, capable of sentience. It is unclear if the murdered Leavitt is merely imitating his final conscious moments as he "suddenly collaps[ed] into a second and final dissolution from which there could be no return" (313) without any further utterances, and the later reanimation of Clapham-Lee's further complicates this, as he also repeats his final (living) utterance immediately upon his resurrection. However, if the narrator's version of events is to be believed, Clapham-Lee at least is clearly capable of subjective action, as is demonstrated by his orchestration of the breakout of the reanimated Halsey from an asylum and of West's own demise. In contrast, the narrator of Lovecraft's "The Outsider" is both corpse and subject.

West's descent into a "morbid and ghoulish curiosity" and a desire for "charnel picturesqueness" imply that West is increasingly willing to throw off the pretense of being scientifically motivated in his experiments in an attempt to gain sensual and aesthetic gratification through his obsessive and (both medically and socially) unacceptable interactions with the dead. This is foreshadowed by the narrator's earlier observation that the process of grave-robbery "might have been gruesomely poetical if we had been artists instead of scientists" (294). Such implications come to fruition in "The Hound," in which necrophiliac engagement with the dead is framed as primarily aesthetic. St. John and the narrator are "Wearied with the commonplaces of a prosaic world" (339) (implying that interactions with the dead are not 'commonplace'), so that "even the joys of romance and adventure [. . .] grow stale" (339); they turn instead to "that hideous extremity of human outrage, the abhorred practice of grave-robbing" (340) and "had assembled a universe of terror and decay to excite our jaded sensibilities" (340). Gratification of the senses is utmost in their pursuits, and they have designed their "museum" (340) of the dead to elicit their perverse satisfaction. They enjoy the sight of displays of human remains, "cases of antique mummies alternating with comely, life-like bodies perfectly stuffed and cured by the taxidermist's art" (340) and "skulls of all shapes, and heads preserved in various stages of dissolution" ranging from "the rotting, bald pates of famous noblemen" to "the fresh and radiantly golden heads of new-buried children" (341). They also indulge their senses of smell and hearing: "the odours our moods most craved" whether that be "the scent of pale funereal lilies, [. . .] the narcotic incense of imagined Eastern shrines of the kingly dead" or "the frightful, soul-upheaving stenches of the uncovered grave" (340) are piped in; and there are "nauseous musical instruments" on which they play "dissonances of exquisite morbidity and cacodaemoniacal ghastliness" (341). Unlike West, who uses and then discards the dead once they have served his purpose, these grave-robbers seek to immerse themselves in the experience of death as fully as possible while still living. Yet though they protest that they are "no vulgar ghouls," and that they "worked only under certain conditions of mood, landscape, environment, weather, season, and moonlight" giving their excursions "a fastidious technical care" (341), they are no more able to view the dead as subjects than West is, with no interest in the individual identities of the deceased but wholly centered on the artistry of their acquirement and display.

Norris notes that Lovecraft appears to use the term "ghoul" in two fashions, as a "distinct designator of a race or creature" (35) as in *The Dream-Quest of Unknown Kadath*, and as "a poetical term" (35) more aligned with its use in the stories analyzed here. While Lovecraft does associate grave-robbery with the figure of the ghoul in a more general way in "Herbert West," the connection between sensual necrophiliac gratification, the consumption of corpses, and the ghoul is more explicit in "The Hound." It is not merely St. John and the narrator who are ghouls by virtue of their grave-robbery, however elevated they may perceive their actions to be by their "fastidious technical care," as their victim, the "one buried for five centuries" whose grave they rob, "had himself been a ghoul in his time" (CF 1.342). Even more explicitly, the amulet they find in the grave bears "the ghastly soul-symbol of the corpse-eating cult [. . .] drawn from some obscure supernatural manifestation of the souls of those who vexed and gnawed the dead" (343). While Norris argues that the lack of "direct evidence that the titular Hound actually eats his victims" (36) and the fact that the protagonists' repertoire of defilement of the dead does not explicitly extend to cannibalism implies that such literal consumption of human flesh "is the work of other orders of being" (37), any attempt to wholly separate the figure of the ghoul into clean categories of human or inhuman or to delineate their consumption of human flesh into strictly literal or symbolic terms is fraught at best, as one sees in "Pickman's Model" or "The Outsider" for instance, whose eponymous characters exist somewhere on the spectrum between human and ghoul. That the grave-ghoul in "The Hound," when the narrator attempts to return the amulet, is discovered to be "not clean and placid as we had seen it then, but covered with caked blood and shreds of alien flesh and hair" (347–48), suggests that he has consumed the flesh of the dead bodies of St. John, who was "seized by some frightful carnivorous thing and torn to ribbons" (345), and the family of the thief (347). It is clear, then, that consumption of the dead is central to Lovecraft's conception of the figure of the ghoul, and this also holds true for St. John and the narrator. Though the narrator notes that their museum gratifies the senses of sight, smell, hearing, and (it is implied) touch with the aestheticized experience of death, there is a conspicuous absence of gratification of the sense of taste. Yet for all that they may not include cannibalism in their necrophiliac practices, they are nonetheless consuming the dead, even if only aesthetically.

Furthermore, the violation or consumption of corpses is implied to be cyclical in nature. As Downing argues, "the true desired outcome of the necrophile's encounter is that it should lead also to his death" in that the "actualization of the desire for death [. . .] announces the foreclosure of desire" (85). As Downing posits, the narrator's desire to join the dead he loves is contradictory: he desires to achieve the state of being dead which emotionally and physically attracts him, but in doing so he will place himself absolutely beyond having desire. Accordingly, it is their interactions with the dead that ultimately and directly lead to the deaths of St. John and the unnamed narrator of "The Hound" and Herbert West.

In "The Hound," the amulet stolen from the ancient ghoul's grave which brings St. John and the narrator's doom appears to be associated with a history of grave-robbery. The grave-ghoul "had stolen a potent thing from a mighty sepulchre" (CF 1.342). The "potent thing" was undoubtedly the amulet, as he suffered the same violent death as St. John at the "claws and teeth of some unspeakable beast" (342) and which the narrator fears for himself. Yet, despite their objectification of the bodies that make up their collection, whose treatment at their hands is clearly abhorrent and therefore inappropriate, St. John and the narrator's deaths are framed as in some ways very appropriate. Though they feel some horror at their predicament, "sometimes it pleased us more to dramatise ourselves as the victims of some creeping and appalling doom" (345), suggesting that on some level they find the death that is stalking them to be desirable, though given the choice, the narrator implies he would prefer to commit suicide rather than die in the same manner as St. John (this is foreshadowed but never fully enacted). Curiously, however, despite their profound disregard for the inviolability of the dead in general, the narrator makes a point to note that he tried to treat St. John's body appropriately to what St. John would have wanted, remarking that he "mumbled over his body one of the devilish rituals he had loved in life" (346). It is still not enough to save the narrator entirely, as the "baying of that dead, fleshless monstrosity" (348) continues to pursue him. Objectification of the dead begets an inescapable cycle in which those who treat the corpse inappropriately are doomed to be the recipients of such treatment themselves.

This is true in "Herbert West" as well: if the narrator is to be believed, West's inappropriate treatment of the dead has created the circumstances for his own inappropriate death, where his body is quite literally disrupted as a consequence of his experimentation on the dead, torn "to pieces," and carried away by the reanimates, as his eyes "hideously blaz[ed] with their first touch of frantic, visible emotion" (CF 1.324). And yet, this is impossible: West's assistant insists that West is taken through a "breach" in the basement wall and yet the plaster there is "unbroken" (324), and the only other evidence of this story, a box sent to West by the deceased Clapham-Lee, has been incinerated. This indicates that there is a greater disruption occurring in the text, a disruption that lies with the narrator. It is for the purpose of proving that "it is a vicious lie" that "it was Herbert West's body which I put into the incinerator" (CF 1.323) that the narrator recounts the entirety of the story. At every turn, West's companion confirms not only his fear of West but repeatedly summarizes preceding events. Though Joshi posits this repeated summarization as a "structural weakness" (375), it also has the effect of suggesting that the unreliable narrator is striving to improve his own credibility through consistent repetition. The narrator's unstable role within the text is also subtly underscored by the contradiction between his descriptions of himself as West's "closest companion" (CF 1.291) and "indispensable assistant" (314) and the entirely passive role that he assigns to himself within his account of the events: he is primarily engaged with observing events, occasionally assisting to transport bodies and, once, pouring "something from one test-tube to another" (296). These details contribute to a distinct sense of instability within the story: West may have been carried off by the reanimated dead through a wall that has mysteriously repaired itself or he may be dead by his companion's hand, incinerated to "unidentifiable ashes" (324), just as he may been the monster he is described as or may not have, in fact, been the perpetrator of the horrors but an ideal scapegoat due to his absence.

Thus, where Bottum finds that the trope of decay "requires something to be lost" (quoted in Douglas 185), it becomes clear that Lovecraft's characters instead find that broken down and decaying bodies are desirable because they are able to refute death and loss through possession of the corpse as object. The only time the grave-robbers in "The Hound" feel alive is through their aesthetic objectification of the dead, and Herbert West's experiments with reanimation both reflect and condemn the medical imperatives that insist on prolonging life 'at all costs' and, in doing so, demonstrate how such an attitude both objectifies the dying/dead body and makes all death inappropriate by removing agency from the patient/family to the professionals of the medical and funerary industries. Theirs may not be an explicitly sexualized desire for the dead, but viewing their actions through the figure of the necrophile enables us to see that it is their objectification of and obsession with the dead, not sexual contact alone, which makes them figures of horror.

Works Cited

Aggrawal, Anil. "A New Classification of Necrophilia." *Journal of Forensic and Legal Medicine* 16 (2009): 316-20. www.sciencedirect.com/science/article/abs/pii/S1752928X08002564. Accessed 3 October 2017.

American Academy of Psychiatry and the Law, jaapl.org/content/jaapl/17/2/153.full.pdf. Accessed 21 November 2017.

Callaghan, Gavin. *H. P. Lovecraft's Dark Arcadia: The Satire, Symbology and Contradiction.* Jefferson, NC: McFarland, 2013. Google Books, www.google.co.uk/books/edition/_/i7xPrPHTLjMC?hl=en&sa=X&ved=2ahUKEwjs3M-JmOrwAhWMT8AKHeNNAUgQ8fIDMBZ6BAgNEAQ. Accessed 27 May 2021.

Cooper, David K. C. "A Brief History of Cross-Species Organ Transplantation." *Proceedings (Baylor University Medical Center)* 25, No. 1 (2012): 49-57. *National Center for Biotechnology Information*, doi:10.1080/ 08998280.2012. 11928783. Accessed 18 June 2021.

Douglas, Katherine. "War Gothic and Bodily Decay: Reshaping Identity in *All Quiet on the Western Front*." *Gothic Studies* No. 2 (July 2020): 183-96. Edinburgh University Press, doi: 10.3366/gothic.2020.0048. Accessed 25 May 2021.

Downing, Lisa. *Desiring the Dead: Necrophilia and Nineteenth-Century French Literature.* Oxford: Legenda, 2003.

Finbow, Steve. *Grave Desires: A Cultural History of Necrophilia.* Arlesford, UK: Zero Books, 2014.

Gilbert, Sandra M. *Death's Door: Modern Dying and the Ways We Grieve.* New York: W. W. Norton, 2006.

Joshi, S. T., ed. *The Call of Cthulhu and Other Weird Stories* by H. P. Lovecraft. New York: Penguin Books, 1999.

Kreis, Henri. "The Question of Organ Procurement: Beyond Charity." *Nephrology Dialysis Transplantation*, 20 (July 2005): 1303-6. Oxford Academic, doi.org/10.1093/ndt/gfh911. Accessed 28 June 2021.

Laderman, Gary. *Rest in Peace: A Cultural History of Death and the Funeral Home in Twentieth-Century America.* Ebook, Oxford University Press, 2003. Oxford Scholarship Online, doi: 10.1093/acprof:oso/9780195183559.001.0001. Accessed 5 June 2020.

Langer, Lawrence L. *The Age of Atrocity: Death in Modern Literature*. Boston: Beacon Press, 1978.

Lovecraft, H. P. *Lord of a Visible World: An Autobiography in Letters*. 2000. Ed. S. T. Joshi and David E. Schultz. New York: Hippocampus Press, 2019.

Mandal, Anthony, and Keir Waddington. "The Pathology of Common Life: 'Domestic' Medicine as Gothic Disruption." *Gothic Studies* 17, No. 1 (May 2015): 43-60. Manchester University Press, doi: 10.7227/GS .17.1.4. Accessed 29 May 2015.

Nguyen, Doyen. "Evolution of the Criteria of 'Brain Death': A Critical Analysis Based on Scientific Realism and Christian Anthropology." *Linacre Quarterly* 86 (2019): 297-313. National Center for Biotechnology Information, doi:10.1177/0024363919869474. Accessed 18 June 2021.

Norris, Duncan. "'Hungry fer Victuals I Couldn't Raise nor Buy.': Anthropopphagy in Lovecraft." *Lovecraft Annual* No. 13 (2019): 27-52.

OED Online, s.v. "ghoul." (December 2022). www.oed.com/view/Entry/78080. Accessed 10 January 2023.

Re-Animator. Directed by Stuart Gordon. Starring Jeffrey Combs, David Gale, Bruce Abbott, Barbara Crampton, and Robert Sampson. Empire Pictures, 1985.

Rosman, Jonathan P., and Phillip J. Resnick. "Sexual Attraction to Corpses: A Psychiatric Review of Necrophilia." *Bulletin of the American Academy of Psychiatry and the Law* 17 (1989): 153-63.

Stearns, Peter N. *Revolutions in Sorrow: The American Experience of Death in Global Perspective*. New York: Routledge, 2007.

Troy, Andy. "'A Stalking Monster': The Influence of Radiation Poisoning on H. P. Lovecraft's 'The Colour out of Space.'" In John Michael Sefel and Niels-Viggo S. Hobbs, ed. *Lovecraftian Proceedings: Papers from NecronomiCon, Providence, 2013*. New York: Hippocampus Press, 2015.

Uttley, Stephen. *Technology and the Welfare State: The Development of Health Care in Britain and America*. London: Unwin Hyman, 1991.

Wasson, Donald L. "Elagabalus." *World History Encyclopedia*, 21 October 2013, www.worldhistory.org/Elagabalus. Accessed 18 September 2021.

"The Call of Cthulhu" and the Rhetoric of Things

Michelle Saavedra
Adjunct Professor of English, Suffolk County Community College

The work of H. P. Lovecraft is most often understood through the lens of literary criticism, but this essay explores "The Call of Cthulhu" and the Cthulhu Mythos through the lens of rhetoric. Rhetoric is commonly known as the study of civic discourse and persuasive language. However, contemporary rhetorical studies take on an expanded view of rhetoric to show how language causes identification and has consequences beyond classical persuasion. To understand Lovecraft's work through the lens of rhetoric, I use Joshua Gunn's framework of occult vs. occultic rhetoric.

Gunn's Framework of Occult vs. Occultic Rhetoric

In recent years, specifically in relation to literary criticism, there has been an increased interest in the occult and the supernatural. According to Joshua Gunn, "there exists a vast, little seen and little known world of occult" ("Occult Poetics" 30). In his book *Modern Occult Rhetoric*, he focuses on "the object of strange, mysterious, or difficult language, including the reasons or forces behind its invention, the experience of reading, interpreting, and reacting to it" (xix). Gunn focuses explicitly on the occult's language and how this language seems to distract readers from receiving the actual messages of occult texts, deliberately driving unknowing readers away from the texts, ones with no previous background in the occult.

However, Gunn's book not only focuses on the occult as simply a cult with a different language; he specifically connects the occult with rhetorical studies. Gunn defines rhetoric in relation to the occult and occultic, stating that rhetoric is defined "as the study of how representations (linguistic or otherwise) consciously and unconsciously influence people to do or believe things they would not otherwise ordinarily do or believe" (xx). Concerning the occult, this definition of rhetoric speaks to its use of "esoteric language" to create new terminology, which "allows the New Age adept and/or occultist to express or perhaps do things that ordinary language does not seem to permit" ("Occult Poetics" 2004, 31).

These challenging types of language are investigated further by an expansive form of rhetorical invention. Historically, the occult can be understood through "Magus Eliphas Lévi's influential 1856 treatise on transcendental magic" interpretation, "which recounts in evocative language the ubiquitous precept of the whole of occultism: the occult concerns secrets" (*Modern Occult Rhetoric* 2005, 3). Using esoteric language and symbolism by the occult becomes an art of invention, which Joshua Gunn coins as occult poetics. Invention is one of the five canons of rhetoric, which deals with discovering new arguments, often influenced by imagination. Gunn creates the term occult poetics for a "mode of invention particular to occultism" (*Modern Occult Rhetoric* 2005, xxvi). However, he "argue[s] that such a poetics is observable in contemporary occultic discourse that many deem to be atheistic or agnostic, such as the disagreements over theoretical jargon in the academy" (2005, xxvi). Occult poetics contains "a logic of rhetorical invention particular or specific to itself" ("Occult Poetics" 41). It functions "as a particular brand of poetics," which transcends vocabularies to "generate a rhetoric distinct from others" (41). Through the rhetoric of invention, the occult sustains "'esoteric language' to describe modern occult discourse as a creative linguistic practice or poetics" (37). Esoteric language is necessary for the occultist to express the ineffable because it functions outside ordinary language, which cannot fully express the occult. In relative terms, Gunn focuses on occult poetics because his argument is "occult discourse can be understood as the end result of a dynamic, generative paradox or antinomy (a stark contradiction between two principles) that structures and in some sense, determines the invention of difficult or strange language" (*Modern Occult Rhetoric* 2005, 37).

In addition to defining what an "occult rhetoric" may entail, Gunn distinguishes between the occult and occultic. He sets out "to distinguish the category of the 'occultic' from that of the 'occult' and 'occultism' because the latter no longer exist as terms for a coherent tradition" (*Modern Occult Rhetoric* xxii). Gunn created "the term 'occultic' . . . from the Latin root *occultus*, which means 'secret,' and which is the past participle of *oculere*, 'to conceal'" (xxiii). He argues that occult rhetoric has transitioned into occultic rhetoric, involving "occultic discourse," which "discriminates among groups of kinds of people with strange or difficult language" (xxiv).

Occultic rhetoric is essentially the transition to an "occult" of contemporary times. This occultic has a different context from "the early twentieth century" (xxiii). Today, the occult is "dominated by image and form" (xxiii). The occult has taken on a new discourse, which refers to "a hidden monster that suddenly appears" or "a hidden door or portal to another world" (xxiii). This new manifestation of the occult, as the occultic, is unlike the interpretation of "traditional occultism" because "it is not concerned with the channeling of preternatural power to effect change by means of spells" (xxii). With a new manifestation in the occult, Gunn creates the concept of occultic for modern occult rhetoric because "as a social form the occult can denote a multitude of objects that have nothing to do, necessarily, with the secret knowledge and practice of magic and mysticism" (xxiii).

The occultic, through the influence of mass media, has become a modern form of occultism, which has lost its purposefulness, meaning, and power (1). Occultic is separate from the occult because it "broadens the more traditional understanding of the centuries-long discourse of secrecy" (xxvii). The occult functioned "as a discrete cultural practice with a long and rich historical legacy" (xxvii). Moreover, as the occult transformed to occultic, "the discourse was reduced to an aesthetic form" (xxvii). In other words, rather than involving cultural practice, the occultic fixates on *appearance* of the occult. One of the influences in moving from occult to occultic is the development and ubiquity of mass media. The presence of mass media undercuts the secrecy of occult discourse, taking away its meaning and ineffability. Instead, mass media replaces secrecy with ubiquitous access to occult ideas.

"The Call of Cthulhu" as Occult Rhetoric

In *Modern Occult Rhetoric*, Gunn mentions Theosophy's use of esoteric language. Theosophy is the "'New Age' system of beliefs" mentioned briefly above and "revealed by a Russian spiritualist and psychic, H. P. Blavatsky" (30). Delving further into the realm of New Age, it is important to note New Age's strong opposition "to the rational outlook of the philosopher, and the verificationist approach of the scientist, rejecting 'the head' in favour of 'the heart' and relying on 'intuition' or inner wisdom'" (Heelas 5). This ideology had "Theosophist vocabulary" or, as Gunn refers to it, "the esoteric language of Theosophy" (*Modern Occult Rhetoric* 30). Lovecraft mentions Theosophy at the beginning of "The Call of Cthulhu," stating: "Theosophists have guessed at the awesome grandeur of the cosmic cycle wherein our world and human race form transient incidents" (CF 2.22). Connecting back to New Age beliefs, these followers "sometimes employ the language of 'new physics' or 'new science': the language of paradigm shifts, quark symmetries, fractals, chaos theory," which is reminiscent of features of Lovecraft's work (Heelas 5).

Francis Wayland Thurston, an occult detective, seeks to understand a manuscript left behind by his grand-uncle George Gammell Angell. Professor Angell's manuscript contains the discovery of an "unpronounceable jumble of letters" (CF 2.26). The danger of foreign words is presented at the beginning of the story when Thurston refers to the manuscript as "the thing" rather than the title of "the main document" called "CTHULHU CULT." Thurston encounters jumbled-up phrases such as "*Cthulhu fhtagn*," finding the "two sounds most frequently repeated" being "those rendered by the letters 'Cthulhu' and 'R'lyeh'" (CF 2.24, 26). The name Cthulhu "appears to contain the beginnings of the word 'chthonic' and most of the word 'thule'" (Tyree 142). The word "chthonic" is an adjective meaning dealing with, belonging to, or occupying the underworld. The word "thule" is a noun describing an area in "the northern most limit of exploration" or region of the ancient world that can still support life (Goho 42). These two words combined into Cthulhu give an origin of where the monster is housed within the mythos. These unpronounceable words are like the esoteric language of Theosophy, which functions as "discriminatory logic of difficult language" and "began as a form of self-protection" (Gunn, "Occult Poetics" 17). Similar to how occult practitioners used complex language to protect themselves, the esoteric language of Cthulhu protects the reader.

Lovecraft's creation of his monster's name is also deliberately unpronounceable to show the inhumanity of the monster. Monsters such as Cthulhu represent "the most dominant motif in Lovecraft's work," "the nameless, ancestral horror lurking beneath the earth, or ready to invade us from the stars; the dethroned but still potent gods of old" (Penzoldt 67). Lovecraft seems secretive in his use of vocabulary surrounding his monster, which aligns with Gunn's "occult discourse" ("Occult Poetics" 31). Occult discourse is "the study of secret or previously secret knowledge, which subsumes the revelations of so-called 'New Age' literature" (31). Gunn states that occult discourse "structures and in some sense determines the invention of difficult or strange language," which "regards spiritual truths as ineffable, but [. . .] assumes that there is much to say about ineffability" (31). Occult discourse seems to function in the rhetorical canon of invention because occult poetics is a form of invention (31). Occult discourse not only creates new languages but occasions "the invention of occult texts: the assumption that spiritual truths are translinguistic paradoxically requires a language for expressing ineffability" (*Modern Occult Rhetoric* 57). Thus, portraying "spiritual truth" requires the "act of speaking or writing," which is contradictory because this truth is ineffable ("Occult Poetics" 43). Therefore, Lovecraft uses invention to create esoteric language, which allows the expression of the supernatural in ways human language does not permit and is simultaneously motivated to generate texts housing the ineffability of Cthulhu.

Lovecraft challenges his readers to come closer to the forbidden knowledge of the occult through their encounter with the monster Cthulhu. The first instance of indirect contact is through Henry Anthony Wilcox's dreamscape creations. Wilcox is "a thin, dark young man of neurotic and excited aspect" who "called upon Professor Angell bearing the singular clay bas-relief" (CF 2.24). This bas-relief has a "modern design" and hieroglyphics, but "a figure of evidently pictorial intent" is present (23). This figure's description is a "symbol representing a monster, of a form which only a diseased fancy could conceive" (23). Wilcox's indirect encounter functions "in terms of ontography" by a term Graham Harman creates in his book, *Weird Realism: Lovecraft and Philosophy*, fittingly called "space" (239). The definition of "space" "embodies the fact that objects spatially removed from us are both absolutely distance (since they are not directly melted together with us), but also near to us insofar as they inscribe their distance in directly assessable fashion." Lovecraft provides a clearer depiction of the creature making "the underlying object [. . .] not entirely unfamiliar, since we are loosely acquainted with the basic ontological style of" one real animal, one mythical creature, and a human (239). Purposefully, Lovecraft focuses on "metaphors in which one of the terms is completely and deliberately unknown, defined not at all by any of the social preconceptions linked with it" (239).

While Wilcox and Thurston's account of the Cthulhu monster is indirect, Lovecraft does allow for one direct experience of Cthulhu. Wilcox's character makes semi-direct contact with Cthulhu in the dreamscape; however, Lovecraft indirectly presents this scene to readers. He uses modes of indirection using his frame narrative to add a layer of terror for his readers while simultaneously protecting them. When Thurston reads about Wilcox's story, he reads through the frame of Professor Angell's research. Readers and Thurston gain a direct encounter with Cthulhu through Gustaf Johansen's account. For the reader, this moment is also indirect. Thurston reads Johansen's encounter in a manuscript left behind before he died. Johansen's manuscript adds another layer to the frame narrative, which he had "written in English" to protect his wife from reading it (CF 2.49). From this manuscript, it is understood that he is the only character to encounter the monster directly in his home of R'lyeh and to survive this encounter, even though it is not for long. From Thurston, Johansen, and Wilcox's encounter with the monster, Lovecraft raises the possibility of an uncertain reality of Cthulhu. Though Lovecraft classifies his writing as fiction, he goes out of his way to present Cthulhu indirectly to his readers, which brings the idea that the same things happening to his main characters could happen to his readers. This idea is an "endeavor to situate the fantastic," which "consists in identifying it with certain reactions of the reader: not the reader implicit in the text, but the actual person holding the book in his hand" (Todorov 34). Fear is able to transcend the work "through reader's individual experience—and this experience must be fear" (Todorov 34). Lovecraft indirectly seems to suggest that that knowledge is so powerful that the Cthulhu Mythos could *actually* transcend the story, creating the fear that "The Call of Cthulhu" and Cthulhu itself are more than mythos.

Cthulhu functions to make humanity feel insignificant because Cthulhu is among the Great Old Ones, creatures seeming to have governed the cosmos before humanity. Cthulhu is a creature human beings cannot understand because "true wisdom and spiritual knowledge cannot be expressed in human language, for it resides beyond or outside human signification. 'The supernatural is by definition the realm of the ineffable,' wrote Burke, and 'language by definition is not suited to the expression of the 'ineffable''" (Gunn, "Occult Poetics" 32). Cthulhu further functions to make readers acknowledge the unhuman. Whether Cthulhu is real or not, the creature signifies this terrible concept of the unhuman, not inhuman. Cthulhu can be classified as unhuman because the unhuman and Cthulhu function outside of humanity. Cthulhu does not simply demonstrate the difference between the otherworldly and human; the unhuman functions outside of humanity and is not merely the difference between what humanity is not.

Invention plays a vital role in tying the unhuman to Cthulhu. Invention not only functions for Lovecraft in describing his monster but also works in inventing the concept of Cthulhu as unhuman. Invention uses imagination, which is "understood as a mental faculty that reproduces images in the mind" (Gunn, "Occult Poetics" 42). Imagination becomes "the generative origin of human existence, especially in magic and art" (42). Lovecraft's creation of Cthulhu is imaginative because the creature is depicted with the features of "an octopus, a dragon, and a human" together in one "caricature" (CF 2.23). In other words, Cthulhu becomes an amalgamation never existing before.

Further, invention being prominent in the psychical creation of Cthulhu, it also is found within the architecture of Cthulhu's domain. Upon Johansen's abduction and interaction with the "Cyclopean masonry" at R'lyeh, the description of the city is a "cosmic majesty" not from "this or any sane planet" (CF 2.50, 51). Johansen describes the city as cosmic and alien-like "instead of describing any definite structure or building, he dwells only on broad impressions of vast angles and stone surfaces" (51). The "architecture is frightening," and Johansen has such a problem explaining the structures in detail because "the ultimate embodiment of fear is non-human architecture, which has no relationship to familiar forms or aesthetics" (Evans 118). The otherworldly architecture makes it impossible to explain because humans do not have the proper language to describe it entirely; after all, the construction is unhuman. Lovecraft created these non-human architectures for his story because he "criticized modern architecture for rejecting tradition" (118). Lovecraft believed "new architecture, to be livable, must draw on traditional symbols (a rather post-modern idea)" (118).

Further, for Lovecraft, "architecture lacking in such symbols would be a terrifying embodiment of cosmic alienage" (118). Instead, the symbols incorporated into the architecture of R'lyeh are "horrible images and hieroglyphs" (CF 2.51). It is no wonder Johansen has problems articulating the words to describe R'lyeh, because the architecture lacks these symbols. Lovecraft deliberately invents R'lyeh's architecture to be otherworldly and new to humanity, thus indescribable to humans. Johansen mentions the "angles" of the structures in R'lyeh, which Thurston finds in correlation to his uncle's understanding of the "geometry" of the dreamscape to be "abnormal" (CF 2.51). Johansen's inhibited description of R'lyeh, which he experiences in person, is like Wilcox's description of his dreamscape. Wilcox describes the "geometry" of the dreamscape as "redolent of spheres and [with] dimensions apart from ours" (CF 2.51), therefore providing a similarly inhibiting description showing the unhuman, outside of Cthulhu's bodily form, through lack of symbolism in connection to traditional architecture in the landscape it inhibits. The unhumanness of R'yleh and the unhuman aspects of Cthulhu all exhibit Lovecraft's use of invention. Furthermore, the story offers opportunities to seek and obscure knowledge, providing a concrete experience of the occult and readers experience of esoteric language, the pursuit of hidden knowledge, and the inventive form of the unhuman.

The Cthulhu Mythos as *Occultic* Rhetoric

The Cthulhu Mythos is different from simply the concept of Cthulhu or the short story "The Call of Cthulhu." The Cthulhu Mythos encompasses these but is not limited to the monster Cthulhu because "Cthulhu hardly forms an important part in the overall Mythos pantheon" (Harms viii–ix). Instead, the Cthulhu Mythos is "a collection of fictional monsters, books, places, people, and other elements which weave together the works of Howard Phillips Lovecraft and other authors through a stream of common references" (vii). Lovecraft created the mythos in two ways: "first, he spun his stories together with a weave of shared allusions" (ix); second, by "its inclusion of others' creations in his work" (ix). Lovecraft's friend Frank Belknap Long was the first author to cross-reference the works in his creation, becoming a phenomenon where Lovecraft and his fellow writing friends borrowed and invented "gods, books and people" (ix). Many other writers took to reinterpreting the Cthulhu Mythos. For example, in the 1970s, writers often reworked different versions of the *Necronomicon*, a fictional book created by Lovecraft but never written by him. As time has advanced, so has the type of media outlet used to reinterpret the Cthulhu Mythos. One of the most influential creations in the Cthulhu Mythos "was the release of the *Call of Cthulhu* role-playing game in 1981" (xv). Sandy Petersen created the game by "combin[ing] the lore from many different Cthulhu Mythos authors to assemble the monsters and books to create the background for his game. 'The Call of Cthulhu' brought Lovecraft and the Cthulhu Mythos to the attention of many who would otherwise not have encountered it" (xv). With new technology and present-day pop culture phenomenon, "new material appear[s] constantly in many different media[s], ranging from computer games to graphic novels" (xv). Lovecraft's creation of Cthulhu and the Cthulhu Mythos

> Further, the open-ended and dynamic quality of his own cosmology has motivated any writers to create their own "Lovecraftian" stories over the years. Lovecraft's world has translated quite naturally into such postmodern phenomenon as role-playing games, Goth and Heavy Metal music, and into new alternative religious movements such as Neopaganism and 'Chaos Magick.' (Evans 128)

Occultic rhetoric is a term created by Joshua Gunn to represent an occult that, instead of focusing on cultural practices, focuses on the *appearance* of the occult. Occultic rhetoric is essential to the Cthulhu Mythos created by Lovecraft because his Cthulhu Mythos changes over time. Through invention, many of Lovecraft's fans and readers turn the Cthulhu Mythos into their creations through the consistent evolution of technology.

However, the Cthulhu Mythos can be classified as occultic rhetoric because it draws on the ways mass media and social form carries only the illusion of the occult. For example, Gunn discusses how modern occultic forms, such as Satanism

> transforms the occult into an imagistic, social form marks its rhetoric as the last or final expression of a logic that began with the popular representations of occultism of the mid-nineteenth century: as the occult became increasingly visible in the mass media, its meaning as the elite study of secrets receded behind the aesthetic value of its imagery. Thus, the occultic was born. (*Modern Occult Rhetoric* 175)

Gunn is helping to bring attention to "occulture," a term presented by Christopher Partridge and defined "as a sociological term, refer[ring] to the environment within which and the social processes by which particular meanings relating, typically, to spiritual, esoteric, paranormal and conspiratorial ideas emerge, are disseminated, and become influential in societies and in the lives of individuals" (116). As Satanism perverts the occult, Cthulhu changes its function in the hands of its fans, both "witnessing a confluence of secularization and sacralization, at the heart of which is a deceptively powerful 'occulture'" (116). Fans of Cthulhu change the monster into a "commodity form" functioning in occulture (Gunn, *Modern Occult Rhetoric* 175). Fans are integral to this transformation due to popular culture influences, whereby "it disseminates and remixes occultural ideas, thereby incubating new spores of occultural thought" (Partridge 116). This occultural movement to an economic view and use of Cthulhu's image shows that "adopting a political-economic perspective requires one to think about occult discourse as a collection of symbols and images that circulate in patterns typical of the media logics of late capitalism" (Gunn, *Modern Occult Rhetoric* 175). Lovecraft's *Necronomicon* functions as an occult discourse, but concerning the Cthulhu Mythos, Cthulhu the monster functions as this symbol. Rather than using Cthulhu as an opportunity to seek knowledge, modern occultic discourse uses the image and idea of Cthulhu (added to other parts of the discourse) as social capital. Therefore, while Lovecraft's story gives an audience the experience of occult rhetoric, the current contemporary fascination with Cthulhu's image and mythos only operates based on occultic rhetoric.

In addition to the way "The Call of Cthulhu" explores a shift to occultic rhetoric, it also offers an opportunity to explore the emerging field of Object

Oriented Rhetoric, where the experiencing human is decentered in favor of knowing what is nonhuman, and in some cases alien. This chapter will explore Cthulhu himself as alien and in connection to a burgeoning interest in rhetorical theory on ontology and post-humanism, as well as suggesting a much earlier connection to Husserlian phenomenology.

History of Rhetorical Ontologies

The term "Rhetorical Ontologies" is a newer form of an already established term called Object Oriented Rhetoric. Object Oriented Rhetoric/Object Oriented Ontologies (OOR/OOO), or now Rhetorical Ontologies, began as a rhetorical movement toward the focus on *things* in the twenty-first century. Things can enact thoughts and emotions, but Rhetorical Ontologies focus less on what these things do to humans, and instead "the story of objects asserting themselves as things . . . is the story of a changed relation to the human subject" (Barnett and Boyle 1). Through this scope of rhetoric, the human becomes decentered in regard to *things* and their relationships. Rhetorical ontologies challenge "epistemological understandings of rhetoric that ground rhetoric's scope and meaning in terms of human symbolic action" (1). This epistemic quality inherent in rhetoric's scope of theories halts rhetorician's "ability to grasp the 'thingness' of things—the way things *are* and the rhetorical force they wield in relation to us and other things" (2). In recent rhetorical scholarship, rhetoricians have begun to question epistemic paradigms where "the human subject occupies a privileged and central position in the rhetorical scheme of things" (3). Our own humanness limits us in regard to rhetorical theory because, with a focus on the epistemic, things matter only in relation to *us*. This epistemological attribute limits rhetorical theory because "we will likely go on believing that human beings alone determine the scope of possibilities of rhetoric and that humans, as a consequence, are the only true legislators of nature" (4). The rhetoricity of things already has scholars such as Doug Hesse, Nancy Sommers, and Kathleen Blake Yancey creating room for the study of things in rhetorical scholarship. As these scholars research things, a first movement in thing theory is created which focuses on personal things "to summon a network of associations and evoke cross-disciplinary inquiries" (4). Within the scholarship of thing theory, "contemporary theorists such as Elizabeth Grosz, Bill Brown, Barbara Johnson, Bruno Latour, and Jane Bennet have each forwarded new conceptions of things that foreground their material agencies and transformational power" (4).

These works constructed by the authors listed above often get their influence from Martin Heidegger's writing on the "thingness of things" (4). In his famous essay "The Thing," Heidegger asked one simple but very important "question, 'what is a thing'" (4). Heidegger in the essay takes an etymological look at the word 'object,' which suggests "an opposition between subject and object, with the object construed as 'that which stands before, over against, opposite us'" (4-5). Heidegger also takes a particular look at the word *Ding*, where a different meaning is found in relation to an object or thing constituting "'a gathering to *deliberate* on a matter under discussion, a contested matter'" (5). Heidegger explains to his readers that "'thing,' in this sense, denotes 'a matter of discourse'" (5). Bruno Latour furthered Heidegger's concepts of thingness to leave scholars with the concept that "rhetoric facilitates the fathering of people and things around *matters of concern and matters of interest*" (5). This ultimately delivers power to things, a "'thing power' in the way they gather forces and actors and in so doing 'affect other bodies, enhancing or weakening their power'" (5). An example of thing power at work is suggested by Graham Harman in the relationship between fire and cotton. The example is demonstrated as follows: "when fire encounters cotton it 'relates' to the cotton primarily by way of its flammability. All of the other aspects of cotton's being—its color, usability, smell etc.—withdraw from the fire's relation with cotton" (7). The thing here, being fire, has thing power in relation to cotton, because it enhances the already present state of cotton. Without the presence of fire using its thing power on another actor, specifically cotton, the presence of cotton's flammability would be absent (or at least less present to us). The fire does not merely replace the thing of cotton. Additionally, the fire does not fully know the thing of cotton. Instead, from this example readers can understand that "things have a depth to their being that is never fully revealed or exhausted in their dealings with other things or human beings" (7). Thus, the very act of naming something a thing versus an object matters, and it indicates a contingency, a gathering, a discussion of a thing's thingness. Thing theory and Rhetorical Ontologies is important to the study of Cthulhu because it will allow us to position "The Call of Cthulhu" and Cthulhu himself as a thing rather than a text or an object.

Before the introduction of Rhetorical Ontologies, rhetorical theory was regarded as "the study of human symbol use, which posits at the center of 'the rhetorical situation' a knowing subject who understands himself (traditionally, it is a *he*), his audience, and what he means to communicate" (Barnett and Boyle 1–2). But Rhetorical Ontologies takes away the self-importance of the subject. To better incorporate a place for thingness in rhetorical scholarship, the field of Rhetorical Ontologies was theorized. Rhetorical Ontology is a "relational framework that harnesses the energies of past and present theories of materiality in rhetoric but also anticipates possibilities for new rhetorical approaches to materiality going forward" (2). Material rhetoric already has a place within the field of rhetoric; however, Rhetorical Ontologies makes a space for rhetoric without the human. Further, Rhetorical Ontologies is able to function and be classified as an ontology because it "builds on the philosophical definition of ontology as the study of being, or 'what is,' to develop an inclusive rhetorical theory and practice" (2). In conclusion, understanding Rhetorical Ontology is to understand that it "highlights how various material elements—human and nonhuman alike—interact suasively [sic] and agentially [sic] in rhetorical situations and ecologies" (2). Thus, understanding this field will give us a sense of the larger suasory force that Cthulhu exerts as a thing.

Connections to Phenomenology

Although Rhetorical Ontologies do not explicitly acknowledge its debt to phenomenology or philosophy, these two fields of study intersect. This section focuses specifically on Don Ihde's teachings of phenomenology. Ihde offers phenomenologists for his readers to reference, such as "Edmund Husserl, Martin Heidegger, and Maurice Merleau-Ponty" (4). Rhetorical Ontologies and phenomenology intersect through trying to know a way of being and "being in the world" developed by Heidegger, who in turn built his interpretation of phenomenology based on Husserl's founding methodology. Heidegger's "being in the world" called for an ontological view of the world; therefore, it may be important to consider the connections between Rhetorical Ontologies and phenomenology briefly.

Don Ihde argues that "without doing phenomenology, it may be practically impossible to understand phenomenology" (1). Ihde encourages his readers to participate in phenomenology through multiple examples of variable analysis. The following variable analysis of a line drawing of Cthulhu provides a phenomenological viewpoint. A line drawing was selected as the simplified way of approaching the phenomenon of Cthulhu as a starting point. It parallels Ihde's objects of study in *Experimental Phenomenology*, where he conducts variable analysis on three-dimensional line drawings of cubes and geometric shapes.

In phenomenology, all objects have relational distinctions defined as *"every experiencing has its reference or direction toward what is experienced, and, contrarily, every experienced phenomenon refers to or reflects a mode of experiencing to which it is present"* (25). This refers to the "intentional or correlation apriori," which Husserl splits into two separate sides—the noema or noesis. The noema, also referred to as noematic correlate, refers to "what is experienced" (25). The noesis, also referred to as noetic correlate, refers to "the mode of experiencing which is detected reflexively" (25).

Figure 1. Line Drawing of Cthulhu

In what follows, I will demonstrate my initial variable analysis examining noema and noetic context for Figure 1, the simplistic line drawing of Cthulhu in Table 1, my variable analysis.

Table 1. Variable Analysis.

Level	Noetic Context	Noema
I	Literal-mindedness	octopus, bat
II	Polymorphic-mindedness	human
III	Polymorphic-mindedness open search (upside-down)	goat/devil, whale

If one were to apply Cthulhu to a phenomenological approach, a variable analysis of the sketch of Cthulhu may result. (Readers need to have an experiencing phenomenon of Cthulhu; therefore, some phenomenon representative of an encounter is necessary.) In the table above, the level refers to the differing levels one can view in the Cthulhu line drawing. The noetic context refers to the distinct movement between the ways the Cthulhu line drawing is "being experienced" (26). The noema, specifically concerning the Cthulhu line drawing, "has its own specific character as imagined" (26). For the Cthulhu line drawing to continue its phenomenological presence, those experiencing the object "must actively renew [noema] imaginatively" (26). The consistently reimagined object is diagrammed by the different levels (I–III) and specifically exhibited in the noema in Table 1. In the variable analysis, "what is experienced (the noema) is placed on one side of a correlation, then the mode of its being experienced (noesis) is always strictly parallel to it. One does not, and cannot, occur without the other" (26). What can be gained from a variable analysis of Cthulhu is the shift in noetic context and noema, and that one cannot occur without the other.

It is also important to note that while phenomenology and Rhetorical Ontologies borrow from a similar tradition in the works of Heidegger and Husserl, they are fundamentally in disagreement. Rhetorical Ontologies draws on many of the same thinkers as phenomenology. However, methodologically and epistemologically they differ. Phenomenology deeply questions the ability to know anything outside the lens of ourselves. In other words, while Rhetorical Ontologies seeks to know a noema without a human noetic context, phenomenology would question if that is relevant, rigorous, or even possible.

While the rest of this chapter will return to rhetorical theory, it is also important to note the long-standing disagreements between philosophy and rhetoric. From the time of ancient rhetorical scholarship, such as in the works of Plato and Aristotle, both philosophy and rhetoric were interested in similar concepts of truth, the human condition, emotions, and phenomena. However, philosophy and rhetoric were consistently proposed as being at odds with each other. Therefore, while there could be a rich cross-disciplinary communication between these fields, rhetoric and philosophy have largely remained separate. Although it would be interesting to see these fields in closer interdisciplinary communication in the future, the remainder of this essay will focus on the opportunities Cthulhu brings specifically to Rhetorical Ontologies. In other words, what can be gained from the attempt to isolate Cthulhu in its material force as a thing, beyond and outside of human understanding?

Rhetorical Ontologies

From Rhetorical Ontologies' scholarship, Thomas Nagel's article "What Is It Like to Be a Bat?" concerns consciousness, not of humans, but of animals. Conscious experience is not exclusive to human experience; "it occurs at many levels of animal life, though we cannot be sure of its presence in the simpler organisms" (436). Due to this awareness of organisms having consciousnesses, one must take away focus from "the relation between mind and body" because there is "no conception of what an explanation of the physical nature of a mental phenomenon would be" (436). However, when trying to understand Cthulhu through a Rhetorical Ontology, one must go beyond the mental and physical barriers placed upon people by their humanness. Subsequently, looking back at mental capacity shows "the fact that an organism has conscious experience *at all* means, basically, that there is something it is like to *be* that organism" (436). Therefore, it is possible to try and conceptualize what it is like to be a thing, but any organism trying to be like another will ultimately fail.

Nagel uses the example of a bat as an organism he tries to imagine being. However, Nagel and readers "must consider whether any method will permit us to extrapolate to the inner life of the bat from our own case, and if not, what alternative methods there may be for understanding the notion" (438). Imagination, being human, is limited by individual experience. Nagel tries to understand

> what it is like for a *bat* to be a bat. Yet if I [Nagel] try to imagine this, I am restricted to the resources of my own mind, and those resources are inadequate to the task. I cannot perform it either by imagining additions to my present experience, or by imagining segments gradually subtracted from it, or by imagining some combination of additions, subtractions, and modifications. (439)

As a human being, it is impossible to understand what it is like to be anything else but human. *Homo sapiens* are limited by their humanness and those physical qualities that determine individuals as human. Any organism "cannot form more than a schematic conception of what it *is* like" to be anything (439). The example Nagel provides that puts this concept into context is the bat's use of echolocation. A bat processes outgoing impulses using echoes to maneuver through its environment; human beings are unequipped to process sonar. Due to humanness, it is impossible to possess the ability to interpret sonar because it "is not similar in its operation to any sense that we possess, and there is no reason to suppose that it is subjectively like anything we can experience or imagine" (438). Although echolocation allows bats to move through their environment safely, it is not comparable to human eyesight. Bats can also view their environment through their eyesight and utilize their echolocation for hunting. Understanding what it is like to be any other thing is "permanently denied to us by the limits of our nature," human nature (440). The conclusion from Nagel's attempt to understand being a bat is

> the nature of beings access to humanly inaccessible facts is presumably itself a humanly inaccessible fact. Reflections on what it is like to be a bat seems to lead us, therefore, to the conclusion that there are facts that do not consist in the truth of propositions expressible in a human language. We can be compelled to

recognize the existence of such facts without being able to state or comprehend them. (441)

Concerning Cthulhu, although the truths of Cthulhu's *being* cannot be interpreted through a human lens and human language is limited in describing these truths, people may be able to ask through Rhetorical Ontologies what it is like to be Cthulhu. The existence of truth surrounding Cthulhu is present. However, from Thomas Nagel's conclusion, it is impossible to state these facts by limiting human language and comprehension.

Another work of scholarship often cited about Rhetorical Ontologies is Ian Bogost's book *Alien Phenomenology; or, What It's Like to Be a Thing*. The book furthers Rhetorical Ontologies through the relation of objects and metaphors. Bogost explains that phenomenology does not deal with human concepts of the universe. With the existence of things, objects do not exist for human use. This concept puts into question human existence. The human becomes an object just as much as a table is an object; "the object-oriented position holds that we do not have to wait for the rapturous disappearance of humanity to attend to plastic and lumber and steel" (8). Bogost also critiques those that consider an object's force (like an apple) only to relate it to human practices (like ecology and horticulture). He says that people do not need to discard the concept of humans completely "but we can no longer claim that our existence is special *as existence*" (8). Human beings can only see things through the human perspective; therefore, they relate objects to themselves. People make themselves the center through human perspective, but they are merely objects relating to other objects, which are also associated with other objects. Human beings are one object in a sea of objects. This idea concludes that "all things equally exist, yet they do not exist equally" (11). Though the human and the table are both objects, they are not the same; people cannot reduce the table to human encounters, nor can the table reduce human beings. Bogost references Latour, the founder of Actor Network theory, who states, "nothing can be reduced to anything else" (19). Bogost is showing his readers that "the world [. . .] does not exist" (12).

The human world and universe are not a "super-object that would gather all objects," the super-object does not exist (12). Through Thomas Nagel's article "What Is It Like to Be a Bat?," readers learn that an animal like a bat has a sense human beings are unable to understand because it is "a sense that's totally alien from a human perspective" (63). This example shows readers that there are some phenomena, as human beings, that *Homo sapiens* cannot experience. However, "alien phenomenology accepts that the subjective character of experiences cannot be fully recuperated objectively, even if it remains wholly real" (64). In a literal sense, "the only way to perform alien phenomenology is by analogy," where Bogost introduces metaphors (64). Bogost notes that "metaphorism offers a method for alien phenomenology that grasps at the ways objects bask metaphorically in each others' . . . attributes for a real object by means of metaphor itself, rather than by describing the effects of such interactions on the objects" (67). Metaphors allow human beings to approach an object's perspective toward other objects, which enables readers to understand that the object functions as a *thing*.

Although the article has referred to OOO/OOR as Rhetorical Ontologies, the terms of the same field will split to show that there are also key theoretical differences. While all these terms represent the same field, the following are a few theoretical considerations that Barnett and Boyle consider important. With a movement toward Rhetorical Ontologies comes a trend of new materialism. This new materialism focuses on the object and its relation to other things. New materialism, constructed by Coole and Frost, takes "vibrant materialisms, object-oriented ontologies, epistemology of the concrete, multiple ontologies, etc." and concludes three key features: "1) a posthumanist commitment to taking physical materiality more seriously; 2) a focus on biopolitical and bioethical dimensions of the human; and 3) a renewed engagement with economic materiality" (Graham 109). In his chapter in *Rhetoric, Through Everyday Things*, S. Scott Graham focuses on the relationship between materiality and ontology. Here he deals with a two-world diagram, one being modernity and one being postmodernity. This diagram shows that "the subject and the object forces a constant reengagement with the question of whether or not the subject has access to the object" (110). The object transforms through the two-world theory into

> the question of the object, of what substances are, is subtly transformed into the question of how and whether we know objects. The question of objects becomes the question of a particular relationship between humans and objects. This, in turn, becomes a question of whether or not our representations map onto reality. (110)

From the two-world theory comes the creation of the four-world theory. Metaphysical and epistemic inquiries need to be removed from Rhetorical Ontologies. However, specifically metaphysical inquiry demonstrates that "an object's being (noumena), and those features that exist in the object's appearance (phenomena)" (111). Epistemic inquiry, to be stripped away, necessitates the simultaneous removal of metaphysical inquiry. By attempting to strip away epistemic inquiry without metaphysical inquiry, "the problem of access despite removing it from the order of representation" becomes duplicated (111). The metaphysical inquiry becomes a fallacy that "is the root of the four-world problem" (111–12). The four-world problem due to metaphysical fallacy demonstrates "two simultaneous moves within new materialisms," including "1) the thingectomy; and 2) the reverse-Cartesian lobotomy" (112).

The thingectomy refers to the epistemic inquiry fallacy, which new materialists attempt to understand through *materia ontologica*. Heidegger presents a solution to the epistemic fallacy in his famous thing theory, "which posits a dualist unit of being. In short, Heidegger makes a critical distinction between the thing (Ding) and the object (Gegenstand)" (112). From Heidegger's *Being and Time*, a distinction is made between the terms "*vorhanden* (present-to-hand) and *zuhanden* (ready-to-hand). The importance of these terms from Heidegger's thing theory and *Being and Time*, exhibits "to be an object, to be *vorhanden*, is to stand against (*Gegenstand*) a subject in the order of representation" (113). Thing theory can offer aid to materialism and rhetorical theory, but "their current instantiation in much new materialisms inquiry provides the root of the metaphysical fallacy" (113). Thing theory, specifically its presence in "new materialisms fails on two accounts: 1) as Harman recognizes, Heidegger's *Ding* never fully disengages with the human; and 2) the cult of the z-axis ground ontological authenticity in reference to the horizon of subject-object entanglement" (114). The z-axis deals with "notions of withdrawal, depth and/or transcendence are used to make both and ontological and a qualitative distinction between the thing and the object" (114). Z-axis movement and thing theory operate together because "the essential aspects of a thing are those which recede from or transcend subjectivity and representation" (114). Thus, the z-axis functions to remove the subject and replaces it "with the horizon of subjective interaction as a new subject, a new reference object. In distancing itself from epistemology and the subject, the thingectomy still relies on the subject-object relationship as the index of being. The horizon of subjectivity creates the boundaries of the thing" (114).

The reverse-Cartesian Lobotomy is described as "representation is split from affect once the two-world problem becomes fully four-world" (114). This comes from the concept of thing theory with Heidegger's use of *Ding* and *Gegenstand*. These terms help to reflect "back on the subject and creates two poles of interaction: one representational and another sensual" (115).

Through the four-world model created by Harman, the "model makes a firm distinction between the real and sensual profiles of objects in interaction. Theory only emerges (as he says above) from the a priori sensual entanglements as projected from real objects" (115). Even in attempting a flat ontology, rhetoricians end up participating in a reverse-Cartesian Lobotomy.

The solution to the reverse-Cartesian Lobotomy, thingectomies, and metaphysical and epistemic fallacy is through a movement S. Scott Graham creates called thing-oriented ontologies. He believes that Heidegger's thing theory needs to be explored further, with a new interpretation that does not separate thing from object (thingectomy). Instead, the object functions as a thing. It becomes important to join object and thing because

> if the classification of articulations is considered a secondary step of metaphysical methodologies that might (or might not) follow from ontology, then human engagement with the world is not treated as a special case, and language and representation are not the accidental epiphenomena of more authentic precognitive sensual engagements. (121)

Thing-oriented ontology becomes a methodology that deals better with metaphysical fallacy and thing theory issues. Thing-oriented ontology makes words a thing and is "stripped down ontologies" (120). A stripped-down ontology deals with the articulation of "the preconditions of being, preconditions from which localized, context (articulation)-specific metaphysics can arise" (120). Bogost refers to thing-oriented ontologies as tiny ontology because they are simplistic. Thing-oriented ontologies are a relatively new theory; because of this, "there is not a great deal of rhetorical new materialism that move in the direction" of this theory (120). Thing-oriented ontology is something to look to in the future, but as of now exists as a singular proposal within the already incredibly new scholarship of OOO/OOR.

Cthulhu and Rhetorical Ontologies

While Cthulhu is perhaps phantasie more than phenomenon, he still allows people to conceptualize some of the possibilities and challenges involved in Rhetorical Ontologies. Some of this goes back to phenomenology and the issue of the self. Some extends from indigenous rhetorics and other rhetorical concerns with dislocating the human. However, Cthulhu brings to these conversations a sense of being the utmost limit of phenomenon.

Within *Alien Phenomenology; or, What It's Like to Be a Thing*, Bogost discusses the concept of "daisy chains." He focuses on an object's thingness through metaphors and furthers this analysis using "daisy chains." Daisy chains are the interwoven connections between two or more objects. For example, this daisy chain is used to phenomenologize Cthulhu. The different levels in the variable analysis chart, Table 1, of objects in use when viewing Cthulhu are instead the chains. Daisy chains are made up of conjectures for multiple types of relations between objects. Thingness through metaphors results in daisy chains or "sensual object relations, each carrying an inherited yet weaker form of metaphor with which it renders its neighbor" (81). These metaphors work to

> set up nested metaphorical renderings. The relationship between the first object and the second offers the clearest rendition, insofar as a metaphor is ever really clear. The next is rendered not in terms of the second object's *own* impression of the third but as the second's *distorted* understanding of its neighbor seen through the lens of the first. (81)

An example given by Bogost of this phenomenon is the example of the "sensor-puppy relation" (80). This relation moves from looking at the relation between photographer and puppy to the relation between sensor and puppy. The photographer and puppy's relationship is the first chain of the daisy chain, and the sensor and puppy's relationship is the second chain. This example continues to be chained out to other network relationships, like sensor-to-shutter digital encoding. The idea behind the daisy chain is the proposition of "what it is like to be a sensor in relation to the puppy?" or "binary code in relation to an image?" Although human beings cannot answer the question through limited human experience, asking the question shifts the focus of attention to different ways of being in the world.

Relating this notion of daisy chains to "The Call of Cthulhu," in specific terms of Cthulhu, let us consider the first and potentially the only encounter in-person with Cthulhu. This moment is the encounter of Cthulhu by Gustaf Johansen in "The Madness from the Sea." When Thurston meets Johansen's wife, he receives "a long manuscript—of 'technical matters' as he said—written in English, evidently to safeguard her from the peril of casual perusal" (CF 2.49). Readers get the relation between Johansen's account, written in a different language from Johansen's native tongue to Thurston's experience reading Johansen's account. Thurston already learned from his research that the *Alert* "held up" the ship Johansen voyaged on called the *Emma* (CF 2.50). Johansen speaks of the *Alert*'s crew "with significant horror" before the ship lands on "a coast-line of mingled mud, ooze, and weedy Cyclopean masonry" or "the nightmare corpse-city of R'lyeh, that was built in measureless aeons behind history" (50). Johansen described his first sight of Cthulhu and the otherworld gods "hidden in green slimy vaults" (50).

Readers get an understanding of Thurston's influential viewpoints upon Johansen's account by describing Cthulhu "sending out at last, after cycles incalculable, the thoughts that spread fear to the dreams of the sensitive and called imperiously to the faithful to come on a pilgrimage of liberation and restoration" (50). This is information that Johansen would not know of. However, Thurston clears this up for readers by saying "all this Johansen did not suspect, but God knows he soon saw enough!" (50). In one sense, removing experience from the narrator (Thurston commenting on and filtering Johansen's account) is a matter of the frame narrative; however, this removal shows how the focus on human characters denies readers some of the richness of the experience of Cthulhu. The characters can be distractions in relating the true story of Cthulhu, not helpful actors. To further pursue an encounter with Cthulhu, though, one cannot only look at the relations of humans.

Johansen (as paraphrased by the narrator) states that "there is no language for such abysms of shrieking and immemorial lunacy, such eldritch contradictions of all matter, force, and cosmic order. A mountain walked or stumbled" (CF 2.53). Cthulhu is described as a mountain here because no true language describes the creature. Instead, Johansen uses metaphors to place the object of Cthulhu in a way for human beings to understand it. Johansen makes it to the boat, but "three men were swept up by the flabby claws before anybody turned" (53). Johansen states that "Cthulhu slid greasily into the water and began to pursue with vast wave-raising strokes of cosmic potency" (54). During this pursuit of the ship, it is important to note later, Cthulhu changes the momentum of normal ocean tides, described as "wave-raising" (54). Going off this metaphor, one can deduce the waters must have been choppy, similar to, if not worse, if the ship was stuck in a storm. In his rendition, it is essential to note that Johansen often refers to Cthulhu as "the Thing" (54). Johansen describes himself as "setting the engine full speed" and he "reversed the wheel" (54). Johansen eventually recounts his attack on Cthulhu when he

> drove his vessel head on against the pursuing jelly which rose above the unclean froth like the stern of a daemon galleon. The awful squid-head with writhing feelers came nearly up to the bowsprit of the sturdy yacht, but Johansen drove on relentlessly. There was a bursting as of an exploding bladder, a slushy nastiness as of a cloven sunfish, a stench as of a thousand opened graves, and a sound that

the chronicler would not put on paper. For an instant the ship was befouled by an acrid and blinding green cloud, and then there was only a venomous seething astern; where—God in heaven!—the scattered plasticity of that nameless sky-spawn was nebulously *recombining* in its hateful original form, whilst its distance widened every second as the *Alert* gained impetus from its mounting steam. (54)

A focus through this rendition is on Johansen's fear of Cthulhu and R'lyeh and the literary elements within the short story. However, from the perspective of Rhetorical Ontologies, if the concept of daisy chains is taken seriously, readers may want to shift focus and attunement from Johansen to the "things" of this encounter. To pursue this as a daisy chain further, one might look at other aspects, specifically objects of Johansen's account. One can propose the following daisy chain (my creation). Readers can consider the steering wheel's relation from the boat to the choppy ocean waters to the form of Cthulhu. Rather than trying to know the encounter between these objects, a daisy chain wants to focus on the boat's experience or the steering wheel's experience. This may ask readers to contemplate further the non-Euclidean geometry of the water over R'lyeh or sound of the ocean churning over the "exploding bladder of slushy nastiness." Several chains take Johansen out of this moment because humans could be distracted from the experience of those "eldritch contradictions" Lovecraft seeks to engender (CF 2.53). The focus becomes the experience of things and becomes a domino effect on seemingly less important objects of focus.

Through the Rhetorical Ontological approach to "The Call of Cthulhu," a shift in attention to a thing's experience of a moment opposing human language occurs. One does not gain a description of the boat's experience with the architecture in terms of course of navigation. The architecture instead functions with Cthulhu, both things indescribable by human language. Thurston uses the term "futurism" in his description of the architecture (CF 2.23). He describes the architecture by not defining any "structure or building, he dwells only on broad impressions of vast angles and stone surfaces—surfaces too great to belong to any thing right or proper for this earth, and impious with horrible images and hieroglyphs" (CF 2.51). This interpretation is Thurston's viewpoint of Johansen's manuscript. Thus, Thurston notes to readers "that the *geometry* of the dream-place he saw was abnormal, non-Euclidean, and loathsomely redolent of spheres and dimensions apart from ours" (51), to make connections between Wilcox's dream R'lyeh and Johansen's physical R'lyeh. Wilcox's and Johansen's renditions are strikingly similar in the feelings they invoke. The architecture of the city of R'lyeh invokes Gothic terror, and the structure's description can be Gothic. Human beings cannot explain or understand it, so the architecture is as alien as Cthulhu. However, by proposing a daisy chain, attention is not only called to focus on relationships between human beings and the alien but also between things and the alien thing in a flat ontology. Thus, if people ask themselves what a boat's experience is, not including architecture and Cthulhu, it causes them to ask other questions. These questions may focus on movement, direction, orientation, force, navigation, or mobility. They might also become overwhelming or lost if the only focus is on people as readers thinking about non-Euclidian architecture.

This concept can also be applied to lesser moments in the story, such as Wilcox and the bas-relief, and Johansen's written account of his experience of Cthulhu, functioning as a thing. The bas-relief description of "a rough rectangle less than an inch thick and about five by six inches in area; obviously of modern origin. Its designs, however, were far from modern in atmosphere and suggestion" (CF 2.23). The art style description is "cubism and futurism" (23). The writing on the bas-relief is not human; it is "prehistoric writing. And writing of some kind the bulk of these designs seemed certainly to . . . failed in any way to identify this particular species, or even to hint at its remotest affiliations" (23). The depiction of Cthulhu on the bas-relief is "a sort of monster, or symbol representing a monster" (23). Its features represent "an octopus, a dragon, and a human caricature" with a "pulpy, tentacled head surmounted a grotesque and scaly body with rudimentary wings" (24). The scariest part interpreted by Thurston on the bas-relief is "the *general outline* of the whole which made it most shockingly frightful. Behind the figure was a vague suggestion of a Cyclopean architectural background" (24). By utilizing the notion of daisy chains, the following is proposed: the bas-relief relating to the representation of architecture, the architecture relating to hieroglyphs, the hieroglyphs relating to writing, and the writing relating to the material of the carving. Rather than concentrating on reader's impressions of the bas-relief as a piece of art, daisy chains for the nonhuman things ask about relationships between symbols, materials, and representation.

A last important point: Rhetorical Ontologies circles back to the idea of language as a thing and makes strange the idea of communicative expression at all. The last two examples, Wilcox's idol and Johansen's manuscript, are arguably the most critical contributions Lovecraft makes in "The Call of Cthulhu" because they reverse the human notion of language as purely symbolic. While Rhetorical Ontologies often deals with things easily considered material as objects or as things, what it offers to the interpretation of "The

Call of Cthulhu" is that words and language are a thing, a material thing. While "The Call of Cthulhu" at the surface can be interpreted as a story about the alien, thing, other; Rhetorical Ontologies can lead to the argument that the story's heart is language itself. Rather than focusing on the text as an object or the noetic context of the reader or author, perhaps it is possible to re-approach literature through a more Rhetorical Ontologies dislocation of the human. This may cause readers to ask different questions through the experience of texts and question the notion of language and words as "thing."

The rhetorical situation is classically a relationship between text, author, and audience; however, it is not a simple relationship. Often, Cthulhu is referenced within pop culture as an icon, more so than a creature created in Lovecraft's story. Most people know Cthulhu without knowing anything about Lovecraft. The relationship between Lovecraft's text and authorship becomes complicated due to the intertextual relationship among friends. For example, Lovecraft's text often has illusions to the works or ideologies of Edgar Allen Poe. Lovecraft and his contemporaries contributed to the pulp-fiction magazine *Weird Tales*, often referencing invented works created by Lovecraft in his stories and vice versa. Lovecraft's text also uses elements to create an experiential notion of the thing, the alien, and the other. This study of "The Call of Cthulhu" has been a theoretical exploration of the rhetorical situation, which "developed significantly since Lloyd Bitzer's influential formulation" (Barnett and Boyle 141). The rhetorical situation is often discussed in ancient theory to more contemporary theory, which is also the commonplace of this Rhetorical Ontological approach to tie some seemingly separate theoretical trajectories. Additionally, by seeing a more complicated sense of the rhetorical situation as a basis for Rhetorical Ontologies, these methods may apply to notions of reading other works of literature.

Works Cited

Barnett, Scott, and Casey Andrew Boyle, ed. *Rhetoric, Through Everyday Things*. Tuscaloosa: University of Alabama Press, 2016.

Bogost, Ian. *Alien Phenomenology; or, What It's Like to Be a Thing*. Minneapolis: University of Minnesota Press, 2012.

Evans, Timothy H. "Tradition and Illusion: Antiquarianism, Tourism and Horror in H. P. Lovecraft." *Extrapolation* 45 (2004): 176-95.

Goho, James. "What Is 'the Unnamable'? H. P. Lovecraft and the Problem of Evil." *Lovecraft Annual* No. 3 (2009): 10-52.

Graham, S. Scott. "Object-Oriented Ontologies Binary Duplication and the Promise of Thing-Oriented Ontologies." In Scott Barnett and Casey Andrew Boyle, ed. *Rhetoric, Through Everyday Things*. Tuscaloosa: University of Alabama Press, 2016. 108-24.

Gunn, Joshua. "An Occult Poetics; or, The Secret Rhetoric of Religion." *Rhetoric Society Quarterly* 34, No. 2 (2004): 29-51.

———. *Modern Occult Rhetoric*. Tuscaloosa: University of Alabama Press, 2005.

———. "Refiguring Fantasy: Imagination and Its Decline in U.S. Rhetorical Studies." *Quarterly Journal of Speech* 89 (2003): 41-59.

Harms, Daniel. *Cthulhu Mythos Encyclopedia*. Lake Orion, MI: Elder Signs Press, 2008.

Harman, Graham. *Weird Realism: Lovecraft and Philosophy*. Winchester, UK: Zero Books, 2012.

Heelas, Paul. *The New Age Movement: The Celebration of the Self and the Sacralization of Modernity*. Malden, MA: Blackwell, 2005.

Ihde, Don. *Experimental Phenomenology: An Introduction*. Albany: State University of New York Press, 1986.

Nagel, Thomas. "What Is It Like to Be a Bat?" *Philosophical Review* 83 (1974): 435-50.

Partridge, Christopher. "Occulture Is Ordinary." In Egil Asprem and Kennet Granholm, ed. *Contemporary Esotericism*. New York: Routledge, 2013. 123-43. EBSCO*host*.

Penzoldt, Peter. *The Supernatural in Fiction*. 1952. Extracts in S. T. Joshi, ed. *H. P. Lovecraft: Four Decades of Criticism*. Athens: Ohio University Press, 1980. 63-77.

Todorov, Tzvetan. *The Fantastic: A Structural Approach to a Literary Genre*. Tr. Richard Howard. Ithaca, NY: Cornell University Press, 2007.

Tyree, J. M. "Lovecraft at the Automat." *New England Review* 29 (2008): 137-50.

Lovecraftian Elements in the Philosophy of Nick Land and the Cybernetic Culture Research Unit

Robert Landau Ames
Harvard University

"Engagement with Bitcoin brings us into communication with hidden inclinations..."

—Nick Land, *Crypto-Current: Bitcoin and Philosophy*

This paper argues that a Lovecraftian reading of the corpus of British philosopher Nick Land (b. 1962) and the Cybernetic Culture Research Unit (CCRU, sometimes styled CCRU) with which he was affiliated, can, despite the apparent discontinuities between the works within this corpus, establish a continuity between them. Land and the CCRU's deployment of Lovecraftian figures was particularly explicit in a brief series of articles published online ca. 1998-99, and Lovecraft references abounded in Land's late 2010s online output; but beyond these more obvious appeals to Lovecraft, an effort to champion unthinkable or otherwise inhuman forces whose description resembles deities found in Lovecraftian fiction persists throughout Land's corpus, even in texts that do not explicitly mention them. In "Origins of the Cthulhu Club," a ca. 1998-99 work of theory-fiction in which the CCRU discusses Lovecraft explicitly, one of its characters notes that in their work and Lovecraft's alike, "nonhuman cultural factors are seen to play a decisive role in large-scale historical developments" (CCRU 44). However, this commonality between Land and Lovecraft extends beyond this one work. Throughout Land's corpus, "nonhuman cultural factors," but also, crucially, economic factors, "are seen to play a decisive role in large-scale historical developments." This commonality persists in the face of apparent ruptures such as Land's 2010s neoreactionary turn, on which much recent Land scholarship has focused.

Background on Land

Land first came to prominence as a scholar of Continental philosophy at Warwick University in the 1990s, where he took up the leadership of the CCRU after the departure of its founder, feminist theorist Sadie Plant. While Land and the CCRU's work from that period until Land's 2013 publication of the neoreactionary text *The Dark Enlightenment* attracted some attention for its radicalism, the work (and Twitter output) following Land's rightward turn has attracted more attention, perhaps in part due to the perceived rupture with the previous decades' Deleuzianism (which many observers tend to assume leans left), though its somewhat sensationalized links to cultural traumas ranging from Donald Trump's 2016 electoral victory to murders committed by open neo-Nazis are probably the major drivers of this recent attention. A 2017 *Quartz* article attempts to link Land to Steve Bannon on the basis of a *Politico* article's claims that Bannon had, like Land, engaged with the thought of Mencius Moldbug (Goldhill). Aria Dean identifies Land as "a leading neoreactionary thinker" due to his right accelerationism, which "advocates that capitalism be encouraged to run wild" in "Notes on Blacceleration," another 2017 article. Meanwhile, a 2019 *Vox* article suggests that Land's role in the development of accelerationism as a philosophical position may also be in part responsible for the murders linked to the neo-Nazi organization Atomwaffen Division on the ground that some of its members and observers have described its sociopolitical strategy as accelerationist (Beauchamp).[1] Whatever the differences in the particular contours of the accusations stemming from Land's right-wing associations, those associations loom large in discussions of his public persona.

However, the apparent rupture involved in Land's right turn is probably a major factor in the attention it has attracted. McKenzie Wark notes in a 2017 Verso Books blog entry that "Land achieved notoriety in recent years as a prophet of Neo-reaction," in stark contrast to "The Land of the eighties," who

---

1. As an aside, it bears noting that the Atomwaffen Division's use of the term accelerationism differs considerably from philosophers' use of it: philosophically, the term refers to a position that favors increasing the speed of technocapitalist development, while the Atomwaffen Division and similar groups use it to refer to a view that favors acts (including murder) that could hasten the collapse of current institutions on the grounds that state failure will facilitate the foundation of a white ethnostate. Both endorse the acceleration of processes that are already in motion, but despite that broad similarity, they have few particulars in common.

"still thought of unbinding the laws of both Kant and capital" in the name of "A radical international socialism" manifested in the form of "a program of collectivity or unrestrained synthesis that springs from the theoretical and libidinal dissolution of national totality"; the Land between those two periods "owes a lot to Deleuze and Guattari, but read not through Bergson's vitalism but through Nietzsche's will to power, and Bataille's reading thereof." Similarly, an *Art Monthly* article from April of that year identifies Land both as a "proponent of accelerationism" and "a long-term darling of the art world and academia because of his work with the Cybernetic Cultures Research Unit [sic] in the 1990s," going on to contrast the CCRU's work, which earned Land his darling status, with his current interests, which "have seen him become a philosophical guru for elements of the so-called 'alt-right' groups of white supremacists and nationalists" (Gogarty 8). Much writing on Land within academia has also dwelt on his relationship to accelerationism and possible influence on the far right, but, when less immediately concerned with Land's right turn, it has tended to focus upon his more obvious philosophical influences (especially Deleuze, Bataille, and Kant) instead of the Lovecraftian implications of his work, framing the latter as a device employed in service of the former.

Land and Accelerationism

Like the discussions of Land in the popular press cited above, accelerationism looms large in recent academic discussions of Land. Katerina Kolozova identifies Land with accelerationism in "Metaphysics of Finance Economy: Of Its Radicalization as the Method of Revoking Real Economy" (2015), going so far as to call accelerationism his theory and noting the "revolutionary potential" in its insight that "An apocalyptic landscape is, evidently, necessary for a new political horizon to appear" (Kolozova 24-25). As its title suggests, Sam Sellar and David R. Cole's "Accelerationism: A Timely Provocation for the Critical Sociology of Education" (2017) also limits its discussion of Land to an explanation of his role in the development of accelerationism, noting that his description of acceleration as "techonomic time" raises a central question for the authors study, that of the "potential divisibility of technology and capital" and in particular its "relevance for critical sociology of education," which they argue depends "on whether technological development in education can be accelerated separately from commercialisation" (39). Of Land, Sellar and Cole conclude that his "concept of techonomic time" can offer "a useful reference point for theorising this process and potential responses to the technological reworking of labour and education" because it "provides an apt description of the potential for machines to displace the middle class" (42). In "Accelerationism, Hyperstition and Myth-Science," Simon O'Sullivan addresses Land's influence upon Srnicek and Williams's accelerationist work with greater breadth than other sources, engaging not only with Land's treatment of acceleration, but with its links to other concepts Land helped develop, including one of the CCRU's key contributions, hyperstition. Discussed in greater depth below, the term, in brief, refers to a process by which the fictional becomes real. However, O'Sullivan does not address the Lovecraftian dimension of hyperstition. The description of hyperstition available on the CCRU's website (which O'Sullivan quotes in full) reads as follows:

> Element of effective culture that makes itself real.
> Fictional quantity functional as a time-traveling device.
> Coincidence intensifier.
> Call to the Old Ones. (CCRU website)

Of these, O'Sullivan discusses the first three, but does not engage with the obviously Lovecraftian mention of "the Old Ones," instead only mentioning Lovecraft in passing when noting that Land's more recent neo-reactionary work often links the "trichotomy" (the three dominant tendencies within neo-reaction: the religious/traditionalist, the ethno-nationalist, and the techno-commercialist) to "more established myth-systems such as Hinduism with its caste system and, invariably, Lovecraft's Cthulhu" (28). Another 2017 article, Frederick Harry Pitts and Ana Cecilia Dinerstein's "Corbynism's Conveyor Belt of Ideas: Postcapitalism and the Politics of Cocial Reproduction," both identifies Land with accelerationism and limits its discussion to the right-wing affiliations to which it led him, alleging that accelerationism "takes on a distorted expression in 'right accelerationism', associated, via one of its chief instigators Nick Land, with the so-called 'alt-right' of bedroom-bound neo-nazis" (426-27). While still focused on Land's accelerationism, in "Arguments within English Theory: Accelerationism, Brexit and the Problem of 'Englishness,'" Benjamin Noys acknowledges the centrality of genre fiction to Land's corpus, but focuses on cyberpunk rather than Lovecraft: Noys highlights cyberpunk's role in shaping Land's vision of a techno-capitalist future rather than Lovecraft's role in shaping Land's presentation of the inhuman forces at work in culture and the economy (588). In

"Accelerating Down a Road to Nowhere: On *Inventing the Future* by Nick Srnicek and Alex Williams" (2020), meanwhile, Florence Gildea appears to cite connections to Land and accelerationism to discredit Srnicek and Williams's political project. Of it, Gildea alleges, "Rather than being rooted in the concerns and interests of the populace at large, this project is ideological. Yet the name of the philosophy which shapes *Inventing the Future*—accelerationism—is notable for its absence." Of this philosophy, Gildea writes, "accelerationism has split into left-wing and right-wing variants and CCRU's leader Nick Land has since become associated with the alt-right" (360).

Land and Continental Philosophy

In "Plotting Nature's Havoc: Potential Realisms between Transcendental Materialism and Transcendental Dynamism" (2011), Ben Woodard mainly presents Land as a successor to Deleuze and commentator upon Kant, noting similarities in Deleuze's and Land's positions regarding transcendence: "Deleuze's (and Land's) Transcendental Materialism begins from the regime of sense and excavates the material which is cemented in the immanent" (81). Woodard argues that Land "expands on Deleuze's materialism and shows its radical difference from Kant through Lands [sic] critique of the critical project;" Land "engages the relation between judgment and aesthetics (via the sublime) making this the jumping off point for diagnosing the limitations of Kant's structured reason yet, at the same time, it questions the limits of sense in Deleuze," as "Deleuze's ontology relies problematically on the pseudophysicalized empirical namely in terms of the concept of sense and, even more specifically, intensity" (82-84). By utilizing sense and synthesis, however, Land "further problematizes the immanence-transcendence relation as it crosses the connection of thinking to being" (85). In "Professor Nobody's Little Lectures on Thomas Ligotti's Supernatural Horror," Roger Luckhurst writes somewhat dismissively of Land when surveying the place of weird fiction in contemporary philosophy: "In the 1990s, Nick Land and members of his Cybernetic Culture Research Unit . . . began to write intense and mildly unhinged horror theory-fictions probably best understood—as they were written—under the influence of amphetamines" (3). Despite the article's focus on horror, Lovecraft only appears briefly and at a few degrees of separation from Land: aside from noting the obviously Lovecraftian title of one CCRU essay, Luckhurst only mentions Lovecraft in connection with the CCRU when he notes that the journal *Collapse*, which another CCRU member edited, published American philosopher Graham Harman's earliest work on Lovecraft (4).

In his review of Gabriel Catren's *Pleromática o las mareaciones de Elsinor*, Alan Ojeda frames Catren's work as the product of his engagement with authors linked to the "speculative turn" in Continental philosophy, including Land and fellow members of the CCRU, claiming that these authors, despite their differences, were all motivated by a common passion: "returning to speaking of the Great Outside (the real, the in-itself), from which philosophy appeared to have resigned since the seventeenth century" (367). However, the author leaves the possible Lovecraftian valences of this "Great Outside" unexplored.

The Cthulhu Club

While the recent scholarship discussed above tends not to discuss the connections between Land and Lovecraft at length, the CCRU's late-nineties theory-fiction and the characters it features explicitly engage with Lovecraft. One of the main characters in "Lemurian Time War" and "Origins of the Cthulhu Club," Captain Peter Vysparov, grows "increasingly convinced that the works of author H. P. Lovecraft and their developed feedback between Scientific rationality and Occult cosmic-horror were more than fiction" after a deployment to a pacific island during the Second World War, which exposed him to a local tribe's occult system (Cabrales 25). "Origins of the Cthulhu Club" takes the form of an epistolary short story, and, as the title suggests, its references to Lovecraft are quite explicit. In the first letter ("Captain Peter Vysparov to Dr Echidna Stillwell, 19th March 1949"), Vysparov explains that he served in the Eastern Sumatran region of Dibboma and conducted a mission "of attempted cultural manipulation, with the aim of triggering a local insurgency against the Japanese occupation." This mission leads Vysparov into contact with, and weaponization of, "Dibboma witchcraft," culminating in the incapacitation ("by severe mental break-down") "[i]n just two weeks—between March 15th-29th 1944" of "three consecutive Japanese commanders." In a postscript, Vysparov concludes, "I cannot help noticing that the dates concerned—as also of this letter [19th March 1949]—are strangely Lovecraftian" (CCRU, 43). While Vysparov only elliptically indicates the Lovecraftian resonances of the dates, in her response to it Stillwell elaborates, noting that they are "what in Northern latitudes constitutes the Spring Equinoctial period," the period that "is so emphatically stressed in Lovecraft's 'The Call of Cthulhu.'" Stillwell then notes that the location of Vysparov's deployment was also Lovecraftian, as "Lovecraft had a peculiar obsession with the

South-Seas, a thematic coalescence of almost hypnotic ethnographic fascination with the most abysmal and primitive dread" (CCRU 44). To be even more explicit than Echidna Stillwell, I will note that in "The Call of Cthulhu," many of the significant events occur from March to April 1925. Wilcox first calls upon Angell on 1 March 1925, then falls into a delirium on 22 March, and comes out of it on 2 April. Wilcox's delirium leads Angell to compile correspondence and press clippings attesting to a more widespread outbreak "of panic, mania, and eccentricity during the given period" (CF 2.29). Then, of course, the narrator's subsequent research leads to the revelation of Second Mate Johansen's collision with Cthulhu upon the latter's rise from his home in R'lyeh in the same period.

In the final letter of the series ("Echidna Stillwell to Peter Vysparov, 28th May 1949"), Stillwell explicitly situates Cthulhu within Dibboma lore and comments upon Lovecraft's depiction of Cthulhu's rising:

> According to the Nma she is the plane of Unlife, a veritable Cthelll—who is trapped under the sea only according to a certain limited perspective...That her submerged Pacific city of R'lyeh is linked to a lemuro-muvian culture-strain seems most probable, but the assumption that she was ever a surface-dweller in a sense we would straightforwardly understand can only be an absurd misconstrual. It is much more likely that Cthulhu's rising—like that of Kundalini as it was once understood—is a drawing down and under, a restoration of contact with abysmal intensities. Why would Cthulhu ever surface? She does not need rescuing, for she has her own line of escape, trajected through profundity. (CCRU 48)

While "Origins of the Cthulhu Club" discusses Lovecraft and "The Call of Cthulhu" by name, it is not first and foremost a work of Lovecraft scholarship. Instead, it, along with another text, "Lemurian Time War," is a work of theory-fiction that simultaneously introduced and performed "hyperstition," one of the CCRU's major conceptual innovations.

In "Lemurian Time War," the CCRU claims that one William Kaye, an associate of the aforementioned Peter Vysparov, provided it with information attesting to "William Burroughs' involvement in an occult time war" and that as a result of this involvement, "The Ghost Lemurs of Madagascar" (a Burroughs story published in 1987) "had been an exact and decisive influence on the magical and military career of one Captain Mission, three centuries previously" (CCRU 24). Kaye reports "that Burroughs, like Vysparov, was interested in the 'hyperstitional' relations between writing, signs and reality." This interest provokes Vysparov and Kaye's interest in Burroughs, and drives

Vysparov's engagement with Lovecraft: "interest in Lovecraft's fiction was motivated by its exemplification of the practice of hyperstition, a concept had been elaborated and keenly debated since the inception of the Cthulhu Club. Loosely defined, the coinage refers to 'fictions that make themselves real'"; this account of hyperstition proceeds from the recognition that "fiction is not opposed to the real," but that reality is instead, "composed of fictions—consistent semiotic terrains that condition perceptual, affective and behavioral responses" (CCRU 25). In contrast to the "equation of reality and fiction" in the form of "'postmodern' ontological skepticism," Burroughs took the equation "in its positive sense, as an investigation into the magical powers of incantation and manifestation: the efficacy of the virtual" (CCRU 25). Writing is therefore an expression of this efficacy; "realism merely reproduces the currently dominant reality program from inside," naively taking a side "in magical war, collaborating with the dominant control system by implicitly endorsing its claim to be the only possible reality." Hyperstitional fiction like Burroughs's "seeks to get outside the control codes in order to dismantle and rearrange them" (CCRU 25). Linear time is one of the dominant reality program's major control codes, so its subversion is central to Burroughs's attempt to "dismantle and rearrange them": "[b]y formatting the most basic biological processes of the organism in terms of temporality, Control ensures that all human experience is of—and in—time" (CCRU 30). Control's universe—the "One God Universe" of linear time—"is a prerecorded universe" in which humanity is "the 'time-binding animal'" in a "double sense": human beings are binding time for themselves in that they "can make information available over any length of time to other men through writing," but they are also "binding themselves into time, building more of the prison which constrains their affects and perceptions," as a result of which Burroughs "saw what time-binding really was, all the books, already written, time bound forever" (CCRU 30). Burroughs's works were "technologies for altering reality," weapons in a cosmic war against the fiction of the One God Universe (CCRU 30). Thus, from the perspective of "Lemurian Time War," the inclusion of a three-century-old copy of "Ghost Lemurs of Madagascar" within that story reflects an effort to use fiction writing to rearrange temporality. Burroughs's cut-up technique was another such weapon in this time war: by cutting up and rearranging texts, Burroughs sought to resist the time-binding imposed upon humanity in the One God Universe, the cutting up and rearranging of books' contents representing the attempt to undo the already-written.

"Lemurian Time War" presents "The Ghost Lemurs of Madagascar" as an example of another hyperstitional technique: it first frames itself as a historical narrative, but then inserts itself into the text of the story, blurring the distinctions between both reality and fiction and past and present. In Burroughs's story, after establishing an anarchist colony on Madagascar (the island to which Lemurs are native), the late seventeenth-century pirate Captain Mission develops an "unwholesome concern with lemurs" (Burroughs 51). While this interest, in Kaye-via-the CCRU's telling in "Lemurian Time War," takes on a more Lovecraftian coloring, a discussion of which will follow shortly, an encounter with a Lemur Mission calls Ghost also sets the scene for the appearance of "The Ghost Lemurs of Madagascar" within itself:

> Mission sat at the table beside his phantom, his Ghost, contemplating the mystery of the stone structure. Who could have built it? Who? He poses the question in hieroglyphs . . . a feather . . . he chooses a quill pen. Water . . . the clear water under the pier. A book . . . an old illustrated book with gilt edges. *The Ghost Lemurs of Madagascar.* (Burroughs 52)

So in Burroughs's work, we already have a work that purports to be nonfiction (it concludes with an appeal that readers support the Duke Lemur Center, an actual institution), but contains a narrative that we would conventionally call fiction, which additionally references itself when its seventeenth-century protagonist discovers it in the form of "an old illustrated book with gilt edges." The CCRU, however, builds on this. It locates a 1789 edition of the story in Vysparov's library and then claims that the agents of the One God Universe arranged its 1987 publication under Burroughs's name as an attempt to "Defend the integrity of the timeline" (CCRU 33-34). However, according to the CCRU, Burroughs subverted this attempt by publishing a revised and expanded version of "The Ghost Lemurs of Madagascar" as the 1991 novella *The Ghost of a Chance*, which concludes with the phrase, "People of the world are at last returning to their source in spirit, back to the little lemur people" (Burroughs 54). The CCRU adds further Lovecraftian significance to this passage, framing it as an attempt at "masking the return of the Old Ones" in "seemingly innocuous words" that really indicate that "Things that should have been long finished continued to stir. It was as if a post-mortem coincidence or unlife influence had vortically re-animated itself"; when Burroughs republished "The Ghost Lemurs of Madagascar" as *The Ghost of a Chance,* "a strange doubling occurred" (CCRU 34).

The CCRU presents Burroughs's Lemurs as similar, and connecting humans, to Lovecraft's Old Ones by way of the Lovecraftian device of dream communication. Of Captain Mission's relationship with the Ghost Lemurs, the CCRU writes, "Lemurs became his sleeping and dream companions. He discovered through this dead and dying species that the key to escaping control is taking the initiative—or the pre-initiative—by interlinking with the Old Ones" (CCRU 31). Both classes of being are also similar to each other in that they are so ancient as to perceive and value worldly affairs differently from human beings because they have lived on a different time scale. Of the Old Ones, Lovecraft's Inspector Legrasse reports in "The Call of Cthulhu" that cultists he questioned claimed that

> They worshiped . . . the Great Old Ones who lived ages before there were any men, and who came to the young world out of the sky. Those Old Ones were gone now, inside the earth and under the sea; but their dead bodies had told their secrets in dreams to the first man, who formed a cult which had never died. (CF 2.37-8)

Meanwhile, of Lemurs, Burroughs writes,

> The Lemur People are older than Homo sap, much older. They date back sixty million years to the time when Madagascar split off from the mainland of Africa. They might be called psychic amphibians-that is, visible only for short periods when they assume a solid form to breathe, but some of them can remain in the invisible state for years at a time. Their way of thinking and feeling is basically different from ours, not oriented toward time and sequence and causality. They find these concepts repugnant and difficult to understand. (Burroughs 54)

Aside from this link between Lemurs and the Old Ones, it bears noting that the attachment of occult significance to Lemurs predates both Lovecraft and Burroughs: H. P. Blavatsky, founder of the Theosophical Society (and therefore a major influence on a spectrum of Western religion ranging from the late nineteenth-century ceremonial magic of the Golden Dawn to a wide variety of twentieth and twenty first-century New Age communities), posited that Lemurians (denizens of the lost continent of Lemuria) were one of humanity's root races, leading Burroughs and the CCRU alike to link Madagascar's prosimians, by wordplay if nothing else, to Blavatsky's race of human beings "possessing intellect and hermaphroditic biological structure" (Cabrales 22). While the CCRU dwells more on this occult-Lemurian connection, a line of dialogue in Burroughs's story may also allude to Theosophical Lemurians' hermaphroditism—a character at one point says the following of a Lemur named Big Ghost: "Her He. For Big Ghost is the same" (Burroughs 50). Lovecraft, too, references Theosophy when discussing incomprehensibly ancient beings in "the Call of Cthulhu," where the narrator notes, "Theosophists have guessed at the awesome grandeur of the cosmic cycle wherein our world and human race form transient incidents. They have hinted at strange survivals in terms which would freeze the blood if not masked by a bland optimism" (CF 2.22).

The Thirst for Annihilation

While the CCRU's work on the Cthulhu Club may be among the more explicitly Lovecraftian content Land was involved with producing, his engagement with Lovecraftian themes may both pre- and post-date it. Land has only published one book-length academic monograph over the course of his career, *The Thirst for Annihilation: Georges Bataille and Virulent Nihilism* (1992). In it, Bataille appears for Land as something of a philosophical Cthulhu: a figure that inspires expectation of a time when humanity would, like the Old Ones, "have become . . . free and wild and beyond good and evil, with laws and morals thrown aside and all men shouting and killing and revelling in joy . . . and all the earth would flame with a holocaust of ecstasy and freedom" (CF 2.39–40). We see this particularly in Land's linkage of Bataille to Nietzsche and Sade.

Early on in *The Thirst for Annihilation*, Land positions Bataille as an heir to Nietzsche. Both, according to Land, emphasized the dimensions of philosophical concepts that exceed or transgress the bounds of conventional reason or morality, framing the "'[n]oumenon' as an energetic unconscious." In this account, "Nietzsche's genealogy of inhuman desire . . . feeds in turn into Bataille's base materialism, for which 'noumenon' is addressed as impersonal death and as unconscious drive" (8). Impersonal forces are quite central to the Land of *The Thirst for Annihilation*. A subsequent passage champions "A Dionysian economy" as "the flux of impersonal desire" (26). Banham explains that this passage "assimilates Nietzsche's thought of eternal return with Bataille's account of global economy" (58).

The Marquis de Sade's influence on Bataille only appears slightly later on, in Land's discussion of the role of criminality in Bataille's atheism:

> What is suggested by the Sadean furore is that anyone who does not exult at the thought of driving nails through the limbs of the Nazarene is something less than an atheist; merely a disappointed slave. Amongst the diseases that Bataille shares with Nietzsche is the insistence that the death of God is not an epistemic conviction, but a crime. (62–63)

In Land's treatment, Bataille's atheism demands not that the atheist accept the death of God as a fact, but instead, participate in it by exulting "at the thought of driving nails through the limbs of the Nazarene." This exultation leads Land to observe that an "illimitable criminality" drives "Bataille's writing," provoking "no hint of repentance ... Lacking the slightest interest in justification, innocence is not an aspiration he nourishes" (63). Because, "[i]n a broadly Nietzschean fashion, Bataille understands law as the imperative to the preservation of discrete being" and "[l]aw summarizes conditions of existence and shares its arbitrariness with the survival of the human race," Bataille celebrates transgression of the law as a function of an impulse to do away with discrete being, an impulse at work in both the erotic and thanatotic drives (64). This celebration of violations of the law in service of "inhuman desire" or "unconscious drive" bears similarities to the above-quoted passage from "The Call of Cthulhu," in which the Great Old Ones' human partisans express hope for a time when they can cast aside law and morality in service of impulses toward "shouting and killing and revelling in joy" amid "a holocaust of ecstasy and freedom" (CF 2.40). Land's depiction of "tragic community" (an elaboration upon Nietzsche's treatment of the tragic in *The Birth of Tragedy*) is more similar still: "Tragic community is not the affirmation of a collective identity, but rather the dissolution of all identifiable traits in an uncircumscribable movement of catastrophe and festival; catastrophe of the individuated self, festival of anonymous flow" (82). What is a "holocaust of ecstasy and freedom" if not "an uncircumscribable movement of catastrophe and festival; catastrophe of the individuated self, festival of anonymous flow"?

Building on this initial celebration of transgression, Land's reading of Bataille leads him to link economic forces and criminal impulses. Transgression is not only the human expression of inhuman drives in the sense that these drives can lead to outcomes conventional morality deems undesirable. Rather, these drives are additionally inhuman in that they precede and exceed any particular human and can, for example, operate on and through individuals from without by means of economic transformations. For example, early modern French serial killer Gilles de Rais was for Bataille a "sacred monster." Of this status, Land says,

> The tragedy of de Rais, which Bataille extends to the nobility as a whole, was that of living the transition from sumptuary to rational sociality. He was dedicated by birth to the reckless militarism of the French aristocracy ... that honour and prestige is incommensurable with the calculations of utility is an insistent theme in Bataille's work, as pertinent to the interpretation of polatch amongst the

> Tlingit as to the blood-hunger and extravagance of Europe's medieval nobility... The feudal aristocracy held open a wound in the social body, through which excess production was haemorrhaged into utter loss. (67)

So de Rais's post-military career in serial murder was just an exaggeration of the impulse to waste that was already at work in his class's consumption habits and notions of martial valor; he simply "embraced this dark heart of the feudal world with particular ardour" (67-68).

The relationship between death and production, however, changed with the advent of capitalism and modernity.

> Like zero, money is a redundant operator; adding nothing in order to make things hum. When Marx associates capital with death he is only drawing the final consequence from this correspondence. Surplus value comes out of labour-power, but surplus production comes out of nothing. This is why capital production is the consummating phase of nihilism, the liquidation of theological irreligion, the twilight of the idols. Modernity is virtual thanocracy guided insidiously by zero; the epoch of the death of God. There is no God but (only) zero—indifferentiation without unity—and *nihil* is the true religion. (90-91)

> Capital attains its own 'angular momentum', perpetuating a run-away whirlwind of dissolution, whose hub is the virtual zero of impersonal metropolitan accumulation. At the peak of its productive prowess the human animal is hurled into a new nakedness, as everything stable is progressively liquidated in the storm. (113)

The Land of the 2010s, especially in his writing on cryptocurrency, appears to touch on similar themes when celebrating cryptocurrency as representing the consummating phase of nihilism, as capital production *par excellence*. It is not only a means of "impersonal metropolitan accumulation," but one whose "productive prowess" is such that it does not even require inputs from "the human animal" to generate capital. Land's use of "impersonal" in the above passage can bring the Lovecraftian dimension of all this to the fore: capital is impersonal as the Old Ones are inhuman; it is cosmic for Land as they are cosmic forces for Lovecraft. Capital is an inhuman force, or capitalism an inhuman algorithm. While some Marxists a few years Land's senior may have advanced such a claim as a critique of capitalism, Land lauds the inhumanity of capital, advocating the liberation of the means of production by removing constraints on capital rather than their seizure by the proletariat in the name of humanity. Land specifically highlights cryptocurrency's potential as capital's perfectly inhuman apotheosis in his 2018 work, *Crypto-Current*.

Crypto-Current

While *Crypto-Current*'s philosophical interests are basically Kantian, two of the text's major features, cryptocurrency's independence from human oversight (and, therefore, its basic inhumanity) and its relationship to time (its instantiation of absolute succession) reveal the persistence of Lovecraftian concerns into the most recent phase of Land's career. The text's basic target is the very notion of trusted third parties and its basic contrast is between fiat currency, where a trusted third party determines the amount in circulation, and Bitcoin (which Land uses to represent cryptocurrency more generally), where an algorithm limits the amount that can ever circulate. Additionally central is the double-spending problem: because electronic data is usually quite cheap, the costs of lying about purely electronic currency have traditionally been low, as a result of which, fraud has been a persistent concern for digital payment systems. One of the most basic forms of fraud would be double-spending: transmitting the same units of currency to two different recipients. Crucially, there is a temporal dimension to double-spending, as one claimed transfer would need to occur before the other. Bitcoin's solution to the double-spending problem is, more generally, a solution to the Byzantine Generals Problem.

In its basic form, the Byzantine Generals Problem is this: four generals need to decide when to launch a simultaneous attack from four different positions. How can they decide when the attack will take place, if each is in a different camp? They can send messengers to one another, but what if messages reach different generals at different times? Speaking philosophically, this is the question of how to relate time to space. Can you have a true, absolute temporal order among all the nodes in a spatially distributed network? Bitcoin's 2008 inaugural white paper offered a solution to the Byzantine Generals Problem. If, when a general receives a message, he has to perform a series of arbitrary, time-consuming calculations before he can re-broadcast the time to the rest of the network, this can force the generals to converge on the same time; the required calculations make it too costly for the majority of nodes in the network to diverge from the earliest possible time. Because of this solution, according to Land, Bitcoin is a distributed truth machine in that it establishes the absolute order of transactions. It verifies who made what currency transfer first: records contradicting the order will simply be discarded by the rest of the network because they will clearly have deviated from the protocol (Murphy, "The Bitcoin Whitepaper, Nick Land, and Kant").

A blockchain is a record of transactions, each of which receives a unique hash that incorporates the time of the transaction into the cryptographic identity its algorithm assigns to that transaction. Land describes crypto-current as "a flow of time, electricity, and cash—a turbulent conceptual confluence. Current events are the only kind. If we are unable to step into the same current twice, it is because of what irreversibility has secured in the past" ("Crypto-Current"). Irreversibility is a reference to the blockchain, since blocks, once added to the chain, are immutable and the transactions they represent are irreversible. Land further presents this as a vindication of Kant, in that Kant had a precise philosophy of time as a category fundamentally different from space, which marks a strong contrast with the generally accepted post-Einstein view that treats space and time as a continuum. Because Bitcoin restores time's independence by establishing absolute succession among spatially distinct nodes in a network.

Despite its staid, Kantian appearance, *Crypto-Current*, too, has Lovecraftian resonances, framing cryptocurrency as a link to inhuman forces. For example, the centrality of automation to the above-described process can, by extension, highlight its inhumanity. Hashes are algorithmically generated, and as a result, so is Bitcoin mining. The creation of new bitcoin is not subject to human influence, unlike fiat currencies, which human institutions issue: central banks still employ human beings, after all. So what we see here is a system not just for severing time from space, but for severing capital from human oversight. To this end, in *Crypto-Current* Land writes:

> No bio-historically generated intelligence—including that of man—is even automatic. Such beings are denied access to automatism. Closure of the intelligenic loop requires a further step, through which self-improving intelligence becomes a practicable end for itself. Contra the Kant of the practical philosophy, man cannot be an end-in-itself, but at most the precursor to such a thing, or—perhaps more probably—an obstacle to it. . . .
>
> The blockchain is not 'mere' code—even highly automated code. It cannot be anything, determinable within an ontology established at a superior level to itself. Nakamoto Consensus is less an object for philosophy than a virtual criterion: a fundamental, obliquely mechanized decision procedure for settling the nature of truth. In other words, Bitcoin is a transcendental operation, before becoming the topic for one. The primary meaning of 'transcendental' is ultimate, which can be clarified negatively by the absence of any higher or superior tribunal. There is no place from which to consistently or authoritatively second-guess the blockchain. By implementing a "fully peer-to-peer" system, which subtracts the role of "third party" monitoring and adjudication, the Bitcoin protocol automatically places itself beyond external oversight. Its criterion of validation is radically immanent.

In these two sections, Land positions the independence of Nakamoto Consensus (the Bitcoin protocol's solution to the Byzantine Generals Problem) from human oversight as a step toward (if not a case of) the development of a nonhuman, self-improving intelligence. Just as engagement with hidden forces drove Wilcox and Cthulhu cultists alike in "The Call of Cthulhu," according to Land, "Engagement with Bitcoin brings us into communication with hidden inclinations," inclinations with a particular significance in reference to time, as their "indicators mark . . . temporalizations" and "Current emerges from the machinery of time" ("Crypto-Current"). These temporalizations take the form of absolute succession:

> A cultural side-product of the Bitcoin protocol, then, is a cryptographic definition of time. Punctual-geometric 'now', as marked on a 'time-line', is replaced by an atomic unit of irreducible duration, coinciding with the completion of a block, and ordered successively on the chain. Between duration and succession, the relation is synthetic. The blockchain is constituted by a series of durations, which are not inter-convertible, or mathematically transformable into each other. Hash-time has ceased to be accurately representable as a dimension. A time-line merely analogizes it, to what is an ultimately inadequate level of definite fidelity.

In a later podcast interview, Land made more explicit the opposition between the absolute duration of the blockchain and relative time (he goes so far as to suggest that this duration may disprove Einstein), which, unlike absolute duration, depends upon the perspective of (presumably human) observer (Murphy, "Ideology, Intelligence, and Capital with Nick Land"). In this, Land may be more Lovecraftian than Lovecraft: while, "Philosophically Lovecraft is quite different [from Shelley] as the horror and any destruction in his tales are purposefully and necessarily removed from humanity in following the tenets of cosmicism" (McCammon 15), his use of time travel and explicit engagement with relativity in "The Shadow out of Time" suggest that Lovecraft's time operates in relation to the human subject more than the blockchain's absolute duration does for Land.

Conclusion

Land's celebration of, and discovery of philosophical significance in, cryptocurrency's absolute independence from human input (whether in the Bitcoin white paper's solution to the Byzantine generals problem or in the inability of policymakers' decisions to directly impact its value) not only appears to strike tones that readers familiar with Lovecraft's cosmicism would probably recognize but may, moreover, inasmuch as they are economically prescriptive, indicate greater willingness to engage with inhumanity than even Lovecraft himself exhibited. It may bear noting that despite the apparent affinities between Land and Lovecraft's politics, by the end of his life Lovecraft favored considerably more state intervention in the economy than one would expect from cryptocurrency's more ideologically motivated adopters.

A contemporary reader could easily assume that the notoriously racist Lovecraft and a writer whom many contemporary commentators have come to regard as neoreaction's philosopher-in-chief would hold similar positions. However, as Tyler Wolanin has demonstrated, in the wake of the Great Depression Lovecraft's personal correspondence in the 1930s indicates that he came to embrace the New Deal and advocate for some degree of socialism as a means of avoiding either another market collapse like that witnessed in 1929 (which Lovecraft understood to be a product of unrestrained capitalism) or a turn to more revolutionary socialist currents. However, for many of its advocates cryptocurrency's major appeal is its independence from the state, if not human institutions more generally. While cosmicism may have led Lovecraft to write a great deal of fiction that depicts encounters between human characters and the Outside (the inhuman and indifferent realities at work in the greater cosmos), the Outside does not appear to have intruded on his political opinions. This intrusion, however, appears to be central to Land's philosophy as reflected in "Crypto-Current." The two developments Lovecraft hoped this measured form of socialism would forestall, meanwhile, could easily stand in for approaches right and left accelerationists would favor. Lovecraft's apparent distaste for revolutionary upheaval of any sort marks a strong contrast between him (or at least his personal views) and Land either in his early or late periods (if, his neoreactionary turn aside, we take him to be the founder of accelerationism left and right). An accelerationist, whether left or right, would probably have accepted the Great Depression as a natural consequence of capitalism, either because, on the right, the market simply does not make mistakes regardless of the human costs of market events, or because, one the left, adverse market events can serve to heighten capitalism's contradictions, driving toward revolution.

However, some hesitation in marking this contrast between Lovecraft and Land merits consideration, as it opposes positions drawn from Lovecraft's personal correspondence to those taken in Land's philosophical work. However, given that those philosophers who have engaged with Lovecraft have drawn on literary output rather than his personal correspondence, that correspondence may be less relevant to this discussion.

While Lovecraft's influence on some of the output of Nick Land and his collaborators is fairly obvious, previous scholarship has not recognized its full extent. The CCRU and mid-2010s Land alike have referenced Cthulhu explicitly, which the scholarship has acknowledged, but it has not previously discussed the less obviously Lovecraftian dimensions of Land's *Thirst for Annihilation* or "Crypto-Current." Both texts do, however, have Lovecraftian valences: in *The Thirst for Annihilation*, Land's interpretation of Bataille's fascination with Giles de Rais strikes a tone similar to Inspector Legrasse's description of cultists' views of the Old Ones, and in "Crypto-Current," Land celebrates the process of generating cryptocurrency for its inhumanity, which Lovecraft took to be the defining feature of the cosmos itself.

Work Cited

Banham, Gary. "Review of French Philosophy of the Sixties: An Essay on Antihumanism; the Thirst for Annihilation: Georges Bataille and Virulent Nihilism." *Journal of Nietzsche Studies* 11 (1996): 53–63, www.jstor.com/stable/20717642. Accessed 8 January 2022.

Beauchamp, Zack. "Accelerationism: The Idea Inspiring White Supremacist Killers Around the World." *Vox* 11 (November 2019), www.vox.com/the-highlight/2019/11/11/20882005/accelerationism-white-supremacy-christchurch.

Burroughs, William S. "Ghost Lemurs of Madagascar." *Omni Science Fiction* (April 1987): 48–54, 118.

Cabrales, Robert Elio. "The Hyperstitional Philosophy of Time-Travel Cybernetics: Theosophy, the CCRU, and Black-Box Poiesis." *Plutonics* (March 2021): 7–36.

Cybernetic Culture Research Unit. *CCRU Writings: 1997–2003*. Time Spiral Press, 2015.

CCRU website. "Ccru-Cybernetic Culture Research Unit." *Ccru.net*, 2022, ccru.net/syzygy.htm. Accessed 5 January 2022.

Dean, Aria. "Notes on Blacceleration." *e-Flux*, e-flux.com/journal/87/169402/notes-on-blacceleration/. Accessed 21 January 2022.

Gildea, Florence. "Accelerating Down a Road to Nowhere: On *Inventing the Future* by Nick Srnicek and Alex Williams." *Political Quarterly* (10 April 2020) 10.1111/1467-923x.12850. Accessed 12 May 2020.

Gogarty, Larne Abse. "The Art Right." *Art Monthly* No. 405 (April 2017): 1–10.

Goldhill, Olivia. "The Neo-Fascist Philosophy That Underpins Both the Alt-Right and Silicon Valley Technophiles." *Quartz*, qz.com/1007144/the-neo-fascist-philosophy-that-underpins-both-the-alt-right-and-silicon-valley-technophiles/. Accessed 2 January 2022.

Hull, Thomas. "H. P. Lovecraft: A Horror in Higher Dimensions." *Math Horizons* 13, No. 3 (2006): 10–12. JSTOR, www.jstor.org/stable/ 25678597. Accessed 31 May 2022.

Kolozova, Katerina. "Metaphysics of Finance Economy: Of Its Radicalization as the Method of Revoking Real Economy." *Identities: Journal for Politics, Gender and Culture* 11 (2015): 19–31. Accessed 3 January 2022.

Land, Nick. "Crypto-Current: Bitcoin and Philosophy." *Desearch and Revelopment* (31 October 2018), Crypto-Current: Bitcoin and Philosophy. etscrivner.github.io/cryptocurrent/. Accessed 25 January 2022.

———. *The Thirst for Annihilation: Georges Bataille and Virulent Nihilism: An Essay in Atheistic Religion*. London: Routledge, 1992.

———; Mackay, Robin, and Ray Brassier. *Fanged Noumena*. Cambridge, MA: Urbanomic, 2011.

Luckhurst, Roger. "Professor Nobody's Little Lectures on Thomas Ligotti's Supernatural Horror." *Dark Arts Journal* (2019). thedarkartsjournal.wordpress.com/ligotti-post-truth/professor-nobodys-little-lectures-on-thomas-ligottis-supernatural-fiction/

McCammon, Garrison. "Quantum Physics and Relativity in Lovecraft's Fiction" (2017). *English Summer Fellows* 14, digitalcommons.ursinus.edu/english_sum/14

Murphy, Justin, host. "Ideology, Intelligence, and Capital with Nick Land." *Other Life* (19 July 2018), www.podcasts.apple.com/us/podcast/ ideology-intelligence-and-capital-with-nick-land/id1195362330

———. "The Bitcoin Whitepaper, Nick Land, and Kant." *Other Life* (10 December 2021), www.podcasts.apple.com/us/podcast/other-life/id1195362330

Noys, Benjamin. "Arguments within English Theory." *Third Text* 32, No. 5–6 (2 November (2018): 586–92. 10.1080/09528822.2018.1558645. Accessed 28 April 2020.

O'Sullivan, Simon. "The Missing Subject of Accelerationism." *Mute* (9 December 2014) www.metamute.org/editorial/articles/missing-subject-accelerationism.

O'Sullivan, Simon. "Accelerationism, Hyperstition and Myth-Science." *Cyclops Journal* No. 2 (August 2017): 11-44, www.cyclopsjournal.net/downloads/CYCLOPS_JOURNAL_Issue_2_ONLINE.pdf. Accessed 4 January 2022.

Ojeda, Alan. "Pleromática O Las Mareaciones de Elsinor de Gabriel Catren." *Revista CHUY* 5, No. 5 (December 2018): 366-74.

Pitts, Frederick Harry, and Ana Cecilia Dinerstein. "Corbynism's Conveyor Belt of Ideas: Postcapitalism and the Politics of Social Reproduction." *Capital & Class* 41, No. 3 (October 2017): 423-34, 10.1177/0309816817734487. Accessed 29 April 2020.

Sellar, Sam, and David R. Cole. "Accelerationism: A Timely Provocation for the Critical Sociology of Education." *British Journal of Sociology of Education* 38, No. 1 (2 January 2017): 38-48, 10.1080/01425692 .2016.1256190. Accessed 27 July 2020.

Wark, McKenzie. "On Nick Land." *Verso Books*, www.versobooks.com/blogs/3284-on-nick-land. Accessed 2 January 2022.

Wolanin, Tyler L. "New Deal Politics in the Correspondence of H. P. Lovecraft." *Lovecraft Annual* No. 7 (2013): 3-35.

Woodard, Ben. "Plotting Nature's Havoc: Potential Realisms between Transcendental Materialism and Transcendental Dynamism." *Identities: Journal for Politics, Gender and Culture* 8, No. 2 (1 June 2011): 81-96, 10.51151/identities.v8i2.266. Accessed 3 January 2022.

Firearms in the Life and Works of H. P. Lovecraft

N. R. Jenzen-Jones
Editor, Armax: The Journal of Contemporary Arms

George Colclough
Independent Researcher

Hans-Christian Vortisch
Independent Researcher

The writings of H. P. Lovecraft are not commonly associated with gunplay. Even though his fiction found publication primarily in pulp magazines, even his lesser works exude more sophistication than most of the dime-a-dozen stories with which they were printed. Lovecraft's works nevertheless feature firearms often. In keeping with their common theme of humanity confronting the seen or unseen *other*, many of his tales feature characters wielding weapons. True to Lovecraft's American heritage and the times in which he lived, this means, more often than not, that the protagonists reach for their guns. Just like real people of his era, they arm themselves upon taking action—or when they are frightened. These actions are often only circumstantial—what good is a revolver against an intangible, ancient evil?—but are sometimes essential to the plot or ending. In spite of the regular presence of firearms in his work, Lovecraft's portrayal of guns has been largely overlooked by scholars. The one story that features an actual gunfight has been criticized for it. Indeed, Lovecraft himself—the bibliophile, the withdrawn gentleman, the sickly shut-in—appears an unlikely gun enthusiast. And yet, as we will see, Lovecraft not only enjoyed guns, collected guns, and shot guns, he also portrayed them often and in sometimes remarkable detail throughout much of his diverse œuvre.

Firearms in the Life of H. P. Lovecraft

> As for the necessary accomplishments of a young gentleman . . . I loved firearms, & could scarcely count the endless succession of guns & pistols I've owned.
> —H. P. Lovecraft, 24 March 1933 (JVS 124)

Lovecraft seemingly developed an affinity for firearms from a young age. Just before his second birthday, in the summer of 1892, he was vacationing with his family in Dudley, Massachusetts, when another boy allowed him to play with a "small rifle" under his mother's supervision (JVS 219). Lovecraft's references to this encounter are sparse and there is little indication as to the type of firearm he handled. We can infer that for the rifle to have appeared small, even to a toddler, it is likely to have been a rifle of the sort broadly intended for use by children (marketing firearms expressly for use by children was relatively commonplace during this period; see, for example, Albers; Witkowski; Figure 1).[1] Common examples of the period include single-shot rifles like the Merwin, Hulbert & Company (Merwin & Hulbert) Junior and the J. Stevens Arms & Tool Company (Stevens) series of Boys Rifles, most often chambered[2] for the .22 Short, .22 Long, or .22 Long Rifle rimfire cartridges.[3] Another possibility is that the item in question was not a firearm at all, but an air weapon[4] like one of the popular models made by the Daisy Manufacturing Company or the Quackenbush Company. Of course, Lovecraft's being so young at the time means that he was most likely relying on family recollec-

---

1. Although uncommon today, firearms intended for children are occasionally still advertised. The WEE1 Tactical JR-15, for example, offers a "small size, lightweight rugged polymer construction and ergonomics are geared towards smaller enthusiasts." It is also said to feature a "tamper resistant safety that puts the adult in control of the firearms safety switch" (Wee1 Tactical 1–2).

2. A firearm's chambering describes the cartridge it is designed to accept (e.g., .357 Magnum). A firearm chambered for .357 Magnum ammunition thus is one which is intended to primarily use that cartridge, even if it could theoretically fire another cartridge (see Jenzen-Jones 120).

3. Small-calibre cartridges are defined as those of less than 20 mm in calibre (i.e., most firearms ammunition) (Jenzen-Jones 43, 133). Rimfire cartridges are those in which the primer compound is contained within the rim of the cartridge; today, most cartridges use the centerfire system, with a central primer (Jenzen-Jones 42–43).

4. An air weapon is "a barrelled weapon shooting potentially lethal projectiles by meansof compressed gas," rather than relying upon the expansion of gases caused by the combustion of propellant, as in a firearm (Jenzen-Jones 105 cf. 34).

tions of the event. Nonetheless, this encounter appears to have set the stage for his continued connection to firearms.

Figure 1. An advertisement for Stevens rifles, 1909 (source: Wikimedia Commons).

As Lovecraft grew up, he acquired what he referred to as the "necessary accomplishments of a young gentleman," and later wrote that he "loved firearms, & could scarcely count the endless succession of guns & pistols [he] owned" (JVS 124). Lovecraft eventually owned a firearm collection that S. T. Joshi describes as "fairly impressive" (IAP 108), although the quantity, quality, or diversity of these arms are not enumerated in Joshi's account. After the death of his maternal grandfather, Whipple Van Buren Phillips, on 28 March 1904, Lovecraft inherited several weapons. Not quite fourteen years old, Lovecraft held tremendous affection for his grandfather, and it is possible that Phillips's interest in arms was passed down to young Howard in much the same way as the older man's appreciation of classical literature. This bequest seemingly elevated a pre-existing interest in firearms to new heights, as, later that year, Lovecraft began purchasing his own firearms to expand the collection, apparently buying and selling guns frequently. He became a reasonably good shot until, around 1910, worsening eyesight forced him to quit. Over the years, the increasing financial difficulties that beset Lovecraft and his family following the death of his grandfather eventually forced him to sell off almost all his guns. By 1910, he had only one (non-functioning) firearm remaining in his collection. Piecing together snippets of information from his letters and other documents, a general understanding of the composition of Lovecraft's collection can be attempted, although it should be noted that this is necessarily an incomplete list.[5]

The first firearm owned by Lovecraft may have been a revolver that he acquired no later than the age of thirteen (in 1903), as part of his play in the "Providence Detective Agency." Writing to August Derleth in 1931, Lovecraft recalled:

> Our force had very rigid regulations and carried in its pockets a standard working equipment consisting of police whistle, magnifying glass, electric flashlight, handcuffs ... tin badge ... tape measure ... revolver (mine was the real thing, but inspector Munroe (at 12) had a water-squirt pistol while Inspector Upham (at 10) worried along with a cap-pistol. (ES 321)[6]

The make and model of this revolver is unknown, but in light of his youth and the fact that Lovecraft appeared to view the revolver primarily as part of his "standard working equipment," it seems reasonable to assume that it was a small-caliber,[7] lightweight, and above all inexpensive firearm. A number of American manufacturers based in New England[8]—such as the Harrington & Richardson Arms Company, Hopkins & Allen Arms Company, and Iver Johnson's Arms & Cycle Works—produced dozens of candidate models. The

---

5. Moreover, it is not always possible to discern which of the arms enumerated below were inherited from Phillips, and which were later purchased or traded for by HPL.

6. The inclusion of "the real thing" in HPL's detective kit may suggest a lack of instruction and parental oversight, although this would not have been uncommon at the time.

7. The caliber of a weapon is, strictly speaking, a measurement of the diameter of the bore of a gun (in the case of firearms, this is typically expressed in either decimal fractions of an inch or millimeters). In practice, this is rarely a precise usage, and the term is often employed to describe the cartridge a firearm chambers (for a more nuanced definition, see Jenzen-Jones 119).

8. Throughout HPL's lifetime, practically the entire American firearms industry was located in New England—a fact that certainly didn't escape his notice.

generally higher-quality products of the Colt's Patent Fire Arms Manufacturing Company (Colt) or Smith & Wesson (S&W) were typically four or five times as expensive, and are thus less likely to have been carried by Lovecraft in his early teenage years. During this period, inexpensive firearms were sold by department stores throughout the country. The Sears, Roebuck & Co. (Sears) catalogues from the early 1900s featured half a dozen pages offering handguns, many of them priced within the range of children eager to spend their allowance. A representative example of the type of revolver likely owned by Lovecraft is the Harrington & Richardson Young America double-action[9] revolver, a seven-shot weapon chambered for the .22 Short (5.6 × 11R mm)[10] cartridge. The marketing for this firearm was specifically aimed at boys, with advertisements extolling its potential use in celebrating the Fourth of July (see Figure 2). The Young America was introduced commercially in 1884 and sold for decades (see NRA Museums). In 1903, it was available from Sears for the eminently affordable price of $1.50 (Sears 306).[11] While the Young America and similar revolvers were also available in .32 rimfire and centerfire chamberings, Lovecraft wrote to J. Vernon Shea that, when he was young, even .32-caliber handguns felt too loud (JVS 190). A .22-caliber chambering thus seems most likely.

Lovecraft owned at least one other handgun, of which we know a little more. This is because he offered it for trade on 14 May 1905, listing it in the *Rhode Island Journal of Astronomy*, an amateur offering that Lovecraft himself edited and published between the ages of thirteen and nineteen (Lovecraft, *Rhode Island Journal of Astronomy* (2). The advertisement read:

> **WANTED TO TRADE** Stevens $5.00 Diamond Model .22cal target pistol only shot 2 or 3 times for an astronomical eyepiece of 150 power.
>
> Apply R.I. Journal

---

9. A double-action revolver is one which can either be manually cocked (and then fired using the trigger—i.e., single-action operation) or both cocked and fired simply by pulling the trigger (Jenzen-Jones 122). Note that this terminology has changed over time (see Jenzen-Jones 38, n. 55).

10. For more on small-calibre cartridge notation, see: Jenzen-Jones, *Weapons Identification: Small-calibre Ammunition* 137–139; 144.

11. The model was offered for sale by Montgomery Ward for $4.50 in 1895, and by Sears for $4.50 in 1897; by 1902, Sears charged only $3.85 (Colclough 6).

Figure 2. A 1905 advertisement for the Harrington & Richardson Young America revolver, offering both .22 (rimfire) and .32 (rimfire and centerfire) chamberings. (Source: Colclough.)

This weapon was a Stevens No. 43 Diamond Model, a single-shot target-shooting pistol chambered for the .22 Long Rifle (5.6 × 15R mm) cartridge (see Figure 3 for a representative example). The Diamond Model had been introduced commercially in 1888 and was widely offered for sale by Stevens and their distributors (Hatcher 173; Smith & Smith 121). This pistol may have been part of Lovecraft's inheritance, since he suggests that the gun had been bought for (or was valued at) $5, but the price of the weapon at the major retailers was already less than $4 by 1900 (Colclough 6). Lovecraft, aged fourteen at the time of the publication, appears not to have been particularly enamored with this pistol, having only shot it two or three times.

Figure 3. A Stevens No. 43 Diamond Model single-shot pistol. (Source: Rock Island Auction Company.)

Lovecraft may well have owned at least one larger-caliber handgun. He wrote to J. Vernon Shea in 1933 that "by the time I was 13 or 14 I could stand an ordinary .32 or .38 pistol shot" (JVS 190). While he might have fired firearms belonging to other people, it seems likely that he owned at least one .32-caliber or .38-caliber handgun at some point. There was a huge selection of modestly priced revolvers in these calibers available at the time, and a potential customer could simply drop into a hardware store or pawnshop and emerge with a serviceable handgun for a few dollars—or have it shipped to his home from one of many mail-order suppliers (Colclough 3–4, 6). Such a weapon would be more suited to self-defense (including defense of the home) than any of the .22-caliber models, although there is no evidence to suggest Lovecraft routinely, or even frequently, carried a firearm beyond his boyhood years. Nonetheless, at least under certain circumstances Lovecraft appears to have believed that the use of firearms against other individuals could be justified. In a letter to Robert E. Howard on 10 November 1932, he described a duel in which his maternal great-grandfather, William Allgood, drew pistols with another man after "reasonable provocation":

> The only duel in my family of which I have any knowledge was fought in 1829, in upper New York State, by my father's maternal grandfather William Allgood [. . .] The affray, as reported by family tradition, was the outgrowth of unpleasant remarks on national differences (memories of the War of 1812, in which the Americans vainly tried to conquer and annex Canada, were then fresh in Northern N.Y.) exchanged with a citizen of Rochester. Pistols were used, both participants were slightly grazed, and everybody appears to have been satisfied,

since no more of the matter had been reported to posterity. It appears that my forebear was the challenger in this matter—though not without reasonable provocation. (*A Means to Freedom* 480)

While handguns appear to have been important in his formative years, Lovecraft's collection was primarily composed of "a long succession of 22-calibre [sic]¹² rifles" (*JVS* 139). These must be considered the core of his arsenal, and rifle-shooting seems to have been his most enduring firearms-related interest. S. T. Joshi went as far as to call it "the only sport that might remotely be said to have interested Lovecraft" (*IAP* 108).¹³ Specific details on the makes and models of these rifles have not yet been uncovered by the present authors, and the vast proliferation of .22-caliber rifles of varying types during the period would in any case complicate definitive identification. One common firearm of this type that may well have formed part of Lovecraft's collection is the Winchester Model 1890 pump-action rifle, chambered for the .22 Short or .22 Long Rifle cartridge. This was a popular gallery gun produced by the Winchester Repeating Arms Company, a fixture in American shooting galleries of the day (Boorman 69). However, at more than $10 in those years this would be a rather expensive weapon for young Lovecraft (Colclough 6; Sears 302). A selection from the numerous single-shot rifles available from makers such as Merwin & Hulbert or Stevens probably comprised the bulk of Lovecraft's collection. These could be had for as little as $2 (Colclough, 2, 6). In one of his letters Lovecraft wrote that he wished he "hadn't given away [his] last Remington" (*JVS* 124), indicating that at least some of the rifles in his collection—and, in any case, some that might be reasonably considered amongst his favorites—were made by the Remington Arms Company.¹⁴ A possible candidate rifle would be the Remington No. 6, a single-shot rifle chambered for the .22 Short cartridge. Introduced to the market in 1901, it retailed for around $4 (Figure 4).

---

12. A "22-calibre" rifle would, strictly speaking, be one with a bore diameter of 22 inches, rather than .22 inch. Nonetheless, this formulation was common at the time and is unlikely to speak to any lack of technical understanding on HPL's part.

13. HPL seems to have been even fonder of bicycling, however. He wrote to Maurice Moe: "My greatest exercise was bicycle-riding, which I pursued from 1900 to 1913. I cultivated high speeds, and managed to cover a large and picturesque area of countryside" (*MWM* 302-3).

14. Incidentally, Remington also manufactured the typewriter HPL used from 6 July 1906 until his death, a Standard No. 6 model.

Figure 4. An advertisement for the Remington No. 6 rifle in the Sears, Roebuck & Co. catalogue No. 112 of 1902. (Source: Sears, *1902 Catalogue* 299.)

The predominance of .22-caliber weapons in Lovecraft's arsenal was no accident. Small arms chambered for this caliber were popular throughout the United States during this period, and .22-caliber rimfire cartridges were readily accessible, had modest recoil and sound report (in a time before hearing protection was commonly used when shooting), and were cheap—the perfect ammunition for a teenager of limited means.[15] However, despite their diminutive size, the lead bullets fired by these guns could still be lethal out to a considerable distance. These were real firearms that necessitated the proper application of safety precautions—they were not toys. Such .22-caliber rifles were often used as squirrel guns, being widely employed to hunt a variety of small game. Lovecraft himself only hunted once, apparently. He wrote to Maurice Moe on 5 April 1931: "The lore of hunting allured me, and the feel of a rifle was balm to my soul; but after killing a squirrel I formed a dislike for killing things which could not fight back, hence turned to targets" (*MWM* 302). Lovecraft nonetheless appears to have maintained a respect for the practice of hunting with firearms. In letters to Helen V. Sully (26 May 1934) and Elizabeth Toldridge (29 December 1934), Lovecraft praises the hunting skills of R. H. Barlow, going so far as to call the books Barlow bound in the skins of the snakes he shot "masterpieces" (*WBT* 357; *ET* 284).

Not all of Lovecraft's rifles were of such small caliber, as he also owned a military surplus single-shot carbine produced by the Sharps Rifle Manufactur-

---

15. .22 Short cartridges cost 19 cents for 100 rounds in 1902, whilst .22 Long Rifle cartridges could be had at 100 for a quarter (Sears, 1902 Catalogue 311).

ing Company (Lovecraft, *Rhode Island Journal of Astronomy*, 7 May 1905).[16] Lovecraft describes this as a "Sharps 50-70 breech loading rifled carbine," which can be identified as a Sharps New Model of 1863 Carbine that has been converted from a breech-loading, .52-caliber percussion rifle to chamber the .50-70 Government (12.7 × 45R mm) centerfire cartridge under a U.S. Government contract (Madaus 176) (see Figure 5 for a representative example). This new conversion was quickly replaced in military service by a succession of more advanced weapons, and most of the converted guns were never issued. By the 1900s, these carbines were sold off in mail-order catalogues for less than $3, including twenty cartridges (Sears, *1902 Catalogue* 298). Lovecraft listed this firearm for trade—seeking "astronomical goods"—in the *Rhode Island Journal of Astronomy* on 7 May 1905, a week before offering his Stevens Diamond. The rifle appears to have seen little use by Lovecraft as he described it as "new" (*Rhode Island Journal of Astronomy*, 7 May 1905). Reasons for his disposing of the weapon might have included its considerable report and recoil, but also the cost of the ammunition (which, at about 60 cents for twenty rounds, was substantial). With the firearm's long history as a half-century-old military piece, a description of "new" may sound strange. However, it is entirely possible that the weapon was new old stock that had never been fired in military service—and perhaps not even by Lovecraft.

Figure 5. A Sharps New Model 1863 Carbine converted in 1867 to chamber the .50-70 Government centerfire cartridge (source: Rock Island Auction Company).

By 1910, Lovecraft had only one firearm remaining. This he kept at least until 1933: "As it is, I possess only an ancestral & unshootable flintlock musket" (*JVS* 124). A "flintlock" is a firearm with "a firing mechanism which utilises the interaction of a hardened steel component and piece of siliceous stone (typically flint) to create sparks for the ignition of a priming charge" (Jenzen-Jones 123). A "musket" is a type of military, smoothbore muzzle-loading firearm

---

16. A carbine is generally understood as a short and compact rifle, and in military use often denotes a shortened version of a longer rifle (Jenzen-Jones 60).

(Jenzen-Jones 77–78). Flintlock muskets were commonplace during the American Revolution, but were antiquated by Lovecraft's day. Lovecraft most probably possessed a military surplus firearm, perhaps an example of the most common weapon of the American Revolution: the Land Pattern Musket (known colloquially as Brown Bess) that was British Army issue (Ferguson 50). This was copied in the United States and spawned a series of American military musket models from the M1795 (see Figure 6 for a representative example) to the M1840 (Madaus 53–64). Lovecraft's claim that the musket was "ancestral" could suggest that the weapon was a century-old family heirloom connecting him to his forefathers. Alternatively, it may simply mean that it had come to him via his grandfather. Old flintlock firearms from the Revolutionary War period were sold off cheaply by mail-order companies in the late nineteenth century (Colclough 7). In 1902, Sears still offered a "revolutionary flint lock musket"—actually a European import that had almost certainly not seen use or issue on American soil—for just $2.65 (Sears, *1902 Catalogue* 296). Either way, Lovecraft put it on his wall and presumably still owned it when he died in 1937. Its present whereabouts are unknown.[17]

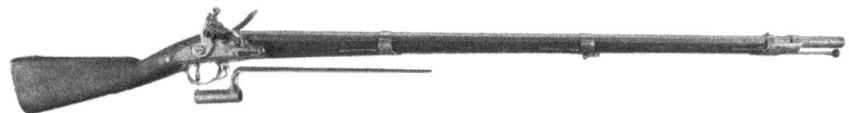

Figure 6. A U.S. M1795 musket produced at Harper's Ferry, West Virginia, in 1801. (Source: Rock Island Auction Company.)

Eventually, it was not just his financial situation that prevented Lovecraft from indulging in his interest in firearms. In 1910, he would stop shooting on account of his diminishing eyesight, explaining to J. Vernon Shea that his "eyes played hell with [his] accuracy" (JVS 189). To Maurice Moe he wrote: "My eyes troubled intermittently, and I wore glasses most of the time. Around 1906 I was a good rifle shot, but by 1910 my skill had declined" (MWM 303). Despite these limitations, Lovecraft's letters allude to a continued appreciation of firearms, as and when he happened to encounter them in the course

---

17. For the researcher this is perhaps the most tantalizing of the known firearms with a personal connection to HPL. It very likely connects him directly to his grandfather, at the least, and quite possibly to earlier ancestors. Should any reader have a lead on the final disposition of this artefact—or, indeed, any firearm with a connection to HPL—the authors would be very interested to hear from them.

of his life. In a letter to Helen Sully, dated 26 May 1934, for example, Lovecraft espoused the various merits of his friend R. H. Barlow, appearing to place "crack rifle shot" on an equal footing with being a bibliophile and chess expert (*WBT* 358).

Firearms in the Works of H. P. Lovecraft

> Inconceivable events and conditions have a special handicap to overcome, and this can be accomplished only through the maintenance of a careful realism in every phase of the story *except* that touching on the one given marvel.
> —H. P. Lovecraft, "Notes on Writing Weird Fiction" (CF 2.177)

Befitting a man who held an interest in firearms from a young age, a selection of guns appear with some regularity in the works of H. P. Lovecraft. A variety of firearms terminology is employed by Lovecraft, ranging from the general (gun, firearm) to the more specific (revolver, big-game rifle). The authors have surveyed all Lovecraft's original stories, as well as his collaborative works, conducting word searches for key firearms terms and reading the text with a view to assessing the technical nuance and impact of Lovecraft's depiction of firearms. The results of this analysis are presented below. Futuristic and unconventional weapons, such as the "poison darts" and "flame pistols" of "In the Walls of Eryx" (CF 4.598, 599) are excluded.[18] Poems and other works were not examined.

A "gun" is simply a "weapon which uses the combustion of a propellant to generate high-pressure gas in a sealed chamber in order to accelerate a projectile in a controlled manner" (Jenzen-Jones 34), applying to large and small weapons alike. The term "gun" is used by Lovecraft once in each of "The Curse of Yig," "The Last Test," and "The Temple." The universal application of this term is especially apparent in the last case, where Lovecraft employs it to refer to the 8.8 cm deck gun—a large-caliber cannon—of the *U-29* submarine (CF 1.156). Derived terms are also used, with gunpowder and gunfire mentioned repeatedly in *The Case of Charles Dexter Ward*, and gunfire occurring once in "The Whisperer in Darkness" (CF 2.494). The term "firearm" (meaning, specifically, a "man-portable gun" [Jenzen-Jones 34]), is used only once in Lovecraft's work, in "The Call of Cthulhu."

---

18. The authors also do not assess the Crookes-tube-derived "ray gun" devised by the protagonists in "The Shunned House," but commend to the reader T. R. Livesey's article on this device (3–9).

A more common term to be found in Lovecraft's writing is "pistol." This was a synonym during the period for handgun; a "firearm which is grasped by placing both the control hand and support hand around the pistol grip, and which may be readily fired with one hand" (Jenzen-Jones 36). "Pistol" occurs twelve times in the surveyed works, appearing three times in "The Horror in the Museum," twice in "The Temple," once in "The Beast in the Cave," once in *The Case of Charles Dexter Ward*, once in "The Dunwich Horror," once in "The Ghost-Eater," once in "The Last Test," once in "The Lurking Fear," and once in "The Shadow over Innsmouth." Identifying which type of pistol is meant is more challenging. In the abstract, the term could be applied to a revolver or self-loading[19] (semi-automatic)[20] pistol, or perhaps even to a break-action design, such as a double-barreled derringer or a single-shot target pistol. Most authors—and readers—of Lovecraft's era had limited understanding of firearms terminology. In both contemporary fiction and journalistic writing, a "revolver" was often a catch-all term for any type of handgun, used even when the weapon in question was a semi-automatic pistol. Hugh Pollard pointed this out in his book *Automatic Pistols*, but it remained true throughout Lovecraft's lifetime:

> There still remains a certain amount of confusion in the public mind about the exact difference between an automatic pistol and a revolver. The latter is a hand-operated arm having a revolving cylinder, which is rotated . . . and is not worked by the effect of the recoil. (1)

In the early twentieth century, pistol was generally employed to describe single-shot target-shooting handguns (Smith & Smith 31), while the semi-automatic pistol was called a magazine pistol or automatic pistol. By the 1920s, pistol was commonly used in juxtaposition to revolver—specifically to mean a semi-automatic pistol (Hatcher 134–35; Himmelwright 18–19; Pollard, *Automatic Pistols* 1). Lovecraft, as we have seen, had hands-on experience with firearms, and it is probable he was most often using the term in the more modern sense, as shorthand for semi-automatic pistol. In "The Ghost-

---

19. Self-loading firearm: "A firearm which make use of the chemical energy stored in a cartridge to cycle the weapon's action, extracting, and ejecting the cartridge case immediately after firing, and chambering a new cartridge from the weapon's magazine" (Jenzen-Jones 132).

20. Semi-automatic (action): "A self-loading action which is capable of firing only one shot each time the firing mechanism is activated" (Jenzen-Jones 132).

Eater," for example, the narrator first refers to an "automatic" (CF 4.55; see below) that he later calls simply a "pistol" (CF 4.61) and then an "automatic" again (CF 4.62). Lovecraft does employ the generic usage, however. In "The Beast in the Cave," he used "pistol" (CF 1.24) when he was probably referring to a revolver. That story was written in 1905, when semi-automatic pistols were still rare.[21] In "The Dunwich Horror," Wilbur Whateley arms himself with a "pistol" in 1915 (CF 2.427) yet leaves a "revolver" when he disappears in 1928 (CF 2.438). The time elapsed certainly allowed for these to be different weapons, but it could also represent another case of Lovecraft's more generic use of the term pistol.

A revolver can be defined as a "manually operated handgun with a fixed barrel and a rotating cylinder containing multiple parallel chambers" (Jenzen-Jones 38). In many ways the workhorse firearm for law enforcement, private investigators, and armed civilians during Lovecraft's time, the term "revolver" is used twenty-seven times within the assessed works: six times in "Herbert West—Reanimator," four in "The Electric Executioner," four in "The Whisperer in the Darkness," three in "From Beyond," three in "The Last Test," twice in "The Mound," twice in "Pickman's Model," and once each in "The Disinterment," "The Dunwich Horror," and "The Hound." In "From Beyond," the narrator describes how he had been "prompted to draw from [his] hip pocket the revolver [he] always carried after dark" (CF 1.197). Habitually carrying a revolver in your hip pocket suggests that it is both light and small—in other words, a pocket revolver. In 1920, when the story was written, there were numerous firearms of that type available, ranging from the quality Colt Pocket Positive or S&W Hand Ejector double-action models to any one of various cheaper domestic or imported designs, most of them chambered for low-powered cartridges. In "Pickman's Model," we hear that Richard Upton Pickman's revolver had six chambers and was fairly loud (CF 2.70). This probably eliminates many of the smaller-framed weapons available at the time, which typically held seven cartridges in .22-caliber or five in .32-caliber. Pickman probably preferred a medium-sized pattern that was still concealable, something like the Colt Police Positive Special or the S&W Military & Police, both double-action revolvers chambered for the .38 Special (9 × 29R mm) cartridge that could be fired quickly and were still compact enough to stuff into a large trouser or jacket pocket.[22] In "Herbert West—Reanimator," West's re-

---

21. It is unlikely that 15-year-old HPL had much experience with self-loading handguns.

22. Coat, jacket, and even trouser pockets of the time were cut wide and deep enough to

volver is likewise a six-shot model (CF 1.303), suggesting a medium-to-large caliber (relatively speaking). As this part of the story is set in 1905, a model such as the Colt Double Action Constabulary Revolver, chambered for .38 Long Colt (9.1 × 26R mm), or the S&W Hand Ejector in .32 S&W Long (7.65 x 23R mm) would be plausible choices. In "The Electric Executioner," the narrator's revolver in his "right-hand coat pocket" (CF 4.140) could have been any one from a number of pocket revolvers available in 1889. A S&W Safety Hammerless double-action-only[23] revolver chambered for the .38 S&W (9 × 20R mm) cartridge, introduced in 1887, would be especially suitable for concealed carry. The "heavy revolver" of the narrator in "The Mound" (CF 4.222) must have been a larger pattern in a comparatively stout caliber. Considering that it was forced upon him by the sheriff, it might have been a Colt Single Action Army[24] revolver chambered for the .45 Colt (11.43 × 33R mm) cartridge, an obsolescent design dating to 1873 that was nevertheless still in use with rural police forces in 1928, in which year this story was set. The comparatively high frequency with which Lovecraft employs the term revolver mirrors the situation on the American firearms market during his lifetime, during which revolvers still very much reigned supreme.

Automatic pistol—colloquially abbreviated during Lovecraft's era to just automatic—is a period term for a self-loading (semi-automatic) handgun.[25] A self-loading handgun can be defined as a "handgun which makes use of the chemical energy stored in a cartridge to cycle the weapon's action, extracting and ejecting the cartridge case immediately after firing, and chambering a new cartridge from the weapon's magazine" (Jenzen-Jones 40). The term automatic pistol is now anachronistic, as the term "automatic" strictly includes weapons capable of automatic[26] fire (Hatcher 135; Jenzen-Jones 40; Pollard, *A History of*

---

accommodate any of the many relatively short-barreled revolvers or semi-automatic pistols designed just for that purpose.

23. A double-action-only (DAO) revolver is one that can be cocked and fired simply by pulling the trigger, but which lacks a hammer spur and internal mechanism to allow for single-action fire (Jenzen-Jones 122).

24. A single-action revolver is one that must be manually cocked for firing (Jenzen-Jones 133).

25. The term was also applied to revolvers with automatic ejectors, which were sometimes described as automatic revolvers (see, for example, Sears 304).

26. True automatic firearms are self-loading weapons capable of firing multiple shots with a single trigger pull (Jenzen-Jones 76).

Firearms 232; Smith & Smith 36). Lovecraft used the term 'automatic' eight times in his works: twice in "The Ghost-Eater," "The Lurking Fear," and "The Temple," once in "Medusa's Coil," and once in "The Shadow over Innsmouth." The specific makes and models of semi-automatic pistols imagined by Lovecraft remain unclear. We find the most information in "Medusa's Coil," where the narrator mentions that his "automatic" holds at least "twelve steel-jacketed bullets" (CF 4.340).[27] The capacity is oddly specific, and also rather high for the period. Most American semi-automatic pistols of the time were fitted with magazines capable of accepting just six to ten cartridges.[28] The weapon depicted may have been one of several cheap Spanish semi-automatic pistols of the time. These were largely patterned after Browning pocket pistols, and included models such as the Beístugei Hermanos Royal, Echave y Arizmendi Pathfinder, and Manufactura de Armas Demon—all chambered for the .32 ACP (7.65 × 17SR mm) cartridge[29] and using a 12-round magazine (Antaris 679–680). These pistols all look very similar, compact but with an elongated grip. The Demon, made between 1925 and 1933, was marked "Automatic Pistol 'Demon'—32 Caliber Metal Covered Bullet" on the slide. In other words, it fits almost literally the description used by Lovecraft. Spanish pistols were imported in such huge numbers in the period between the Great War and the Spanish Civil War (1936-39) that "Spanish pistol" became a familiar generic term in both police reports and newspaper articles, indicating not a specific make and model but a general type.

The "guardian automatic" in the pocket of the narrator in "The Ghost-Eater" (CF 4.55) is undoubtedly a small semi-automatic pistol, something along the lines of the Colt Pocket Hammerless—a handy, compact weapon that is chambered for the .32 ACP cartridge (with an eight-round magazine) or .380 ACP (9 × 17 mm; seven rounds) (Sapp 132). There were dozens of similar American, Belgian, British, German, Spanish, and other models readily available. The narrator in "The Lurking Fear" is an experienced explorer

---

27. This probably indicates a twelve-round magazine, but could perhaps refer to a weapon fitted with an eleven-round magazine and a user who loaded a twelfth round in the chamber—although this practice was not as common at the time as it is today.

28. A notable exception being the Reising Arms Company Bear, chambered for the .22 Long Rifle cartridge (Scott).

29. In the U.S., the cartridge is given the epithet Automatic Colt Pistol, a reference to the earliest American weapon chambered for the round. In Europe, where it was actually first introduced, the cartridge is called the 7.65 × 17SR mm Browning.

who has survived "a series of quests for strange horrors" (CF 1.349). It appears probable that, not unlike historical figures of the period, his "automatic" (CF 1.372) of choice would be a large-caliber, high-quality, military-type weapon.[30] Famous explorers such as Richard E. Byrd[31] and T. E. Lawrence favoured Colt Government Model self-loading pistols chambered for the .45 ACP (11.43 × 23 mm) cartridge on their expeditions to the dangerous corners of the world (Hoffman; Daley). Other adventurers, including Gordon Mac-Creagh,[32] preferred smaller-caliber weapons such as the Luger Parabellum, chambered for the 7.65 × 21 mm Parabellum cartridge (MacCreagh 9; 154). The exploits of these men—frequently including details of their equipment—were widely publicized, both through contemporary newspaper coverage and in books recounting their expeditions. The "automatic pistol" in "The Temple" (CF 1.160) suggests that Lovecraft might have been aware of the fact that the German navy issued the Luger P.04 semi-automatic pistol (chambered for the 9 × 19 mm Parabellum cartridge) during the Great War (Görtz & Sturgess 877–78) and that officers like the protagonist, *Kapitänleutnant* Karl Heinrich, Graf von Altberg-Ehrenstein, often provided their own semi-automatic sidearms.

Long guns—that is, firearms that are "grasped by placing the control hand and support hand in different locations," and which are "typically fitted with a buttstock intended to be braced against the user's shoulder when fired" (Jenzen-Jones 50)—occur less commonly in Lovecraft's stories than handguns. The rifle, defined as a "long gun with a rifled bore,[33] primarily intended to fire individual bore-diameter projectiles" (Jenzen-Jones 58), is mentioned a total of four times in the surveyed works: twice in "The Whisperer in Darkness," once in "The Curse of Yig," and once in "The Dunwich Horror." Without more descriptive language, rifle is a broad term that does little to hint at any specific make or

---

30. The narrator's two "armed companions" (CF 1.353) in "The Lurking Fear" were probably similarly equipped.

31. Rear Admiral Byrd's Antarctic expeditions were of course an inspiration for At the Mountains of Madness (see, for example, Waugh 91–92; Eckhardt 33–34).

32. MacCreagh was also a prolific pulp author who published in *Strange Tales of Mystery and Terror* and elsewhere (see, for example, MacCreagh 68–84).

33. A weapon with a rifled bore bears rifling: "a pattern of helical grooves in the bore of a barrel which are designed to impart spin to a fired projectile. This rotation provides gyroscopic stability to the projectile, increasing accuracy and precision, and ensuring the projectile flies point-first toward the target" (Jenzen-Jones 132).

model of firearm that Lovecraft had in mind when employing the word, and by itself could refer to anything from an antiquated muzzle-loading hunting rifle to a modern semi-automatic military rifle. Lovecraft provided only limited contextual information to allow us to interpret his meaning in these cases. References are made to "big-game rifles" in "The Dunwich Horror" (CF 2.455) and "The Whisperer in Darkness" (CF 2.493). "Big game" is a term generally used to refer to large wild animals that are hunted for food or sport; in North America, these include especially bear, deer, elk, and sheep (Shields). Lovecraft may have had a specific cartridge in mind that would be employed for the hunting of these animals, such as the .30-06 Springfield (7.62 × 63 mm), .30-30 Winchester (7.62 x 52R mm), or .30-40 Krag (7.7 × 59R mm). Dozens of makes and models of rifles were available chambered for these, or similar, cartridges. We know the weapon in "The Whisperer in Darkness" was a "repeating rifle" (CF 2.493), meaning one in which "the number of cartridges held in the weapon is greater than the number of barrels, one or more cartridges are held elsewhere than the firing chamber, and more than one shot can be fired before the weapon needs to be reloaded" (Jenzen-Jones 131). In other words, it was a rifle fitted with a magazine, rather than a single-shot (or double-barreled) example. This definition can still be applied to a variety of designs, however, including bolt-action,[34] lever-action,[35] pump-action,[36] semi-automatic, and even automatic weapons. All types were commercially available at the time, with both domestically produced and imported options available. There are other hints to the weapon's characteristics, however. The first clue is the fact that Henry Akeley bought spare ammunition for his rifle (CF 2.493) in Brattleboro, Vermont—a town that Lovecraft knew from his visit with Vrest Orton in 1928 (see Figure 7). Brattleboro was a small town with a population of less than 10,000 (Bureau of the Census 1,113), and ammunition would almost certainly be purchased at a hardware store rather than a specialist gun shop. This would imply a relatively common caliber, such as .30-30 Winchester or .30-40 Krag.

---

34. Bolt action: "A type of manually operated firearm action in which the weapon is cycled by manipulating a handle affixed to its bolt. The most common variants are turn-bolt and straight-pull actions" (Jenzen-Jones 118).

35. Lever action: "A type of manually operated firearm action in which the weapon is cycled by manipulating a lever, usually operated by the control hand" (Jenzen-Jones 126).

36. Pump action: "A type of manually operated small arm or light weapon action in which the weapon is cycled by manipulating a handgrip, usually grasped by the support hand, in a linear fashion" (Jenzen-Jones 130).

Further, we know that Akeley drove an "antique" Ford automobile (*CF* 2.537), probably a Model T as introduced in 1908. An older rifle might then be more plausible for such a man; perhaps a U.S. Army-surplus Krag-Jørgensen M1898 bolt-action rifle chambered for the .30-40 Krag cartridge. Surplus Krag rifles were sold in the 1920s for only $6, and widely used for hunting (Poyer 24–25).[37]

Figure 7. Vrest Orton and H. P. Lovecraft on Orton's farm near Brattleboro, Vermont, in 1928. Orton appears to wear a pistol belt with a holster on his right hip. (Source: Wikimedia Commons.)

---

37. A more expensive but still moderately priced option would be a Winchester Model 1894 lever-action rifle chambered for the .30-30 Winchester cartridge, which was the single most common rifle in the United States at that time (Wallack 190). The Winchester retailed for around $40 in the 1920s (Colclough 6).

An older form of firearm, the musket, is mentioned four times in *The Case of Charles Dexter Ward*, three times in "The Street," and once in "The Shadow over Innsmouth." A musket is a smoothbore firearm that does not use self-contained cartridges, instead requiring the separate loading of gunpowder and one or more projectiles from the muzzle-end of the weapon (Jenzen-Jones 77–78). In "The Ghost-Eater," the villagers kill the werewolf by "fill[ing] it with lead" (CF 4.64). The story was written in 1923, and that scene was supposed to have taken place 60 years earlier. In the 1860s, the typical firearms were "caplock" (or "percussion") muskets and rifles, making use of percussion caps, rather than earlier flint-and-steel "flintlock" designs. Of course, villagers may well have had earlier firearms in their possession, too, and it is tempting to imagine Lovecraft picturing his "ancestral flintlock" playing a role in the story.

A common category of firearm that is curiously absent from Lovecraft's works is the shotgun (a "smoothbore long gun, primarily intended to fire multiple projectiles of less than bore diameter ('shot')" [Jenzen-Jones 51]). This is markedly unusual given the rural settings of many of his stories. It may be that Lovecraft never have owned a shotgun himself and was informed by personal experience. Indeed, shotguns were primarily considered hunting weapons (usually intended for small game), and Lovecraft, as we have seen, did not hunt. The closest he comes to including the common shotgun is a reference in "The Street" to a "fowling piece" (CF 1.113), an early term for a smoothbore weapon that fired shot (essentially a precursor to the modern shotgun) that refers to its use in killing game birds (Bosworth 105).

Use of Firearms in Lovecraft's Works

Many of the protagonists in Lovecraft's stories own firearms as a matter of course. Seldom is a weapon acquired only to be used over the course of the story. Twice we read that a protagonist has bought a handgun specifically for self-defense during the task ahead (in "The Dunwich Horror," CF 2.427; and in "The Lurking Fear," CF 1.372). In "The Mound," a handgun is "forced upon" the narrator by a well-meaning sheriff (CF 4.222). Once we read that a narrator acquired a semi-automatic pistol specifically to end his life, in "The Shadow over Innsmouth" (CF 3.229). The only time we hear about a protagonist acquiring a weapon specifically to ward against a known supernatural threat is in "The Shunned House" (CF 1.470), when Dr. Elihu Whipple and his nephew modify a Crookes tube[38] into a weapon and acquire not one but two flamethrowers.[39] All this conforms to the realities of the United States during Lovecraft's lifetime: firearms were readily available everywhere, and to almost everyone. Even weapons that are today restricted in the U.S. (such as automatic firearms and explosives) could be purchased by civilians in Lovecraft's time.[40] Ownership of both handguns and long guns was commonplace and unremarkable, although some larger Eastern cities (including Boston, Chicago, and New York) had started to restrict the acquisition, ownership, and carriage of handguns.[41] Practically, however, everyone who wanted a firearm could access one.

As we have established, Lovecraft held a robust interest in firearms, as well as being possessed of a certain degree of practical experience. Consequently, he was aware of many of the small details surrounding the use of firearms, from their mechanical properties and handling characteristics to their employment and (mis)use. In particular, Lovecraft repeatedly and accurately described what happens when shooters find themselves in high-stress situations. Psychological stress brought on by dangerous circumstances, chaos, confusion, darkness, fear, and other factors (an eldritch horror, say!) may result in perception distortions and perceived time dilation for the shooter—often resulting in an involuntary increase in the rate at which the weapon is fired. William Fairbairn, instructor of the Shanghai Municipal Police, alluded to this in *The American Rifleman* in 1927:

---

38. See Livesey.

39. Flamethrowers are not firearms, but rather belong to the broader class of light weapons. A light (i.e., man-portable) flamethrower is "A man-portable device which ejects a flammable substance (a fuel) towards the target without the use of a delivery munition" (Jenzen-Jones 98).

40. Flamethrowers were—and still are—broadly legal to own in the United States, with the United States Consumer Product Safety Commission even issuing safety guidance in 2018 (USCPSC). A few states and municipalities have made provisions to regulate them locally, but only Maryland has banned the weapons outright (CBS Baltimore).

41. An example is New York's controversial Sullivan Act of 1911, which required a pistol permit for buying, owning, and carrying a handgun and, in 1913, made provisions to exclude applicants without "proper cause" or who were deemed unreliable because of their "moral character" (Sullivan Act 1911). The "proper cause" requirement was struck down by the U.S. Supreme Court on 23 June 2022, for violating the Second and Fourteenth Amendments to the U.S. Constitution (New York State Rifle & Pistol Association, Inc. v. Bruen).

> Take the records of the New York and Chicago police and see if the average distance at which effective shooting has taken place, both at and by the police . . . and we shall be surprised if it is over five feet (*not* yards).[42] It does not take much power of imagination to see that at that distance it is a question of the greatest possible speed, and owing to the disconcerting knowledge of knowing that the other man is trying to kill you, your firing will have to be done instinctively, and the greater the volume of fire you can put in the greater the chance of your living. (17)

Shooters under stress will not only fire faster, they may also continue to fire until their ammunition source is depleted. This phenomenon has been documented in many shootings involving police officers, who will instinctively continue to fire at their target until they are down and/or an officer's weapon empty (McNab 244, 281). Lovecraft appears to have known of this phenomenon, writing in "Herbert West—Reanimator" that "It is uncommon to fire all six shots of a revolver with great suddenness when one would probably be sufficient. . . my friend suddenly, excitedly, and unnecessarily emptied all six chambers of his revolver into the nocturnal visitor" (CF 1.308). Similarly, in "Pickman's Model," he writes: "there was a shouted gibberish from Pickman, and the deafening discharge of all six chambers of a revolver, fired spectacularly as a lion-tamer might fire in the air for effect" (CF 2.70), and in "The Ghost-Eater": "That scream had roused me to action, and in a second I had retrieved my automatic and emptied its entire contents into the wolfish monstrosity before me" (CF 4.62). Similar situations are depicted in "Medusa's Coil" ("Reason deserted me altogether, and before I knew what I was doing I drew my automatic and sent a shower of twelve steel-jacketed bullets through the shocking canvas"; CF 4.340) and in "The Thing on the Doorstep," which again ties the use of unmitigated force to feelings of fear, horror, and dread:

> It is true that I have sent six bullets through the head of my best friend, and yet I hope to shew by this statement that I am not his murderer. At first I shall be called a madman—madder than the man I shot in his cell at the Arkham Sanitarium. Later some of my readers will weigh each statement, correlate it with the known facts, and ask themselves how I could have believed otherwise than as I did after facing the evidence of that horror—that thing on the doorstep. (CF 3.324)

In all the above cases, Lovecraft depicts shooters under traumatic stress. They fire "with great suddenness," "in a second," or in "a shower"—as fast as they can squeeze the trigger of their revolver or semi-automatic pistol. These

---

42. Five feet equals approximately 1.5 meters; five yards is approximately 4.5 meters.

depictions convey important information about the mental states of the shooters, but also accurately reflect the mechanical capabilities of the firearms involved. Any double-action revolver or semi-automatic pistol can be emptied very quickly. According to Edward Farrow, instructor at the U.S. Military Academy at West Point, even an early Colt Military Model semi-automatic pistol (.38 ACP, 7-round magazine) could be emptied *on target* in just 1.4 seconds (Farrow 150).

Most of the gunplay in Lovecraft's work is necessarily one-sided—the protagonist uses a firearm to ward off a supernatural threat. "The Whisperer in Darkness" is the only story that features an actual gunfight between at least two shooters:

> About the same time bullets came through the window and nearly grazed me. What was up there I don't know yet, but I'm afraid the creatures are learning to steer better with their space wings. I put out the light and used the windows for loopholes, and raked all around the house with rifle fire aimed just high enough not to hit the dogs. (CF 2.495)

Here we have two parties firing at each other, with Henry Akeley even using cover and varying shooting positions to his advantage. Note the tactically sound move of extinguishing the light, which allowed Akeley to move from position to position without silhouetting himself. It probably also allowed him to see his opponents better, at least as shadows in the night. To S. T. Joshi, the gunfight discredits the story: "Their gun-battle with Akeley takes on unintentionally comic overtones, reminiscent of shoot-outs in cheap western movies" (*IAP* 763). While it is uncharacteristic for Lovecraft to detail a fight from beginning to end, it fits the narrative in this case, depicting Akeley desperately and literally fighting for his life and humanity—with human cunning very much on display.

A detail that commonly escapes authors (and readers) without first-hand shooting experience is just how loud firearms are. A shot from an ordinary larger-caliber handgun produces more than 150 decibels (dB), a sound well above the pain threshold (Paulson 6), especially indoors. Lovecraft himself could not tolerate larger-caliber handgun shots during his childhood, as we have seen. We hear echoes of this this in the "deafening discharge" of the revolver in "Pickman's Model" (CF 2.70)—the sound no doubt exacerbated by the firing of not just one but six shots. Lovecraft also observes that loud gunfire will attract unwelcome attention unless the shooter is in a suitably isolated location, such as the cottage in "Herbert West—Reanimator" (CF 1.304), or the sound can be covered by something else, such as a thunder crash in "The Lurking Fear" (CF 1.349). In *The Case of Charles Dexter Ward*, Lovecraft describes how the muskets of the vigilantes "flashed and cracked" (CF 2.259), a vivid description of the action of a flintlock musket, which features a distinctive flash of the powder in the pan igniting before the sharp report (and muzzle flash) of firing.

In "The Dunwich Horror," Lovecraft accurately describes a common firearm malfunction, a so-called "misfire." Firearms, like any moderately complex mechanical tool, can fail to function as intended in a variety of different ways. In this case, Lovecraft depicts a cartridge malfunction with a dud round: "Near the central desk a revolver had fallen, a dented but undischarged cartridge later explaining why it had not been fired" (CF 2.438). This is an excellent detail, lending verisimilitude to a scene depicting inexplicable events—in other words, exactly the sort of detail that Lovecraft suggested made for good weird fiction ("Notes on Writing Weird Fiction," CF 2.177). He could probably draw directly from own experience, since the rimfire cartridges used in most of his personal firearms were especially prone to this kind of malfunction due to the way these cartridges are manufactured (Jones).[43] The dent in question is a result of the striker, firing pin, or hammer of a firearm hitting the cartridge case head, which should have initiated the priming compound contained therein.

Lovecraft is also eminently practical in addressing another neglected aspect of writing firearms in fiction: target acquisition under low-light conditions. The now well-known pairing of the handgun with the portable electric flashlight is portrayed several times in Lovecraft's stories. In "The Whisperer in Darkness," Professor Albert Wilmarth describes himself as "gripping in my right hand the revolver I had brought along, and holding the pocket flashlight in my left" (CF 2.528). In "Herbert West—Reanimator," West "had in his hands a revolver and an electric flashlight" (CF 1.308); while in "The Lurking Fear," the narrator carries a semi-automatic pistol and a "pocket-light" (CF 1.371). In "Pickman's Model," Richard Upton Pickman carries a revolver and a "flashlight" (CF 2.63), while in "The Dunwich Horror," Dr. Henry Armitage, Dr. Francis Morgan, and Professor Warren Rice bring at least one "electric flashlight" (CF 2.455). In "The Mound," the narrator carries a revolver and "electric torches" (CF 4.222).[44]

---

43. Other factors, such as environmental and storage considerations, as well as the firearm itself, can also play a role.

44. An earlier combination of tools is also depicted; in *The Case of Charles Dexter Ward*,

Firearms are often used to end the supernatural or otherworldly threat in Lovecraft's tales—if only partially or temporarily. In "From Beyond," the narrator uses a revolver to destroy the noxious machine (CF 1.201). In "Herbert West—Reanimator," the titular character uses a revolver to kill a zombie (CF 1.308), while the narrator in "The Lurking Fear" uses a semi-automatic pistol to kill one of the Martense descendants (CF 1.372). In "Pickman's Model," Richard Upton Pickman uses a revolver to kill a ghoul (CF 2.70); in "The Whisperer in Darkness," Henry Akeley uses a repeating rifle to destroy at least one of the Mi-Go (CF 2.493). In "The Thing on the Doorstep," Daniel Upton uses a handgun to dispatch an animated corpse (CF 3.356), and in the "The Ghost-Eater," the villagers had used firearms to kill the werewolf (CF 4.64). In "The Horror in the Museum," Orabona uses a handgun to kill Rhan-Tegoth (CF 4.448). In "Medusa's Coil," the narrator uses a semi-automatic pistol to destroy the painting (CF 4.292). These cases show at least some success in fighting off the unknown terrors of Lovecraftian design. Then again, in "The Dunwich Horror," we are reminded "that no material weapon would be of help" (CF 2.455)—including Dr. Francis Morgan's big-game rifle—other than to boost morale.

Conclusion

> To his readers he might be a source of fascinated speculation, for the intensity of his writings in unusual fields hinted at delvings into black magic, but to his correspondents his views were well-known—even the apparent contradictions in his nature, such as the military streak that made him love firearms and volunteer for a war his intellect assured him was senseless. . ."
>
> —J. Vernon Shea, "The Necronomicon" (54)

As demonstrated, Lovecraft's use of firearms in his stories is varied and knowledgeable. In the authors' view it can be safely assumed that this represents a conscious effort on the author's part to create contrast between the plausible actions of his protagonists and their interactions with material culture, and the surreal, often inexplicable nature of the weird. Lovecraft's personal experience—most probably supported by his propensity for reading and researching a broad range of practical and theoretical topics—informs his portrayal of firearms throughout his works and speaks to a nuance acquired in part through practical, first-hand experience. It is therefore surprising that

---

there are "parties of men with lanterns and muskets" (CF 2.250).

this aspect of Lovecraft's writing has been overlooked in Lovecraftian scholarship thus far. It is the authors' hope that this preliminary analysis will generate further exploration of Lovecraft's relationship to firearms, and a more detailed analysis of their symbolism and connotations in his published works.

Works Cited

Albers, Rachael Kay. "American as Apple Pie: How Marketing Made Guns a Fundamental Element of Contemporary Boyhood." *JSTOR Daily* (19 October 2022). daily.jstor.org/american-as-apple-pie.

Antaris, Leonardo M. *Astra Firearms and Selected Competitors*. Davenport, IA: FIRAC, 2009.

Anuschat, Erich. *Pistolen- und Revolverschießen im Polizei- und Sicherheitsdienst*. Berlin: Gerstmann, 1928.

Boorman, Dean K. *History of Winchester Firearms*. Guilford, CT: Lyons Press, 2001.

Bosworth, N. *A Treatise on the Rifle, Musket, Pistol, and Fowling-Piece: Embracing Projectiles and Sharp-shooting*. New York: J. S. Redfield, 1846.

Bureau of the Census. "Population, Volume I: Number and Distribution of Inhabitants" in *Fifteenth Census of the United States: 1930*. Washington, D.C., 1931.

CBS Baltimore. "State Fire Marshal Reminds Marylanders That Flamethrowers Are Illegal Following Elon Musk Sale." 3 February 2018, www.cbsnews.com/baltimore/news/flamethrower-warning/.

Colclough, George. *Small Arms Pricing in 19th Century American Catalogues and Advertising*. Unpublished background paper, 2023.

Daley, Jason. "Bullet Helps Revive Lawrence of Arabia's Reputation." *Smithsonian Magazine*. Digital edition: 5 April 2016. www.smithsonianmag.com/smartnews/bullet-helps-revive-lawrence-arabias-reputation-180958662/.

Eckhardt, Jason C. "Behind the Mountains of Madness: Lovecraft and the Antarctic in 1930." *Lovecraft Studies* No. 14 (Spring 1987): 31–38.

Fairbairn, W. E. "Pistol Shooting." *American Rifleman* 75, No. 3 (March 1927).

Farrow, Edward S. *American Small Arms*. New York: Bradford, 1904.

Ferguson, Jonathan. "'Trusty Bess': The Definitive Origins and History of the Term 'Brown Bess.'" *Arms & Armour* 14, No. 1 (Spring 2017): 49–69.

Görtz, Joachim, and Geoffrey Sturgess. *The Borchardt & Luger Automatic Pistols–A Technical History for Collectors from C93 to P.08, Vol. II.* Galesburg, IL: Brad Simpson Publishing & G. L. Sturgess, 2011.

Hatcher, Julian S. *Pistols and Revolvers and Their Use.* Marshallton: Small-Arms Technical Publishing Company, 1927.

Himmelwright, A. L. A. *Pistol and Revolver Shooting.* New York: Macmillan, 1920.

Hoffman, George Amin. "T. E. Lawrence (Lawrence of Arabia) and the M1911." *SightM1911.* n.d. sightm1911.com/lib/history/telawrence.htm.

Jenzen-Jones, N. R. "Weapons Identification: Small-calibre Ammunition." In N. R. Jenzen-Jones and M. Schroeder. *An Introductory Guide to the Identification of Small Arms, Light Weapons, and Associated Ammunition.* Geneva: Small Arms Survey, 2018. www.smallarmssurvey.org/resource /introductory-guide-identification-small-arms-light-weapons-and-associated- ammunition.

———, ed. *The ARES Arms & Munitions Classification System (ARCS).* Perth: Armament Research Services (ARES), 2022.

Jones, Allan. "How to Prevent Rimfire Misfires." *Shooting Times* (17 October 2012).

Livesey, T. R. "Lovecraft and the Ray-Gun." *Lovecraft Annual* No. 3 (2009): 3-9.

Lovecraft, H. P. *A Means to Freedom: The Letters of H. P. Lovecraft and Robert E. Howard: 1930-1932,* ed. S. T. Joshi, David E. Schultz, and Rusty Burke. New York: Hippocampus Press, 2017.

———. *Rhode Island Journal of Astronomy* III, No. IV (7 May 1905). Ms., John Hay Library, Brown University.

———. *Rhode Island Journal of Astronomy* III, No. V (14 May 1905). Ms., John Hay Library, Brown University.

MacCreagh, Gordon. "Dr. Muncing, Exorcist." *Strange Tales of Mystery and Terror* 1, No. 1 (September 1931): 68-84.

———. *White Waters and Black.* Garden City, NY: Doubleday, 1961.

Madaus, H. Michael. *American Longarms.* New York: Warner, 1981.

McNab, Chris. *Deadly Force: Firearms and American Law Enforcement from the Wild West to the Streets of Today.* Oxford: Osprey Publishing, 2009.

New York State Rifle & Pistol Assn., Inc. v. Bruen. 597 U. S., 2022.

NRA Museums. "Harrington & Richardson Young America." n.d. www.nramuseum.org/guns/the-galleries/innovation,-oddities-and-competition/case-26-the-booming-arms-industry/harrington-richardson-young-america.aspx.

Paulson, Alan C. *Silencer–History and Performance, Volume 1.* Boulder, CO: Paladin Press, 1996.

Pollard, H. B. *Automatic Pistols.* London: Pitman & Sons, 1920.

———. *A History of Firearms.* London: Geoffrey Bles, 1926.

Poyer, Joe. *The American Krag Rifle and Carbine.* Tustin, CA: North Cape Publications, 2017.

Sapp, Rick. *Standard Catalog of Colt Firearms.* Iola, WI: Gun Digest, 2007.

Scott, Macgregor. "The Reising .22 Semi-auto Pistol: A Bit of Handgun History." *American Handgunner.* n.d. americanhandgunner.com /handguns/ exclusive-web-extra-the-reising-22-semi-auto-pistol/.

Sears, Roebuck & Co. *1902 Catalogue*, No. 112. Chicago: Sears, Roebuck & Co, 1902.

Shea, J. Vernon. "The Necronomicon." *Dragon & Microchips: Le Seul Fanzine Qui Rêve.* No. 14 (June 1998): 54–61.

Shields, G. O. *The Big Game of North America: Its Habits, Habitat, Haunts and Characteristics; How, When and Where to Hunt It.* Chicago: Rand, McNally & Co., 1890.

Smith, W. H. B., and Joseph E. Smith. *Book of Pistols and Revolvers.* Harrisburg, PA: Stackpole, 1968.

Stanford, Andy. *Fight at Night: Tools, Techniques, Tactics, and Training for Combat in Low Light and Darkness.* Boulder, CO: Paladin Press, 1999.

Sullivan Act 1911 ("An Act to amend the penal law, in relation to the sale and carrying of dangerous weapons"). *Laws of New York* Vol. 134 (1911), chap. 195. 442-45.

United States Consumer Product Safety Commission. "Flame Throwing Device Safety." 2018. www.loc.gov/resource/gdcebookspublic.2019666988/

Wallack, L. R. "Sixty Million Guns." 1983. In H. A. Murtz, ed. *Gun Digest Treasury: The Best from 45 Years of Gun Digest.* Northbrook, IL: DBI, 1994.

Waugh, Robert. "Looming at the Mountains of Madness: Lovecraft's Mirages." In David Simmons, ed. *New Critical Essays on H. P. Lovecraft.* New York: Palgrave Macmillan, 2013. 91-103.

Weel Tactical. 'JR-15 .22 Long Rifle' [product flyer]. Heber, UT: Weel Tactical, 2023.

Witkowski, Terrence H. "Guns for Christmas: Advertising in *Boys' Life* Magazine." *Journal of Macromarketing* 40, No. 3 (2020): 396–414.

Authors' Note

This article is derived from a research paper written by N. R. Jenzen-Jones and George Colclough and presented by Jenzen-Jones at the 2022 *Armitage Memorial Symposium* (19–21 August). In preparing this extended article, Messrs. Jenzen-Jones and Colclough were delighted to enlist the help of Hans-Christian Vortisch, who has examined Lovecraft's relationship to firearms and made many valuable contributions to this work.

Transdimensional Voices in Weird Fiction: Reverb, Echo, and Delay in Sound-Related Texts

Nathaniel R. Wallace
Independent Scholar

> It is almost erroneous to call them *sounds* at all, since so much of their ghastly, infra-bass timbre spoke to dim seats of consciousness and terror far subtler than the ear; yet one must do so, since their form was indisputably though vaguely that of half-articulate *words*. They were loud—loud as the rumblings and the thunder above which they echoed—yet did they come from no visible being.
> —H. P. Lovecraft "The Dunwich Horror" (CF 2.463)

An under-examined aspect of weird fiction and affiliated genres is the interjection of sound and sound description to disrupt temporal and spatial conventions. This analysis specifically seeks to examine the presence of the transdimensional voice, a voice emanating from another dimension, in various texts. Sound of this nature, intended by the author or artist to evoke a sense of the universe, outer space, or speaking from outside our own reality, is not medium-specific. It can exist as a description in literature, a sound effect, or a musical composition in media such as television, film, and radio drama. When examined through the field of sound design, the manipulation of space and time associated with the transdimensional voice has a significant correlation with effects of reverb, echo, and delay in creating two or more distinct spaces on a spectrum, from dry to a gradient of wet signal with varying degrees of delay. The placement of sound in contrasting spatiotemporal origins creates a challenge for listeners, as they attempt to understand spatial relation of the sounds heard simultaneously (polyphony) or in sequential order. These irreconcilable differences in sound placement are granted even more substance where there is a diegetic presence of a voice without reference to a body, further displacing sound from spatial and temporal origins.

Elements of these sound effects associated with transdimensional voices were first described and used in media. They established a "fictional novum," as Trace Reddell defines it, "an analogic and metaphorical device used to identify the fictive newness at the core of a science fiction text's narrative and thematic extrapolations" (8). Through experimentation and technological development, new methods for disruption were invented by authors, screenwriters, and sound artists who invested the fictional novum, in this case the transdimensional voice, with more sophisticated spatio-temporal techniques derived from recording, mixing, and editing practices that produced certain effects on the part of the audience. As novel sounds were created through experimentation and the use of technology, they became associated with certain speculative scenarios and technologies, engaging audiences in a derived culture of collective knowledge that grows in number and potential complexity from previous iterations. In terms of novelty, there are parallels between concept and the unknown as Lovecraft defined the supernatural, or "obscure" as Edmund Burke defines it in his treatise on the sublime.

Of particular importance to this analysis is Ambrose Bierce's story "Whither?" (1888), as it predates the "split between an original sound and its electroacoustical transmission or reproduction" described by R. Murray Schafer in his *The Soundscape: Our Sonic Environment and the Tuning of the World* (90). The decoupling of sound from its origins in space and time occurred with the invention and widespread use of broadcasting and recording technology. Once sound could be isolated and manipulated, it was a natural development to employ the effects of reverb, echo, and delay to give it a spatial dimension. This was especially true with regard to science fiction television and film productions during the 1960s in the United States such as *The Twilight Zone* and *The Outer Limits*. The examples analyzed here have something common: a privileging of the human voice, the very sound that triggers recognition, only undermined and distorted in the context or mask of reverb, echo, and delay. These and other examples will be examined for their use of the sound effects of reverb, echo, and delay on the human voice and the manner in which experimental techniques and new sound technology create a sense of wonder and awe in the audience. The feelings of wonder and awe take the form of a displacement that arises from the juxtapositioning of different spatial and temporal points, both through simultaneous expression and sequentially through connections with a potential image or lack thereof.

Reverb, Echo, and Delay in Literature and the Arts

Artists can use the effects of reverb, echo, and delay in sound to manipulate the listeners' perception of space and time through literary references to acoustics, actual or simulated, creating a geography of sound that subverts and offers a juxtaposition to conventional sound for the audience.[1] The rendering of sound through reverb and echo has the ability to position objects spatially for the listener. Neil Verma explains, "Reverberation . . . situate[s] voices in a vivid world," lending an "audioposition" indicated through the use of varying levels of reverb to echo (37, 38). These effects taken together can be thought of as a spectrum that contrasts from a dry, unmasked sound to that which is considered wet with sound effects of this nature. As the listener moves further away from a potential source of sound, the sound accumulates distance and potentially reverberation, in further distances and larger spaces, an echo. Similarly in this dynamic, there potentially accumulates decay time, reflected sound, the sense of space and distance, and echoes, represented by a progressively wet sound.

The significant though subtle distinctions between these concepts are best demonstrated by J. Sheridan Le Fanu's short story "The Familiar" (1872), in which the ominous pursuing footsteps are described as "other footfalls, pattering at a measured pace" (212), indicating they are coming from a nearby but hidden source. At this dry end of the spectrum there would be a clear and immediate sound with little to no reverberation. As the protagonist proceeds through a row of houses, the sounds of his own footsteps are amplified by the constructed residential spaces, adding a reverberation that characterizes his steps. Sounds in this context would possess a longer decay time and a more spacious sound as these footfalls reflect off the walls and ceiling of the space. Finally, the protagonist attempts to comfort himself by making louder footsteps, creating an echo that confirms he is the source, not some external phenomena, resulting in distinct, delayed repetitions of the original sound that gradually fade away. Echoes are a distinct repetition that occur after a sound wave has bounced off a reflective surface and returns to the listener. Often heard in large open spaces, such as canyons or concert halls, they provide an audible sense of distance or spaciousness. In this context, the echo imbued in sound bears similar qualities to the geographies that Lovecraft praised as the "scenes—landscapes & architecture" in a letter to Clark Ashton Smith (25 January 1924; *DS* 66). On a similar note, Burke said of such geographies, "Greatness of dimension, is a powerful cause of the sublime" (7). Reverb and

---

1. HPL opined in a letter to Frank Belknap Long (13 May 1923) regarding his role of challenging conventional spatio-temporal conditions, "What I am, is a hater of actuality—an enemy to time & space, law & necessity" (*SP* 110).

echo are essentially different points on a gradient of reflected sound against a direct and unreflected sound; however, with the former there is no whole reiteration of the original sound as it is reflected by too many surfaces, or "the reflective surfaces are too near the listener to allow subjective aural separation" (Doyle 38).

The elements of reverberation, echo, and delay have long been a prominent aspect of the arts, literature, and performance, especially in religious texts and speculative fiction. From the very origins of humanity, Schafer contends, "The desire to dislocate sounds in time and space had been evident for some time in the history of Western music, so that the recent technological developments were merely the consequences of aspirations that had already been effectively imagined" (90). In parallel, these aspirations often take the form of speculations in the realm of literature. Authors have detailed novel sounds and effects through description, sometimes taking concepts practiced during their lifetimes and expanding on their use in other art or music forms. Though some authors would confine their speculations to the page, Athanasius Kircher, a musician writing in the seventeenth century, not only methodically documented his speculations on the subject of reverb, echo, and delay in his *Phonosophia Anacamptica*, particularly in the chapter "The Science of Sound from the Perspective of the Echo," but he also put these ideas into practice through his experiments (Tronchin 12). Before the advent of television and film, authors relied on text to create atmosphere, evoke emotions, and immerse readers in their stories. At the same time, advancements were being made in the field of acoustics, theatrical productions, and sound that would bring these elements into performances on the stage and later into sound recordings.

Connected with the distance expressed through varying degrees of reverb to echo, there is an increase of the presence of delay on the sound emitted from a given position of the spectrum. Indeed, delay is often used to create a sense of space or depth in music production, as well as to create rhythmic patterns or complex textures. Placing a sound in a sequence of repetition can provide a structure of repetitive iterations for the listener. Returning this discussion to "the sublime," it is noteworthy that Edmond Burke indicated that such further reiterations offered by the effect of delay and repetition is internalized by the one who experiences it:

> Whenever we repeat any idea frequently, the mind by a sort of mechanism repeats it long after the first cause has ceased to operate. After whirling about; when we sit down, the objects about us still seem to whirl. After a long succession of noises, as the fall of waters, or the beating of forge hammers, the

hammers beat and the water roars in the imagination long after the first sounds have ceased to affect it; and they die away at last by gradations which are scarcely perceptible.... The senses strongly affected in some one manner, cannot quickly change their tenor, or adapt themselves to other things; but they continue in their old channel until the strength of the first mover decays.[2] (9)

This very technique was used to great effect in Ambrose Bierce's story "An Occurrence at Owl Creek Bridge" (1890), in which "a sharp, distinct, metallic percussion like the stroke of a blacksmith's hammer upon the anvil" repeated to the narrator, to the point at which "the intervals of silence grew progressively longer" (109), causing in him a sort of madness in the process. Similarly, the imagined heartbeat of the old man in Edgar Allan Poe's "The Tell-Tale Heart" continues unabated getting increasingly louder, causing the protagonist much agony and agitation until he confesses to murder. An echo with a repetition through delay can cause a similar agitation in the listener, though perhaps in accelerated surges and feedback.

Heard But Not Seen: A Disembodied Voice with Transdimensional Origins

The human voice is one of the most compelling sounds a listener can experience in that it demands to be heard and processed. Indeed, Julian Treasure has expressed the agency of the human voice in a hierarchy of sounds for listeners, stating, "There is no sound more powerful than the human voice" (83). David Toop makes the case for human beings privileging sound and the human voice in that such experiences extend all the way back into the womb (28). On a cosmic spectrum, the human voice registers as divergent, in that it is intimately connected to the human body and is thus known. Indeed, one must recognize that the human voice can be a powerful means of demonstrating the unique properties of the space in which it is expressed, a potential fulcrum for heightening the dynamic of the known, represented here by the human voice, versus the unknown and unseen, represented by a transdimensional space. Sound scholar R. Murray Schafer has detailed how small communities from the beginning of human history would gather in caves to tell stories and conduct religious and cultural-related ceremonies. During such gatherings there was an urge to create differences in the human voice that

---

2. This phenomenon is very much like that in Mark Twain's "A Literary Nightmare" (1876) and Henry Kuttner's "Nothing but Gingerbread Left" (1943) in creating a type of earworm that is difficult for listeners or readers to get out of their minds.

captured the divinity vocal performances using novel techniques, tools, and structures. Indeed, Schafer points to the cave of Hypogeum on Malta, dating to 2400 B.C.E., which had unusual properties in that if a person possessing a deep voice spoke slowly in a low register, his voice would be amplified considerably and a "deep ringing sound" would resonate throughout the chamber (217). Historically, the divine of our ancestors gave way to the transdimensional that has marked speculative fiction.

The early development of echoes and the voice in Western culture can be traced through literary examples from ancient Greece to the Roman era. In Homer's *Odyssey*, the Sirens sing their enchanting song, described as "Celestial music [that] warbles from their tongue," to lure Odysseus and his crew into peril. As they make their escape from the creatures by sailing past the threat, "the distant sounds decay" (314). Significantly, the Sirens' bodies are not described in this scene, leaving their remarkable voices and implied threat as the focus of their representation in the text. Later, Ovid's *Metamorphoses*, Book 3, written in 8 C.E., furnishes an example of the first explicitly transdimensional voice in extant literature. Ovid includes a description of the ancient Greek goddess Echo, who was denied the ability to speak but could only echo the last phrase or set of words of others. Her story in many ways is the first iteration of the trope of a disembodied voice used in modern fiction: she falls madly in love with Narcissus, he denies her affection, and from thereon out, due to her inability to come to terms with this rejection, she loses her corporeal form. As a result, "Only her bones and the sound of her voice are left. Her voice remains, her bones, they say, were changed to shapes of stone. She hides in the woods, no longer to be seen on the hills, but to be heard by everyone. It is sound that lives in her" (92). Here, in contrast to later speculative tales, her being loses its physical dimension and exists only as sound without a corresponding foundation in space.

Later myths and fictional stories would provide additional miraculous qualities and transdimensional contexts to the voice. In Poe's "The Fall of the House of Usher" (1839), the narrator hears "a long tumultuous shouting sound like the voice of a thousand waters" (183) whose speaker is not defined, adding to the disturbing atmosphere of the story. Fred Botting has pointed out the references to reverberations in Poe's story, remarking,

> Uncanny reverberations are part of the tale's phantasmagoria of doublings and crossings between internal and external realms, perceptual and medial registers, imagination and reality in movements that never quite restore conventional boundaries between cause, effect, truth, convention or fiction. Strange sounds...

may echo from another dimension or duplicate imagined fictional sounds so intensely that they become present to the ear. (75)

In "The Great God Pan" (1894), Arthur Machen writes: "suppose that such a man saw uttermost space lie open before the current, and words of men flash forth to the sun and beyond the sun into the systems beyond, and the voice of articulate-speaking men echo in the waste void that bounds our thought" (3), a concept that makes it appear as though there are higher order beings that inhabit the purposeless that underlies reality. In Algernon Blackwood's "A Victim of Higher Space" (1914), Racine Mudge's voice changes as his body moves through dimensions: the use of reverb and echo is associated with the disorienting experience of transdimensional travel. When Mudge disappears from the external world, his voice no longer sounds in the air but instead echoes within the depths of the doctor's own self. The voice is described as a "faint singing cry" that sounds like a "voice of dream, a voice of vision and unreality" (122). Later in the story, Doctor Silence experiences a similar phenomenon when a "thick, whispering voice" cries out from deep within his own consciousness, repeating the words "Gone! gone! gone! [. . .] Lost! lost! lost!" (124). The voice grows fainter and fainter until it disappears into nothingness, taking the last signs of Racine Mudge with it.

These descriptions of echoing and reverberating voices suggest that the experience of transdimensional travel is disorienting and unsettling, as the normal boundaries between external reality and internal consciousness are blurred. The literary references to the effects of echo and reverb creates a sense of unreality and dislocation, for the voices referenced heighten the nature of their origins from a strange and unfamiliar space. In H. F. Arnold's widely anthologized short story "The Night Wire" published in *Weird Tales* (September 1926), two night wire operators receive a report regarding a strange fog taking over a town called Xebico, but also some unusual vocal activity. Specifically they receive a report during their shift that contains references to voices with a heavy echo effect: "From the outskirts of the city may be heard cries of unknown voices. They echo through the fog in queer uncadenced minor keys. The sounds resemble nothing so much as wind whistling through a gigantic tunnel. But the night is calm and there is no wind" (156). In his story "More Light" (1970), James Blish includes the following passage after the protagonist reads *The King in Yellow*: "Odd noises rang through my pounding head; sometimes I thought I could hear lines from the play being spoken, as if in an echo chamber, or, sometimes, even being sung" (110). It is not clear that these voices come from outside the body or within, yet they are disembodied and are represented through a reference to echo.

One of the more novel fictional works that incorporates a transdimensional voice is Ambrose Bierce's short story trilogy "Whither?," originally published in the *San Francisco Examiner* in 1888. Later renamed "Mysterious Disappearances," it appears in his collection *Can Such Things Be?*, which contains short stories that detail fictional accounts of individuals physically disappearing into a liminal space. Of these stories, "Whither" in particular contains an example of sound that demonstrates novel properties connected to reverb, echo, and delay. The story recounts the disappearance of a family's son who walked into the wilderness, leaving tracks which abruptly end in the snow:

> Four days later the grief-stricken mother herself went to the spring for water. She came back and related that in passing the spot where the footprints had ended she had heard the voice of her son and had been eagerly calling to him, wandering about the place, as she had fancied the voice to be now in one direction, now in another, until she was exhausted with fatigue and emotion. (101)

Her family and neighbors attribute her experience with Ashmore's voice to a hallucination, a product of grief and loss of her son. From Bierce's description of the situation the scenario is, in more contemporary terms, similar to a ping-pong delay effect within two channels, bouncing sound from one to the other.[3] The result creates juxtapositions within space, of sound coming from different directions and thus different locations. As the narrative continues, the reader learns:

> for months afterward, at irregular intervals of several days, the voice was heard by the various members of the family and by others. All declared it unmistakably the voice of Charles Ashmore; all agreed that it seemed to come from a great distance, faintly yet with entire distinctness of articulation. Yet none could determine its direction, nor repeat its words. (101)

This sounds again like a ping-pong arrangement, but here it is distinct and the reverberations high, while obscuring the communicative aspect of the

---

3. In terms of technology able to replicate this effect, the first two-channel sound delivery system was unveiled by Clément Ader in 1881, and later modern stereophonic sound was invented in the 1930s by Alan Blumlein, a sound engineer from the UK (Rapoport 2014). One of the first electronic devices that could create the ping-pong effect described in "Charles Ashmore's Trail" was the Lexicon Prime Time Model 93, invented by Gary Hall and released in 1978 (Schlarb).

words spoken by Ashmore. The acoustic description of this scenario is reminiscent of the structure in ancient Greece known as "odeia," a form of concert hall with strong reverberation qualities mostly used for musical performances rather than speeches or dramas; thus excessive reverberation of a sound source somewhat displaces the original sound, stretching it out, while undermining its discernibility among the audience (Mourjopoulos).

In "Whither?," the delay expands in reiteration to the point of termination. Bierce writes, "The intervals of silence grew longer and longer, the voice fainter and farther, and by midsummer it was heard no more" (101). The overall experience seems to embody reverb, extending an echo to a repeated delay. Here, the definition of reverb aligns with this process; Tony Gibbs's definition of reverberation as "the way in which a sound dies away in a real or virtual space" (170) bears a strong resemblance to this concept, only expanded upon in scope. The key element here is the word "intervals" and the manner in which the supernatural unknown, or unknown status of the boy, goes from within the dimension of the story to the outside of it, accumulating an effect in the process, better known as decay. R. Murray Schafer distinguishes echo from reverb, explaining, "Echo differs from reverberation in that it is a repetition or partial repetition of sound, due to reflection off a distant surface" (130). In this framework of reflective surfaces, Ashmore is entering into a more vast transdimensional space, which is causing an increase in the delay in echo, until it completely terminates, indicating no further sound emanations. Daniel von Rudiger has stated of such a repetition, "Rhythm presupposes a temporal repetition of objects" and their relation to one another in time and space whereby "These relations describe a structure and rules can be derived from it" (66). The structure in this case is of two dimensions, where one is leaking sound into the other, to create a juxtaposition representing contrasts within an unseen but heard spatial configuration in a way that Lovecraft stated he enjoyed in the pictorial realm with "new juxtapositions" and "new effects."[4] In Bierce's story, the structure of the contrasts in sound is the most

---

4. In a letter to Zealia Bishop (13 February 1928) regarding landscape and architecture and the importance of contrasts, HPL wrote: "I am above all else *scenic and architectural* in my tastes. It might quite justly be said that the only genuine motivating element in my existence is a quest for novel adventures in landscape, panorama, and lighting-effects: new combinations of hill and river-bend and wooded valley, new juxtapositions of winding road, stone wall, and half-embowered farmhouse roof, or new effects of slanting late-afternoon sunlight over the spires, roofs, and terraced gardens of some marvellous city I have never seen before" (*Letters to Woodburn Harris and Others* 355).

significant expression of the unknown.

In an invented text at the end of "Whither?," similar to Lovecraft's *Necronomicon*, Bierce tied his stories concerning mysterious disappearances together by the inclusion of a pseudo-science column replete with fake references. It is conveyed to the reader that spaces outside known reality are accessed through "void places" where both living and non-living things "may fall into the invisible world" and "be seen and heard no more" (102). This is equivalent to Lovecraft's notion of "the unechoing emptiness of infinity" ("Celephaïs," CF 1.186) or his original inspiration—Lord Dunsany—for a passage from his short story "The Nameless City," "the unreverberate blackness of the abyss," which has no walls or surfaces to generate successive sounds (CF 1.237). Sound within this context is more intelligible, but it would not have much of a sonic footprint beyond the initial sound. Peter Doyle reflects that "if all real-world sounds were to be somehow stripped of their cloaking of reverberation, it would be a wholly disorienting, dead, almost spaceless and depthless world," and according to Gautam Pemmaraju, a scenario of "reverberation (echo being a type) [that] would render perception of our surroundings as dimensionless" (38). This dimensionless quality, specifically of the voice, is highlighted in God's voice in ancient Jewish scripture. Indeed, according to Hayim, "God's voice is not an 'echo' in the sense that it is not a part of the general 'noise' generated in the universe whether natural or human made, whether accompanying the human voice or any other sound."[5] The type of sound environment that contains such a voice, a sort of anechoic chamber, would seem to be the end point after the initial decay effect of Ashmore's voice as he moves through a reality possessing normal acoustics into a delay and later to inhabit the void place without echoes, or reverberations, at least any heard by the narrator.

Richard Matheson's story "Little Girl Lost," first published *Amazing Stories* (October/November 1953), contains a similar transdimensional voice-related scenario. The story is significant for its affinities to "Whither?," except that it takes place in the domesticated space of an American suburb of the 1950s. However there are no specific references to unusual acoustic phenomena beyond that of a lost child who can be heard but not seen, a reversal of the fifteenth-century proverb "Children should be seen and not heard." Rod

---

5. Hayim refers to Resh Lakish scholarship and quotes his interpretation of the matter, "If one man calls to another, his voice has a Bat Kol [i.e., an echo]; but the voice proceeding from God has no Bat Kol."

Serling's introduction to the story in *The Twilight Zone* broadcast in 1962 makes this connection clear. He elaborated: "Bettina Miller can be heard quite clearly, despite the rather curious fact that she can't be seen at all."[6] In "Little Girl Lost," Bierce's disappearance scenario is brought into the suburban home of a couple, their daughter Tina, and their dog. Tina and the sound of her voice bear similarities to the concept of the voice of God, an omniscient voice that has been used in theater, radio dramas, television, and film. This voice is one that, without connection to a diegetic body, relays information to or expounds on elements of the plot for the audience. Significantly, Tina's decoupled voice is adjacent to the concept of Bat Kol, the indirect echoes of the voice of God from the Old Testament, spoken largely by angels, that translates to "daughter of voice" (Jillions 176). It is Tina who exists only as a voice for much of the duration of the episode.

The two soundmen for "Little Girl Lost," Franklin Milton and Bill Edmondson, created whirling echo on all diegetic voices in the alternative dimension, a technique that set the delay time to a relatively short value.[7] The episode starts with Tina crying for her mother while the couple are present in the living room. Her voice is distressed, but it sounds as though she is present in the same room. However, after the introduction by Rod Serling, when the couple goes looking for their daughter, her voice is modified through the use of reverb, placing her in a different space from what is depicted on camera. It is difficult to know exactly what specific reverb was used on the recorded vocals on this scene; however, at the time Paul Theberge explains the proliferation of one particular brand: "EMT 140 was introduced in 1957 by the German company Elektro-Mess-Technik, and it quickly became one of the most popular plate reverbs ever produced. Well-known studios such as Abbey Road in London and CBS Records in New York used them, as did many smaller facilities" (330). Through their use of reverb, Milton and Edmonson segregated the characters living in conventional reality from the little girl and

---

6. The actress playing the girl, Tracy Stratford, is only visible at the climax of the episode when the audience is shown this third dimension. Prior to that, the actress playing the role, only purely vocally, was Roda Williams, who supplied the cues during the filming and later recorded her parts in a studio to be included into the soundtrack during the editing process (Grams 498).

7. Peter Wolfe attributes the distortion to director Paul Stewart, who very well could have requested the effect of Milton and Edmonson, but without full documentation, it is difficult to determine (195).

even the family dog who have entered another. Once Tina disappears, there is a distinct echo, indicating her presence in an even larger space out of sight, as well as delay, with a high level of feedback that changes her voice, just as Bierce described in "Whither?" Whether the duo employed the Binson Echorec, commercially available in 1950s and early 1960s, Charlie Watkins's Copicat (1958), or Echoplex by Mike Battle and Don Dixon (1959; created by Market Electronics of Cleveland), there is a use of echo delay technology exhibited in "Little Girl Lost" but taken to the extreme in the service of introducing weirdness into the conventionalized audio of the episode (Hughes). Indeed, the manner in which Milton and Edmonson utilized reverb, echo, and delay in this segment on Tina's voice is much in line with Steve Goodman's assertion that "the conceptual power of such effects is in their potential to preempt virtual sonic spaces that do not yet actually exist, populating real spaces with audio hallucinations" (159). Note that this reference to hallucination is much in line with "Whither?" and the behavior exhibited by Ashmore's mother in hearing echoes of her son's voice.

It is significant to provide context to this scenario of sound by highlighting the work of sound artists such as Karlheinz Stockhausen, Pierre Schaeffer, and John Cage, who were among the pioneers experimenting with electronic effects including reverb, delay, and echo, just prior to the airing of "Little Girl Lost." Milton and Edmonson were only building upon their earlier efforts, this time in a different medium, television. Of particular relevance to their techniques is Stockhausen's seminal piece "Gesang der Jünglinge" (1956), which used tape manipulation and electronic effects to create a complex and otherworldly sound environment, including the use of reverb and delay that has elements of what was demonstrated in "Little Girl Lost." This other fictional dimension not only takes on a visual characteristic in the episode based upon the episode's script, which described this other dimension using only the words "INTERIOR: LIMBO," but, more importantly for the purpose of this analysis, that of sound (Wolfe).[8]

The transmission of "Little Girl Lost" in 1962 brought a formerly obscure audio effect into the living rooms of millions. Music listeners would later hear it in popular psychedelic songs in the late 1960s, such as Led Zeppelin's "Whole Lotta Love" (1969), but at the time it was not a common effect in

---

8. Buck Houghton mentioned this passage from the original script of the episode written by Richard Matheson, the author of the original story, in an interview included in Grams's *The Twilight Zone: Unlocking the Doors to a Television Classic* (498).

American music. Its exposure to the masses introduced another example in the language of science fiction audio but was essentially a refinement of the original scenario using modern sound technology. The transdimensional trope had a definitive sound, one later employed by Lovecraft adaptations in the 1960s, such as in the coven scenes in the UK version of *Curse of the Crimson Altar* (1968) and the cult scenes in *The Dunwich Horror* (1970) and *All the Colors of the Dark* (1972). In each film, reverb and echo are explored equally throughout their respective soundscapes, and there is a definitive connection with the human voice and transdimensional space.

The juxtaposition of conventionally recorded dialogue, filtered through reverb, echo, and delay, provides "Little Girl Lost" with a steady contrast building to a crescendo once the father enters the alternative dimension to retrieve his daughter. The dynamic of conventionally recorded vocals contrasts with that of the daughter's sound effects-altered voice as she speaks to the dog from another dimension, thus setting up a contrast between the conventional and unconventional using effect. Lawrence Krauss writes that the episode is an example of other dimensions featured in media:

> By the 1960s, however, one finds a growing and more realistic use of the intimate connection between space and time exposed by special and general relativity. Perhaps this was driven in part by the new opportunities for creative expression as special effects in movies began to blossom in the 1950s and '60s, and as television emerged as a key medium. With new graphic opportunities came new stories that exploited them. (144)

The transdimensional voice in material terms is obscured through reverb and later distorted by echo and delay while being juxtaposed with the conventional, what was intended to be symmetrical and provide a point of identification for the viewing audience. William Whittington states, "When ambient sound effects are deployed, cognitive geography is offered through echoes, reflections, and reverberations, which create spatial anchors or cues. Spaces, then, can exist without image-based referents. No image is necessary" (126), and indeed in "Little Girl Lost," the audience is not shown the aforementioned character until the later climax of the episode, and her reverb, echo, delay vocals stand in for her for most of the episode. It is not just the image that has been excised, it is a decoupling of the human body and manipulation of the voice that is reversed in time for the climax and its resulting catharsis for the audience. More importantly, the decoupling of the voice from the body hints at the technique of a voice over, a perspective of a God's-eye view of the narrative proceedings.

Repetition within the Overall Soundscape of "Little Girl Lost"

At the beginning of "Little Girl Lost," the dialogue among the parents, their daughter, and the scientist is "clean," or at least a replication of what the sound designers' standards were of "clean." However, as the episode progresses, their exchanges start to create a dynamic that repeats until one reverb delay signal creates a sense of distance or detachment from the original sound. This makes it seem as though their exchanges are happening in a different space or time, similar to the illustration by Ernő Juhász featured in Figure 1. In this case, there are persons in conventional reality, and a girl and her dog in a transdimensional space. This conventional recording of dialogue at the beginning of the episode is contrasted heavily with the transdimensional sound of the daughter, who initially is coded as normal and, once passing through to another dimension, is coded as transdimensional using delay.

Figure 1. Ernő Juhász—"Little Girl Lost." 2023.

The dynamic of this back-and-forth between the conventional-sounding voices of the father, mother, and scientist, contrasting with the reverb and delay-heavy voice of Tina, forms a series of juxtapositions, much in line with what Linda Hutcheon establishes as a "rhythm and tempo" of expression in order to "create the psychological/emotional engagement with the audience (42). Notably, Susanne Schmidt and Martin Eisend have studied the impact of exposing phenomena, especially advertising, to an audience and the number of exposures necessary to have an influence on the audience. They have found that three exposures, advocated by the minimalist school of advertising, are not sufficient to effect recall and that ten times is the ideal number to "maximize effects on attitudes" in a potential audience (426). This dynamic is also much in the vein of Trace Reddell's argument that "science fiction requires the manufacture of realistic codes as a way to promote the audience's investment in the fantastic, futuristic, and alien" (373). The use of reverb, delay, and echo technology as a means of coding the other coupled with naturalistic codes, which are assumed by the conventional sound recordings of the episode, are probably shared among the entire series. A voice with characteristics that depart from convention creates a dynamic that Lovecraft described as a process that would "concoct something realistic & coherent enough to fool the rest of my mind & make me swallow the marvel" (*DS* 244 193). The reverb in and echo of Tina's voice, especially later in the episode, goes beyond merely replicating a space and edges into an expression of sound that is highly artificial.

Tony Gibbs has outlined some of the pitfalls in creating artificial environments outside of the known, explaining:

> The basic technique here is reverberation: many systems exist that simulate real and imaginary environments and the best of these are capable of excellent performance. Where many fall short is that they create 'spaces' that are impossible or unbelievable and, whilst these are immediately attractive, their artificiality may make them unsatisfying in the longer term. (84)

The extreme delay and echo effects placed on the father and Tina's vocals that led to feedback sound, of the artificial sort Gibbs describes, is countered by the presence of the human voice. Its mere presence forces the audience to try to discern and interpret what is being said.

When reverb or echo effects are applied to a sound source such as the father and Tina's vocals, they create a trail of sound that continues after the original sound has stopped. If the sound trail is picked up by a microphone, it can be amplified and then re-amplified by the reverb or echo effect, creating a loop of sound that gets louder and louder until distortion is created in an oscillating manner. The episode "The Borderland" (1963) of *The Outer Limits* television series includes the use of heavy echo on the vocals of the character Professor Ian Fraser, who enters another dimension through a magnetic field. As with "Little Girl Lost," it sounds as though there is a short delay applied to the echo of the voice, just enough to cause a segmentation and multiplication of repeated iterations.

In demonstrating the evolution of the transdimensional voice, it is notable that "Little Girl Lost" had a strong influence on Stephen Spielberg's *Poltergeist* (1982) (Grams 500). Alan Howarth, the famed sound designer in the 1980s and 1990s who contributed to weird-related films such as *Star Trek: The Motion Picture* (1979), *The Thing* (1982), *Twilight Zone: The Movie* (1983), and *Phantasm II* (1988), used reverb in *Poltergeist*, adding a twist with reverse reverb inspired by the Led Zeppelin song "Whole Lotta Love" and used on Robert Plant's voice mid-song. The exact method has been widely debated. This effect involves running the recorder backward and adding echo, and then playing the track forward so that the echo precedes the actual dialogue. As R. Murray Schafer has said of the separation of sound from its origins through transmitting or recording, "When, following the Second World War, the tape recorder made incision into recorded material possible, any sound object could be cut out and inserted into any new context desired" (90). This is a clear case where popular music helped complete the language of a certain transdimensional phenomena, building on the qualities of the medium to be rendered in a way that never could have been achieved to such a technical degree by pure speculation in the distant past.

In more recent years, the Netflix television show *Stranger Things* (2016) contains specific references to other dimensions. Here the sound designer Craig He asked the producers whether this dimension was reverberant or "dead dry." Upon learning the sound was supposed to be "wet," He used "something between a reverb and a delay," running it through comb filtering, again using a technique established by former sound designers but tweaking it to furnish something new for a contemporary audience (Walden). In *Spider-Man: No Way Home* (2022), the sound team led by Kevin O'Connell implemented a technique known as the reverse reverb to create an otherworldly effect when characters, such as Doctor Strange, enter the mirror world or experience astral projection. According to O'Connell, they treated these voices with delay, but the most notable effect was achieved using a technique that he had seen applied in his role as a mixer on *Poltergeist*. In the case of *Spider-Man: No Way Home*, O'Connell notes that he was able to achieve this effect electronically, eliminating the need for analog manipulation (Mavity). Indeed, the ability to recreate this process has become much easier, potentially allowing for further widespread adoption within sound production culture, increasing associations with the effect among the public with the transdimensional, and lessening its novelty with each exposure.

Reverb, Echo, and Delay in the Age of Machine Learning

This analysis has traced the advent of the effects of reverb, echo, and delay in both acoustic spaces and literature in a historical context, demonstrating the mythological and fiction-based origins of transdimensional representation in sound that is connected with locating the human voice in another space. This fictive novum, probably first expressed in Ovid's *Metamorphoses* in relation to Echo, was constantly re-explored and reiterated by sound artists once transposed into the new media forms that developed and flourished in the nineteenth century in radio drama, television, and film. The decoupling between origins of sound and sound that R. Murray Schafer mourns was celebrated and taken advantage of by numerous artists who took up the challenge of total manipulation of a sound recording that has become more complex and sophisticated with each new generation of technological advancement. What perhaps has not changed is the compelling nature of the human voice and its attraction to by listeners, hence the use of the human voice to as a point of manipulation continues to hold such high potential in engaging contemporary audiences. With the increased presence of artificially intelligent generated content in media connected with sound, it is clear that reverb, delay, and echo will play an important role in offering spatial context to these new creations, especially in potentially offering new configurations of their use to affect the audience in novel ways. The continued experimentation and development of technologies in the area of reverb, echo, and delay will further give sound designers the ability to stay ahead of the fictional novum familiar to audiences of television, film, and radio drama, especially those familiar with this speculative sound language.

Works Cited

Arnold, H. F. "The Night Wire." 1926. In Ann VanderMeer and Jeff VanderMeer, ed. *The Weird: A Compendium of Strange and Dark Stories.* New York: Tor, 2011.

Bierce, Ambrose. "An Occurrence at Owl Creek Bridge." 1890. In Bierce's *Collected Fiction*. Ed. S. T. Joshi. New York: Hippocampus Press, 2020. 2.109–18.

———. "Whither?" 1888. In Bierce's *Collected Fiction*. Ed. S. T. Joshi. New York: Hippocampus Press, 2020. 1.97–103.

Blackwood, Algernon. "A Victim of Higher Space." 1914. In Henry Bartholomew, ed. *Dangerous Dimensions: Mind-Bending Tales of the Mathematical Weird*. London: The British Library, 2021. 101–24.

Blish, James. "More Light." 1970. In Robert M. Price, ed. *The Hastur Cycle*. 2nd rev. ed. Oakland, CA: Chaosium, 1997. 95–122.

Burke, Edmund. *A Philosophical Inquiry into the Origin of Our Ideas of the Sublime and Beautiful*. 1757. Charlottesville, NC: Ibis, 1989.

Doyle, Peter. *Echo and Reverb: Fabricating Space in Popular Music Recording, 1900–1960*. Middletown, CT: Wesleyan University Press, 2005.

Gibbs, Tony. *The Fundamentals of Sonic Art and Sound Design*. New York: Watson-Guptill, 2007.

Goodman, Steve. *Sonic Warfare: Sounds, Affect, and the Ecology of Fear*. Cambridge, MA: MIT Press, 2010.

Grams, Martin, Jr. *The Twilight Zone: Unlocking the Door to a Television Classic*. Churchville, MD: OTR, 2008.

Hayim, Etz. "The Bat Kol–Daughter of a Voice." *Tree of Life* (14 January 2013). www.etz-hayim.com/resources/articles/bat_kol.php.

Homer. *Odyssey*. Tr. Alexander Pope, 1725. thewritedirection.net, 2004.

Howarth, Alan. "Alan Howarth Interview about Sound Design for Poltergeist Movie "Carolanne Voice." *YouTube* (3 October 2020). www.youtube.com/watch?v=MezJBEhvPCA.

Hughes, Tom. "Echoes of the Past and Future." *Premier Guitar* (27 August 2014). www.premierguitar.com/gear/echoes-of-the-past-and-future.

Hutcheon, Linda. *A Theory of Adaptation*. New York: Routledge, 2006.

Jillions, John A. *Divine Guidance: Lessons for Today from the World of Early Christianity*. New York: Oxford University Press, 2020.

Juhász, Ernő. "Little Girl Lost." 2023.

Krauss, Lawrence M. *Hiding in the Mirror: The Quest for Alternative Realities, from Plato to String Theory*. New York: Viking, 2009.

Le Fanu, J. Sheridan. "The Familiar." 1872. In *Best Ghost Stories of J. S. Le Fanu*. Ed. E. F. Bleiler. New York: Dover, 1964.

"Little Girl Lost." *The Twilight Zone*, created by Rod Serling. Season 3, episode 26. CBS, 1962.

Machen, Arthur. "The Great God Pan." 1894. In *The Three Imposters and Other Stories*. Ed. S. T. Joshi. Oakland, CA: Chaosium,, 2001. 1–50.

Matheson, Richard. "Little Girl Lost." *Amazing Stories* 27, No. 7 (October/November 1953): 50–59.

Mavity, Will. "A Behind-the-Scenes Look at This Year's Oscar Contenders for Best Sound." *NextBestPicture.com* (31 January 2022). nextbestpicture.com/a-behind-the-scenes-look-at-this-years-oscar-contenders-for-best-sound.

Mourjopoulos, John. "5aMU3—The Origins of Building Acoustics for Theatre and Music Performances." *Journal of the Acoustical Society of America* 137 (2015): 2427. acoustics.org/the-origins-of-building-acoustics- for-theatre-and-music-performances-john-mourjopoulos/.

Ovid. *Metamorphoses* Tr. A. S. Kline. Ann Arbor, MI: Borders Classics, 2004.

Pemmaraju, Gautam. "Reverberance, Reverence, Deliverance: Echoing the Otherworld." *3 Quarks Daily: Science Arts Philosophy Politics Literature* (14 April 2014). 3quarksdaily.com/3quarksdaily/2014/04/reverberance-reverence-deliverance-echoing-the-otherworld.html#more-15218.

Poe, Edgar Allan. "The Fall of the House of Usher." 1839. In *The Complete Tales and Poems of Edgar Allan Poe*. Edison, NJ: Castle Books, 2002. 171–84.

———. "The Tell-Tale Heart." 1843. In *The Complete Tales and Poems of Edgar Allan Poe*. Edison, NJ: Castle Books, 2002. 199–202.

Rapoport, Bob. "Essence Reveals the History of Stereophonic Sound." *Essence: For Hi Res Audio* (15 August 2014). www.essenceelectrostatic.com/ essence-reveals-history-stereophonic-sound.

Reddell, Trace. *The Sound of Things to Come: An Audible History of Science Fiction Film*. Minneapolis: University of Minnesota Press, 2018.

Schafer, R. Murray. *The Soundscape Our Sonic Environment and the Tuning of the World*. Rochester, VT: Destiny, 1994.

Schmidt, Susanne, and Martin Eisend. "Advertising Repetition: A Meta-Analysis on Effective Frequency in Advertising." *Journal of Advertising* 44, No. 4 (2015): 415–28. doi:10.1080/00913367.2015.1018460.

Schlarb, Chris. "Lexicon Prime Time 93 Digital Delay." *Music from Big Ego*, 2023. musicfrombigego.com.

Stockhausen, Karlheinz. *Gesang der Jünglinge.* "Song of the Youths." 1956.

Theberge, Paul. "The Sound of Nowhere: Reverb and the Construction of Sonic Space." In Robert Fink, ed. *The Relentless Pursuit of Tone: Timbre in Popular Music.* New York: Oxford University Press, 2018. 323-44,

Toop, David. *Sinister Resonance: The Mediumship of the Listener.* New York: Continuum, 2010.

Treasure, Jullian. *Sound Business: How to Use Sound to Grow Profits and Brand Value.* Gloucestershire, UK: Management Books 2000, 2011.

Tronchin, Lamberto. "Athanasius Kircher's *Phonurgia Nova*: The Marvelous World of Sound During the 17th Century." *Acoustics Today* (January 2009).

Verma, Neil. *Theater of the Mind: Imagination, Aesthetics, and American Radio Drama.* Chicago: University of Chicago Press, 2012.

Von Rudiger, Daniel. "Rhythm as the Intermediary of Audiovisual Fusions." In Andrew Knight-Hill, ed. *Sound & Image: Aesthetics and Practices.* New York: Routledge, 2020. 65-82.

Walden, Jennifer, and Asbjoern Anderson. "How the Outstanding Sound for 'Stranger Things' Is Made." *A Sound Effect* (2016). www.asoundeffect.com/stranger-things-sound.

Whittingon, William. *Sound Design and Science Fiction.* Austin: University of Texas Press, 2007.

Wolfe, Peter. *In the Zone: The Twilight World of Rod Serling.* Bowling Green, OH: Bowling Green University Popular Press, 1997.

Digital Dream-Quests: A Collaborative Project in Lovecraftian Game Studies

Daniel J. Holmes
Professor, New England Institute of Technology

Blueprints of the Witch House: Identifying a Method

The influence of H. P. Lovecraft on video game development and design has been prodigious, if perhaps a touch ironic. It seems unlikely that an author so proudly technophobic would be enthusiastic to learn of the digital reception of his works; one may consider how he dismissed the "utter and unrelieved hokum of the moving picture" because it "cheapens and degrades any literary material it gets hold of" (quoted in Menegaldo 56). Despite Lovecraft's aversion to new forms of media, the Cthulhu Mythos has extended its public-domain tentacles into almost every corner of the gaming market. As early as 2010, studies cited roughly 10% of commercial horror games as invoking Lovecraft or his creations by name, with an even more substantial number clearly appropriating his narrative mechanics by telling stories of "investigator characters who go mad" through interactions with "ancient, sleeping gods under different names" (Lessard 4).[1] In the decade since Lessard's publication, this figure has proliferated dramatically, swelling beyond the confines of the horror genre and establishing Lovecraft as the obvious choice for the American author with the greatest influence on game design.[2]

At the same time, the popularity of Lovecraftian gaming has recently opened new and terrifying vistas in Lovecraft scholarship, with several critics using games to expand our understanding of the source texts. In response to this trend, the New England Institute of Technology is seeking to connect

---

1. (French: "Anciens Dieux en dormance nommés autrement . . . personnages enquêteurs qui deviennent fous.")

2. I would suggest J. R. R. Tolkien as the only English language author with a comparable influence (primarily identifiable in the genre of the fantasy RPG).

undergraduate researchers in video game design with the wider community of weird scholarship. Among other useful resources, the website for the Digital Humanities Research Initiative (DHRI) includes an index of relevant publications and a fully playable library of open-source games inspired by Lovecraft's fiction. The key contribution of the project, however, is the inclusion of player-submitted records of major Lovecraftian titles. These field journals are designed to promote future scholarship by rendering the electronic game as a textual document, making it accessible to non-players. This preliminary paper will describe the methodology for the project, then outline some of the aesthetic and thematic content that defines the Lovecraftian game as a genre.

The basis for this project is an inversion of Thomas Hawranke's methodology of "esoteric computer game research," which he evocatively refers to as "dreaming in the Witch House" (242). In Hawranke's formulation, there is a necessary tension between the player and the designer of a computer game, with the latter traditionally holding the position of privilege. Hawranke's "esoteric" method focuses on aesthetic experimentation that subverts the expectations and limits of the game's programming. He describes this as "an approach similar to the research of Lovecraft's characters: in order to find something new, we have to create an unfamiliar and uncertain surrounding, exchange the comfort of our home for the menacing angles of the witch house gable" (245). By repurposing the game from the confines it was marketed with, this method encourages players to "create our own witch houses, meditate in the corners of their architecture, and stroll through them without purpose" (246).

The DHRI will invert Hawranke's methodology in order to introduce an *exoteric* mode of gaming research. Instead of liberation from the text, this method will seek to reduce the computer game to a textual record, something that future critics may analyze and cite just as readily as Lovecraft's own fiction. In contrast to walkthroughs and plot summaries, this exoteric approach will introduce a focus on the mechanical and aesthetic values present in these games (which critics have suggested receive comparatively less attention in scholarly literature than narrative content) (Bridgett 127). Video games depend upon the interplay of these elements on a formal basis: like the Wagnerian "artwork of the future," the medium can be defined as a network of intersecting aesthetic elements, ranging from music to the digital arts. In order to provide a framework for this investigation, this paper will identify certain benchmarks in mechanical, graphical, and audio design which typify the genre.

At the Mechanics of Madness: Virtual Insanity

Expanding upon Hawranke's framework, it is easy to imagine the console (or computer) as a "witch house" of its own: it is a geographically stationary and geometrically unthreatening structure that is nevertheless capable of transporting the player to any number of hostile alien worlds. Because the details of these worlds are conditioned by the capabilities of the devices that host them, there exists a unique degree of synergy in this medium between the aesthetic vision of the creator and the material through which it is created. Games are not merely fashioned *out of* material, but actually require the independent participation of a material object (the console) in order to generate an aesthetic effect. The mode of relation here is often less like that of the *Pietà* to its marble than of a stage play's script to its director.[3] From the artificial intelligence required to control the behavior of enemies and other non-player characters, to system-operated random number generators used to create the impression of chance, the narrative experience provided by a video game is generally conditioned by the "choices" of its own programming.

In most contexts, the player can act with the assumption that the game will make these decisions in a more or less consistent way, creating a ludic status quo with which to interact. Games based on the works of Lovecraft, however, have developed a reputation for subverting these player expectations, often through the use of sanity mechanics. Indeed, outside of thematic content inspired by the Cthulhu Mythos, the most distinctive hallmark of the Lovecraftian ludonarrative seems to be the incorporation of sanity as a gameplay element. The tenuous threshold between reality and madness is a perennial theme in the works of Lovecraft, whose own perspective on the subject was undoubtedly influenced by his father's hospitalization (and eventual death at Butler Hospital) following a mental breakdown.

Considered broadly, these mechanics typically follow a reliable format: player characters begin the game mentally sound, with some numerical representation (typically either a meter or point system) keeping track of their "sanity." As characters experience emotionally or mentally traumatizing stimuli, this meter gradually decreases, exposing players to simulated symptoms of psychosis. These "sanity effects" can vary wildly from game to game, though certain audio and visual effects (blurred vision, hallucinations, and intrusive

---

3. To extend the metaphor, one might imagine the player as the actor and audience combined.

sound effects such as footsteps or conspiratorial whispering) seem ubiquitous. Many games treat the sanity meter as a secondary system of hit points, such that the total depletion of sanity results in a game over screen, suggesting that the player character has become incurably insane. The flowchart in Figure 1 is taken from the original patent for a sanity mechanic system granted to Nintendo of America in 2005, and typifies the operation of this system as a gameplay element.

The spread of this content has been noted by a number of critics recently, as have the problems inherent in "gamifying" mental health in this manner. A study by Ferrari et al. concluded that roughly 13% of games published on the online sales platform Steam between 2016 and 2017 incorporated a sanity mechanic of some sort. (It is interesting to note that Nintendo's patent on sanity mechanics did not expire until 2021, but does not appear to have restricted the proliferation of the mechanic.) Of these games, 97% "portrayed mental illness in negative, misleading, and problematic ways ... [including] as manifestations or consequences of supernatural phenomena or paranormal experiences ... [with] little or no hope of recovery" (Ferrari et al. 2–3).

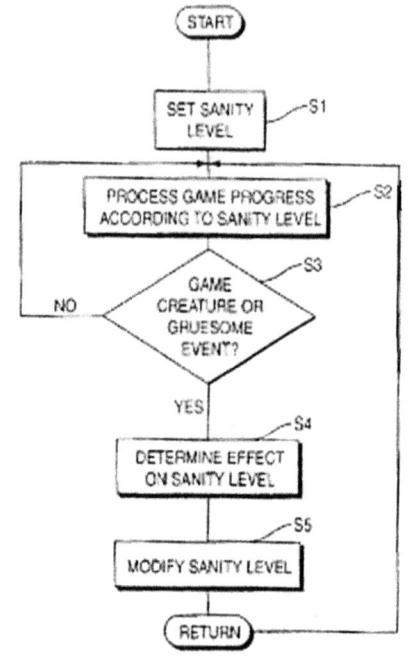

Figure 1. "Sanity System for Video Game," Nintendo of America, Inc. (US Patent 6935954B2)

The past several years have witnessed a broad cultural shift in the reception of mental health issues. It remains to be seen to what extent this will trickle down to popular culture (including video games). In the meantime, it is interesting to note certain contrasts between this quintessential element of Lovecraftian gaming and the source texts. Although the Cthulhu Mythos is replete with dangerous "madmen" lurking on the fringes of society, or with asylums full of the "psychically hypersensitive," insanity typically extends the narrative rather than interrupting it. Notably, Lovecraft's narrators more frequently express their madness in behavioral than in perceptual terms; scientists may run shrieking through the Antarctic wastes, reciting the names of subway stations in a bizarre effort at self-soothing, but the terrifying sights that provoke this behavior are implicitly depicted as real. Far more frequent than narrative hallucinations are passages in which narrators consciously attempt to reclassify their experiences as insane, such as the hapless sailor of "Dagon" who struggles to convince himself that what he saw was "pure phantasm—a mere freak of fever as I lay sun-stricken and raving in the open boat" (CF 1.58).

Critics of these game effects have made the observation that, despite their regular disclaimers of having been driven insane, Lovecraft's narrators typically present cogent, detail-rich accounts of their experiences that give no indication of florid psychosis (Fox and Annison). Rather than serving as a barrier between the intellectual subject and the apperception of reality, Lovecraftian madness typically proceeds from an *overdose* of reality, dangerously moving the narrator closer to a true adequation of the thing and the intellect. The most famous opening lines from Lovecraft actually recast sanity itself as being an incoherent mental state, made possible only by "the inability of the human mind to correlate all its contents" and leaving most of humanity stranded "on a placid island of ignorance in the midst of black seas of infinity" (CF 2.21).

As "games," however, electronic narratives openly operate upon a reduced degree of reality than other forms of fictive media; not only are they virtual, they present themselves as objects of *play*. In comparison to textual narratives (even those that are not merely fictional but fantastic), video games have traditionally struggled with audience disbelief: there seems to be something significant in the fact that books striving for realism and accuracy are called "nonfiction," whereas the most faithfully realistic electronic narratives are still called "simulations." Perhaps the reception history of the video game as a "toy" continues to color audience expectations for virtual worlds.

Sanity effects seem to bridge that generic gap by complicating the toy's intended function of play. By continually forcing players to assess whether what is happening on the screen is "real" or not, these mechanics distract players from the fact that *nothing* they are experiencing is actually real. Digital hallucinations of monsters exist on precisely the same ontological plane as "real" digital monsters; by forcing players to create two separate intellectual categories for virtual objects of perception, games with sanity mechanics redefine the terms for suspending disbelief.

The genealogy of the sanity mechanic traces back to tabletop role-playing games, such as Chaosium's *The Call of Cthulhu* (1981). It made a transition to digital format two decades later, with a patent issued to Nintendo of America in 2005; this would serve as the basis for the Silicon Knights–developed title *Eternal Darkness: Sanity's Requiem*. The game received extensive attention from both academic and industry critics and is frequently cited as one of the most influential survival horror titles of all time. Its complex, branching narrative is clearly inspired by the Lovecraftian fragment "History of the 'Necronomicon,'" tracing the history of the eponymous "Tome of Eternal Darkness" over the course of more than a thousand years. Players take on the role of a series of unlucky souls to have interacted with the book during that span, shifting locations from Persia to France to Cambodia to Rhode Island. Along the way the game features elements adapted from "The Call of Cthulhu" (opening with the investigation of one Inspector Legrasse into the murder of a professor), "The Rats in the Walls" (the professor's granddaughter inherits the family estate, built atop an eldritch subterranean secret), and "The Nameless City" (reimagined as the Persian "Forbidden City").

The patent issued to Nintendo does not actually mention *Eternal Darkness*; in fact, the included concept art appears to depict a scene from *The Legend of Zelda*, a series that has never included sanity mechanics. It also contains references to a number of features that do not appear in the final game. The most Lovecraftian of these is an abandoned "research" feature that would have allowed players to reduce their loss of sanity by studying and academic investigation. Few cosmic horror games have required players to engage directly in research activities, despite the central role that such work plays in the Cthulhu Mythos. Indeed, the most successful of Lovecraft's protagonists (such as Dr. Armitage's team in "The Dunwich Horror" or Dr. Willett in *The Case of Charles Dexter Ward*) are those who do their research beforehand so that, as described in the patent, the "character knows exactly what is to be faced, [and] the effect on [their] sanity may be reduced" (Nintendo 2).

Although this element ultimately did not appear in *Eternal Darkness*, the game's sanity system is nevertheless framed upon an essentially Lovecraftian sense of human psychological frailty. "The human mind is a somewhat fragile control system," reads the unusually literary patent. "When circumstances beyond imagination are encountered, the brain must attempt to deal with the improbable and impossible as reality" (Nintendo 1). The sanity effects of *Eternal Darkness* attempt to disrupt this control system, in a manner that is "decidedly non-diegetic, directed at the *player*, rather than at the character" (Wilson and Sicart 4). *Eternal Darkness* does include a number of perceptual sanity effects, but the title's most iconic moments are those in which the material components of the game system appear to rebel against the player. Volume settings on the television may suddenly appear to adjust themselves, the controller may suddenly cease responding (or appear to have become stuck vibrating), or the game may act as though it has unexpectedly reset, bringing the player back to the start menu. The most engaging examples are those that feign a critical hardware error, such as having deleted the contents of players' memory cards (losing not only their progress in this game, but in every game they have ever saved).

Steven Conway refers to this phenomenon as a "contraction of the magic circle," a moment in which the game "inverts the hierarchy of control, taking it away from the player" (150). There is actually one fleeting instance in which the game openly reveals this foundation of its ludic values. One of the game's sanity effects is the sudden intrusion of a blue error screen, as though it were a computer that had crashed. Although it appears to display appropriate text at first, the player is eventually given the nonsensical instruction to "Press CTRL+ALT+DEL" (an impossible operation to perform on a Nintendo GameCube). The faux hardware error then takes a frighteningly introspective turn, encouraging the player to "Press CTRL+ALT+DEL over and over to assert your authority over the Operating System guidelines in a futile attempt to regain control."

In addition to evoking the nearly universal feeling of helplessness in the face of malfunctioning technology, this particular effect helps to explicate the aesthetic basis of the sanity effect. It will be helpful here to borrow vocabulary from Bill Brown and say that this represents the moment in which the console transitions from being an *object* to becoming a *thing*. Brown explains his "Thing Theory" with the analogy of a window that gradually becomes occluded by filth. While clean, the window can be *objectified* by human subjects, serving their needs and offering no ontological resistance: it impedes drafts without impeding vision. When a window becomes filthy, however, it becomes a *thing*, alienated from its essential function and therefore resistant to human efforts at objectification. In his 2001 essay Brown writes:

> We look through objects because there are codes by which our interpretive action makes them meaningful, because there is a discourse of objectivity that allows us to use them as facts. A *thing*, in contrast, can hardly function as a window. We begin to confront the thingness of objects when they stop working for us... The story of objects asserting themselves as things, then, is the story of a changed relation to the human subject. (4)

In the context of electronic gaming, the screen functions as a "window" into a virtual world, capable of rendering digital code in a way that creates meaning. The console asserts itself as a *thing*, however, when it begins to undermine the player's ability to apperceive that meaning. Sanity effects dramatically shift the relation of the console to the human subject, causing players to become the *objects* of play. Players may attempt to "assert [their] own authority over the Operating System," but sanity effects prove just how limited the illusion of player freedom really is.

The Horror in Pixels: Graphical Reticence and Perceptual Control

Despite their widespread popularity as source material, the weird tales of H. P. Lovecraft are notoriously resistant to graphic representation. As a medium, text allows Lovecraft to introduce his panoply of "indescribable" horrors with only a loose delineation of abstract qualities, hiding them behind language that is emotionally rather than visually evocative. Few readers are likely to develop any clear mental picture of a shoggoth after reading of "a shapeless congeries of protoplasmic bubbles, faintly self-luminous, and with myriads of temporary eyes forming and un-forming as pustules of greenish light" (CF 3.150). Despite this, the bubbly behemoths have continued to terrify and fascinate readers in the ninety years since *At the Mountains of Madness* was first published. Similar, perhaps, to the chronic physical instability that Milton and C. S. Lewis describe the denizens of hell as suffering, or to the "flickering" effect that Dickens gives to the first of his three Christmas spirits, Lovecraft succeeds in his description of the shoggoth by offering a series of concrete yet irreconcilable images.

Text can accordingly be considered the natural home of the Old Ones and their ilk. This may explain why interactive fiction was the first format of electronic game to incorporate Lovecraftian themes, and it remains a popular genre for cosmic horror even to the present day. *Eye of Kadath* (Musgrave, 1979) is widely considered the first game inspired by the Cthulhu Mythos, and its "graphics" clearly depend upon the same tricks Lovecraft used to hide his monsters behind text. The shoggoth that serves as the game's only non-player character is described in language not only inspired by Lovecraft, but also clearly borrowing (if intermittently misspelling) his vocabulary (Figure 2).

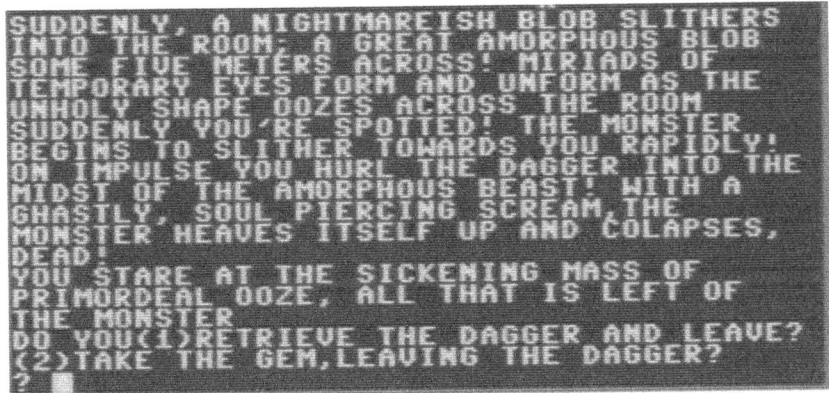

Figure 2. The First "Appearance" of a Lovecraftian Creature in an Electronic Game. *Eye of Kadath*, Musgrave (Commodore 64).

For the *video* game, however, graphic depiction is inevitable—a problem shared by other forms of visual media. In the context of film, Gilles Menegaldo notes that "while Lovecraft avoids, by using suggestion or a rhetoric of the implicit and the unnameable, a graphic representation of the monster or alien entity, cinema must at some point, show the monster, even if this revelation is delayed" (59). The filmmaker, however, at least has the benefit of total control over the audience's perspective, giving them final authority over how their work appears on the screen. By virtue of interactivity, the game designer often cedes control of perspective to the player, which can undermine a reliable visual presentation of the horror. The advantage of cinema in this regard is so profound that initial entries into the survival horror genre experimented with "imposing different camera angles onto the viewer's perspective, withholding visual information and creating a pronounced effect of enclosure. Like a film, [these games] structure space and the player's experience through editing and fixed framing" (Krzywinska 13).

Early titles from the *Resident Evil* (Capcom) and *Silent Hill* (Konami) franchises cemented the popularity of fixed angles in horror games, although the introduction of the trope is typically credited to *Alone in the Dark* (Infogrames, 1992). This feature, together with its "tank controls" (which restricted movement by separating the commands for rotating and walking), induced a sense of helplessness in the player that has led many critics to identify *Alone in the Dark* as the first true survival horror game.[4] Perhaps the most important mile-

---

4. Other elements featured within the game, such as an emphasis on item collection and puzzle-solving, a strict scarcity of ammunition in order to raise stakes during combat, and a

stone achieved by *Alone in the Dark*, however, was proving the commercial viability of a Lovecraftian video game adaptation—and introducing a visual idiom to guide it. The French title found international success, selling more than two million copies and leading to numerous sequels and Hollywood adaptations. With its regular references to Lovecraft, Edgar Allan Poe, Robert Bloch, and Clark Ashton Smith, the game showcased survival horror's uniquely literary genealogy. Several enemies are clearly modeled after Lovecraftian creations such as night-gaunts and Deep Ones, while copies of the *Necronomicon* and *De Vermis Mysteriis* can be found in the library of the game's mansion. The result is a "treatment of horror that is as much psychological and literary as it is physical and graphical" (Roux-Girard 149).

Director Frédérick Raynal has stated that this Lovecraftian content was "grafted" onto the game fairly late in the development process, insisting that the Cthulhu Mythos was used merely to "add creatures to the bestiary" rather than serving as the initial inspiration (Roux-Girard 151). Despite this, it is not merely the graphic *content* of the game that resembles Lovecraft's works, but its graphical *style* as well. Similar to Lovecraft's characteristic refusal to allow his readers a clear "vision" of the horrors in his narratives, *Alone in the Dark* maintains its brooding, threatening atmosphere through the persistent threat of unseen enemies—which can be heard approaching well before they appear onscreen. Scenes in the game were created by combining pre-rendered two-dimensional backgrounds with animated three-dimensional assets, something that critics have suggested heightens the sense of perceptual helplessness in the player:

> This hybrid engine allowed characters and items to be rendered. . . and move to and from any position, whereas the environments or rooms could be shown only from a certain fixed camera angle. . . . [This] allowed for dramatic, predetermined camera angles, but also meant that the player didn't always have a clear view of the action . . . you know something is around the corner, but can't make it out until it is too late. (Loguidice 274)

Bernard Perron connected the sense of tension in *Alone in the Dark* with Bonitzer's concept of "blind space," which allows "the enemy to be virtually anywhere." This graphical reticence is naturally in keeping with the Lovecraftian theme. The scope of *cosmic* horror is made possible by the fact that its horrors extend beyond the narrator's field of vision, making it impossible to consign them within any set geographical radius. In "The Statement of Ran-

---

pervasive sense of isolation, also became hallmarks of the emerging survival horror genre.

dolph Carter," Randolph Carter never actually views a single one of the "hellish things" (CF 1.138) lurking beneath the abandoned cemetery, but the knowledge of their presence entirely blasts the young dreamer's fragile psyche. Francis Wayland Thurston, for his part, cannot "think of the *extent* of all that might be brooding" under the ocean's waves without "wish[ing] to kill [himself] forthwith" (CF 2.51). It is narrative invisibility that allows the Old Ones to pervade their cosmos, even rendering "the skies of spring and flowers of summer" as "poison" to those who have not seen, yet must believe.

An inverted form of this mechanic can be found at work in the more recent title *Dagon*, released by Polish development company BitGolem in 2019. Billed as a "visual novel" (and compatible with virtual reality headsets), the game gives players control over nothing *except* perspective. Although they can rotate the camera freely, players have no control over the movement (or, by extension, the fate) of the protagonist and can do little more than observe the series of animated, three-dimensional scenes presented to them. This is accompanied by an abridged audio recording of the short story that inspired the game, with footnotes to the text hidden in clickable assets scattered throughout each scene.

The game serves as an example of how digital and interactive media adaptations can sometimes improve our understanding of the source texts that inspired them. The arrangement of the digital assets within the game closely mirrors Lovecraft's narration, revealing a tension between enclosure and open space implicit in the short story. Within game design, this approach to level construction is often inspired by English geographer Jay Appleton's Prospect/Refuge Theory—the idea that common aesthetic preferences regarding landscapes have an evolutionary basis. Based on instincts of self-preservation, human beings are naturally attracted to places of *refuge* (enclosed areas that offer a sense of privacy and protection) and to *prospects* (locations with a vantage point that provides knowledge of the surrounding environment and advance warning of any imminent threats). The most aesthetically pleasing landscapes and environments are those that simultaneously achieve both goals, allowing one to "see without being seen" (Appleton 91). The influence of Appleton on video game level design has been widely noted, with critics suggesting that the theme of "enclosure" is specifically problematized within the survival horror genre (Kramazewski and De Nucci). There has not, however, been much critical work connecting his ideas to the creation of haunted literary environments.

Dagon opens with a depiction of the claustrophobic hotel room that begins and ends Lovecraft's story. Although in shabby disrepair, the room superficially conforms to both of Appleton's criteria: it is enclosed, providing an initial sense of *refuge*, and it offers an immediately identifiable *prospect* in the form of a large window (the first thing the player sees upon beginning the game). Lovecraft's opening lines, however, immediately resituate the window as a threat, informing players that by the end of the game their character will "cast [himself] from this garret window into the squalid street below" (quoted in BitGolem). For Appleton, vantage points improve a creature's odds of survival because of the knowledge they can provide; in the Lovecraftian cosmos, where knowledge always comes at a deadly price, they are transformed into "terrifying vistas of reality, and of our frightful position therein" (CF 2.22).

As the game continues, the tension between enclosure and open space becomes even more apparent: players emerge from the tightly confined quarters of a German U-boat to gaze out upon the boundless expanse of the open sea; they huddle beneath the makeshift shelter of their lifeboat, helplessly surveying the "monotonous, roiling plain" of "black slime" they have been shipwrecked upon; they dart between hiding places formed from the enormous remains of decaying sealife, some readily identifiable as fish or whales, others blending visual attributes of crustacean, mammalian, and "less describable things ... protruding from the nasty mud" (CF 1.53). As in the source text, the only constant feature of the amorphous landscape is the "faraway hummock which rose higher than any other elevation on the rolling desert" (CF 1.54; see Figure 3). The uninterrupted movement toward this place of prospect serves as the main narrative arc of both the story and the game.

Figure 3. Screenshot from *Dagon: By H. P. Lovecraft* (BitGolem).

Upon attaining the summit, of course, players do not gain any knowledge beneficial to their survival; instead of locating a path back to the sea, they stand helplessly as "the thing slid[es] into view." Over the remainder of the game, the player's vision becomes increasingly blurry, probably the most commonly utilized visual sanity effect in the genre. By the time they have returned to the hotel room, their entire field of vision begins to shift and roil like the gelatinous surface of the island. As the unendurable knowledge of what exists on that island finally begins to intrude upon players' last place of refuge, they use a point of prospect to seek the only type of escape left: "I hear a noise at the door, as of some immense slippery body lumbering against it. It shall not find me. God, that hand! The window! The window!" (CF 1.58).

Although many games have channeled Lovecraft's graphical reticence by restricting player control, an alternate approach some game developers have employed is conditioning players to restrict their own field of vision. This frequently involves punishing them with sanity effects: an early example can be found in *Call of Cthulhu: Dark Corners of the Earth* (Headfirst Productions, 2005), in which players can incur a sanity penalty whenever they view something frightening. This is often unavoidable in a shooting game (which forces players to aim carefully at the repulsive creatures pursuing them through Innsmouth), but several uncanny sequences in the title exist solely to punish curiosity. Peering into a basement window might reveal a murder scene, for instance, causing the player's sanity to decrease. These occurrences train players to suppress their own investigative instincts and avoid potential points of prospect.

This technique was famously employed by *Amnesia: The Dark Descent* (Frictional Games, 2010), which drops players in an isolated German castle to be hunted by monsters they cannot fight. By eliminating combat mechanics, the title removes any need for the player to focus visually upon the creature threatening them. Staring at these horrors will cause the sanity meter to deplete rapidly; this restricts players to stealing fleeting glances behind them during the game's frequent chase sequences. The roughly stitched-together bodies of these creatures (resembling the monsters of *Frankenstein* or "Herbert West—Reanimator") feature unusual contours and variegated details that impede visual classification, especially when the player is prevented from inspecting these assets directly (Figure 4).

Instead of gazing at the monster, players are instead encouraged to invest their attention into analyzing their surroundings. Assets of these environments are fully manipulable and contain clues needed to piece together dissociated information and reveal the details of the game's plot. This emphasis on hiding the monster and diverting audience attention to the environment mirrors the style of Lovecraft himself—so it is appropriate that Frictional Games should have named their in-house game design software the HPL Engine. Thomas Grip, the co-founder of the Swedish company, succinctly summarized the graphical ethos he and the author share in an interview, saying:

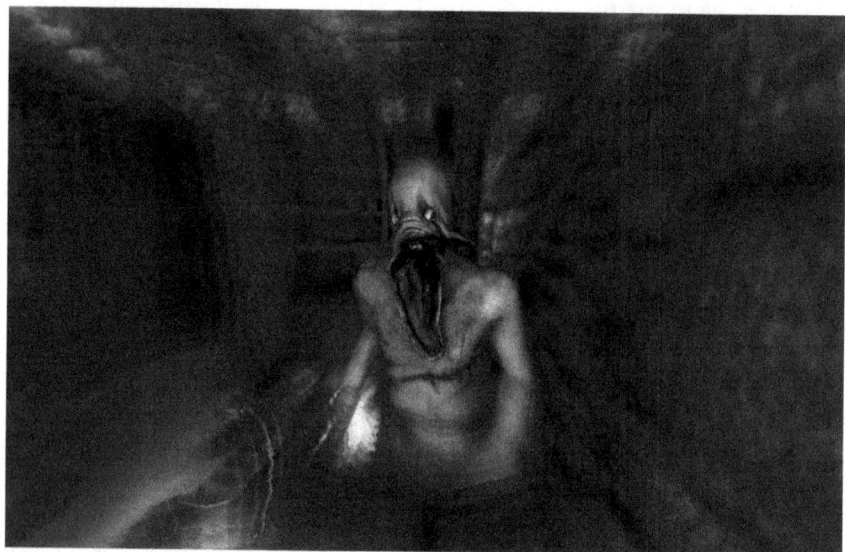

Figure 4. Box art depicting a "Gatherer" from *Amnesia: The Dark Descent* (Frictional Games).

> You cannot just have the monster pop into full sight. The player will easily see all of the imperfections, and their imagined beast is replaced by a much more boring one. So you have to thread somewhere in-between. The player must face the creature, but not enough for it to spoil their imagination. (Quoted in Moser)

Beyond the graphical influence, the HPL Engine shares an interesting thematic similarity with the works of its namesake: since it was made open source, the engine has been adopted by an extensive community of modders and independent game designers, much the way the Cthulhu Mythos has become an "open source" body of mythic details shared by a wide community of writers.

Whispering in Darkness: Soundscapes and Audio Design

So far, this paper has discussed Lovecraft's influence on gaming and cinema, but the pop cultural impact of the Mythos is hardly restricted to the screen.

Countless would-be Erich Zanns from various genres have taken inspiration from H. P. Lovecraft, dating back at least as far as the 1960s acid rock group named after him. Just as cinematic techniques served as the basis for the videographic style of the earliest Lovecraftian games, the soundtracks for these titles owe a clear debt to the ways popular music has interpreted the Cthulhu Mythos.

The most celebrated example of this is probably the soundtrack of the 1996 title *Quake* (id Software), composed by Nine Inch Nails frontman Trent Reznor. Reznor's involvement with the project marked one of the earliest examples of a high-profile popular musician composing video game music, establishing a trend that would culminate in the introduction of a Grammy Award for Best Video Game Score this past year (2023). The soundtrack was a significant emphasis in id Software's marketing of *Quake*: the original CD-ROM for the game was fully playable in a conventional audio CD player, and ammunition boxes in the game were embossed with the Nine Inch Nails logo (Collins 8). In an era when "background" music was still largely regarded as an afterthought in game design, the *Quake* soundtrack broke new ground.

Although the famous "*Quake* Theme" features the heavy, droning guitar riffs and throbbing industrial beats fans might expect from Nine Inch Nails, other tracks from the album display a more subtle, understated approach. Several of these introduce techniques in ambient sound mixing that would later win Reznor Academy Awards for the musical scores of *The Social Network* (2011) and *Soul* (2020). This audio dichotomy mirrors the gameplay experience, which includes both frantic first-person shooting sequences and the exploration of a foreboding, non-Euclidean levelscape. Players take on the role of Ranger (voiced by Reznor), a futuristic soldier tasked with traveling between dimensions to eliminate a malevolent entity codenamed "Quake." By the end of the game, this is revealed to be Shub-Niggurath, the Great Old One mentioned in tales by Lovecraft and others.

Actually defeating this Black Goat of the Woods requires players first to fight their way through her Thousand Young. The process is not a quiet one: id Software director John Romero told Reznor that "everything should make a sound," leading to an unprecedented scope of sound effects (Menegus).[5] As in *Alone in the Dark*, these sound effects often serve as a warning of oncoming

---

5. Menegus identifies one notable example, the grunting "Hup!" exclamation that Reznor made to signify that the character was jumping, and which has since become a staple of action games.

enemies: in between these waves, the soundtrack lapses into a silence that "puts the player on edge rather than reassuring him that there is no danger in the immediate environment ... The appearance of danger is therefore heightened in intensity by way of its sudden intrusion into silence" (Roux-Girard 151).

Silence is a key component of the game's surprisingly understated audio. Compared to the polyphonic, looping melodies of the 8-bit era, *Quake*'s soundtrack features an innovative use of ambient tones and atmospheric effects, designed to be immersive rather than entertaining. In interviews, Reznor has said that his goal for the game's audio was to augment the player's apprehension in a way that "allowed the environment to be the soundtrack ... it's not that dissimilar to how I approach writing songs: I usually dress the set and then stick a song in there" (quoted in Thomas 12). In addition to musical elements such as synthesizers and distorted guitars, the acoustic "set dressing" for the album includes various mechanical and organic sound effects. These acoustic textures are layered in ways that provide a sense of depth to the digital world players must navigate and survive.

Several of these soundscapes are directly suggestive of Lovecraftian themes. The track used for the beginning of each level is dominated by a slowly pulsing pneumatic tone, counterbalanced by a dull mechanical rumbling (Nine Inch Nails, Track 5). Though it could also suggest the sound of breathing, the track's hypnotic rhythm distinctly calls to mind the ebb and flow of the tide. Other elements of the soundscape—such as musical/mechanical peals resembling whale song—extend the thalassophobic themes even further. The track "Hall of Souls" is overlaid with a "hollow, unearthly, gelatinous" audio filter reminiscent of the voice that speaks to Randolph Carter through the radio at the end of his "Statement." The warbling filter is combined with reversed samples of the members of Nine Inch Nails whispering to one another, which (when played in stereo) create a disorienting surround-sound effect. Given that the game requires players to listen carefully to detect imminent threats, effects like these wandering whispers (or quiet, footstep-like tapping) can easily cause them to doubt whether they are in fact alone. Instead of a mere accompaniment to game mechanics, *Quake*'s soundtrack actually represents one of the game's challenges, something hinted at by American McGee in an essay he composed as liner notes for the album's 2020 vinyl release:

> Earlier games and music lacked the fidelity to move you emotionally in the way Quake and its soundscape did. ... In the dirty, fuzzy output from id and NIN

was something perceived as sharper and more real than the individual bits. It required your brain to work and to fill in the spaces with imagined shadows and barely heard whispers behind a maelstrom of chainsaw buzzes and flying gore. (4)

The influence of the *Quake* soundtrack on horror games continues to be felt today, both in acoustic style (an emphasis on alternating discordant and disorienting audio textures with periods of silence) and in terms of its thematic content. In fact, later video game composers would expand upon what it means for sound design to "require [the player's] brain to work" in order to progress through the narrative. One fascinating example can be found in the demo for the canceled Konami title *Silent Hills*. Produced through collaboration between *Silent Hill* creator Hideo Kojima and Lovecraftian film director Guillermo del Toro, *P. T.* (for "Playable Teaser") was released by Konami in 2014 and featured complex audio puzzles by sound designer Akira Yamaoka, who had also worked on previous titles in the franchise.

Yamaoka has described the original *Silent Hill* (Konami, 1999) as an effort to reinterpret themes from Lovecraft and Stephen King "through Japanese eyes" (Pruett 4). A 2015 article by Ruiz and Bienvenido situates *P. T.* within this Lovecraftian tradition, making a valuable connection between Lovecraftian epistemology and the narrative structure of the game, something that depends upon Yamaoka's sound design for its aesthetic effect.

As a "playable teaser," *P. T.* lasts only 30 minutes and lacks gameplay mechanics beyond movement and the ability to zoom the camera in to inspect the environment. This environment is extremely limited, consisting of only a single, L-shaped hallway in a typical suburban home. Although the hallway appears normal at first, its architecture quickly betrays an influence from MC Escher: upon stepping through the doorway at the end, the player inexplicably finds themselves back at its beginning of the hall. This continues with each trip through, with details about the hallway changing each time—at first subtly, then in increasingly dramatic (and disturbing) ways. The most threatening change is the eventual emergence of a ghost (Lisa) who stalks players and will attack them if they turn around to look at her—a reimagining of the Orpheus narrative owing a clear debt to the videographic player-conditioning techniques described previously. Despite the absence of any clear allusions to Lovecraft in *P. T.*, the game adapts his narrative techniques in an innovative way, as Ruiz and Bienvenido note:

> Although the way the player discovers the story in *PT* is not similar to the way they might read a Lovecraft story (instead requiring them to uncover the story

through the exploration of interactive space), it does come close to the way in which Lovecraft's characters discover mysteries. Like the protagonists of stories like *The Call of Cthulhu*, who reconstruct history from diaries, newspapers, and other documents, interaction with the disparate elements of *PT*'s environment is necessary to reconstruct the events that took place in the cursed house. (110)[6]

P. T.'s narrative is entirely implicit, requiring players to "piece together dissociated information" in the classic Lovecraftian style. Each trip through the hallway uncovers a new clue hinting at the game's backstory, ranging from cryptic notes that appear scrawled on the wall to subtle changes in the photographs and paintings that decorate the house. By far the most significant set of clues are auditory in nature, many of them being provided by a radio at the end of the hallway. In fact, a broadcast within the first ten seconds of the game explains the plot in full, although its full significance does not become apparent until much later. As players round the corner in the hall for the first time, they hear a news report describing a local man who hanged himself after murdering his pregnant wife and their two children. By the end of the game it becomes clear that the player is in fact the murderer himself, walking through the scene of his crimes in a hellish cycle of being pursued by the ghost of his slain wife.

Specific acoustic details about these radio broadcasts create a horror idiom that, although verbal, could never be recreated in a textual format. In his description of the murder, for instance, the radio reporter pronounces "911" as "nine-eleven"—an extremely unusual way to refer to emergency services in America, and one bearing horrific connotations of a different sort altogether. Because the radio is not tuned in very well, snippets of other programs occasionally cut in over the news bulletin; during one trip through the hallway, the phrase "umbilical cord" floats in during a portion of the newscast that usually describes the murderer as hanging himself with a garden hose (themes of birth and pregnancy are a recurring motif throughout the *Silent Hill* series). In a later trip through the hallway, the radio suddenly begins to skip like a record player after mentioning that the killer's daughter attempted to "hide in the bathroom, but . . . he lured her out by telling her it was just a game." The monotonous repetition of this line (which occurs after an especially nerve-wracking sequence) does much to undermine players' confidence that what they are experiencing is in fact "just a game."

This murder in the bathroom is also the basis for what is likely to be the most effective audio sequence in the game: on one walkthrough, players no-

---

6. Translated from Spanish by the author.

tice that a peephole has appeared where a painting had previously been hanging. Peeking through the hole will cause the sounds of the murder to begin playing; first-time players will probably begin casting their gaze around frantically upon hearing the screams and sounds of bloodshed, but there is actually nothing to see through the peephole (looking through it only triggers an audio cue). Players are forced to participate imaginatively in reconstructing the murder, creating the nauseous visual accompaniment needed to interpret the audio and echoing McGee's suggestion that an effective Lovecraftian soundtrack forces the listener to "fill in the spaces with imagined shadows."

Beyond the Walls of Author Intent: Cross-Cultural Cthulhiana

As the DHRI continues to receive field journals from player-researchers, our understanding of Lovecraft's influence on game design will continue to grow. At the outset, however, it seems fair to define the following as suitable generic benchmarks for the Lovecraftian video game: 1) a narrative emphasis on the Cthulhu Mythos or another Lovecraftian theme; 2) a mechanical structure that incorporates or simulates insanity as a player condition; 3) a graphical design that increases player helplessness by restricting vision of antagonists; and 4) an audio design that interrupts or complicates play rather than simply serving as "background" music.

These benchmarks will represent a shared frame of reference to guide player research. Over time we hope that additional trends will become apparent. In particular, the DHRI hopes that this project will be able to explore the ways that game designers from widely different cultures have adapted characters and plots from a notoriously xenophobic writer like Lovecraft. Indeed, several regions where Lovecraftian games have become extremely popular (such as Eastern Europe and the Middle East) are cultures with negative or problematic representations in the author's fiction. A careful study of these games, therefore, may do much to move the Mythos forward and bring the world together in fear.

Works Cited

Amnesia: The Dark Descent. [PC]. Frictional Games, 2010.

Appleton, Jay. "Prospects and Refuges Re-Visited." *Landscape Journal* 3, No. 2 (1984): 91–103. JSTOR, www.jstor.org/stable/43322970. Accessed 5 Mar. 2023.

Bethesda Softworks. *The Call of Cthulhu: Dark Corners of the Earth.* [PC]. Headfirst Productions, 2005.

Bridgett, Rob. "Dynamic Range: Subtlety and Silence in Video Game Sound." In Karen Collins, ed. *From Pac-Man to Pop Music: Interactive Audio in Games and New Media.* Aldershot, UK: Ashgate, 2008. 127-33.

Brown, Bill. "Thing Theory." *Critical Inquiry* 28, No. 1 (2001): 1-22. doi:10.1086/449030.

Collins, Karen 2008. "Grand Theft Audio?: Video Games and Licensed IP." *Music and the Moving Image*, Vol 1/1 (University of Illinois Press). mmi.press.uiuc.edu/1.1/collins.html S

Conway, Steven. "A Circular Wall? Reformulating the Fourth Wall for Videogames." *Journal of Gaming & Virtual Worlds* 2, No. 2 (2010): 145-55.

Dagon: By H. P. Lovecraft. [PC]. BitGolem, 2019.

Eye of Kadath. [Commodore 64]. Gary Musgrave, 1979.

Ferrari, M., S. V. McIlwaine, G. Jordan, J. L. Shah, S. Lal, and S. N. Iyer. "Gaming with Stigma: Analysis of Messages about Mental Illnesses in Video Games." *JMIR Mental Health* 6, No. 5, e12418. doi.org/10.2196/12418

Fox, Josh, and Rebecca Annison. "Mental Health and Lovecraft." *Black Armada* (17 December 2019), blackarmada.com/mental-health-and-lovecraft/.

GT Interactive and Bethesda Softworks. *Quake.* [MS-DOS] id Software, 1996.

Hawranke, Thomas. "Dreaming in the Witch House." In Marc Bonner, ed. *Game | World | Architectonics: Transdisciplinary Approaches on Structures and Mechanics, Levels and Spaces, Aesthetics and Perception.* Heidelberg: Heidelberg University Publishing, 2021. doi.org/10.17885/heiup

Konami. *P.T.* [Playstation 4]. Kojima Productions, 2014.

Kramarzewski, Adam, and De Ennio Nucci. *Practical Game Design: Learn the Art of Game Design through Applicable Skills and Cutting-Edge Insights.* Packt Publishing Ltd., 2018. O'Reilly Learning.

Krzywinska, Tanya. "Hands-on Horror." *Screenplay: Cinema/videogames/interfaces* (2002): 206-23.

Lessard, Jonathan. "Lovecraft, le jeu d'aventure et la peur cosmique." *Loading* 4.6 (2010): Special Issue—Thinking After Dark: Welcome to the World of Horror Video Games. journals.sfu.ca/loading/index.php/loading/article/view/89

Loguidice, Bill, and Matt Barton. *Vintage Games: An Insider Look at the History of Grand Theft Auto, Super Mario, and the Most Influential Games of All Time.* Boca Raton, FL: CRC Press, 2012.

Nine Inch Nails. Soundtrack to Quake. id Software, 1996.

McGee, American. "Merged Almost Perfectly." Liner notes, *Quake Remastered.* Nine Inch Nails, 2020.

Menegaldo, Gilles. "H. P. Lovecraft on Screen, a Challenge for Filmmakers (Allusions, Transpositions, Rewritings)." *Brumal: Revista de Investigación Sobre Lo Fantástico* 7, No. 1 (2019): 55. doi.org/10.5565/rev/brumal.591

Menegus, Bryan. "A History of Hup, the Jump Sound of Shooting Games." *Wired* (26 March 2022). www.wired.com/story/hup-history-jump-sound-video-games/?fbclid=IwAR1huN12ijZSShTpwsZMIkD8B-kEp22TiS-2U_nAuqoRq2-FJQCDO2S4tbg

Moser, A. J. "How H. P. Lovecraft's Horror Crafted a Subgenre of Video Games." *Game Informer* (16 August 2016) www.gameinformer.com/b/features/archive/2016/08/16/how-h-p-lovecrafts-horror-crafted-a-subgenre-of-video-games.aspx.

Nintendo of America, Inc. *Eternal Darkness: Sanity's Requiem.* [Nintendo GameCube]. Silicon Knights, 2005.

———. "Sanity System for Video Game." US Patent 6935954B2, 2005 (Exp. 2021). Henry Sterchi, Edward Ridgeway, and Dennis Dyack, inventors. patents.google.com/patent/US6935954B2/en

Pruett, Chris. "The Anthropology of Fear: Learning about Japan through Horror Games." *Loading... Special Issue: Thinking After Dark.* 2010.

Roux-Girard, Guillame. "Plunged Alone into Darkness: Evolution in the Staging of Fear in the *Alone in the Dark* Series." In Bernard Perron, ed. *Horror Video Games: Essays on the Fusion of Fear and Play.* Jefferson, NC: McFarland, 2009. 156-67.

Ruiz, Marta, and Héctor Bienvenido. "Fantastic Universes and H. P. Lovecraft in Survival Horror Games. A Case Study of P. T." (Silent Hills). *Revista de Investigación Sobre Lo Fantástico* 3, No. 1) (Brumal 2015): 95-118. doi.org/10.5565/rev/brumal.177

Thomas, M. "Music in Video Games." *International Journal of Urban Labour and Leisure* 6, No. 1 (2004): 1-20.

Wilson, Douglas, and Miguel Sicart. "Now It's Personal: On Abusive Game Design." In *Proceedings of the International Academic Conference on the Future of Game Design and Technology*. miguelsicart.net/publications/Abusive_Game_Design.pdf

Hereditary Memories of Fright: The Gaming Industry's Response to Lovecraft's Xenophobia as Viewed through Most Recent Major Releases

Joshua E. Shockley IV
Old Dominion University

Relatively obscure during his own life and almost forgotten about in the decades since, the early twentieth century writer of weird tales and cosmic horror, H. P. Lovecraft has seen a renaissance of interest within the past decade. This last year has seen the first-time publication of a starter-set for the long running tabletop role-playing game *Call of Cthulhu*, as well as the release of two major video games directly pulling from Lovecraft's fictional universe (referred to as his "Mythos"): *Call of Cthulhu* (Cyanide Studio) and *The Sinking City* (Frogwares). Lovecraft's Mythos has been fruitful stomping grounds for small, "indie" game developers, and it is not often that larger studios tackle his writings (for good reason, as we shall see). While both games received generally a positive response from fans and critics alike, many of the reviews either gloss over or ignore entirely how the games address one of the most prominent issues surrounding the author: the specter of Lovecraft's blatant xenophobia and racism, which has been an uncomfortable reality in much of the media inspired by his writings.

For most of the decades since his death, Lovecraft's collected works had enjoyed (or languished in) the freedom from serious scholarly review, partly because his writing was considered too crude and "schlocky" and partly because of his position as an underground, countercultural icon emerging in the late 1960s (Poole 212). In recent decades, however, an explosion of Lovecraft-inspired properties has made it impossible to ignore the author's influence on popular culture.

Today, the Cthulhu Mythos exists not only as an ever-growing body of literature but also in the forms of games, toys, music, internet memes, movies, and more ... bands such as Metallica, Blue Oyster Cult, and Black Sabbath have written songs about Lovecraft and his tales. Cthulhu has made cameos on both *The Simpsons* and *South Park*, while TV personalities including Stephen Colbert and Craig Ferguson have been known to drop the occasional Cthulhuvian reference on their shows. The Cthulhu Mythos also served as a key inspiration behind the hit HBO original series *True Detective* as well as the popular internet podcast *Welcome to Night Vale*. (Mullis 514-15)

With this newfound fame, the implications of Lovecraft's legacy, which fans had long managed to ignore, came to the forefront as conflicts began to arise. One of the more public ones came in 2015 when the World Fantasy Convention announced it would no longer feature a bust of H. P. Lovecraft as the shape of their prestigious award. This arose out of concerns voiced by many writers of African descent as well as other ethnicities toward whom Lovecraft was well known to be prejudiced (Flood).

The argument over Lovecraft and his xenophobia is still a complex one, as many such as S. T. Joshi, perhaps the most preeminent Lovecraft scholar, argue, "Lovecraft's ethnocentric views were typical of his time, his social position, his milieu; it is not that his views were more pronounced than other, 'Old Americans' of the early twentieth century, but that they were repeatedly, coordinately, and strongly expressed on paper" (Faig and Joshi 14). While Lovecraft's complicated life and personal beliefs will continue to be debated, the purpose of this article is not to focus on the man but on how his work is being interpreted in the modern day. With two video games being released on the heels of each other in 2018 and 2019, it is the first time in over a decade that major game releases have attempted to draw directly from Lovecraft's stories. My interest lies in how both *Call of Cthulhu* and *The Sinking City* address the issues that have become one of the focal points of the dialogue surrounding Lovecraft, and what this says about the gaming industry making them—an industry that, in many ways, is similar to fans of Lovecraft in how it has often pretended that these issues of race do not exist.[1]

At first glance, the games seem to present a paradox in their approach to Lovecraft's mythos. *The Sinking City* is a veritable checklist of his stories, ranging from the best-known to some of the more obscure. In doing so, it fore-

---

1. There could also be parallels drawn between this approach and how gaming culture is often portrayed as a haven for "incels" and alt-right ideology. Unfortunately, due to space and time constraints, such investigation is outside the scope of this paper.

grounds many of the author's more controversial artifacts in a way that few representations of Lovecraft have been willing to do. More surprising is how *The Sinking City* does not shy away from the issue of racism but claims to confront it head-on. *Call of Cthulhu* conversely largely chooses to ignore the author's xenophobia, preferring to isolate the player in a small New England fishing village and to isolate *itself* from much of Lovecraft's universe, being only tangentially connected to the mythos. By creating a homogeneous setting and lore, *Call of Cthulhu* follows the path of many Lovecraft-inspired games that have come before it. To what degree each game is more "Lovecraftian" than the other is up for debate among the fans, but how these two games tackle the issues of race speaks more to today's gaming industry than to the author himself. Initially it would appear that the two games take drastically different approaches to the problems, yet I would argue that neither game truly confronts the racism inherent in their source material. Both the attempt at correcting Lovecraft's racism and the complete overlooking of it reveal an industry struggling between its traditionally seen role of video games as just mindless fun and its newly emerging role as influential media.

The Sinking City and *Call of Cthulhu* follow many of the tropes common to Lovecraft's Mythos. In both games the player controls a white, male, World War I veteran, now turned private investigator, with a generous helping of PTSD and supernatural abilities. He is sent to solve a mystery of the weird kind on a small, isolated fishing town off the coast of Massachusetts. Though this does seem very much in keeping with the traditional Mythos setup seen in many Lovecraft games, it does raise questions as to why such a trope is still maintained. Traditionally, the white male protagonist has been a staple in video games since graphical allowances have made it possible to represent race (Mou 929). For much of video game history, this was just assumed to be the norm. As Anna Everett and S. Watkins write, "At least some of the absence of discussions of race in public and policy dialogues about video games can be attributed to the fact that the use of racially marked characters, themes, and environments, historically speaking, is a relatively recent development in video games" (143).

Yet, as the push for greater racial (and gender) representation in gaming has gained traction in recent years, *The Sinking City* and *Call of Cthulhu* still cannot break away from the narrow character representation common to the stories they were based on. The argument could be made that the games are trying to capture Lovecraft's original style, yet this reasoning does not hold up, especially when applied to *Call of Cthulhu*. One of the co-creators of the game is Chaosium Inc., which is also the publisher of the widely successful *Call of Cthulhu* tabletop role-playing game the video game was heavily inspired by. For many years, Chaosium has made headway in expanding from the Caucasian, New England men who had dominated the genre. "Strong, central female characters have become an important part of Chaosium's RPGs. Female scientists, researchers, authors, and a 1920's flapper packing heat are playable characters in the enormously popular board games ... [t]he new editions of *Call of Cthulhu* [Tabletop RPG] also add an African American surgeon and 'a torch singer and actress'" (Poole 259). Whereas it is understandable that both Cyanide Studio and Frogwares are smaller companies without the resources of major gaming studios, by keeping this artifact of how Lovecraft's world has been traditionally shown it merely reinforces the racial and gender exclusion that the genre has been accused of.

As mentioned above, while *Call of Cthulhu* falls back on the conventional Mythos setting of a homogenous New England village, with no racial minorities, and few women (though the ones who are present are major characters), *The Sinking City* addresses the author's legacy almost immediately. In an unskippable text screen after starting the game, it states:

> Inspired by the works of H. P. Lovecraft, *The Sinking City* depicts an era in which ethnic, racial, and other minorities were frequently mistreated by society. These prejudices were and still are wrong, but have been included for an authentic depiction of that time, rather than pretend they never existed. (Opening Credits)

It is an admirable statement, especially when such introspection has been rarely applied to either Video Games or to the Mythos of H. P. Lovecraft.

However, upon arriving in the town of Oakmont, Massachusetts, one finds it is surprisingly progressive. Not only is there a large population of African Americans for a 1920s New England fishing town, but they also hold a wide variety of jobs. Exploring the town, the player finds both black men and women in positions of authority, such as policemen, doctors, and the head of the town newspapers. This equality is not only acknowledged in *The Sinking City* but flaunted, as Anna (local spokeswoman for the Esoteric Order of Dagon) informs the protagonist, "You'll find here on Oakmont a woman can achieve much more than on the mainland. Our University has always accepted women with open arms" (Case 3: Quid Pro Quo). This society certainly is the antithesis of Lovecraft's beliefs as, even though his opinions toward other minorities may have changed over the course of his life, his view on African Americans did not. "Lovecraft retained to the end of his days a belief in the biological inferiority of blacks and also of Australian aborigines . . . Lovecraft advocated an absolutely rigid color line against intermarriage between blacks and whites, so as to guard against 'miscegenation'" (*IAP* 936). Gone are the degenerate "mulattos" and swarthy immigrants of such tales as "The Horror at Red Hook," threatening to undermine white civilization with blasphemous rites. Instead, it is a non-issue, for both the town and the player. How then is this a representation of the mistreatment of minorities as the game promised to present? What *The Sinking City* gives the player is not an immersion into the rampant racial discrimination of Lovecraft's day, but a fantasy far removed from reality.

Instead, *The Sinking City* chooses to confront issues of race and xenophobia not through humanity, but through the monstrous in both the Throgmorton clan and the displaced Innsmouthers. This is first encountered in the character of Robert Throgmorton, head of one of Oakmont's wealthiest families and de facto leader of the town. It is obvious that he is not a normal human being at all, with prominent apelike features clashing starkly with his genteel speech. Later in the game, the player learns that this appearance is a result of Throgmorton's father copulating with a "great white ape." As absurd (or disturbing) as this may seem, Lovecraft was no stranger to white apes. Throgmorton is directly inspired by the story "Facts concerning the Late Arthur Jermyn and His Family," in which the title character kills himself after discovering that one of his ancestors had bred with a "white ape of some unknown species, less hairy than any recorded variety, and infinitely nearer mankind" (*CF* 1.182).

The use of apes a source of horror was a common trope within Victorian literature from which Lovecraft heavily drew. Mainly, as the theory of evolution began became commonly accepted, the growing fear was of how close humanity truly was to the animal, and if it were possible to slip back into the bestial. This fear was heavily tied into nineteenth-century ideas of racial theory (from which Lovecraft also drew), as it was believed that degeneration into the "sub-human" was easier for blacks as they were closer to the bestial than more evolved whites. "By the end of the 19th century the identification of the 'lower' modern races with the early ancestors of all mankind was widespread. The Australians and Tasmanians in particular were singled out as having smaller brains and more ape like features" (Bowler 727). This sentiment is echoed in the game as insults such as "ape-face" and "brute" are levied against Throgmorton. One of the greatest fears for Lovecraft was that the white races were not immune to degeneracy and could join the level of sub-human that many in the nineteenth century saw Africans as. In "The Lurking Fear," he describes an isolated New England family having changed, through generations of inbreeding and cannibalism, into subterranean white apes as "the ultimate product of mammalian degeneration" (CF 1.373).

While Lovecraft used the trope of degeneration to invoke horror and disgust, *The Sinking City* takes almost the opposite tone with the idea. Robert Throgmorton does not shy away from his simian heritage; instead, he (as well as the game) openly embraces it. While in the Lovecraft story the Jermyn family is only marked by a "subtly odd" (CF 1.177) appearance that inspires an unplaceable fear, the game chooses to make the resemblance to ape undeniable. Throgmorton relishes in his hybridization, claiming that it is "proud and powerful blood" that flows in his family's blood. "My father united with a certain royal family, which has blessed all our offspring with these exquisite features," he openly tells the player (Case 1: Frosty Welcome). In none too subtle hints throughout the rest of the game, Throgmorton makes it clear that he believes his ape lineage to be superior to that of normal human beings, even going as far as wanting to put the trapped soul of his deceased half-brother into a body befitting a "trueborn Throgmorton"—an orangutan (Through the Looking Glass). He is the antithesis of Lovecraftian degeneracy, where "the human can become the subhuman through uncouth and primitive practices" (Joshi, *The Weird Tale* 198); instead, Throgmorton subverts the ideas of bestial generation, replacing it the source of his bloodline's strength.

It is a confusing transference of discrimination that the game tries to present. Throughout *The Sinking City* there are continual references to how the Oakmont residents are bigoted against Throgmorton and his family, with many refusing to do business with the "crazy-ape." If the game is trying to make the philanthropist a stand-in for the racism present in Lovecraft's writings and the 1920s toward African Americans, then it raises far more issues than it addresses. Even as the game tries to present Throgmorton in a positive light and takes strength in a such blending where Lovecraft and the Victorians would have seen degeneracy, it still cannot remove itself from the pall of nineteenth-century racial theory. That it is still a "white" ape as taken from the story is a necessity, since a "black" ape is too far down the evolutionary ladder to be considered, the white being is closer to human than the black. It echoes Lovecraft's own fear of miscegenation, undermining any message the game might have been trying to imply about racial intermarriage. Throgmorton's appearance brings an uncomfortable reminder of common racist imagery of blacks and apes (with the former often being portrayed closer to the latter) that was used in much of the nineteenth and twentieth centuries. Finally, it raises the question that, if the developers of *The Sinking City* wished to have Throgmorton be an example of racial discrimination of the time, why did they not actually make him African American? As evident with *Call of Cthulhu*, the Mythos is still a genre where minorities are often underrepresented (if represented at all). What could have been an opportunity to address discrimination for a game that wished to represent the reality of the time is instead transformed into something unrecognizable as any kind of comparison.

The Sinking City again tries to tackle Lovecraft's xenophobia with another hybridity drawn directly from one of his stories. The player finds Oakmont inundated with refuges from the city of Innsmouth, trying to eke out a living within the town. With troubles including rising sea level and the appearance of monsters all over town, the Innsmouthers are often the brunt of scapegoating and discrimination. With accusations of the newcomers taking work away from native residents and causing rising crime rates, it is not hard to draw comparisons with many of today's discourses. It is yet another odd choice by the game developers as the refugees from Innsmouth are truly alien, in all senses of the word. Taken from Lovecraft's story "The Shadow over Innsmouth," they all bear the infamous "Innsmouth look," as its described: "'[s]ome of 'em have queer narrow heads with flat noses and bulgy, stary eyes that never seem to shut, and their skin ain't quite right. Rough and scabby, and the sides of their necks are all shrivelled or creased up. Get bald, too, very young'" (CF 3.163).

With obvious fishlike features they are the embodiment of the alien other that Lovecraft feared as new waves of Slavic and Eastern European immigrants arrived in America. In the story, this is a result of the Innsmouthers being the offspring of human beings and Deep Ones, an amphibious, alien race that dwells beneath the sea. In both "The Shadow over Innsmouth" and *The Sinking City*, at first glance they look to portray a caricature of racial and cultural othering. "They are, for all intents and purposes, racially marked immigrants overtaking and, according to the initial response of the narrator, polluting and degrading Innsmouth's Anglo-Saxon stock, sapping the citizenry's humanity in both appearance and behavior" (Bealer 31).

Within the game, however, the Innsmouthers are not just the monstrous hybrids of the original story but are actually portrayed as sympathetic. A refugee pleads for mercy when confronted by the player, as he has a family and children. The Innsmouthers have started a charity to feed many of the townsfolk hurt by the recent disasters, and the player meets one of its members who makes toys for a local orphanage. There is even a darker turn in one mission when it is discovered that a local chapter of the Ku Klux Klan has started attacking the "fish faces," even presenting the disturbing imagery of lynched Innsmouthers straight out of the darkest days of the Jim Crow South (Nosedive). Through its humanizing, *The Sinking City* at first manages to evoke commentary on how the Other is often made into the monstrous and has the potential of creating a counterpoint to Lovecraft's xenophobic legacy.

Yet once again, by trying to keep true to the source material, *The Sinking City* weakens its own humanizing efforts. Within Lovecraft's writings, one of the main reasons why the Innsmouthers and Deep Ones are so terrible is the plans they have for humanity. In "Dagon," the narrator has a premonition of the day when the Deep Ones would "drag down in their reeking talons the remnants of puny, war-exhausted mankind" (CF 1.58), and it is clear from "The Shadow over Innsmouth" that the Innsmouthers/Deep Ones are slowly but surely planning an invasion of the surface world. The charitable organization started by the refugees is revealed to be the Esoteric Order of Dagon, a cult that is kidnapping townsfolk to use as sacrifices to the god Dagon, and to acquire women for breeding. While many of the Innsmouthers appear to be ignorant of the evils committed by the cult and are often shown to be friendly, the player now cannot trust them as the game itself chooses to stay true to the original story. The reason why Innsmouthers are refugees to begin with is that their town was raided by the federal government, in keeping with what was described in "The Shadow over Innsmouth." *The Sinking City* does not give any further insight into the destruction of Innsmouth, so the player is left to assume it was for the reasons Lovecraft originally stated. In this light, any humanizing of the Innsmouthers is completely undone; instead of sympathy at the racism directed against them, it appears instead to be a necessity if humanity is to survive. These revelations even go so far as to place upon the player the uncomfortable realization that, despite the game's obvious indications to the contrary, siding with the KKK may actually be the lesser of two evils.

While endemic problems with the presentation of Throgmorton and the Innsmouthers in *The Sinking City* could have been resolved with further departure from Lovecraft "canon," it is arguable that the greatest detriment to either it or *Call of Cthulhu* is placing it anywhere in the author's overarching universe. Any attempts at presenting a message or morality contradictory to Lovecraft's racism is immediately undermined by the core value of his secondary world: that nothing matters. The cornerstone of Lovecraft's Mythos, which has been dutifully followed by acolytes and imitators alike, has always been the inherent and inescapable nihilism of his secondary world. It is what gives his monsters true cosmic horror, as readers discover that, despite mankind's achievements, institutions, and religions, we are an accident of nature (or, more precisely, an accidental creation of an alien race that got loose) and of no more concern to other cosmic entities than ants are to us. In Lovecraft's own words:

> Now all my tales are based on the fundamental premise that common human laws and interests have no validity or significance in the vast cosmos-at-large. . . . To achieve the essence of real externality, whether of time or space or dimension, one must forget that such things as organic life, good and evil, love and hate, and all such local attributes of a negligible and temporary race called mankind, have any existence at all. (*Letters to Woodburn Harris* 60)

For *Call of Cthulhu*, this does not affect the game's inherent themes, as it follows the traditional Lovecraftian setup of embracing universal meaninglessness. Characters with whom the protagonist has formed bonds will ultimately die in horrible ways, no matter what is done to save them. The multiple endings range from the implied destruction of humanity through the summoning of Cthulhu, to suicide, to the "good" ending that leaves the protagonist alive but permanently insane. For *The Sinking City*, however, any hope of subverting Lovecraft's intrinsic racism is ultimately lost as the game plainly states that the player's actions, for good or ill, are of no importance. Eventually the protagonist discovers it is not by accident that he has been brought to Oakmont. Instead, he is but one in a long line of "Chosen Few" who are able to release the gates that are preventing a sleeping Eldritch Horror from destroying humanity. "You can close them, and cling to mankind's misery for a few more cruel centuries. Or you can open them and end it" (Deal with the Devil), states the Faustian, Van der Berg, revealing that the events surrounding the player are merely a cycle that has repeated for countless centuries.

Whatever choices or sacrifices the protagonist/player makes, ultimately the gates will be opened and mankind will be doomed. Much like *Call of Cthulhu*, there are different endings to *The Sinking City*; but it is clear in each of them that no matter what course the player takes, the end is ultimately the same. Any messages about the evils of racism or the importance of humanization are rendered moot by being placed in a reality where they are of no more value than evils committed by the Esoteric Order of Dagon or the KKK. Whether the alien Other conquers the white homogeny of Lovecraft's world or they are ultimately destroyed does not matter against cosmic indifference.

While the cosmic horror of Lovecraft is what provides the genre with much of its power and lasting influence, by its nature no system of morality can survive contact with it. "Lovecraft does not offer humanity hope in the end," writes S. T. Joshi, "we shall either be wiped out by those unassimilable nuclei of aliens on the fringe of our civilization or destroy ourselves through repeated miscegenation" (*The Weird Tale* 227).

As video games grow in scope and complexity, other studios besides Frogwares are realizing that the long-held belief of video games being completely free of the real world may not actually be true. They are beginning to understand that "[g]ames are also necessitated and deeply informed by the epistemic contours of contemporaneous American culture and its history" (Higgins 23). This has led a few studios to try to address issues of race and politics within their own games. One that bears a striking similarity to *The Sinking City* is *BioShock Infinite*, produced by 2K Games in 2013. Its setting is also a fictionalized American city in the interwar years and also relying on a "young, white male avatar, a former Pinkerton Agent named Booker DeWitt to exercise its social critique" (Mafe 90). But like with *Call of Cthulhu* and *The Sinking City*, this is where the similarities end, both in setting and execution. I, with author Diana Mafe, would point to *BioShock Infinite* as demonstrating that video games can be successful in addressing difficult conversations on race and politics.

While the white homogeny of *Call of Cthulhu*'s town of Darkwater is a simulacrum created by what is not included (blacks and other minorities), the hyper-nationalistic white city of Columbia maintains homogeny through the open oppression and subjugation of minorities. Unlike the fantasy-like utopia created by *The Sinking City*, the blatant racism passed off as natural within *BioShock Infinite* rings truer as the player sees it as a closer reality than the transplanted racism of Oakmont. "The game thus encourages is player to see beyond what is in plain sight-to look past the contents of the fishbowl and make out the hidden structure" (Mafe 101). Instead of ignoring race or transposing xenophobia onto a literal other, *BioShock Infinite* incorporates them into every part of the game, from combat to moral decisions, making their evasion far more difficult (Mafe 108). It is fair to point out, however, that *BioShock Infinite* has a freedom of storytelling that neither *Call of Cthulhu* nor *The Sinking City* are afforded, as it is not based on a pre-existing property. Yet this could have been an even greater opportunity for both Lovecraft games to address the issues in their source materials as part of a genre that is often sorely lacking in introspection. Instead of transferring the issues of race or ignoring them outright, *BioShock Infinite* manages to maintain an intelligent dialogue. As Diana Mafe writes, "While the game clearly condemns racism, it nonetheless encourages players to come away with their own conclusions about the politics of racial identity and the ways in which those politics shape nationhood (108).

It is also unfortunate that *The Sinking City* could not use its ideas of subverting the monstrous in H. P. Lovecraft's tales to address ideas of xenophobia and othering. The use of Throgmorton and the Innsmouthers as a means of dialogue about racism only ended in confusing its own message by keeping too close to Lovecraft's Mythos. It is not only the video game industry that has to deal with problematic source material. The 2011 film *Rise of the Planet of the Apes* and its subsequent sequels share many of the same issues with *The Sinking City*. While being a reboot of the original 1986 Charlton Heston film, the 2011 film still walks the line of having what is now considered heavily racialized subject material to draw from while trying to address and even subvert these themes. much like how the white ape and Innsmouthers represent the decadent and invading other within Lovecraft:

> ... *Apes* (1968) actively reinforces contemporary audience members' fears of real-world upheaval and insurgence on the part of the racial Other. Framing its ape characters as analogical counterparts of the Black male, the work unsettles viewers by presenting a speculative future in which the world has been turned upside down in violent, terrifying fashion—a world in which the racial/hegemonic center has been pushed to the fringes and the putative Other has seized the reins of power. (Chidester 6)

It is through the white males' perspective that the horror and sympathy of the audience is gained as he struggles to reassert the natural homogeny that has been seized (6). For both Lovecraft and the 1968 *Planet of the Apes*, this latent fear of invasion and conquest by the other is inescapable. Within *The Sinking City*, despite the game's attempt at humanizing both Throgmorton and the Innsmouthers, there is still the lurking fear of the invading other. By trying to overcome the symbology of the ape in Victorian literature, Throgmorton's claims at superiority contain a threatening note as to what may become of normal "inferior" human beings (especially when the idea of giving humans new ape bodies is put on the table). The Innsmouthers and their link to the sea cannot be disconnected with the slowly encroaching tide as it subsumes Oakmont, delivering it unto the creatures of the deep.

What separates *Rise of the Planet of the Apes* from *The Sinking City* in terms of executing a successful subversion of sympathetic others is the moving of the audience outside of the human characters and into the apes.

> A telling example of this subtle shift of perspective can be found in the films' depictions of various characters at opposite ends of an attack by a high-pressured hose. In *Planet of the Apes* (1968), Taylor is assaulted by a gruff ape who gleefully blasts him to the back of his cage.... Yet because viewers have long since been invited to identify with the [2011] film's chimp characters instead of its human ones, the abuse is still coming at the hands of the Other. As a result, when Caesar exacts revenge later in the film by using the same hose to electrocute his handler, the audience cheers this moment of sheer brutality as a just end. (Chidester 8)

For the player in *The Sinking City*, the monstrous other can never be anything different, as the protagonist is still approaching the narrative from the view of a white male human being. Any attempt at giving power to Throgmorton or the Innsmouthers, no matter how well-intentioned and noble it may appear on the surface, will still invoke the anxiety of invasion from the player. They both threaten destruction of the current power structure of white Anglo-American society, and thus the races they were intended to replace are put back upon them, negating the shift entirely. In the 2011 *Apes* film, initially, there is the threat of conquest and destruction of the familiar normative structures. By the final act it seems assured that the apes will literally and figuratively smash through the last bastion of society and realize the assumed conquest of the other. Instead, they go around it and, "[h]aving discovered a completely unexpected way to subvert the existing power structure, the apes in the redwoods are now poised to introduce a new brand of 'reality' into civilized (White) American society" (Chidester 11). If the racialized other is to be addressed and overcome within incarnations of Lovecraft's work, *Rise of the Planet of the Apes*'s ability to be inspired by but still adapt its source material may be key in confronting the xenophobia inherent in his Mythos.

Though they handle the source material in different ways, neither video game manages to escape Lovecraft's ideologies. For *Call of Cthulhu*, in trying to avoid the realities of the inherent racial prejudices within the source material and setting the game in the homogenous setting of New England, it does the opposite. Removing African Americans and other racial minorities from the narrative only serves to bring the issue to the foreground as it creates a blackless world. Ironically, *Call of Cthulhu* becomes a world closer to what Lovecraft himself would have preferred, by removing those he viewed as racially inferior. Players, in participating in this world, "(re)produce socially prescribed and technologically mediated notions of race" (Everett and Watkins 149). *The Sinking City*, for all its issues, is open about attempting to address the prejudices of both Lovecraft and his era. It tries to create a dialogue on Throgmorton's hypocrisy toward the Innsmouthers, as he is discriminating against them the same way many of the townsfolk do toward him. The game attempts to reclaim the Victorian "ape narrative" and transform it as a positive representation of the blackness associated with it. It even manages to make the alien sympathetic with the Innsmouthers and their plight. Yet, even with these modifications to Lovecraft's stories, the underlying racial binaries of the source material remains. By moving the racism and xenophobia from the actual minorities present in the game, *The Sinking City* creates a fantasy just as removed from reality as *Call of Cthulhu*. This suspension of disbelief causes the player to "take in not only the realistic and fantastic game elements but also the meanings underlying the representation" (Schwartz 315).

With the success of properties like the Marvel cinematic universe and J. R. R. Tolkien's *Lord of the Rings*, stories once thought untouchable are being dredged up in the hopes of finding the next big hit franchise. Yet, in this haste to resurrect the next story, controversies that may exist within them are often pushed aside, such as racist, sexist, and colonialist ideals that were often common in nineteenth- and twentieth-century fiction. By examining how *Call of Cthulhu* and *The Sinking City* address these issues embedded within Lovecraft, it is clear that there is no easy solution to the problem. Either by ignoring these ideologies (as traditionally has been done with Lovecraft) or by attempting to address them, both present problems. With Lovecraft's popularity continuing to grow, it is doubtful we have seen the end of video games inspired by his Mythos. Though it may be easier to ignore these latent ideologies, it is encouraging to see games like *The Sinking City* not shy away from them. Though not perfect, it may be the first step in leaving behind H. P. Lovecraft's antiquated beliefs and using his stories to confront issues of race and bigotry that still exist today.

Works Cited

Bealer, Tracy. "The Innsmouth Look: H. P. Lovecraft's Ambivalent Modernism." *Journal of Philosophy* 6, No. 14 (2011): 44-50. ProQuest, eres.regent.edu:2048/login?url=https://search-proquest-com.ezproxy.regent.edu/docview/855603381?accountid=13479.

Bowler, Peter J. "From 'Savage' to 'Primitive': Victorian Evolutionism and the Interpretation of Marginalized Peoples." *Antiquity* No. 252 (1992): 721-29. doi:10.1017/S0003598X00039430.

Chidester, Phil. "The Simian That Screamed 'No!': Rise of the Planet of the Apes and the Speculative as Public Memory." *Visual Communication Quarterly* 22, No. 1 (2015): 3-14.

Cyanide Studios. *Call of Cthulhu*. Focus Home Interactive, 2018. Microsoft Windows.

Everett, Anna, and S. Craig Watkins. "The Power of Play: The Portrayal and Performance of Race in Video Games." In Katie Salen Tekinbas, ed. *The Ecology of Games: Connecting Youth, Games, and Learning*. Cambridge, MA: MIT Press, 2008. 141-66.

Faig, Kenneth W., Jr., and S. T. Joshi. "H. P. Lovecraft: His Life and Work." In S. T. Joshi, ed. *H. P. Lovecraft: Four Decades of Criticism*. Athens: Ohio University Press, 1980, 1-19.

Flood, Allison. "World Fantasy Award Drops HP Lovecraft as Prize Image." *The Guardian* (9 November 2015), www.theguardian.com/books/2015/nov/09/world-fantasy-award-drops-hp-lovecraft-as-prize-image.

Frogwares. *The Sinking City*. Bigben Interactive, 2019. PlayStation 4.

Higgin, Tanner. "Blackless Fantasy: The Disappearance of Race in Massively Multiplayer Online Role-Playing Games." *Games and Culture* 4, No. 1 (2009): 3-26.

Joshi, S. T. *The Weird Tale*. Austin: University of Texas Press, 1990.

Lovecraft, H. P. *Letters to Woodburn Harris and Others*. Ed. S. T. Joshi and David E. Schultz. New York: Hippocampus Press, 2022.

Mafe, Diana Adesola. "Race and the First-Person Shooter: Challenging the Video Gamer in BioShock Infinite." *Camera Obscura: Feminism, Culture, and Media Studies* 30, No. 2 (2015): 89-124.

Mou, Yi. "Gender and Racial Stereotypes in Popular Video Games." Ph.D. diss.: Michigan State University, 2007. ProQuest Dissertations and Theses.

Mullis, Justin. "Playing Games with the Great Old Ones: Ritual, Play, and Joking within the Cthulhu Mythos Fandom." *Journal of the Fantastic in the Arts* 26, No. 3 (2015): 512-30. JSTOR, www.jstor.org/stable/26321173.

Poole, W. Scott. *In the Mountains of Madness: The Life and Extraordinary Afterlife of H. P. Lovecraft*. Berkeley, CA: Soft Skull Press, 2016.

Schwartz, Leigh. "Fantasy, Realism, and the Other in Recent Video Games." *Space and Culture* 9 (2006): 313-25.

Asexual Possibility in the Life and Fiction of H. P. Lovecraft

Riley Chirrick
Independent Scholar

At first glance it might be difficult to imagine that Lovecraftian studies and queer theory[1] have any intersection whatsoever. Lovecraft was at one point a married man, a man obsessed with duty and heritage, a man who balked at effeminate men and staunchly claimed the inferiority of women.[2] He was a strong supporter of the traditional family, a firm believer in the importance of class and station, a proud descendent of aristocratic ancestors, and, most ironic of all, in the words of Bobby Derie, he "viewed homosexuality as a perversion"[3] (41). All in all, a plethora of evidence seems to put Lovecraft squarely at odds with anything queer.

On closer inspection, however, Lovecraft's life and work quite often intersect and reflect queer ways of living and thinking. His obsession with time, his own past, the future, and the unknown are in direct conversation with

---

1. Queer theory is the study of queer people, their lived experiences, gender, sex, and sexuality. Queer theorist Eve Kosofsky Sedgwick defines queer as "the open mesh of possibilities, gaps, overlaps, dissonances and resonances, lapses and excesses of meaning when the constituent elements of anyone's gender, of anyone's sexuality aren't made (or can't be made) to signify monolithically" (6). Asexuality, defined more fully later in this paper, falls under the umbrella of queer, and thus it is important to discuss queer theory as a whole before narrowing scope.

2. In a 1923 letter to Frank Belknap Long, he said, "I do not agree with you regarding the Merit of the Female Mind. In my opinion, 'tis not only not more imaginative than that of Men, but vastly less so." He later goes on, "[Women] are by Nature literal, prosaic, & commonplace, given to dull realistick Details and practical Things, & incapable alike of vigorous artistick Creation & genuine, first-hand appreciation" (SP 127).

3. While HPL did hold all these views at one point or another, it is important to note that he recanted or reconsidered many of them over time.

queer theory concepts such as queer temporality and melancholia.[4] His stories overwhelmingly featured powerless, feminine-coded male heroes contrary to what were the contemporary masculine and heroic ideals of his time.[5] And, most striking of all, he was consistently, continuously uninterested in and repulsed by sex, believing it an animalistic act in reality and featuring it as a cause and perpetrator of horror in his fiction.

Lovecraft's contemptuous perspectives on sex would not only be considered non-normative[6] today but certainly within early twentieth century society, and it is this non-normative outlook that echoes queer theorist Kathryn Bond Stockton's work *The Queer Child, or Growing Sideways in the Twentieth Century*. In it she introduces her concept of "thinking sideways," a way to define the ways queer people live their lives aslant of the normative. It reflects the way queer people have historically needed to think about the world and move through it differently from their heterosexual or cisgendered peers, all in order to protect and enrich themselves in a society where they were not and are not considered the norm.

In *Thinking Sideways, or an Untoward Genealogy of Queer Reading*, queer theorists E. L. McCallum and Tyler Bradway extrapolate on this concept of sideways thinking, suggesting that "scholars and activists seized on the term 'queer' as a way to describe not fitting in, not being fully intelligible to mainstream demands for comportment, and even to question those demands for normativity in our desires, pleasures, bodies. As queer, we may be able to articulate how we are not fitting in" (3).

As difficult as it might be for some to imagine that Lovecraft was queer, it should be even harder to imagine that he fit in neatly with the sexual expectations and mores of his time. In fact, the way he disavowed sex, avoided sexual relationships with women (and men), and endured ribbing from friends about his known lack of interest in sex[7] all deserve an exploration that goes

---

4. The works of queer theorists Jack Halberstam, Judith Butler, and Elizabeth Freeman are good places to start with queer temporality and melancholia. In short, these concepts investigate how queer people move differently and uniquely through time and space. A particular concept of note is chrononormativity, or the typical life path that includes birth, schooling, employment, marriage, and having children. Queer people often deviate from this path, and HPL did as well.

5. More about this in Morgana LaVine's excellent essay "Lovecraft and the Male Gender Role."

6. Cambridge dictionary defines *non-normative* as "not relating to what is considered the usual or normal way for people to look, act, or behave."

7. In an interview conducted by R. Alain Everts decades after HPL's death, his ex-wife

beyond simple accusations of puritanism or gentlemanly aesthetic. This paper examines Lovecraft's life and fiction—filled as it is with asexual utopias, acts of monstrous breeding, and sex as eldritch ritual—to examine how his stated and implicit views on sex and sexuality can be viewed as asexual.

Why Queer Lovecraft?

The application of a queer theory lens to the examination of a subject is often called *queering*. It is a way to explore that sideways thinking, to look at something—such as a piece of literature or a movie—from an angle that might be little explored or overlooked, especially as pertaining to gender, sex, sexuality, and queer affect.[8] Queering examines ways in which something speaks to queer experiences, resonates with queer people, and reflects qualities that make it itself queer. When talking about *queer* as a way of examination, McCallum and Bradway posit, "Queer marks an opportunity for reinterpretation. In this sense, queer is not an identity, a thing, or an entity but an *activity*" (3).

It is, however, considered more difficult and controversial to queer a historical figure, even among queer theorists. While unpacking an artistic work and assessing how it might speak to the queer is commonplace, there is debate over whether it is ethical or even valuable to queer a person's life, especially a long-dead person. This debate is complicated by the fact that queer does not have a historical archive. Persecution of queer people throughout history necessitated keeping queerness secret, and because of this, queer acts and persons go largely undocumented. The language we use today to discuss matters of queerness was not available even a hundred years ago, making the examination of what little documentation is available an effort in decoding and deciphering.[9] Even Lovecraft himself, surrounded by friends and corre-

---

Sonia Davis said that "when the boys and HPL used to meet in his [Sam Loveman's] studio room on Clinton Street, when I was not there—whether they did it on purpose or to tease him, they would open a conversation re sex, knowing that HPL did not like to listen to such stories . . ."

8. Queer affect describes feelings unique or partial to the queer experience, and investigates the types of actions, ways of living, and ways of thinking that evoke both what it means to feel queerly and to respond to something queerly. See queer theorist Sara Ahmed's *The Cultural Politics of Emotion*.

9. It is this lack of visibility and historicity that makes it appear as though "homosexuality is something alien to the American experience—an intruder that inexplicably gate-crashed America in 1969" (Hari). This is of course not true. Queerness has always existed. Nota-

spondents who were themselves queer,[10] had "never heard of homosexuality as an actual instinct till [he] was over thirty" (JVS 146).

In part because of this ethical question and this lack of historical understanding of queer lives, there might be those who level "who cares?" at the notion that Lovecraft may have been asexual, as though being so would have been as remarkable and as significant to his life as the shape of his big toe.[11] But it is important to consider just how integral queer identity—much like any identity—is to one's life, and that considering the evidence of whether Lovecraft may have been queer could shed new light on how his cosmic horror spoke so strongly to the fringes, to the liminal, to the melancholy, to the temporally displaced—all those things queer people often feel when they are not fitting in.

If we consider the evidence that points to even the possibility that Lovecraft may have been asexual, we may be able to interrogate with more purpose some interesting aspects of his life and work: first, that there was a notable absence of sex or interest in sex in his life; second, that there is a prevalence of sexually charged orgies and acts of monstrous breeding in his works, and that when he did write about utopias, they were asexual. Queer theory's emphasis on sex and sexuality makes it uniquely suited as a framework through which to examine these aspects.

Since Lovecraft is dead, there will be no confirming whether he himself was asexual, but examining the *possibility*, especially alongside elements of asexuality in his fiction, should bring to the surface new questions and considerations about one of the world's most beloved authors.

---

bly, this lack of a historical archive contributes to the fallacy that queer identities are a fad, a belief some have adopted in response to the increasing prevalence of queer-identifying people. One who holds this notion might wish to examine the ways in which historical social consequences for coming out pressured queer people not to do so, or how those consequences pressured queer people to comport themselves in ways that aligned with societal expectations, thus reducing their apparent number. The queer experience cannot be removed from these pressures and must be examined together.

10. Samuel Loveman and R. H. Barlow were among the most notable of HPL's queer friends; August Derleth, whom he never met, was bisexual. There are others, but that's another paper.

11. This echoes Robert M. Price's question in his essay, "Homosexual Panic in 'The Outsider'": "ultimately, who cares [if HPL was gay]?" Amusingly, he writes after, "Indeed, the close correspondence between the story's character and the experience of many gay people is most likely purely coincidental. But in any event, the parallel is plainly there, and gay readers of HPL will probably wonder why it has taken the rest of us this long to see it."

Asexuality in Lovecraft's Life

The Asexual Visibility and Education Network (AVEN) defines an asexual person as "a person who does not experience sexual attraction." While this a common and well-understood cornerstone of asexuality, queer theorist and asexual studies expert Ela Przybylo pushes back against defining asexuality purely by these conditions. She laments that focusing solely on sex as a nonsexual act instead of as an act decoupled from the sexual hemisphere entirely has the result that "even nonsexual action becomes 'sexual' such that an absence of a sex drive (or asexuality) is understood as 'repression' of one's sexual instincts" (20).[12] Przybylo calls this *compulsory sexuality*, defining the normative societal compulsion as "the ways in which sexuality is presumed to be natural and normal to the detriment of various forms of asexual and nonsexual lives" (1). Ergo, it is so natural to the sexual person to *be* and *feel* sexual that the assumption becomes that *everyone* is sexual and everyone must feel some sexual drive, even if that is demonstrably not the case.

As a remedy to this compulsory line of thinking, Przybylo suggests that we look at asexuality as a way of thinking about intimacy differently—and indeed separately—from the sexual at all. Many asexual people have deep friendships and even romantic relationships, she explains, but they often express and feel intimacy apart from the erotic. Consider the following quote:

> Love is generally linked with subsidiary conditions such as pride, admiration, eroticism, intellectual congeniality, and in practice it may be taken for granted that all other things being equal, the possessor generally prefers to have the object close at hand, although a purely ethereal and imaginative force such as real love is sometimes independent of time, space, or corporeal existence. True love thrives equally well in presence or absence, proving that the force is an exalted and imaginative one, and directed toward the most permanent spiritual and aesthetically responsive part of the personality. It need not disavow a parallel erotic appreciation but it inwardly eclipses and transcends it. (Derie 24)

This is not a quotation from Przybylo, or any queer theorist, but from Lovecraft in a letter to Sonia H. Greene in 1922. In it we can see how he is defining his sense of intimacy and love, notably that it is a "purely ethereal and imaginative force" and that it can be "independent of time, space, or corporeal existence." He contends that some who possess feelings of love ("the possessor") want the thing, experience, or person they love ("the object") to be

---

12. This accusation has often been leveled at HPL.

close, but that it is not necessary for that love to exist, that it "thrives equally well in presence or absence." This force of love "need not disavow a parallel erotic appreciation"—suggesting that love is entirely decoupled from the erotic, that it is a parallel feeling, not a conjoined one—but it "eclipses and transcends it." For Lovecraft, love and intimacy are "directed toward the most permanent spiritual and aesthetically responsive part of the personality," not the erotic, nor even proximity, which in fact became a sticking point in his and Sonia's marriage years later:

> I told him I did everything I could think of to make our marriage a success, but that no marriage could ever be such, in letter-writing only; that a close propinquity was necessary for a true marriage. Then he would tell me of a very happy couple whom he knew, where the wife lived with her parents, in Virginia, while the husband lived elsewhere for reasons of illness, and that their marriage was kept intact through letters. My reply was that neither of us was really sick and that I did not wish to be a long-distance wife "enjoying" the company of a long-distance husband by letter-writing only. (Quoted in Derie 24)

One can hardly blame Sonia, though she certainly demonstrates a different (and indeed more normative) way of thinking about marriage and intimacy than Lovecraft. He seemed perfectly content to be apart from Sonia, as his letter of 1922 forewarned. Even marriage did not change how he felt about or expressed intimacy, and though he seemed happy to discuss *love* as a theoretical concept, he evidently expressed it in ways differently from the norm. Years after Lovecraft's death, Sonia said of him that "He never used the word 'love': his idea of verbal love-making was to say: 'My dear, you don't know how much I appreciate you'" (quoted in Derie 26). L. Sprague de Camp noted that Lovecraft's "efforts at affectionate physical contact consisted of wrapping his little finger around hers and grunting 'Unh!'" (200).

It appeared even to Lovecraft's friends that he and Sonia were not entwined in any way deemed to be typical. Asked how he would assess Lovecraft's relationship with Sonia during his panel at the 1990 Centennial Conference, Frank Belknap Long said, "He really liked her very much, from the first. He never changed in that respect, but it was no romantic relationship"[13] (Joshi,

---

13. It might be wise here to carefully consider what Long considered a "romantic" relationship. It is very likely that he shared Sonia's typical assessment of the need for proximity and overt erotic interest, given that he was married for 34 years until his death to Lyda Arco. However, as noted, sexuality is mistakenly considered to be necessary and normal for intimate relationships. It is possible he knew of HPL's and Sonia's lack of erotic intimacy, and chalked that up to a lack of romantic interest. The evidence shows that HPL did express

Centennial Conference Proceedings 29).

While Lovecraft may not have met Sonia's needs for a thriving marriage, the evidence suggests he did express intimacy—just in his own way, which was considered atypical. This seems to echo Przybylo's conditions for non-normative intimacies decoupled from compulsory sexuality—and therefore possible asexuality. But the well-read Lovecraftian might by now be thinking about AVEN's definition of a "person who does not experience sexual attraction," and about how—wait a minute!—Lovecraft *did* have sex! Indeed, in 1969 Sonia recalled Lovecraft as an "adequately excellent lover" (Everts), though while interviewing Sonia years later, Everts clarified, Lovecraft "never once made any sexual overtures to his wife—she, Sonia, always had to make the overtures for their sexual relations."

One might imagine that having sex (even if only "adequately" excellently) proves once and for all that Lovecraft was not asexual, just as a gay man being married to a woman makes him undeniably heterosexual.[14] But some asexual people do or have had sex, which is part of the reason Przybylo urges the viewing of asexuality as less rigid and more defined by non-normative expressions of intimacy over a purely *sexual or nonsexual* discourse.

It is also important to consider that even if Lovecraft was uninterested in sex, he might have participated in it to fulfill what even Sonia, in the same interview with Everts, called his "husbandly duty." Lovecraft was certainly a dutiful man, and it is not difficult to imagine that he would have tried to perform for Sonia even if (as the evidence suggests) he was not eager to do so.

However, perhaps AVEN's definition—one that most people can probably accept more readily than Przybylo's—needs more weight in this conversation. Many have suggested that Lovecraft was simply sex-repressed, or perhaps too much of a gentleman and prude to discuss sexual matters openly—even with his wife. This would certainly be in line with his old-world aesthetic and outlook, and is a due point of consideration. Perhaps, underneath the shy, intellectual exterior, Lovecraft had a perfectly typical sexual appetite. For this, let us turn away from intimacies for a moment and look at something simple: what Lovecraft thought about sex.

He once wrote that "Eroticism belongs to a lower order of instincts, and

---

intimacy and affection for Sonia, however, just in non-normative, very possibly asexual ways.

14. Such marriages—known as "lavender marriages"—did exist, and they did not make their gay participants any less gay. See "When Hollywood Studios Married Off Gay Stars to Keep Their Sexuality a Secret" on History.com.

is an animal rather than a nobly human quality" (RK 152. He recounted to J. Vernon Shea how as a child he looked up the act of sex in his family library. Of the experience he said:

> instead of giving me an abnormal & precocious interest in sex (as *unsatisfied* curiosity might have done), it virtually killed my interest in the subject. The whole matter was reduced to prosaic mechanism—a mechanism which I rather despised or at least thought non-glamourous because of its purely animal nature & separation from such things as intellect & beauty. (JVS 220)

Lovecraft found sex repulsive at worst and a prosaic mechanism at best. The use of "mechanism" here is important, as he was not blind or ignorant of sex's biological necessity, a point that comes up time and time again in his fiction.

Lovecraft confessed to Rheinhart Kleiner: "I am coming to be convinced that the erotic instinct is in the majority of mankind far stronger than I could ever imagine without wide reading and observation; that it relentlessly clutches the average person—even of the thinking classes—to a degree which makes its overthrow by higher interests impossible" (RK 177). This is possibly the most vital piece of evidence in considering whether Lovecraft was asexual. His claim is telling: without seeing sexuality everywhere around him, he could not possibly believe that such an urge existed naturally. This suggests that these erotic interests were foreign to him, that the lack of his own interest was not due to prudishness, but simply a lack of sexual urge. He could not comprehend how natural it was for others to be sexually interested; it was an alien consideration—perhaps even a horrifying one.

Asexuality in Lovecraft's Fiction

It is important not to conflate authors with their work, but in Lovecraft's case it can be difficult to separate the two entirely. There are some grounds for this: Lovecraft was not shy about using his personal experiences in his fiction; he based stories in the places he visited and in his hometown of Providence; he used historically significant events such as the Antarctic exploration of his era, as well as his fascination for and amateur understanding of various sciences; he even turned his dreams into stories, and quite purposefully drew direct parallels between characters and friends.15 For Lovecraft, his fiction and his life were intertwined.[16]

---

15. "Hypnos" is a notable example of this, as is "The Statement of Randolph Carter."

16. There are many academic studies of this, but "Personal Elements in Lovecraft's Writ-

In "Haunted Castles, Dark Mirrors: On the Penguin Horror Series," horror luminary and Lovecraft admirer Guillermo del Toro calls horror fiction a "dark mirror" (xii). Expanding on the themes of Lovecraft's "The Outsider" del Toro explains that the allure of horror is the fear and excitement of approaching a story (the mirror) and realizing that the figure staring back from the darkness is us. He writes, "To learn what we fear is to learn who we are. Horror defines our boundaries and illuminates our souls" (xii). This may be distinctly true for *writers* of horror, and for Lovecraft especially. His stories were not only fiction, but a reflection and sometimes an outright pronouncement of his beliefs, political views, and greatest anxieties.

Knowing this, we can take the statements he made about sex, as well as the way he expressed intimacy in his one romantic relationship, and hold them up to his stories. We can ask of his prolific body of work: In what ways was this a dark mirror?

Sex serves two primary functions in Lovecraft's stories. The first is as prosaic mechanism: procreation. In these cases, the act of sex itself is largely implied, never shown. While Lovecraft himself admitted to not understanding "erotic interests," he doubtless understood *how babies are made*, that ancestry simply does not exist without the sexual act. This is of course the *mechanism* component of his stated lack of interest that sex is necessary for human propagation.

We can see this understanding of sex as prosaic mechanism doing work in such stories as "Facts concerning the Late Arthur Jermyn and His Family." In it a string of dubious mating choices with a "daughter of a gamekeeper," "the daughter of the seventh Viscount of Brightholme," and of course the "ape-princess" all lead to the climactic and unsettling conclusion of the Jermyn family's monstrous interbreeding and resulting ancestry (104-6). Very often—and certainly in this case—if a woman is included at all in a Lovecraft story, it is for the purpose of bearing children and delineating an ancestral connection. The deaths and disappearances of various women throughout this tale invite no sense of intimacy or mourning; they are hardly referred to at all outside the explanation of who is which man's wife or mother.[17]

---

ings," a presentation by David E. Schultz for the 1990 Centennial Conference, is a great place to start for more information.

17. "The Shadow over Innsmouth" is similar in its use of sex as prosaic mechanism. The narrator seeks out his ancestry, getting waylaid to the coastal town of Innsmouth where he is tempted by fate to discover its horrifying secret: the entire community has interbred

In "The Dunwich Horror," another tale of monstrous interbreeding, Lavinia Whateley has (implied) coitus with Yog-Sothoth, bearing as a result Wilbur Whateley and the titular Dunwich Horror. Henry Armitage, the story's hero, expresses extreme disgust that such a creature as Wilbur could come to be, but interestingly, the fact that Lavinia had sex with an *eldritch being* is decidedly glossed over. Armitage's worry is less about the woman and her questionable dating choices and more about the creature that mated with her: "But what thing—what cursed shapeless influence on or off this three-dimensional earth—was Wilbur Whateley's father? . . . What walked on the mountains that May-Night? What Roodmas horror fastened itself on the world in half-human flesh and blood?" (CF 2.436). To the sexual among us, it perhaps feels a bit as though Lovecraft has buried the lede.[18]

Now, one could very likely identify *heritage* as the cause of Lovecraft's anxiety in these texts, not sex. But we have discussed what heritage cannot exist without. While there are certainly ancestral tensions in these stories, his handling of sex as a mere tool for propagation and heritage echoes his view of sex as a prosaic mechanism. That the horror of these stories is more about the ancestry than the sex itself is quite telling when we consider that learning about sex as a child "killed [his] interest in the subject." We might deduce that he would not have been inclined to explore the sexual in his work because he was not interested in exploring it in his life. And so, sex as prosaic mechanism is an implied act that lacks intimacy, a hand-wave, a biological imperative.

The second primary function of sex in Lovecraft's work is as horror. It is what he intends to evoke when writing about the sexual *explicitly*, instead of as implicit mechanism. There are references to orgiastic[19] acts in several Lovecraft stories, but there is none more pronounced than in "The Horror at Red Hook":

---

with or are the result of interbreeding with underwater monsters. At the end of the story, the main character learns the unfortunate truth: he, too, by acts of implied sex, shares this heritage.

18. This gap has been filled in by many Lovecraftian erotica writers over the century since his death. A particularly explicit and harrowing example is Alan Moore's *Neonomicon*, in which one of the main characters is shown to be raped by a Deep One.

19. While orgy in its historic use is not necessarily sexual, HPL combines other sexually telling imagery and tone around such cases to evoke sex and animalistic nature in his scenes. The fine, obfuscated line in these cases only serves the mysterious, dangerous nature of the mythos' cults.

In an instant every moving entity was electrified; and forming at once into a ceremonial procession, the nightmare horde slithered away in quest of the sound—goat, satyr, and aegipan, incubus, succubae, and lemur, twisted toad and shapeless elemental, dog-faced howler and silent strutter in darkness—all led by the abominable naked phosphorescent thing that had squatted on the carved golden throne. (CF 1.500).

The language in this passage alone alludes to a sexual act—an electrified moving horde that slithers after a naked thing—but references to satyrs, incubi, and succubae ground it in the undeniably sexual. Incubi and succubae—whose sexually charged roots go all the way back to Mesopotamia—are commonly known as demonic or spiritual entities that tempt human beings into illicit acts of sex. Satyrs, a Greek mythological creature, are "characterized by riotous merriment and lasciviousness" and are sometimes pictured with "a perpetual erection" (Wiktionary).

Later in the same passage, Malone, the protagonist, hears "chanted horrors and shocking croakings," the "whine of ceremonial devotion" (500), "whistling sigh[s]," and the name *Mormo* "repeated with ecstasy" (501)—all visceral, erotically charged sounds even on their own, and doubly so when written in combination with the visually stimulating satyr and incubus. There are also mentions of Lilith in this passage, another widely known and cited she-demon who has been a source of both the sexual and the fearful in cultures both ancient and modern. For almost two pages Lovecraft paints arguably his most evocative, powerful, and controversial scene of horror, and it is firmly rooted in the erotic.

There is of course another theme in this work, another anxiety of Lovecraft's: his fear and disgust of immigrants. There is no denying that his various deprecating ways of referencing "mongrel hordes" are rooted in racism and a sense of racial supremacy. In their essay "Lovecraft's Most Bigoted Story, No Really: 'The Horror at Red Hook,'" Ruthanna Emrys and Anne M. Pillsworth note that this is the "the nadir of Lovecraft's nastiest themes. Civilization—modern, Aryan civilization—is the only bulwark against primitive cults and superstitions and sacrifices—and the least tolerance of variation will let those things slip into the cracks and destroy the world." They also note that the story is very much about "sex [as] death," and indeed, sex is being used to demonstrate the reprehensible nature of the cultists. The racism in the story does not overshadow the horror of the sexual, but compounds it. Lovecraft viewed sex as animalistic, as separate from human beauty and intellect. For him, what better way could there be to showcase the abhorrent nature of Suydam's cult?

While Lovecraft wrote a number of such stories that feature both implicit and explicit acts of sex, he also wrote stories that emphasized a lack of sex, or asexuality at its most plain. These stories usually feature utopic alien civilizations that, as S. T. Joshi writes in "Lovecraft's Alien Civilizations: A Political Interpretation," are "vastly superior to men . . . It is a fact of no small interest that all three of Lovecraft's comparatively utopian societies have done away with sex in the normal fashion" (10).

One such story is "The Mound," in which the Spanish explorer Zamacona comes across an alien utopia under the earth. He notes with fascination that the alien people there "no longer grew old or reproduced their kind" (CF 4.233) and that in their society, "art and intellect, it appeared, had reached very high levels" (254). The people in their underground city of Tsath engaged in "religious exercises, exotic experiments, artistic and philosophical discussions, and the like" (254).

While this society is hardly perfect (and is in fact the story's antagonistic force), it is easy to draw parallels between its utopic veneer and Lovecraft's values: art, intellect, and, quite possibly, a lack of sexual need or interest. Not only do the highly esteemed alien people not engage in sex themselves, but they have enslaved their rival societies and forced sex upon them, "interbreeding them with certain horned and four-footed animals" (252), so as to create "a sort of half-human slave class which also served to nourish the human and animal population" (253). Sex here is used both as a tool to further degradate those whom the people of Tsath have enslaved and as a prosaic mechanism to generate a resource. Sex therefore becomes weaponized in the story, where a lack of need or interest in it becomes a mark of the higher class and the superior race.[20]

Conclusion: A Matter of Legacy

By both AVEN's and Przybylo's definition, Lovecraft seemed to live his life and express his views on the erotic in an asexual way, and for a man who so frequently instilled his beliefs about the world in his fiction, it is no surprise to find that these asexual views are mirrored in his work. While these evidences alone may paint a compelling picture of possible asexuality, there is one more thing to consider.

---

20. "The Mound" is full of many other interesting queer ideas. In its utopian society, "family organization had long ago perished, and the civil and social distinction of the sexes had disappeared." (254)

This paper began by listing the ways in which Lovecraft resists queerness, and it should be ended in a way that marks him alongside many who are queer: Lovecraft did not have children. Not having children is queer in that many queer people do not have biological offspring, but also in that not having children deviates from a hetero- and chrono-normative lifepath, especially in the early twentieth century, and especially for a man of Lovecraft's aristocratic heritage. Queerness can be explored as a lack of legacy, paralleling being queer itself with its own unfortunate lack of historicity.

Lovecraft was a gentleman, a man of duty who clearly valued not only his specific heritage but the general idea of ancestry. He wrote that "it is ever part of the exemplary citizen to sustain with equanimity his share in the production of the coming generation" (quoted in de Camp 193). He appeared to have everything he needed to manifest this duty; he moved to New York with a job and a supportive wife who was also a willing sexual partner, and yet it is clear that he made no real moves to produce children with her. Why would Lovecraft not have jumped at the ample opportunity to fulfill the duty of an exemplary citizen, to one day be "Grandpa" to more than just his young correspondents (and his elderly aunts!) but his own line? And say that he simply did not like Sonia. Why then is there no evidence of any other romantic entanglement over the course of his entire life?

Lovecraft is one of the most prolific letter writers in history. Researchers are lucky to have well-documented records of almost every major life transition, political view, and even his favorite and least favorite foods. It is not difficult to chart Lovecraft's life path through his letters alone, and so the absence of lamentation over not having offspring or a typical marriage is conspicuous. Instead of these types of evidences, we find that post-marriage, Lovecraft went on to cultivate his friendships, to become a mentor to R. H. Barlow, to express intimacy as confidant and intellectual only. Is this not a form of intimacy that Przybylo would want considered of someone asexual? A form of intimacy that is decoupled from sex and romantic relationships entirely?

One possible explanation is that Lovecraft held conflicting desires: the desire for legacy, for his own line, or at least for meaningful impact on the world, and yet an utter lack of desire to copulate. His legacy, as befitting for many who share queer identities, was carried on by friends and correspondents, by a community of writers and intellectuals whose lives he touched.

Over decades of study, researchers have accused Lovecraft of being sex-inhibited, sex-repressed, and in some cases, perhaps unwittingly, asexual. It is time to consider the value of legitimizing queerness in a figure so widely considered to be such, and to swing open the door of what the consideration of that queerness might bring to the future of Lovecraftian studies. Because maybe, just possibly, Lovecraft was not just sex-repressed; he was asexual.

Works Cited

Ahmed, Sara. *The Cultural Politics of Emotion*. New York: Routledge, 2015.

The Asexual Visibility and Education Network. www.asexuality.org/. Accessed February 2023.

Bradway, Tyler, and E. L. McCallum. "Introduction: Thinking Sideways, or An Untoward Genealogy of Queer Reading." In Tyler Bradway and E. L. McCallum, ed. *After Queer Studies: Literature, Theory and Sexuality in the 21st Century*. Cambridge: Cambridge University Press, 2019.

de Camp, L. Sprague. *Lovecraft: A Biography*. 1975. London: New English Library, 1976.

del Toro, Guillermo. "Haunted Castles, Dark Mirrors: On the Penguin Horror Series." In Edgar Allan Poe. *The Raven: Tales and Poems*. New York, Penguin Books, 2013. lx–xxx.

Derie, Bobby. *Sex and the Cthulhu Mythos*. New York: Hippocampus Press, 2014.

Emrys, Ruthanna, and Anne M. Pillsworth. "Lovecraft's Most Bigoted Story, No Really: 'The Horror at Red Hook.'" *Tor.com* (21 September 2020. www.tor.com/2015/03/03/lovecrafts-most-bigoted-story-no-really-the-horror-at-red-hook/. Accessed February 2023.

Everts, R. Alain. "Howard Phillips Lovecraft and Sex: Or the Sex Life of a Gentleman." 1974. *The H. P. Lovecraft Archive*, 22 June 2012, www.hplovecraft.com/study/articles/hpl-sex.aspx. Accessed February 2023.

Hari, Johann. "Johann Hari: The Hidden History of Homosexuality in the US." *The Independent*, Independent Digital News and Media (21 June 2011). www.independent.co.uk/news/world/americas/johann-hari-the-hidden-history-of-homosexuality-in-the-us-2300636.html. Accessed February 2023.

Joshi, S. T. "Lovecraft's Alien Civilizations: A Political Interpretation" *Crypt of Cthulhu* No. 32 (St. John's Eve 1985): 8–24, 31.

———, ed. *The H. P. Lovecraft Centennial Conference Proceedings*. West Warwick, RI: Necronomicon Press, 1991.

LaVine, Morgana. "Lovecraft and the Male Gender Role." *Crypt of Cthulhu* No. 8 (Michaelmas 1982): 14–15.

Morgan, Thaddeus. "When Hollywood Studios Married Off Gay Stars to Keep Their Sexuality a Secret." *History.com* (10 July 2019) www.history.com/news/hollywood-lmarriages-gay-stars-lgbt. Accessed February 2023.

"Non-Normative." *NON-NORMATIVE Definition | Cambridge English Dictionary*, dictionary.cambridge.org/us/dictionary/english/non-normative. Accessed February 2023.

Price, Robert M. "Homosexual Panic in 'The Outsider.'" *Crypt of Cthulhu* No. 8 (Michaelmas 1982): 11–13.

Przybylo, Ela. *Asexual Erotics: Intimate Readings of Compulsory Sexuality*. Columbus: Ohio State University Press, 2019.

Sedgwick, Eve Kosofsky. *Tendencies*. Durham, NC: Duke University Press, 1993.

Stockton, Kathryn Bond. *The Queer Child, or Growing Sideways in the Twentieth Century*. Durham, NC: Duke University Press, 2009.

Wiktionary. en.wiktionary.org/wiki/satyr. Accessed February 2023.

Toward a Definition of Lovecraft Punk

Heather Miller
Independent Scholar

HUMANITY WON'T BE HAPPY UNTIL THE LAST BUREAUCRAT IS HUNG WITH THE GUTS OF THE LAST CAPITALIST.
—Branka Bogdanov, *On the Passage of a Few People through a Rather Brief Moment in Time: The Situationist International 1957–1972*

... In the UK, the term was not favoured by the leading lights of the new movement, and it took a while to stick. For example, in October 1976 a major article by Jonh Ingham in the music weekly *Sounds* was titled "Welcome to the (?) Rock Special," suggesting that at that point nobody quite knew what to call it.

A month later, however, the Sex Pistols swore on live TV. The next day, the word "punk" was all over the newspapers, and—for better or worse—was here to stay.
—Wilcox, Linehan, and Cleary, "From Shakespeare to Rock Music"

Punk, as a music genre and a visual mode attached to a particular attitude, should be no stranger to most Western readers. It developed from an underground musical movement into a freestanding social and cultural form, then over time became a suffix attached to other concepts: steampunk, cyberpunk, and the like. As a genre for those with "nothing better to do / than watch TV and have a couple of brews,"[1] punk was nevertheless a prolific cultural influence: art, music, clothing, and design changed profoundly after its advent, and punk visual referents became part of the common pop cultural language of the West. Punk's longevity led to its subsummation, but a closer look at the gift of fire that punk offered the world will help illuminate its importance to Lovecraftian studies.

We in the West know what punk looked like in visual terms: it was a chaotic, dangerous version of the advice to brides to wear "something old /

---

1. Black Flag's song "TV Party" is a scornful, ironic examination of the induced helplessness modernity brings about and possibly even references Guy Debord's *The Society of the Spectacle*.

something new / something borrowed / something blue," except it tended instead toward "something black / something torn / something messy / something scorned." It was do-it-yourself, immediate, and, above all, young (Worley 77). Punk was disruptive. Grimy, intense, raw, unfiltered. Loud. Unbound by the complications faced by conventional performers in the music industry, punk was an "antidote to egocentric and overly produced progressive rock" (Hodgson). Punk's roots were in the images, sounds, and expressions of the International Situationists movement (Bogdanov), and because of these roots, whose artistic projects laid emphasis on the written word, punk was about the freedom of the individual personality to speak: "The Situationist International project was always a project of communication, an attempt to discover the forms of a new kind of free speech, and then to use them" (Bogdanov). The sheer passion of punk attracted people who sought personalities that resonated with their own. They sought others who shared experiences outside the safe, middle-class world of popular music. Punk was angst, emotion, and volume, "wild energy, chaos, and danger" (Pisado). Its style stood up against capitalism, conformity, and "the establishment" (Hodgson). Punk was a middle finger to the safe, middle-class comforts that many Westerners used to dull themselves to the horrors on the news. Punk wanted above all to be heard.

Whence all this rage, then, when the American project was already about radical individualism and making oneself heard? Would not punk's message have been redundant? Perhaps to an extent it would have been in America, but not in Europe, at least not at first, where punk flourished (see, for example, Worley on the UK political environment of punk's origins). Shane Greene, author of numerous articles on punk in general and punk music in South America in particular, and self-titled "misanthropologist," observes that punk "generates its own set of ideologically constructed values that revolve, however ironically, around the very idea of antinormativity" (271). Punk raged against norms, conformity, and middle-class numbness. To be punk, then, was to embrace some stance that opposed the norm—whichever way those norms faced at the time.

This means that we have some fairly long bridges to cross between punk and Lovecraft. The two do not immediately strike one as having many similarities. We must note carefully how Lovecraft and the Lovecraftian can differ from punk. Lovecraft valued civility and decorum. He was a passionate Anglophile, and in his youth it colored his racial views (although, as S. T. Joshi notes in multiple publications, Lovecraft's stance was ameliorated after his return from New York).[2] Lovecraft was solitary much of the time though an inveterate correspondent, introverted though perfectly charming and outgoing when among friends, and not particularly good at music. He was formal, scholarly, and a bit class conscious. Many of these aspects of Lovecraft's attitudes and personality would be antithetical to punk. Upon closer examination, however, there are key points of overlap, enough so that we will eventually be able to characterize Lovecraft punk as an iteration of punk that shares common ground with it in the mutual battle against inhumanity.

First, though, we must examine some of the context for this idea of Lovecraft punk. In some ways Lovecraft punk was inevitable, given the pervasiveness of Cthulhoid imagery in popular culture. But to approach a definition of Lovecraft punk, we will need to begin by discussing a figure I call "Lovecraft's Hamlet," taken from his discussion of Hamlet in an early letter to Alfred Galpin. After that discussion, we can turn to the ways in which punk culture—a general approach—can be shown to have unexpected but invigorating similarities with Lovecraft's worldview. Note that this study is not about how Lovecraft was a proto-punk: he was unequivocally not one. Nor does this study offer the theory that punk really began in the 1920s; it did not. What this study does is draw some lines between Lovecraft's thought and ways that punk engaged with the world, finding important parallels between the two that have heretofore gone unnoticed and that may provide interesting new routes for future approaches to Lovecraft.

While reading some of Lovecraft's early letters, I came across a passage where Lovecraft discusses his take on *Hamlet*, specifically the moment when Hamlet enters what so many critics have called his madness. In a letter to Alfred Galpin of November 1918, Lovecraft observes:

> [Hamlet] now loses the subtle something which impels persons to go on in the ordinary currents; specifically, he loses the convictions that the usual motives and pursuits of life are more than empty illusions or trifles. Now this is not "madness"—I am sick of hearing fools and superficial criticks [sic] prate about "Hamlet's madness." It is really a distressing glimpse of *absolute truth*. But *in effect* it approximates mental derangement. Reason is unimpaired, but Hamlet no longer sees any occasion for its use. He perceives the objects and events about him, and their relation to each other and to himself, as clearly as before; but his new estimate of their importance, and his lack of any aim or desire to pursue an

---

2. See, for example, Joshi on Houellebecq as well as Joshi's essay on how not to read HPL, both in the Works Cited list.

ordinary course amongst them, impart to his point of view such a contemptuous, ironical singularity that he may well be thought a madman by mistake. (*Letters to Alfred Galpin* 220)

Hamlet's glimpse of absolute truth is an awakening, a moment of conversion. Hamlet's loss of faith in humanity is replaced with new understanding. It is a loss that is also a correction, a falling away that is also an expansion, even though it breeds in him "a contemptuous, ironical singularity." Just as Lovecraft's sense of human insignificance infused his weird fiction with cosmic horror and reoriented the genre,[3] Lovecraft's Hamlet reorients the notion of a tragic hero. This Hamlet is heroic not in his deeds but in his resistance. By recognizing the insignificance of others' beliefs, Lovecraft's Hamlet becomes that contemptuous, ironic, singular figure who is equally important to rock music in general and to punk in particular.[4] Even though this figure does not become part of the lyric inheritance of rock music or punk philosophy, Lovecraft's Hamlet is an important cornerstone for what can later be described as Lovecraft punk.

By embracing madness in order to reveal the truth about the murderers in the royal court, Lovecraft's Hamlet names uncomfortable, inconvenient truths aloud before the powerful, risking the consequences of his brashness for the sake of his integrity. As Lovecraft notes, this Hamlet is not mad; he is well-informed. His madness is that of the visionary who has grasped truths that will eventually become commonplaces. But because his brashness seems like madness to others, he is rejected, just as punk's brashness forced it to the edges of society.[5]

Despite the differences between Lovecraft and punk discussed earlier, the similarities between the two are striking. They both offer an intellectual curiosity that rejects the simple answers offered by positivist, conformist thought; they have at their respective cores the battle of the powerless against the over-

---

3. See Fritz Leiber's famous essay "A Literary Copernicus," available in, among other places, S. T. Joshi's *H. P. Lovecraft: Four Decades of Literary Criticism* (Athens: Ohio State University Press, 1980).

4. The classic example of this is the narrator of "Rise Above" by Black Flag, who howls "Society's arms of control / Rise above, we're gonna rise above / Think they're smart, can't think for themselves / Rise above, we're gonna rise above."

5. The irony of punk's eventual acceptance into mainstream culture is that its superficialities were adopted—torn clothing, brightly dyed hair, spiked jewelry—even as its philosophies of resistance were waved off.

whelmingly powerful; and they engage with and confront inhumanity.

Instead of embracing popular culture and its easy answers at the expense of other cultural forms,[6] both punk and Lovecraft embrace logic, intellectuality, the community of the like-minded, and the importance of uniqueness. Whereas this embrace is well documented in Lovecraft, in punk we see it readily in the lyrics of bands such as Fugazi, the already cited Black Flag, and Bad Religion, whose songs were recognized for their intellectual content and political commentary.

Both punk and Lovecraft question norms, too, with punk's questions about society and Lovecraft's questions about the value of human achievements arising from their mutual awareness of human insignificance in the face of overwhelming power structures. Punk's roots in challenging social power structures is well documented (see Worley's work on punk publications, as well as the punk manifesto of Greg Graffin, the lead singer of Bad Religion).[7] Although punk bands frequently pushed for social progress and broad change, and although Lovecraft cannot be said to have felt similarly until later in his life, punk and Lovecraft respectively observed the dehumanizing, reductive effects of modernity. The Northern Irish punk band Stiff Little Fingers released its debut album *Inflammable Material* in 1979, right in the middle of the Troubles, and its commentary on the effects of the Troubles is unsparing. For both Lovecraft and punk, the horrors are out there, and both confront inhumanity.

This confrontation is not a perfect one, of course. Lovecraft has been widely criticized for his early views on race, while Henry Rollins, punk musician and former leader of the punk band Black Flag, criticizes the constraints on freedom of thought that he sometimes ran into when he was active in punk. He recalls in a column in *American Songwriter* that "[l]yrics were often held to a high degree of scrutiny for their political correctness and anti-establishment quotient, lest they be too happy or shiny. In a genre that was supposed to be so do-what-you-want, the thought police were telling you how it was supposed to be." Punk endured further marginalization by offering song lyrics that reveal the truth about the powerful; similarly, Lovecraft courted rejection from editors and readers by writing weird fiction that emphasized

---

6. Although HPL did not enjoy many of the popular culture entertainments of his day, he did enjoy theater and films, especially the work of Charlie Chaplin, even composing a poem to him (AT 108–9).

7. Graffin's manifesto is on his blog and is listed in the works cited for this study; it was originally published as "EL COURTO!" on urbandictionary.com, 10 December 2007.

human insignificance rather than the raw male heroism commonly enjoyed by those readers. This willingness to state the truth regardless of consequence is an embrace of one's integrity, a matter sometimes lost on critics of both punk and Lovecraft.

Here we have the core of Lovecraft punk. More than a brash two-fingers-up at someone in a suit—which grants nothing but the pleasures of self-aggrandizement—Lovecraft punk sees beyond the superficialities of social class confrontations in Marxist debate, beyond the too-easy stances on politics, economics, and sumptuary codes found in subcultures and online movements. Lovecraft punk recognizes that it is impossible to speak truth to the kind of power that Lovecraft reckons with in his fiction, because those powers rarely, if ever, recognize human existence, much less attribute any value to humanity. And although the latter statement may seem a reversal from a socially engaged realism and a movement back into the basic premise of Lovecraft's weird fiction, keep in mind that the many -isms of our day—sexism, racism, and the like—have taken on a politico-cultural existence separate from people and thus cannot be called to account. Rather than being a reversal, this statement acknowledges that sometimes the battles we fight are within. Arguably, those -isms are the modern-day faceless forces we struggle against, the dehumanizing effects of which Lovecraft punk would recognize.

The powers Lovecraft conjured in his weird fiction may have gone by names such as "daemon-sultan Azathoth," but in reality they were forces that could roll over humanity like a car tire over a beetle. Whereas punk insists that human relevance is axiomatic, Lovecraft punk points out that relevance is manifested, first, in the moment of that beetle's recognition of the car tire's approach, and second, upon the beetle's escape and subsequent diary entry. For Lovecraft punk, some kind of communication of the experience of cosmic horror is critical. Human relevance does not exist solely in movements or masses, but in one human being's grappling with the communicated experience of another. Human relevance is personal, immediate, and connected. In some ways, Lovecraft punk may be that deep, important, human connection we all crave and with which the twentieth and now twenty-first century continue to struggle.

Just as Lovecraft punk needs no axiom, it also needs no audience, though it may publish its own zines and participate in the amateur press, as both Lovecraft and punk culture participants did.[8] Lovecraft punk is self-created,

---

8. See, for instance, numerous letters from HPL to various correspondents describing the

rather than being defined by the values of others, deriving its independence of spirit from Lovecraft's own well-documented independent streak.[9] It sees the reality behind the illusions held by others and, when exposing illusions through its punk prescience, knows that it may be ridiculed. With its independence and openness, Lovecraft punk does not rely on the opinions of others.

Lovecraft punk, then, resists the twentieth century in general: industrialism, modernity, and its knock-on effects—middle-class boosterism, the stultifying effects of middle-class conformity, and the reactionary politics that followed. Quite naturally, this carries over into the twenty-first century, with its ongoing inability to resolve the issues brought about by the end of the social orders that fell, first after World War I, and conclusively after World War II.[10] Our century continues to reckon with the racial and economic divides that were ignored in the twentieth century. Lovecraft's commitment to realism, his sense of place, and his burgeoning mythos, which pointed to humankind's ultimate fate, are each important parallels to punk culture's grasp of its disappearing future. Just as there was no future in punk, for Lovecraft, there is no future for humankind.

More than anywhere else, however, we can expect to find Lovecraft punk in literature, and it should come as no surprise to some readers that Lovecraft punk can be extended to fiction. Jeffrey Thomas's world in his story collection *Punktown* draws on cosmic horror as one of its themes, brought closer to the human scale in stories such as "The Reflections of Ghosts."

In this story, the main character Drew[11] is an artist who uses his own DNA to clone himself, then makes artistic statements with his clones. By manipulating their development, Drew enables some clones to possess full bodies, others only partial bodies. They lack full sentience and free will, a matter

---

publications he produced and distributed himself as a youth.

9. HPL's letters are rife with examples of his independence of thought. For instance, in a letter to Frank Belknap Long (SP letter 29), HPL discusses rejecting superficialities and instead embracing rejected and forgotten aspects of traditions. His doing so was perhaps his own way of raging against the vacuous pseudointellectualities of Modernists. Modernism was carrying the day, and HPL was having none of it.

10. Numerous authors have discussed the social and political changes after the two world wars, a topic that is outside the scope of this study.

11. Unlike other stories in this collection, in "The Reflections of Ghosts" these characters have only one name, reminding the reader of Genesis. Given the context of what little dialogue exists in the story, Drew is probably his first name.

emphasized at multiple points in the story, but they can still react to their surroundings. For Drew, they are all living works of art, and their purpose is to live as such. Some are sold to wealthy patrons, who dispose of them as they wish—the reader learns that they are often hunted, tortured, or killed during parties—while others Drew releases to wander the streets as walking art pieces, dully confused and uncared for. One patron's request, however, changes Drew's emotional connection with his art.

The first clone we encounter, quite early in the story, has been killed and is lying by a curb near Drew's home. To preserve the clone as an artwork, Drew coats the clone's body, right where it lies, in a thick layer of acrylic (Thomas 18-19). He has sold other clones to the wealthy for sexual use at parties, as victims during hunts, and for other equally unsavory pursuits. Yet more clones are on grisly display in his home. Drew has become comfortable with his disposition of his clones because he sees the clones as works of art, not parts of himself.

Drew is a Lovecraftian figure like Richard Upton Pickman of "Pickman's Model" and Crawford Tillinghast of "From Beyond." Drew toils away at a process that is disturbing to his friend and art dealer Sol, who has debated the ethics of it with him (23). Like both Pickman and Tillinghast, Drew is driven by an artist's needs and a scientist's desire to know. His background includes both the arts and medicine (24-25), which makes possible his ability both to clone himself and to make works of art out of the clones. Pickman's art and Tillinghast's machine are devices to mediate their respective creators with things beyond, and Drew's clones fill his need for a similar extension of self that Pickman and Tillinghast experience.

As an artist, Drew has hardened himself so that he can be what he believes is a better artist of his own flesh. He obliterates most of the clones' minds ("nothing more human than a starfish" [21]), changes their appearance so that they no longer resemble him (20), then sells or releases them with no further thought. Because Drew has told himself that they are works of art, not human beings, he believes he bears no responsibility once they are out of his hands (21).

Beyond Pickman and Tillinghast, Drew is the creator, like Victor Frankenstein, whose inhumanity eclipses that of his creation. After recalling one debate with Sol over the ethics of his actions, Drew muses:

> Even if people did not venture close enough to see his branded signature, even if they never knew Drew's name, even if they thought the thing was a painted madman, a mutant, an alien being or a true demon, they would marvel at it, and even if Drew never saw them marvel, he was gratified knowing that they did.

> Whether people gazed in admiration or horror, he knew they gazed, and in gazing at his creations they gazed at him, their creator. (21)

This stance is that of a subject rooted in inhumanity, the gaze of the privileged, the status of sentience and artistic lineage, the perverted valorization of the artist, and ends up as the reversal of the subject and object. Drew receives the gaze of the spectator, which is the traditional position of the object rather than the subject and has traditionally been interpreted as the lesser position. The power in the relationship between subject and object has usually been given to the possessor of the gaze, not its recipient. But here the artist becomes the work of art, in a sense erasing the value of the work by superimposing himself onto it.

Even as he demonstrates repulsive artistic motivations, Drew represents the worst of capitalism. He defines the idea of the "human" largely as a mirror of himself. He plays God with his clones while denying that he is doing so, selling human beings into slavery and torture and forcing other clones into homelessness by pushing them out onto the streets, all the while describing it as "art." He preens himself with the knowledge that his patrons see him as a creator and artist. Drew can maintain this ethical self-delusion for only as long as he remains emotionally disconnected from his work; his mistake occurs when he creates a female version of himself for a patron, a creation with slightly more intelligence than he usually permits his clones to carry.[12]

Drew himself is in no way punk, but his female clone very much is. The girl is necessarily compliant with Drew's wishes but is awakened, dimly, when he has sex with her shortly after he takes her out of the tank of amniotic fluid. The reader is unsurprised when Drew is first sexually, then emotionally attracted to his female clone, given Drew's self-obsession. As the girl grows vaguely more involved with the world around her, she seemingly comes to understand something about her own existence and that of Drew's other clones, though we cannot know precisely what she understands because she cannot speak.

During the days that follow, the reader sees that she vaguely understands the creations in Drew's apartment (29–30), one of which is a clone pinned to the apartment wall with "[i]ts chest . . . opened up in two wide sheets like a spread cowhide, the flaps of a dissected frog belly, spiked to the wall. The ribs showed through a translucent membrane, as did the nest of fat bluish intestines" (23). To amuse his infrequent guests, Drew uses a keyboard to make

---

12. Thomas does not explicitly state it in the story, but the implication is that the girl is the first female clone Drew has created.

the limbs and eyeless head move via electrical spasms. Another creation is a cloned head in a jar that Drew has nicknamed "Robespierre," its eyes rolling open whenever Drew taps on the jar to amuse himself.

One night, the girl releases the crucified clone from its place on the wall and spikes its brain in a mercy killing, then carries Robespierre with her as she jumps off the balcony of Drew's apartment building. Her final act underlines her authority over her own life even as it ends both. The moral gaps in what Drew does are staggering to the reader, and on an individual level, his actions are everything that both punk and Lovecraft would rail against. The girl may not have been able to take to the streets or lead a movement, but she was able to do one of the most punk things of all: look her creator square in the eye and deny his authority to control her.

In Thomas's story, just as in Lovecraft before him, the punk is the one who knows and sees the weird, the fringe, and the border zone and is the first to call out the inhumanity he sees there. Thomas's story forces the reader to consider how humanity treats itself, how it uses itself for terrible ends, how it has utter disregard for itself even as it exalts itself.

"The Reflection of Ghosts" also forces us to question what "real" life is. Is it mere sentience? Are Drew's creations somewhere between man and animal? Does he rightfully maintain the power to do as he wishes with them and to let others do with them as they wish? Are the clones any less valuable simply because they are not artists? Is the degree of ego that Drew exhibits necessary? Does being an artist force a kind of distance from compassion? Does compassion weaken us? Does compassion keep us from finding the answers? Thomas's story rightfully does not attempt to answer these difficult questions but instead leaves them with the reader as signposts or even interpretive placards.

Lovecraft punk asks us to look at the world through different eyes. Mere rebellion is insufficient, and withdrawal leaves the way open for evil. Lovecraft punk does not ask us to entertain hope, but it does ask us to consider courage—the courage to look inside humanity, including meeting our own humanness and hopelessness, and use what we find within to battle the horrors we face without.

Works Cited

Bogdanov, Branka, director. *On the Passage of a Few People through a Rather Brief Moment in Time: The Situationist International 1956–1972*. Institute of Contemporary Art, Boston, 1989. *YouTube*, uploaded by Counter Publics

(4 December 2021). youtu.be/eBlSBI64UxY.

Debord, Guy. *The Society of the Spectacle*. 1967. Tr. Ken Knabb. Berkeley, CA: Bureau of Public Secrets, 2014.

Graffin, Greg. "The True Definition of Punk: A Punk Manifesto." 2007. punxinsolidarity.wordpress.com/2013/10/22/punk-manifesto-by-greg-graffin/. Accessed 4 August 2022.

Greene, Shane. "On Punk and Repulsion: A Misfit Theory of Society." In Gretchen Bakke and Marina Peterson, ed. *Anthropology of the Arts: A Reader*. New York: Bloomsbury Academic Press, 2017. 263–73.

Hodgson, Stewart. "Punk and Disorderly: The Enduring Impact of Punk Rock on Design and Culture." *Punktuation* (1 July 2020). www.punktuationmag.com/punk-and-disorderly-the-enduring-impact-of-punk-rock-on-design-and-culture/. Accessed 10 July 2023.

Joshi, S. T. "How Not to Read Lovecraft." stjoshi.org/review_ruins.html. Accessed 20 February 2023.

———. "Why Michael Houellebecq Is Wrong About Lovecraft's Racism." *Lovecraft Annual* No. 12 (2018): 43–50.

Lovecraft, H. P. *Letters to Alfred Galpin and Others.*, Ed. S. T. Joshi and David E. Schultz. New York: Hippocampus Press, 2020.

Pisalo, Alex. "The Punk Art Movement." *Art Diction* (25 June 2020). www.artdictionmagazine.com/the-punk-art-movement/. Accessed 11 July 2023.

Rollins, Henry. "Henry Rollins on Songwriting." *American Songwriter* 14 (November 2013). americansongwriter.com/songwriter-u-henry-rollins-songwriting/. Accessed 10 August 2022.

Thomas, Jeffrey. *Punktown*. Gaithersburg, MD: Prime, 2005.

Wilcox, Zoe, Andy Lineham, and Stephen Cleary. "From Shakespeare to Rock Music: The History of the Word 'Punk.'" *British Library English and Drama* (26 August 2016). blogs.bl.uk/english-and-drama/2016/08/from-shakespeare-to-rock-music-the-history-of-the-word-punk.html. Accessed 16 July 2023.

Worley, Matthew. "Punk, Politics, and British (fan)zines, 1976–84: 'While the World Was Dying, Did You Wonder Why?'" *History Workshop Journal* No. 79 (2015): 76–106.

The Window to Madness: Creativity in Lovecraftian Fiction

Kyle Gamache
Ph.D., Community College of Rhode Island

The most merciful thing in the world, I think, is the inability of the human mind to correlate all its contents. We live on a placid island of ignorance in the midst of black seas of infinity, and it was not meant that we should voyage far. The sciences, each straining in its own direction, have hitherto harmed us little; but some day the piecing together of dissociated knowledge will open up such terrifying vistas of reality, and of our frightful position therein, that we shall either go mad from the revelation or flee from the deadly light into the peace and safety of a new dark age.

–H. P. Lovecraft, "The Call of Cthulhu" (CF 2.21)

The belief that creativity and insanity are linked has been accepted by society for millennia. Indeed, the speculation and dispute around this supposed link may be the oldest question in behavioral science (Becker "Association" 45). The concept is often presented in one of two ways, leading to two common and interconnected hypotheses. The first is that madness leads to great insight and creativity, the mad-genius motif. The second is that creativity is the cause of insanity, leading to the concept of the tragic, doomed artist. These two themes are interrelated, and elements of both are present in fictional characters and in interpretations of historic artists. This madness-creativity link is frequently presented in media, philosophy, and popular culture, occurring so often that it has become a standard trope in fiction.

The connection between madness and genius is displayed in the weird fiction of H. P. Lovecraft, who was influenced by the voluminous history of the archetype and took it in new directions. This paper explores this connection by discussing the concept in detail with historical context, then exploring its use in Lovecraft's fiction.

The Origins of the Madness-Creativity Link

Antiquity

Most scholarship on creativity and madness traces the origins of the hypothesis to ancient Greece, with Greek philosophers questioning the nature of creativity and the relationship it has with the divine. This led to the dual exploration of *theia mania* and *melancholia*. Plato described *theia mania* as "divine madness," whereby a supernatural servant of the gods (the *daemon*) possessed the poet or philosopher, allowing for the gods to work their will on the world by inspiring the human vessel (Becker, "Overview" 5-6; Plato 244-45, 265; Schlesinger, "Mythconceptions" 62). This "touch of madness" yielded a gift of poetic creativity and prophetic insight, but was temporary, lasting only long enough for the inspired to create their work.

Expanding on this, Aristotle posed the question, "Why is it that all those who have become eminent in philosophy or politics or poetry or the arts are clearly [melancholic]"? (953a10-14; Akiskal and Akiskal 2). Aristotle's reference here is to the Hippocrates' humor theory, in which the human body consists of four humors—fluids that must be in harmony for the individual to be healthy. Imbalance of these fluids results in disharmony and illness. The *melancholic* type of person had an excess of black bile, and this resulted in *melancholia*, a state where an individual experiences intense emotion, sensitivity, and excitement. Aristotle suggests that it is in this state that chaotic creativity can be harnessed (Becker, "Overview" 5-6). Seneca the Younger interpreted Aristotle's meaning with the famous quotation: "No great genius has existed without a touch of madness" (287; Motto and Clark 190).

These two elements probably birthed the creativity-madness association, and out of this the modern negative connotation became attached to it. Over the centuries, Plato's divine madness has been increasingly related to mental illness, particularly disorders involving psychosis and mania (Angst and Marneros 4; Jamison 2-10). Furthering this negative opinion, Christianization in Europe lead to the daemon becoming associated with evil spirits (Becker, "Overview" 5-6). Society also began to see Aristotle's connection of creativity and melancholic states as being associated with clinical illness (i.e., symptoms of melancholy). These two components are frequently cited in the literature as the origin of the creativity-madness link, often with quotations from Aristotle, Plato, or other Greek philosophers. The irony is that this association is probably related to poor interpretations and misunderstanding of the beliefs of the ancient Greeks (Padel 13-20). *Theia mania* was not considered the same as the clinically debilitating syndrome of mania, nor was it considered mental illness; instead, the divine madness was thought of as a true gift of the gods and eagerly sought out. Also, the general melancholic state that Aristotle references is not related to later conceptions of depression but rather is a neutral, if suboptimal, state (Becker, "Overview" 5-6; Schlesinger, "Mythconceptions" 62-63; "Connections" 67-68). These mischaracterizations have strengthened the idea of the mad-genius by adding a veneer of ancient knowledge, entrenching the concept in society's collective memory regardless of the truth of its origins.

Contrasting Perspectives of the Mad-Genius During the Renaissance and Enlightenment Periods

The transition between the benign perspective on creativity and madness of the ancient Greeks to the ominous trope of the mad-genius took centuries to occur. Philosophers of the Roman era generally agreed with their Greek counterparts, with occasional hints at mundane explanations of creativity such as Horace's adage "no poems can please for long or live that are written by water-drinkers" (*Epistles* 1.19.2). In the Middle Ages of Europe, little interest or thought was devoted to the origins of creativity, with the Greek concepts being largely ignored or forgotten (Becker, "Overview" 8-13; "Association" 46-53).

The Renaissance brought renewed interest in art and philosophy and with it a renewed investigation into the origin of creativity and the concept of genius. Whereas the Greeks' interest lay in intellectual and dramatic pursuits, the Renaissance also supported manual artistic endeavors such as sculpting and painting. As the Renaissance progressed, creativity was tied to the concept of the *genio*—an individual of vastly superior creativity with the ability to mimic the virtuosi of old and imitate the splendor of nature (the *imitation-ideal*). Later during the period, the focus on imitation was challenged and gradually replaced with the more contemporary need for unique creation and personal vision (Becker, "Overview" 12-13).

An early shift in the creativity-madness hypothesis can be seen with the writings of Marsilio Ficino (1433-1499), the Italian scholar and priest. Ficino returned to the Greek attribution of melancholic states as being related to creativity. This *pazzia*—or madness—was closely aligned with Greek perspectives of *theia mania* and differentiated it from the state of illness (Becker, "Overview" 12-13; Schlesinger, "Connections" 68). Again, as with the Greeks, melancholic states were not generally associated with the grim melancholy of the later Romantic period, and were viewed in a positive light. Indeed, a brooding and moody persona became popular, as it was increasingly associated with greatness (Babb 66, 71; Becker, "Overview" 12-13; Wittkower and Wittkower 93-101). It is worth noting that Ficino suffered from depression and alluded to the notion that great geniuses (like himself) often had some element of emotional disruption associated with the Aristotelian melancholia (Radden 87-93; Wittkower and Wittkower 93-101). At the close of the English Renaissance, Robert Burton stated that his creativity held his depressive melancholia at bay, perhaps setting the stage for the later link between creativity and illness (408-10; Schlesinger, "Connections" 68).

Echoing the Greek philosophers that preceded them, and significantly opposing the Romantic and contemporary views that would follow them, philosophers of the Enlightenment viewed creativity and genius as a hallmark of health. Additionally, creativity/genius was no longer defined by the *imitation-ideal* but instead was regarded as the creation not only of something beautiful but also something unique and novel. Exemplifying this core perspective of the Enlightenment, the creative genius needed to be rational, balanced, and probably drawn from the cultural and social elite (Becker, "Overview" 12-13). Blaise Pascal (1623-1662), mathematician and philosopher, noted that to use their talents, geniuses needed to resist the intoxicating lure of unfettered imagination. Thus, the emotional instability or insanity later associated with melancholia is incompatible with the genius of the Enlightenment, with the artist needing stability and rational judgment in order to constrain the chaotic energies of raw creativity. William Duff expanded on this in his *Critical Observations* (1770), reflecting directly on genius and madness, stating that there was little relationship between creativity and disorder. Nodding to the melancholic state described in the Renaissance, Duff noted that geniuses experienced emotion and drive more intensely and needed to subdue their passions to focus their energy. Following great creative effort, they could then descend into a calming and "sublime" melancholy to soothe themselves (262-69). This is obviously far from the troubled artist of the mad-genius model in later centuries, as the Enlightenment thinkers characterized artistic geniuses as almost superhuman in their composure and connection to divine Nature (Becker, "Overview" 12-15; "Association" 46).

The Romantic Notion of the Doomed Artist

The creativity-madness hypothesis, and the accompanying mad genius–doomed-artist character truly became solidified in the Romantic period of the nineteenth century. Rejecting the rationality and positivism of the Enlightenment, Romantic authors applauded rampant creativity, emotion, irrationality, and the almost reckless pursuit of truth and experience (Becker, "Overview" 10-13). The "gentleman genius" of the seventeenth and eighteenth centuries was replaced by poets and men of letters who often were not members of the aristocracy nor had great personal wealth or fame. In their rebellion against reason and order, Romantics abandoned control over creative impulses and the theories of the Enlightenment, leaving themselves at the mercy of chaotic imagination. While the Romantics embraced the ancient notions of melancholia and divine madness, organic mental illness increasingly was believed to be the cost of such creativity (Becker, "Overview" 10-13; "Association" 46).

This darkening perspective on creativity was on display in the works of Romantic authors as well as in the lives of the authors themselves. The archetype of the Romantic hero came into vogue: brooding heroes who have both rejected and been rejected by society, leaving them alone on their personal journeys. Often these characters experienced misfortune and loss, linking their passion and imagination with a tragic fate. Examples of this can be seen in characters in famous Romantic works, such as the titular characters in *Eugene Onegin* (Pushkin) and *Frankenstein* (Shelley), as well as Captain Ahab of *Moby-Dick* (Melville). Lord Byron further contributed with the variant "Byronic hero" with *Don Juan* and *Childe Harold's Pilgrimage*, a moody and darkly passionate character who incorporated elements of Byron's own persona (Poole).

With the Romantic hero, the creativity-and-madness link became established enough to birth the archetypes of the mad-genius and the doomed-artist, suggesting that the price of greatness was calamity and that there was a tragic beauty in artists suffering for their art. Alongside their creations, Romantic poets and men of letters equally contributed to the archetype with embellished and scandalous reports of their private lives. Several of the most influential writers, such as Byron, Percy Bysshe Shelley, and Oscar Wilde, appeared to revel publicly in personal chaos; like the gloomy melancholic of the Renaissance, the flamboyant and passionate writer became a sensational cultural icon (Becker, "Overview" 10-14; Chadwick 50; Schlesinger, "Connections" 68). Indeed, Lord Byron certainly contributed with his own bravado and with quotations such as: "We of the craft are all crazy. Some are affected by gaiety, others by melancholy, but all are more or less touched." The antics and musings of the Romantics, coupled with their profound influence and early deaths, entrenched the archetype in the public mind and it would eventually become a treasured pulp icon.

Edgar Allan Poe

In this review of Lovecraft's influences and the creativity-madness link, Edgar Allan Poe (1809-1849) deserves special focus. Poe was a pillar of the Romantic and Gothic literary traditions, an incredibly versatile writer who is credited with creating modern detective fiction. His grim explorations into the darkness of the human psyche were popular, and he remains a central figure in American literature (Meyers 280-99).

Poe is often remembered for his Gothic horror stories and his works often centered around gloomy topics. Two prominent stories that feature madness as a quality of the characters are "The Tell-Tale Heart" (1843) and "The Black Cat" (1843). In "The Tell-Tale Heart," the unnamed narrator obsesses about and murders a former friend due to his revulsion of this friend's eye. Similarly, in "The Black Cat," the unnamed narrator explains the brutal torture and killing of his formerly beloved cat. Both stories involve protagonists that succumb to sudden, murderous insanity, leaving their otherwise rational confessions disturbing and unreliable. The murderers are consumed with guilt and paranoia, and their crimes revealed. This frightening notion that madness was something that struck otherwise healthy individuals was popular in Poe's day and was in line with the increasingly negative view of divine madness.

Ultimately, while Poe's stories are dark in nature, it was the public's fusing of his work with his personal life that fostered the lasting impact on the mad-genius and doomed-artist archetypes. Poe's life was marked with tragedy and difficulty: poor family relationships, struggles with alcoholism, and the loss of his young wife Virginia. His scandalous affairs with Frances Osgood and Elizabeth Ellet shattered several of his personal relationships and made him the subject of salacious gossip worthy of Byron himself (Meyers 150-69). Also, like Byron and Shelley, Poe's own early, mysterious death as well as his chaotic life led to the public fitting him into the doomed artist motif (Neimeyer 205).

While Poe was living, and since his death, commentators have linked his personal tragedies with his dark writing, seeing it as a personification of his own inner turmoil. Sun (2015) comments that "he was doomed to live a lonely and miserable life all his lifetime. His creation reflected his unique life experience, which laid a strong foundation to the unique style of his work" (97). Poe's mystique and connection to the horror within his stories were further expanded upon by his adversaries, with Rufus Wilmot Griswold writing in Poe's obituary that his doomed and villainous characters contained "traces of his [own] personal character" and that Poe "walked the streets, in madness or melancholy" (2). During Poe's feud with his former friend Thomas Dunn English, English published *1844; or, The Power of the "S.F.,"* a novel focused on a caricature of a drunken Poe that ends with his confinement in a mental institution (1847). Poe certainly contributed to his characterization of "mad," both in his semi-autobiographical story "Eleonora" (1842) and in his responses to English's charges of plagiarism (1846). In "Eleonora," a story about the untimely death of a lover, the narrator states that "[m]en have called me mad; but the question is not yet settled, whether madness is or is not the loftiest intelligence; whether much that is glorious, whether all that is profound, does not spring from disease of thought" (373). Later, in his editorials in the *Spirit of the Times*, Poe describes his own struggles with grief and depression following the death of his wife, noting that he was "constitutionally sensitive—nervous in a very unusual degree" and had become "insane, with long intervals of horrible sanity" ("Poe's Reply").

This attention to Poe's character and connection to his gloomy work focused the study into how mental illness affected the troubled author. Shortly after Poe's death, eminent British psychiatrist Harold Maudsley made a case study of Poe, declaring that he suffered from intense melancholia related to a disturbed family life and grief (369). Maudsley was perhaps the first to diagnose Poe formally, but far from the last. As scholar Benjamin Reiss points out, a great deal of Poe scholarship is devoted to analysis of Poe's possible mental health and retroactive diagnoses (167). Perhaps even more than the Romantics mentioned earlier, Poe himself has been transformed into the archetypal doomed-artist and a mad-genius, and his tragic life and great contributions are often used as an example of the link between creativity and madness (Dietrich 1).

Psychology of Madness and Creativity

The preceding review studies how the creativity-madness link originated from philosophical and literary explorations serving as the basis of public thought on the construct. These allusions are primarily based in seeing madness as a force or characteristic that is closely related to creativity itself (Rothenberg 6). As discussed above, with the Romantic movement madness increasingly became associated with harmful and destructive behaviors, but it was with the budding field of psychology that the leap to clinical illness occurred. As the fields of psychiatry and psychology developed, mental illness was codified into diagnostic categories and behavior pathologized. Early French psychiatrist Louis-Francisque Lélut (1804-1877) is perhaps the first to link genius with madness, with his pamphlets *The Demon of Socrates* (1836) and *The Amulet of Pascal* (1846) claiming that both subjects suffered from mental illness. Lélut's work generated fevered exploration by psychologists to discover the presence of mental illness in the minds of the great geniuses and artists of history, with hundreds of articles giving examples of the now *clinical* creativity-madness relationship. The dominant position within psychological theory was that genius was closely related to, or a form of, pathology (Becker, *Mad Genius*). This obsession was well summarized in an anonymous report: "in many instances it is no longer a question as to whether a certain genius was insane or not. The modern query is: from what form of insanity did he suffer?" (Becker, "Overview" 17).

Italian criminologist Cesare Lombroso (1836–1909) is frequently cited as a foundational theorist driving the creativity and madness link with his phrenological assessments. In addition to skull and facial measurements of living subjects, Lombroso heavily scrutinized biographical data, histories, and communications of hundreds of people in developing his theories. In his often cited treatise *The Man of Genius* (1891), Lombroso observes that abnormality and moral insanity were synonymous with genius and that the more talent a person displayed the deeper his or her depths of depravity and insanity.

While scholars suggest that Lombroso had a profound influence on the pathologizing of creativity (Schlesinger, "Connections" 68), this negative connotation was challenged in early psychological research, most notably by Lewis Terman (1877-1956). Terman's seminal research was a longitudinal study of a large cohort of gifted and intelligent children, identifying common traits between them and arguing that highly gifted people were less likely to suffer from emotional disturbance when compared to the general population. Even with Terman's unfortunate association with the eugenics movement, his challenge served as a foundation for the counter position of the mad-genius debate, one more in line with the perspective of Enlightenment philosophers and later positive psychologists that genius was a trait of healthy individuals.

In the early twentieth century, another psychological movement contributed to the archetype of the mad-genius: psychodynamism. Sigmund Freud (1856-1939) developed a theory that focuses on the duality of the conscious and the unconscious mind, with the unconscious being the source of motivation and emotional energy. The unconscious mind was thought of as a primal force detached from reality, and was able to communicate to the conscious mind through latent means such as dreams. Freud himself was fascinated by art, seeing expression of psychodynamic concepts in the great works of Leonardo da Vinci and William Shakespeare (Rothenberg 50). He stopped short of stating that creativity was directly connected to the unconscious mind, something that his later followers were less shy about (Carson). As psychodynamic theory progressed, more attention was devoted to creativity, suggesting that creative inspiration and effort required a surrender to the tempest of the unconscious mind in the form of regression or ego disinhibition (Carson 200; Rothenberg 50). Thus, creativity and imagination were the domain of the irrational, impulsive, and emotional drives within the mind (Freud; Carson 200). This perspective matured earlier psychodynamic theory linking mental illness with creativity and solidifying the mad-genius archetype.

H. P. Lovecraft and the Creativity-Madness Link

H. P. Lovecraft is considered the father of weird fiction and cosmic horror. He frequently employed variations of the mad-genius and doomed-artist archetypes in his fiction, as well as in his conception of modern horror. His work and perspectives were influenced by multiple sources ranging from his exposure to classic authors to personal experiences in his own life.

Lovecraft, an intelligent youth, had early introduction to classical literature, English authors, and Greek mythology (*IAP* 38). As such, he was exposed to the same sources that shaped the creativity-madness link and the resulting literary characters. By his own recollection, he was obsessed with Greek myth and the *Odyssey* in particular (*CE* 5.143), which thereby connected him with the classic construct of *divine madness* (Maieron). In his seminal "Supernatural Horror in Literature," Lovecraft describes the classic characters of Gothic and Byronic heroes, citing tales of their dark fates as the foundation of modern horror (CE 2.100). The sensational and dramatic works of the Romantics readily developed the doomed-artist and mad-genius motifs, themes that Lovecraft saw as leading toward the developing genre of weird fiction (Pedersen).

Out of the Gothic Romantics, Lovecraft was significantly influenced by Edgar Allan Poe. Poe's writing and personal history forged Lovecraft's own perspective on the creativity-madness hypothesis. Poe's influence on Lovecraft cannot be overstated, as he famously described the unfortunate author as his "god of fiction" (Joshi and Schultz 207), stating that "Poe did that which no one else ever did or could have done; and to him we owe the modern horror-story" (CE 2.100). In "Supernatural Horror in literature," Lovecraft describes Poe's work as brilliantly cerebral, tying the intricacies of mental abnormality with analytical knowledge of true terror. Lovecraft further suggests Poe's influence on the later Decadents and dark Romantics such as Oscar Wilde (1854-1900) and Lord Dunsany (1878-1957), showing further echoes of Poe's influence in Lovecraft's own fiction. Lovecraft also linked Poe's dark genius with the author's unfortunate personal life and possible mental health issues. He states that Poe was constantly thinking about death and morbidity, and this influenced every aspect of Poe's professional effort, branding "his macabre work with the ineffaceable mark of supreme genius" (CE 2.103). Lovecraft lauds Poe's greatness and his departure from the Romantic/Byronic characters, forging his own style of character that is arguably the prototypical protagonist of weird fiction. In "Supernatural Horror in Literature," Lovecraft closes his chapter on Poe by linking his genius and insight to the "psychology of Poe himself, who certainly possessed much of the depression, sensitiveness, mad aspiration, loneliness, and extravagant freakishness which he attributes to his haughty and solitary victims of Fate" (CE 2.104). Here, Lovecraft can be seen exploring the creativity-madness hypothesis as an explanation for Poe's genius, and it is not an exaggeration to suggest that this can be applied to Lovecraft himself.

Like Poe, Lovecraft suffered from a number of tragedies and maladies that may have influenced his life and work. His parents both suffered from mental illness. His father Winfield was afflicted with psychosis, potentially due to syphilis, later being committed to Butler Hospital, where he died in 1898. His mother Sarah was plagued with grief over her husband's death for the remainder of her life, possibly leading to her later psychotic behavior. She was committed to Butler as well and died there in 1921. Lovecraft was profoundly affected by these losses and the effect they had on his family's financial stability. The death of his paternal grandfather in 1904 brought the loss of another father-figure and financial ruin to Lovecraft's family. Lovecraft described this period as the lowest of his life wrought with passive suicidality. He recovered from this, but his own struggles with mental health—probably connected to undiagnosed depression and anxiety—continued and led to a number of nervous breakdowns that disrupted his high school education and also prevented him from entering Brown University. The dissolution of his brief marriage probably further increased loneliness and isolation. Lovecraft died in obscurity and near poverty in 1937. Like Poe, the effect of Lovecraft's personal life and possible mental illness on his work has become a topic of scholarly research and public interest (Barker; Tyree).

Creativity and Madness in Lovecraft's Work

In "Supernatural Horror in Literature," Lovecraft describes the typical protagonist in Poe's work as

> generally a dark, handsome, proud, melancholy, intellectual, highly sensitive, capricious, introspective, isolated, and sometimes slightly mad gentleman of ancient family and opulent circumstances; usually deeply learned in strange lore, and darkly ambitious of penetrating to forbidden secrets of the universe. (CE 2.104)

In this summary of Poe's typical characters, we can see both the blueprint for Lovecraft's literary protagonists as well as the persona to which he may have personally aspired with his Anglophilia and intellectualism. Indeed, several of Lovecraft's protagonists are clearly Poe-esque, notably Edward Derby from "The Thing on the Doorstep" and Henry Wilcox from "The Call of Cthulhu." Lovecraft continues to explore this duality of character and creator in "Supernatural Horror in Literature," stating that to understand the "weird tale" one must have the "requisite sensitiveness" of the mind to perceive the world as it truly is and to explore the fantastic vistas that only come to us in dreams or madness (CE 2.103). This characterization is reminiscent of the earlier concept of "divine madness," and Lovecraft mentions this "sensitivity" several times in his essay, listing it as a requirement for authors, readers, and characters of the weird tale.

Lovecraft clearly believing that he had such sensitivity. This idea is present in many of his stories, often paired with art and creative energy. Creativity leads to the sensitivity to perceive and experience the weird. But, for

Lovecraft, creativity is not a mad gift that tragically burns the artist. Instead, it is a cruel window through which the doomed sensitive is impelled toward insanity and annihilation. In this way, Lovecraft fuses the doomed-artist and mad-genius characters, putting an even darker tint on the creativity and madness hypothesis. Examples are discussed below.

"The Haunter of the Dark" (1935)

In "The Haunter of the Dark," the protagonist Robert Blake is a writer and painter of some prestige, whose work was "wholly devoted to the field of myth, dream, terror, and superstition, and avid in his quest for scenes and effects of a bizarre, spectral sort" (CF 3.452). Blake is drawn to Federal Hill in Providence to compose his greatest work, drawing inspiration from his dreams of the unseen world and painting canvases of foul creatures and strange, alien landscapes. His proximity and sensitivity to these horrific vistas lead to his obsession with the cursed dark church on Federal Hill, which ultimately leads to his doom at the hands of the titular monster. The creativity-madness link is seen with Blake, both as the mad-genius in that his art is enhanced by the insanity of the Mythos, and as the doomed-artist because it is this insight that leads to his destruction.

"The Hound" (1922)

The two ghoulish characters in "The Hound" illustrate the creativity-madness trope, having descended into complete and horrific decadence in their obsession over perverse and morbid art. They gather gruesome charnel artifacts, including in their ghastly collection macabre paintings and foul musical instruments that surround a portfolio bound in human skin containing unspeakable drawings allegedly created by Francisco Goya (1746–1828). Their obsession leads to their doom: after stealing an amulet from a decrepit Dutch graveyard, the spectral guardian destroys both of them.

"The Picture in the House" (1920)

A rainstorm interrupts an afternoon bicycle ride, forcing the narrator of "The Picture in the House" to take refuge in a rotting New England farmhouse. In the house, the narrator meets the ancient resident and his strange book. The tome displays a series of engravings that depict bloody, cannibalistic ceremonies in vivid and incredible detail. The narrator's host explains that there is power in the pictures, implying hidden secrets of eternal life exist within the pages. The narrator believes the old man to be insane and only avoids becoming his next victim because of a lucky lightning bolt. The mad-genius is seen in this story with the art contained in the tome leading to insane and creative insight that allows an old bumpkin to live forever, albeit through ghastly rituals.

"Hypnos" (1922)

With "Hypnos," Lovecraft's protagonist is not a painter as is found in many of his works, but a sculptor of some skill who is drawn by "unsanctioned phrensy into mysteries no man was meant to penetrate" (CF 1.325). A chance meeting at a railway station leads to an intense relationship between the sculptor and a beautiful but strange gentleman. The sculptor becomes obsessed with his companion, thinking him a god, and sculpts him every night. Their discussions and dreams open the sculptor to new and terrible perspectives about reality. The horror of these revelations finally shatters the narrator's sanity. The sculptor summarizes that when he was found by the authorities, they claimed that he never had a friend and instead was obsessing over a sculpture that he had made. In closing, he observes that only "art, philosophy, and insanity had filled all [his] tragic life" (323). Madness is clearly at play in this story, but it is unclear if the sculptor's experiences are supernatural or the product of psychosis, but the result is the same: a gifted artist is driven to lunacy because of his art.

"The Music of Erich Zann" (1921)

The artist at the center of "The Music of Erich Zann" is not the unnamed narrator of the piece, but instead a neighbor in an ancient boarding house. The haunting music of Erich Zann gravely affects the narrator after he moves into the house. The narrator is vague about his origins, but he states that he is a student of metaphysics at a local university who is profoundly sensitive to the strange music of Erich Zann, a supremely gifted musician who plays fantastic and strange music nightly on his viol. The narrator becomes obsessed with the music and the mute musician, with Zann begrudgingly accepting a friendship with him. As the weeks pass, the narrator watches Zann become increasingly haggard and ill as he plays, but the music continues to grow in power. At the conclusion of the story, Zann agrees to explain to the narrator the origin of his eldritch music. His written explanation is interrupted by a mysterious presence at the window, forcing the elder musician to seize the viol and begin the most "fantastic, delirious, and hysterical" music the narrator has ever heard (CF 2.287). The small attic room is plunged into darkness and the narrator experiences horrific howling wind and sinister presences in the room while Zann's viol shrieks. As the narrator escapes, he attempts to bring Zann with him. Finding his friend in the darkness, he discovers that the old musician is dead yet still playing the demonic viol. The character of Zann exemplifies the doomed-artist, his fantastic musical prowess draining him of his health while he attempts to keep the darkness at bay with his viol.

"Pickman's Model" (1926)

Lovecraft's "love-letter" to art, "Pickman's Model," explores the author's fascination with art. The narrator Thurber is discussing art and the local art scene with his friend Eliot. The narrative touches upon some of Lovecraft's favorite artists, notably Goya, Gustave Doré, and Sidney Sime, noting that true artists can capture the horror of the real and fantastic worlds with vivid detail, possibly because both realms coexist. The main subject of the conversation, however, is Richard Upton Pickman, an artistic genius who focuses on grim and disgusting art Pickman's art presents the anatomy of fear in stark and brilliant detail through his gory and sinister paintings. His work unsettles the art community, so that he is kicked out of multiple art clubs and frays the nerves of Thurber. As he continues creating his grotesque art, Pickman experiences a slow, degenerative change. His descent is connected to his art, with Thurber stating that Pickman "wasn't strictly human. Either he was born in strange shadow, or he'd found a way to unlock the forbidden gate" (CF 2.72). Thus it is unclear if Pickman's inhuman nature gave him artistic insight or if his powerful art is gradually transforming him. Either way, Pickman is able to show the unknown horrors of the world as they really are, with Thurber concluding that he was the "greatest artist [he] had ever known—and the foulest being that ever leaped the bounds of life into the pits of myth and madness" (CF 2.72).

Elements of the mad-genius trope are prevalent throughout "Pickman's Model" in Thurber's musings on art and in the character of Pickman. Art is likened to a window into madness, showing us the horrors that exist hidden but all around us. Some of Lovecraft's beloved artists are deliberately mentioned in the piece, and it is noted that they all have the skill and creativity to show the world as it actually exists. Pickman has this ability above all. He is supremely gifted, and it is implied that his gifts come from his possible inhuman nature or his madness or both. For these reasons, "Pickman's Model" is probably the clearest example of the mad-genius in Lovecraft's stories.

"The Thing on the Doorstep" (1933)

"The Thing on the Doorstep" is a perfect example of a Lovecraftian protagonist who is also a "doomed-artist." Edward Pickman Derby is cut from Poe's archetype, being precocious and gifted, but also *sensitive* and delicate. His maladies lead to his being sheltered and coddled, fostering a "strange, secretive inner life in the boy, with imagination as his one avenue of freedom" (CF 3.325). Derby channels his creative energies into crafting fantastic poems of the most morbid and somber quality. Through his work and academic connections, Derby becomes entangled with occult and esoteric circles, ultimately causing him to be drawn to Asenath Waite. Their relationship, and later marriage, is a snare, allowing Asenath's wizard father Ephraim to seize control of Derby's body through foul magic. Derby had been chosen by the old sorcerer because of his sex, his weak will, and his sensitive mind. Thus, Derby is a mad-genius and a doomed-artist, with his vulnerability to the weird world enriching his poetry but ultimately leading to his mind being magically imprisoned in his wife's moldering corpse.

"The Call of Cthulhu" (1926)

A final story to explore is the seminal "The Call of Cthulhu." Arguably Lovecraft's most famous work, this story personifies Lovecraft's perspective on creativity and madness. The subject of the work is the rising of the titular entity, but it is in the monster's "call" that the creativity and madness link is shown. In the weeks leading up to Great Cthulhu rising from the South Pacific, a psychic ripple cascades around the world. The average person is unaffected by this spell, but scientific men were "more affected . . . [glimpsing] strange landscapes" and experiencing feelings of dread (CF 2.28). But, as the doomed narrator recounts, it is the "poets and artists" (28) who are most profoundly affected by the "thoughts that spread fear to the dreams of the sensitive" (50). Worldwide, creative people are struck with horrific dreams, maddening insights, and thoughts of suicide during the short few days when the nightmare city of R'lyeh surfaces. In essence, the more creative people are, the more susceptible they are to the madness and death that Cthulhu brings.

In addition to the general madness that befalls the artists worldwide, the narrator investigates the case of one Henry Wilcox of Providence, Rhode Island. Like many Lovecraftian characters before him, the gifted sculptor Wilcox "was a precocious youth of known genius but great eccentricity" hailing from an "excellent family" (25). Wilcox describes himself as "psychically hypersensitive" (25) and is responsible for sculpting a bas-relief of the monstrous Cthulhu. During the "call," Wilcox is struck with feverish delirium and wracked by terrible dreams that inspire his sculpture (27). Similar to Edward Derby from "The Thing on the Doorstep," it is implied that Wilcox's sensitivity allowed him to see Cthulhu in his dreams and, like the other artists worldwide, fuel his creative impulses towards the macabre and alien subjects.

Conclusion

The idea that creativity and madness are related to each other is ingrained in our culture, having been explored and pondered since antiquity. This has given rise to the two common archetypes of the doomed-artist and the mad-genius; but, in a broader sense, it has solidified in the public's mind the notion that in order to produce great art one must be mad, or that the creation costs artists their health, or both. The main issue with this trope is that it is insidious as, in a way, it glorifies and romanticizes the suffering of people afflicted with mental illness.

A dangerous trend in explorations of creativity and its relationship to mental illness is to utilize well-known artists who suffered from mental illness as proof of a link between illness and greatness. Indeed, some of the most often cited works on the subject (Andreasen's "Creativity and Mental Illness" and Jamison's *Touched with Fire*) discuss fabulous artists whose lives and work were tragically cut short due to suicide or substance abuse. And this perspective glamorizes the suffering of artists such as Sylvia Plath, Sarah Kane, Vincent Van Gogh, and countless others, as if these people were martyrs for their art (Hunt). This leads to the notion that one must suffer for one's art, and that attempts to alleviate suffering (e.g., mental health therapy, medication) will only diminish their artistic ability. This is obviously dangerous because it can result in artists ignoring or embracing their illnesses, often with fatal results. It is important to realize that many troubled artists who are frequently offered as examples of this idea were at their most creative and successful before or between episodes of mental illness (e.g., John Nash), and in essence their mental illness ultimately cut their careers short, robbing them and the world of their genius (Carson 219; Prentky). Still, there is a romance in the notion that artists must in essence be punished for their art, and it allows average people to process possible envy they feel for talents that have been denied to them. Ultimately, Schlesinger places the blame for the creativity-madness myth on the audience, asking whether "Van Gogh's vibrant colors fade [if] you learn that somebody else sliced off his ear?" ("Connections" 72). The objective answer should be no; but perhaps, if we are honest with ourselves, our answer would probably be confirmatory.

Lovecraft's influence on modern horror literature cannot be overstated. To quote Stephen King in *Danse Macabre*:

> [I]t is beyond doubt that H. P. Lovecraft has yet to be surpassed as the twentieth century's greatest practitioner of the classic horror tale. . . . Lovecraft . . . opened the way for me as he had done for others before me. . . . [I]t is his shadow, so long and gaunt, and his eyes, so dark and puritanical, which overlie almost all of the important horror fiction that has come since. (102)

To his credit, Lovecraft's conceptualization of the creativity and madness hypotheses is not supportive of any of his philosophic predecessors, or of the attitude of the general public on the matter. Even though he was well versed in the concept and knew well the public's perceptions of his hero Poe, Lovecraft does not romanticize the idea of illness or expect his protagonists to suffer beautifully for their visions. Creativity opens up the subject to the horrible truth of the cosmos, and it is only through ignorance that we are able to hold onto sanity. For Lovecraft, there is no love for creativity but instead fear about what horrible insights creativity can reveal about unknown and sinister vistas that are better left undisturbed and unexplored.

Works Cited

Akiskal, H. S., and K. K. Akiskal. "In Search of Aristotle: Temperament, Human Nature, Melancholia, Creativity and Eminence." *Journal of Affective Disorders* 100 (2007): 1-6.

Andreasen, N. C. "Creativity and Mental Illness: Prevalence Rates in Writers and Their First Degree Relatives." *American Journal of Psychiatry* 144 (1987): 1228-92.

Angst, J., and A. Marneros. "Bipolarity from Ancient to Modern Times: Conception, Birth and Rebirth." *Journal of Affective Disorders* 67 (2001): 3-19. doi:10.1016/s0165-0327(01)00429-3

Aristotle. "Problems Connected with Practical Wisdom, Intelligence, and Wisdom." Tr. E. S. Foster. In *The Complete Works of Aristotle*, Volume 2. Ed. J. Barnes. Princeton, NJ: Princeton University Press, 1984. 1498-502.

Babb, Lawrence. *The Elizabethan Malady: A Study of Melancholia in English Literature from 1580 to 1642*. East Lansing: Michigan State College Press. 1951.

Barker, Clive. *Clive Barker's A-Z of Horror*, Comp. Stephen Jones. London: BBC Books. 1997.

Becker, George. "A Socio-Historical Overview of the Creativity-Pathology Connection: From Antiquity to Contemporary Times." In James C. Kaufman, ed. *Creativity and Mental Illness*. Cambridge: Cambridge University Press, 2014. 3–24.

———. "The Association of Creativity and Psychopathology: Its Cultural-Historical Origin." *Creativity Research Journal* 13 (2001): 45–53.

———. *The Mad Genius Controversy: A Study in the Sociology of Deviance*. Beverley Hills, CA: Sage, 1978.

Burton, Robert. *The Anatomy of Melancholy*. 1621. New York: New York Review Books, 2001.

Byron, George Gordon, Lord. *Childe Harold's Pilgrimage*. New York: G. Munro, 1886.

———. *Don Juan*. Boston: Phillips, Sampson & Co., 1856.

Carson, Shelly. "Cognitive Disinhibition, Creativity, and Psychopathology." In Dean Keith Simonton, ed. *The Wiley Handbook of Genius*. Chichester, UK: John Wiley & Sons, 2014. 198–221.

Chadwick, Peter. "Decadence as Growth: Oscar Wilde and the Renewal of Romanticism." *Wildean* No. 34 (January 2009): 50–60.

Dietrich, Amy. "The Mythconception of the Mad Genius." *Frontiers in Psychology* No. 79 (2014): 1–3.

Duff, William. *Critical Observations on the Writings of the Most Celebrated Original Geniuses in Poetry: Being a Sequel to the Essay on Original Genius*. London: Printed for T. Becket and P. A. De Hondt, 1770.

English, Thomas Dunn. *1844; or, The Power of the "S.F."* New York: Burgess, Stringer & Co., 1847.

Freud, Sigmund. *An Outline of Psychoanalysis*. New York: W. W. Norton. 1949.

Griswold, Rufus Wilmot. "Death of Edgar A. Poe." *New York Daily Tribune* (9 October 1849): 2.

Horace. *The Satires, Epistles and Ars Poetica*. Tr. H. R. Fairclough. New York: G. P. Putnam's Sons, 1925.

Hunt, M. "It's Time to Finally Retire the Myth of the Tortured Artist." *The Link* (7 April 2020). thelinknewspaper.ca/article/its-time-to-finally-retire-the-myth-of-the- tortured-artist

Jamison, Kay. *Touched with Fire: Manic-Depressive Illness and the Artistic Temperament.* New York: Free Press, 1996.

Joshi, S. T., and David E. Schultz. *An H. P. Lovecraft Encyclopedia.* Westport, CT: Greenwood Press, 2001.

King, Stephen. *Danse Macabre.* New York: Everest House, 1981.

Lélut, Louis-Francisque. *Du demon de Socrate* [The Demon of Socrates]. Paris: Trinquart, 1836.

———. *L'amulette de Pascal* [The Amulet of Pascal]. Paris: Trinquart, 1846.

Lombroso, Cesare. *The Man of Genius.* London: Walter Scott, 1891

Maudsley, Henry. "Edgar Allan Poe." *Journal of Medicine* 6, No. 2 (1860): 328-69.

Maieron, Mario Augusto. "The Meaning of Madness in Ancient Greek Culture from Homer to Hippocrates and Plato." *History of Medicine* 1, No. 2 (2017): 65-76.

Melville, Herman. *Moby-Dick.* New York: Dodd, Mead, 1922.

Meyers, Jeffery. *Edgar Allan Poe: His Life and Legacy.* New York: Cooper Square Press, 1992.

Motto, A. L., and J. R. Clark. "The Paradox of Genius and Madness: Seneca and His Influence. *Cuadernos de Filología Clásica: Estudios latinos* 2 (1992): 189-200.

Neimeyer, Mark. "Poe and Popular Culture." In Kevin J. Hayes, ed. *The Cambridge Companion to Edgar Allan Poe.* Cambridge: Cambridge University Press, 2002. 205-24.

Pascal, Blaise. *Pensées et opuscules.* 1670. Paris: Classiques Hachette, 1968.

Padel, Ruth. *Whom Gods Destroy: Elements of Greek and Tragic Madness.* Princeton, NJ: Princeton University Press. 1995.

Pedersen, Jan B. W. "Howard Phillips Lovecraft: Romantic on the Nightside." *Lovecraft Annual* No. 12 (2018): 165-73.

Plato. *Plato in Twelve Volumes: With an English Translation.* Volume 9. Tr. H. N. Fowler. London: William Heinemann; Cambridge, MA: Harvard University Press, 1914.

Poe, Edgar Allan. "Eleonora." In *The Works of Edgar Allen Poe: The Raven Edition.* Volume 2. New York: Collier & Son, 1903. 373-81.

———. "Mr. Poe's Reply to Mr. English and Others." *The Spirit of the Times* (10 July 1846). www.eapoe.org/works/misc/18460710.htm

Poole, Gabriele. "The Byronic Hero, Theatricality and Leadership." *Byron Journal* 38, No. 1 (2010): 7–18.

Prentky, R. A. "Creativity and Psychopathology: A Study of 291 World-Famous Men." *British Journal of Psychiatry* 165 (1979): 22–34.

Pushkin, Alexander. *Eugene Onegin.* Tr. Walter Arndt. 2nd ed. Ann Arbor, MI: Ardis, 2009.

Radden, Jennifer, ed. *The Nature of Melancholy from Aristotle to Kristeva.* Oxford: Oxford University Press. 2000.

Reiss, Benjamin. *Theaters of Madness: Insane Asylums and Nineteenth-Century American Culture.* Chicago: University of Chicago Press, 2008.

Rothenberg, Albert. *Creativity and Madness: New Findings and Old Stereotypes.* Baltimore: Johns Hopkins University Press. 1990.

Schlesinger, Judith. "Creative Mythconceptions: A Closer Look at the Evidence for the 'Mad-Genius' Hypothesis." *Psychology of Aesthetics, Creativity, and the Arts* 3, No. 2 (2009): 62–72. doi: 10.1037/a0013975.

———. "Building Connections on Sand: The Cautionary Chapter." In James C. Kaufman, ed. *Creativity and Mental Illness.* Cambridge: Cambridge University Press, 2014. 60–75.

Shelley, Mary Wollstonecraft. *Frankenstein; or, The Modern Prometheus.* London: Printed for Lackington, Hughes, Harding, Mavor, & Jones, 1818.

Seneca Lucius Annaeus. *Minor Dialogues: Together with the Dialogue on Clemency.* Tr. A. Stewart. London: Bell & Sons, 1912.

Sun, Chunyan. "Horror from the Soul: Gothic Style in Allan Poe's Horror Fictions." *English Language Teaching* 8, No. 5 (2015): 94–99.

Terman, Lewis. *Mental and Physical Traits of a Thousand Gifted Children: Genic Studies of Genius.* Volume 1. Stanford, CA: Stanford University Press, 1925.

Tyree, J. M. "Lovecraft at the Automat." *New England Review* 29, No. 1, (2008): 137–50.

Wittkower, R., and M. Wittkower. *Born under Saturn.* London: Shenval, 1963.

Lovecraftian Elements in Cormac McCarthy's *Blood Meridian*

Zachary K. Rutledge
Peninsula College

This paper contributes to the research in Lovecraftian intertextual comparison by analyzing the relationship between Lovecraft's texts and Cormac McCarthy's *Blood Meridian*. This may be an unlikely comparison given McCarthy's distance from Lovecraft in terms of time and genre: McCarthy's first novel was published almost three decades after Lovecraft's death, and many of his novels are realistic fiction in the sense that they mostly operate in realistic settings and rarely enter the realm of the fantastic as Lovecraft's works do. *Blood Meridian*, however, introduces a character with seemingly preternatural abilities and uses sweeping and poetic language to suggest alien worlds beyond our knowledge. Indeed, at times the novel reads a bit like the literature of the fantastic in its descriptions. This paper makes no claim that the novel is actually weird fiction; it is not. However, there are instances of common ground with some aspects of Lovecraft's weird fiction that are worth noting in both their use and effect. By making these connections, we can gain greater insight into the nature of Lovecraft's works and how his approaches and the issues he addressed have transformed and found their way into works written much later.

Using existing critical work, four specific characteristics of Lovecraft's writing—or Lovecraftian elements—are identified. Examples of these elements are then located in Lovecraft's texts as well as in *Blood Meridian*. This paper argues that these authors use these elements to communicate and reinforce their common perspectives on the relationship between humanity and the universe. Further, it is shown that both authors denigrate, through parody and inversion, the power of religion to mitigate the horrors of decay, death, and violence.

Given that there are numerous concepts and techniques that might be considered "Lovecraftian," a review and synthesis of relevant literature has led to the following focused list, which serves to highlight some commonalities between the authors' works.

- A materialist perspective that is manifested as an aesthetic, which tends to express the vastness—both historically and physically—of the world in comparison to humanity.
- A grotesque aesthetic that shows the horror of body transformation.
- A parodic evocation of Christian themes and symbols.
- A mythology that includes a gnostic demiurge such as Nyarlathotep.

The first and third elements are derived from S. T. Joshi's analysis of Lovecraft's philosophy and aesthetic in *H. P. Lovecraft: The Decline of the West* (1990). The second element is derived from Victoria Nelson's *The Secret Life of Puppets* (2001).[1] The fourth element is inspired by Leo Daugherty's identification of the judge character in *Blood Meridian* with a gnostic archon and by a realization that the judge and Nyarlathotep are, according to the authors' description and use, similar entities.

Assuming that the reader is probably more familiar with Lovecraft's works than with *Blood Meridian*, a brief summary of the novel is offered. Then the four Lovecraftian elements are discussed in turn by considering their instantiations in the texts of the two authors. The impact of these elements is delineated. Summary and some indications of further research directions are given in the conclusion.

Blood Meridian

Based on historical events, the action in *Blood Meridian* follows a band of killers who have been hired to scalp natives in the deserts of west Texas and northern Mexico circa 1850. Leadership of the band is shared between John Glanton and Judge Holden, the latter of whom is referred to as the "judge" (uncapitalized). Glanton is the organizational leader of the group, and the judge is the spiritual leader. The narration is largely from a character known only as the "kid" (again, uncapitalized), who left his home in Tennessee at the beginning of the novel and is therefore an outsider to the worldscape of the story, bearing witness to its unfolding along with the reader.

---

1. Nelson's work is a study of the Gothic and supernatural in various media.

The novel is about the awful violence committed by this group as it rampages through the bleak landscape. The violence is made all the more terrible in that the story is based on factual events and that Glanton and Holden are historical figures (Sepich). The different ways in which the characters enact or react to the violence are also a subject of the novel. These differences serve as a point of contention between the kid and the judge, the former wishing to remain separate from the cycle of violence and the latter pushing all into acceptance of one general premise: that humanity's truest calling is violence. The conflict between the kid and the judge culminates in an indecisive confrontation, which ends the principal storyline. The novel then picks up with the kid decades later when he meets up with the judge, who has not aged in that time, confirming suspicions created throughout the novel of the judge's preternatural powers. The judge continues the confrontation begun years earlier and murders the kid.

Published in 1985, the novel is McCarthy's fifth novel and represents a break from the previous novels, which were in the Southern Gothic tradition. That said, *Blood Meridian* still creates an atmosphere and situates characters in places that are burdened by their histories in such a way as to summon, at times, a Gothic mode. This mode, as shown in this paper, is not dissimilar in some respects to Lovecraft's.

Cosmicism: The Narrator and the Expanse

In Lovecraft's work, we find narrators who stand at the brink, looking from a vista, and are overwhelmed by the horrifying vastness of a universe that is tinged with threat. It is a moment of revelation for the narrator. It is not unlike the scene in Stephen Crane's "The Open Boat" (1897), in which the narrator lies in the boat, exposed to and helpless against the forces of nature that rage around him. It is an image of the heroic narrator facing down the vastness of the natural world. Indeed, Michael D. Miller recognizes Crane's naturalism as a precursor to "cosmicism" (146). As is shown below, McCarthy exhibits scenes of vastness similar to both Crane and Lovecraft. Thus, it can be argued that McCarthy, too, portrays a form of cosmicism.

But more than just having narrators facing down the expanse, McCarthy and Lovecraft use these scenes to communicate the dizzying vastness of time as well as to serve as the locus of revelation. To understand the latter better, it is helpful to consider Dylan Henderson's comparison of Lovecraft's narrator to the fictional sleuths of popular detective stories; he finds a particular inversion in key events in the detective story format. Unlike the moment of discovery in the detective story—when all the pieces rationally come together and the world is set back in order—the Lovecraftian moments of revealing only serve to delineate the lack of understanding of the narrator/detective. Indeed, what should be a Zarathustrian moment, standing on a grand vista, becomes a horrifying revelation of the narrator's own ignorance of the scope and nature of the universe. Enlightenment comes but it does not change the character for the better.

For example, in "The Haunter of the Dark" (1935), Robert Blake marvels at the grand view offered from his study from which he can see "the far horizon" and the countryside's "purple slopes" (CF 3.453). Seeing the "unknown streets and labyrinthine gables" stretching before him, Blake is reminded of the strange tales he writes and as a result ascribes a sense of alien mystery to his view, ultimately turning to the "grotesque" when the courthouse's floodlights and the Industrial Trust's red beacon are turned on. Finally, a layer of history is imbued on the place as Blake identifies "remnants of older Yankee" houses (CF 3.454).

Much more than just a scene to introduce a particular location, Lovecraft accomplishes at least four things in this well-drawn scene. First, he indicates an expansive world and Blake's relative smallness—similar to Crane's narrator facing down the large bowl of sky. Second, he communicates an expansive *historical* world where remnants of prior culture—in this case, a "Yankee" culture—are still visible beneath more modern structures. Third, he subtly communicates Blake's outsider status in this place by imbuing the city scape with an "alien mystery." Fourth, as night unfolds and the city turns garish and red, Lovecraft foreshadows the threat held in those streets.

In "The Shadow out of Time" (1934-35), the narrator, Nathaniel Wingate Peaslee, attempts to reconstruct the lost memory of his time with the Great Race. In one of his memories, Peaslee finds himself looking across an alien city in a similar fashion as Blake did across Providence. He describes

> vistas from the great round windows, and from the titanic flat roof . . . [a] wide barren area. . . . There were almost endless leagues of giant buildings. . . . Many seemed so limitless that they must have had a frontage of several thousand feet, while some shot up to mountainous altitudes in the grey, steamy heavens. (CF 3.379)

Peaslee also notices a history embedded in the scene: "enormous dark cylindrical towers . . . of prodigious age and dilapidation. . . . Around all . . .

there hovered an inexplicable aura of menace and concentrated fear" (CF 3.379-80). Again, the narrator recognizes the layers of age, indicating the menace of long history as well as of space. In this way, Lovecraft shows that an ancient civilization that dwarfs humanity's efforts is itself proven vulnerable to the ultimate natural power of time.

Finally, in "The Dreams in the Witch House" (1932), the narrator, Walter Gilman, finds himself, like Blake and Peaslee, gazing at a space that is vast, alien, and hostile. Gilman emerges from his sleep on a high "balustraded terrace above a boundless jungle of outlandish, incredible peaks. . . . Looking upward he saw three stupendous discs of flame, each of a different hue, and at a different height above an infinitely distant curving horizon of low mountains" (CF 3.249).

In this scene we have mountains, a distant horizon, and disks that are redolent of some sort of triple sun flaming in the sky. Gilman's altitude provides a dizzying perspective of the distant curvature of the world. This is an incredible image that would probably capture Crane's desire to show humanity's effeteness. The scene ends with Gilman breaking off a statuette mounted on the railing. Waking later from the dream, he finds that he still holds the statue. Donald R. Burleson interprets this as Lovecraft asking whether "dreams may perhaps be a projection of such other worlds really existing" (179). Thus, Lovecraft connects the idea of cognitive revelation to actual physical presence—intertwining the ideas of knowledge and being, which is reminiscent of a gnostic epistemology as discussed later.

Further, the scene approaches the metaphorical language used by McCarthy when describing the kid's ascent of a peak to gain a view of the coming trail. The kid mounts a great altitude and is given a revelatory view of the inchoate hostility of the desert world through which these warring men travel:

> In the evening they came out upon a mesa that overlooked all the country to the north. The sun to the west lay in a holocaust where there rose a steady column of small desert bats and to the north along the trembling perimeter of the world dust was blowing down the void like the smoke of distant armies. The crumpled butcher paper mountains lay in sharp shadowfold under the long blue dusk and in the middle distance the glazed bed of a dry lake lay shimmering like the mare imbrium . . . (110)

As with Lovecraft, this scene does more than just present a panoramic desert landscape. It is a threatening "holocaust" and an expansive, "trembling perimeter" along a dusty "void." A "long blue dusk" enrobes the landscape in crippling shadow. McCarthy describes a vastness that renders the kid truly childlike before its force. Further, the simile comparing the dry lakebed to the "mare imbrium," which is a crater on the moon, communicates the narrator's sense of traveling in an alien landscape.

In another scene the kid, in a sort of reverse Zarathustrian move, climbs the mountain at sunset. At the peak he is treated to an immersive view in which all the signs of life are illusory:

> They crested the mountain at sunset and they could see for miles. An immense lake lay below them with the distant blue mountains standing in the windless span of water and the shape of a soaring hawk and trees that shimmered in the heat and a distant city very white against the blue and shaded hills. . . . They slept among the rocks face up like dead men and in the morning when they rose there was no city and no trees and no lake only a barren dusty plain. (65)

Thus, in McCarthy, the vastness and baleful trickery communicate "a physical—and metaphysical—landscape whose indifference and lack of obligation are its chief characteristics" (Link 155). Similar to a Lovecraft narrator/detective who finds the revelatory information provided by the vista maddening, the kid is left with a similarly maddening conclusion that the world he perceives is an illusion that belies a bleak reality.

The scene also summons an image of the narrator's approach to Innsmouth: "we reached the crest and beheld the outspread valley beyond, where the Manuxet joins the sea just north of the long line of cliffs that culminate in Kingsport Head and veer off toward Cape Ann. On the far, misty horizon I could just make out the dizzy profile of the Head" (CF 3.172). As we know by the end of the story, Innsmouth is the missing piece required for the narrator to understand himself and his history. Thus, in this case, the formulaic scene of revelation is used as a foreshadowing tool at the beginning of the story rather than at the climax.

The kid is presented a view that serves to undermine any perception of the universe as being something other than an uncaring cosmos. It is even more to the point that McCarthy uses these scenes in the beginning of his novel in order to provide the psychological impact of the space on the kid, whose origins are far from this world. In other words, the kid truly is in an alien space just as the Lovecraftian heroes find themselves at those antienlightenment moments when the history, expanse, and hostility of the universe are revealed.

Finally, to emphasize the weight of history in McCarthy's harsh desert-scape, the judge teaches his fellow riders about the previous residents of the valley in the heart of the desert. "The people who once lived here are called the Anasazi. The old ones. They quit these parts. . . . The tools, the art, the building—these things stand in judgement on the latter races. . . . Their spirit is entombed in the stone. It lies upon the land with the same weight" (152).

Just as with Lovecraft, the weight of history is present, waiting to "stand in judgement" against the narrator. This reminds us of the narrator of "The Shadow over Innsmouth" (1931), who must face the judgment of his own family history. We also recall Peaslee, who faces the burden of cosmic history that stands in judgment against his entire species, relegating its history to "the vaults of the lowest or vertebrate level" (CF 3.400).

Descriptive Grotesquerie and the Violence of Transformation

Lovecraft is conservative in his approach to the unrealistic, stating clearly that his preferred method was to maintain absolute reality until the intense encounter with the otherworldly (Joshi 55). McCarthy, in comparison, places the reader in an alien space of death and mayhem in *Blood Meridian* and provides little reprieve. Thus, the descriptive violence in the novel far exceeds anything provided in Lovecraft's works. I argue, however, that, when it does appear, we can identify a similarity in style and language between the two authors.

McCarthy's aesthetic is exemplified in the description of a nighttime scene of slaughter by the company of men. "[T]hey commenced cutting up the gutted antelopes in the floor of the wagon with bowieknives and handaxes, laughing and hacking in a welter of gore, a reeking scene in the light of the handheld lanterns" (45–46). This scene is reminiscent of a ritual sacrifice and the exultation of the worshippers that would follow.

Lovecraft provides a similar scene in "The Call of Cthulhu" (1926) when investigators enter the swamp where cult activities have been reported related to the disappearance of a number of the locals. As the investigators approach the cultists, they see "hybrid spawn . . . braying, bellowing, and writhing about a monstrous ring-shaped bonfire" (CF 2.36) around which a ring of sacrificed and butchered bodies hangs. The narrator further describes the scene as an "orgy" and an "endless Bacchanale."

In both scenes the dominant image is of brutal violence perpetrated in celebration. The cultists performing the acts operate in darkness with primitive lighting. The reader visualizes shadows jumping around as the figures move frantically, their faces partially illuminated and frightening.

But more than just the violence committed, it is important to note that this is violence enacted by an anonymous mob. Paul Neimann identifies the tension between Lovecraft's concern about the influences of "ignorant mobocracy" and his deterministic philosophy (89). Specifically, without a divine ordering at work, there is no one to act as arbiters of value. A purely deterministic philosophy would also need to accept that there is no god to sort out the good from the evil at any level—whether it be the ultimate good and bad of human morality and sin or merely what constitutes good taste in literary practice. Without any such arbiter, it would fall to the mob—as Lovecraft feared—to decide. Therefore, the faceless mob for both authors may represent a common pessimism toward democratic ideals as well as an anxiety towards materialism.

The swamp cults enact rituals to bring about change through grotesque violence. McCarthy, too, embraced the relationship between violence and transformation. Both authors are drawn to the aesthetic of transformation; but it is often horrific, and while metamorphosis in nature can be a signifier of new life, Lovecraft and McCarthy subvert this by locating the violence of their transformations in the degradation of sexual function or in the death of children.

Consider the famous example from the "The Dunwich Horror" (1928) in which Wilbur Whateley's lineage is revealed in the grotesqueness of his body, which "below the waist . . . was the worst; for here all human resemblance left off and sheer phantasy began" (CF 2.439). Nelson sees this scene as a kind of sublimation of sexual energy following a larger trend of "displacement of sexuality in his fictions" (136). Thus the lack of sexuality—in even its mildest non-explicit forms—is viewed from the psychological basis of suppression and finds representation in frightening metamorphosis.

Connecting to *Blood Meridian*, a novel completely devoid of sexual energy, we can find an equally disturbing scene in which the narrator describes the corpses of some of the recently murdered men who were identifiable as such by their beards: they "wore strange menstrual wounds between their legs and no man's parts for these had been cut away and hung dark and strange from out their grinning mouths" (159). Thus, following Nelson, we see that McCarthy too assaults the sexual function with a grotesque aesthetic. The body we inhabit can be the site of horrible transformation—even more horrific if the locus of the change is the generative center.

Nelson broadens the conversation around transformation and places Lovecraft in a tradition of writers that has emphasized metamorphosis in storytelling. Further, she quotes Bruno Schulz, stating that the "migration of forms is the essence of life" (114). Thus the "life" of a being is not the form it takes but is the process of changing from form to form. The metaphysical implication of this statement is that a being can transcend—however horrifically—its current physical manifestation.

Both authors are tapping into the same deep tradition that regards bodily change as symbolic for the cycle of life and death. Indeed, death is the type of "migration" often presented in Lovecraft and almost exclusively so in *Blood Meridian*. In a scene following a confrontation with natives, the scalp hunters find a bush that had been decorated with dead babies, which "had holes punched in their underjaws and were hung so by their throats. . . . Bald and pale and bloated, larval to some unreckonable being" (60).

Through death, McCarthy transforms the babies into creatures—swollen, hairless larvae—that could have appeared in weird fiction. The description is reminiscent of an alien creature made complete with the phrasing "pale and bloated," adding a clinical illness dimension to the visual. The reader is transported to an alien world with these images, and its hostility is apparent.

Throughout the novel we find similar images. In mud huts we see victims lying in their doorways "naked and swollen and strange" (61). In other places "the dead lay with their peeled skulls like polyps bluely wet or luminescent melons cooling on some mesa of the moon" (182). Again, McCarthy details the transformation of the body after violent death along with hints of alien strangeness.

Lovecraft, too, uses similar language to produce images reminiscent of McCarthy's. For example, in *At the Mountains of Madness* (1931), Lovecraft describes the shoggoth as "a shapeless congeries of protoplasmic bubbles, faintly self-luminous, and with myriads of temporary eyes forming and unforming as pustules of greenish light" (CF 3.150). A shapeless thing that consists of collections of bubbles and pustules can be compared to an alien larva as described by McCarthy above. In both there is an image of curved smoothness along with a vocabulary of sickness, invoking words such as "bloated" and "pustules."

Pursuing his attack on humanity and its reproductive predilections, McCarthy continues with descriptions of violence against babies. We see in the remnants of an Apache settlement, the citizens of which were slaughtered by Mexican soldiers: "tiny limbs and toothless paper skulls of infants like the ossature of small apes at their place of murder and old remnants of weathered basketry and broken pots among the gravel" (95).

From "The Dreams in the Witch House," Lovecraft describes the horrific findings in the witch house after its demolition: "the floor was a veritable ossuary of the bones of small children—some fairly modern, but others extending back in infinite gradations to a period so remote that crumbling was almost complete" (CF 3.275).

Both of these passages combine the horrific imagery of children's skulls with a sense of a long history of violence. In addition, both authors reach for the Latinate vocabulary: ossature and ossuary. This gives the reading a scientific quality with the associated objectivity and thus credibility. Further, the use of such formal terms reminds us of the tendency of both authors to utilize archaic vocabulary. As Philip A. Snyder and Delys W. Snyder point out concerning McCarthy, "the archaic words, much like the geological strata, fossils, and petroglyphs in McCarthy's descriptive passages, embed the past within the present, giving the impression of language's timeless immanence in his texts" (36). In McCarthy's work, diction is used to propel the reader back in time. Lovecraft, too, has been well noted for "his absorption in archaic modes of thought and expression" (Joshi 46). As Burleson notes in quoting Lovecraft, the author's work is to create a sense of timelessness—a type of cosmic yearning for the forgotten—in presentation of the everyday (16). Seeking archaic modes also serves to remove the text from mundane fiction, granting it a larger perspective—a view that creates sacredness—just as the archaic language present in ancient holy texts serves to inspire a sense of transcendence in their readers.

Focusing again on the notion of metamorphosis, Nelson also reminds us that from a gnostic perspective to know something is to become something (111). This argument indicates that knowledge acquisition comes along with physical transformation. For Lovecraft there is the correlation of knowledge accumulation by the narrator and the concomitant physical transformation of him or others in his purview. For example, the narrator in "The Shadow over Innsmouth" witnesses his physical transformation into a deep one as he acquires the knowledge of his ancestry. In "The Colour out of Space" (1927), as the increasing effects of the color on the local environment are revealed, increased transformative effects take hold of the family. There is also the psychological metamorphosis of the narrator in "The Dreams in the Witch House" as he studies more and more advanced mathematics. The theme of change—specifically negative or harmful change—concurrent with increased knowledge is in line with the Lovecraftian apprehension of developments or discoveries in science as exemplified by the fate dealt to the exploratory team in At the Mountains of Madness, or similarly, the fate dealt to the Old Ones by their own scientific creations.

Like Lovecraft, McCarthy shows the transformations of bodies—specifically the metamorphosis brought about by death—with great detail. By targeting the reproductive function, these descriptions challenge humanity's drive to transform itself into its next generation, thereby escaping species death. Instead, the authors offer another type of religious transcendence of the physical form—a horrific transformation of the body. The purpose of which is, as opposed to approaching deity, to offer a gnostic understanding of violence by merging with it. Not only do the characters in these stories potentially experience this, but the power of these texts with their archaic-cum-sacred words lies in its ability to offer this mergence, at least vicariously, to the reader as well with horrifying impact.

Christian Parody

Maurice Lévy notes that Lovecraft had an "obsession with infamy and sacrilege which rests on an inverted aesthetic" (88). René J. Weise notes that Lovecraft was well versed in the Bible and advocated for its study from a literary perspective (47–48). Weise argues further that Lovecraft parodies the Holy Trinity with his deities Nyarlathotep, Yog-Sothoth, and Azathoth. Thus, Lovecraft, with a "lifelong hostility to religion" (Joshi 21), was not content to abandon his formidable knowledge of Judeo-Christian mythos in favor of a materialist viewpoint. Indeed, he had a desire to use this knowledge to pervert biblical lore, to invert it, and ultimately to parody it.

Cecelia Hopkins-Drewer documents this desire for playful satire when she recognizes Lovecraft's poem "Festival" as a parody of a nineteenth-century Christian hymn. The parody centers on the telling of the events of a contemporary (relative to Lovecraft) Yule season, liberated from "modern trappings" (54). Yet to tell this story, Lovecraft uses a published hymn as the framework for his poem. Thus, we see a theme in which Lovecraft takes a Christian structure, empties it, and refills it with something pagan or chthonic.

In particular, Lovecraft empties churches and fills them with the horrid. He makes these abodes of Christ a nexus of moral decay. For example, the Esoteric Order of the Dragon from "The Shadow over Innsmouth," although centered in a former Masonic lodge, has co-opted the other churches in town as well. As the young grocer tells the narrator: "the churches . . . were not advisable neighbourhoods" (CF 3.182) as all have been "disavowed by their respective denominations" (CF 3.177). Further, "The Haunter of the Dark" originates in a long-abandoned church, which had been converted by cultist decades earlier to a ritual site. Thus the Christian centers of hope have been subverted by forces that also have rituals and worship but in an inverted way—worshipping blasphemous godlike creatures such as Dagon and Nyarlathotep.

Similarly, McCarthy also describes imagery of desecrated churches. They are often the locus of violent acts that are explicitly stated as opposed to the indirect hints as Lovecraft provides. For example, the kid awakes in a wasted church after a night of debauchery in the following scene: "He woke in the nave of a ruinous church. . . . The floor of the church was deep in dried guano and the droppings of cattle and sheep" (27). After entering the sacristy, the kid observes that the "domed vaults overhead were clotted with a dark furred mass that shifted and breathed and chittered. . . . [A]long the back wall lay the remains of several bodies, one a child." And on the outside door, he sees a "carved stone Virgin held in her arms a headless child."

Not only is there a theme of desecration and decadence, but even the shifting shadow in the vaults of the high ceiling is reminiscent of when Blake hears "a soft stirring sound [that] seemed to come from the steeple's eternal blackness overhead" (CF 3.465). Both examples turn to parody the notion of what a church should do, which is provide comfort and hope.

Later in the novel, the kid finds another desecrated church that had been used as a last refuge from an attack.

> The savages had hacked holes in the roof and shot them down from above. . . . The altars had been hauled down and the tabernacle looted and the great sleeping God of the Mexicans routed from his golden cup . . . and a dead Christ in a glass bier lay broken in the chancel floor. The murdered lay in a great pool of their communal blood. (63)

The parody in these scenes exists in the conversion of houses of worship into houses of death. The damage done to this structure would amount to sacrilege, but McCarthy intensifies the attack on religion by filling the pews with corpses rather than hopeful supplicants.

McCarthy clarifies his commitment to religious parody through his use of carnivalesque symbols and references. As Steven Frye notes, "McCarthy's awareness of the history of the carnivalesque seems obvious, as well as its association with religious celebration and a peculiar form of contained and aesthetically constituted transgression of normative behavior" ("*Blood Meridian*" 116). Indeed the "carnival permitted . . . a burlesque parody of the sacred" (115). The key tie to Lovecraft is the idea of parody and religion. And now we see that McCarthy has a similar desire to besmirch the religion of Christ.

Throughout *Blood Meridian* there are allusions to medicine shows and carnival. Fellow travelers with the gang include entertainers who "were dressed in fools costumes with stars and halfmoons embroidered on" (93). But perhaps the most stunning use of the carnival aesthetic is a scene occurring early in the novel in a battle between the native Americans and a U.S. army regiment. The natives are described as "clad in costumes attic or biblical or wardrobed out of a fevered dream . . . one in a stovepipe hat and one with an umbrella and one in white stockings and a bloodstained weddingveil . . . grotesque with daubings like a company of mounted clowns, death hilarious" (55).

The word "hilarious" is offered, but this is a serious scene that descends into violence and death. By showing the warriors as participants in some ancient Saturnalian feast of fools, McCarthy turns a religious celebration into a festival of death and bloodshed. The parodic element offers a challenge to the seriousness of the historically based novel and presents a risk that the reader may feel the novel loses legitimacy in its endeavor to maintain the gravity of the material.

Lovecraft, too, can operate in a nexus of parody and sublime horror in which he inserts playful allusions. As Steven J. Mariconda suggests, the "concept of *play* is central to Lovecraft's art" (77), and readers who have misjudged Lovecraft's grandiloquent style may have not "caught onto the game" (80) that Lovecraft was playing.

Mariconda focuses on Lovecraft's use of verbal irony, but it would not be unfair to include in this interpretation those great parodic jabs at religion that Lovecraft makes at the end of "The Shadow over Innsmouth" and "The Dunwich Horror." As Burleson notes, the ending to the former is a "delectable parody of the ending of the 23rd Psalm" (176). And, in the latter, Lévy observes that the final cries of the Dunwich Horror are an allusion to the Gospels of Jesus Christ (96)–a move by Lovecraft that would be difficult not to comprehend as satirical.

The Demiurge

McCarthy's judge serves as an anti-saint as well as a symbol of the carnival. He emerges in the desert in vengeful pursuit of the kid. He carries a parasol to protect him from the sun. It is fashioned from "rotted scraps of hide stretched over a framework of rib bones" with a handle made from "the foreleg of some creature." Holden also has a captured "idiot" man and leads him on rawhide leash. The scene makes Holden appear to be a "degenerate entrepreneur fleeing from a medicine show" (310).

The surreal image of Holden described above is McCarthy at the height of his carnivalesque aesthetic. It is comical and scary. The umbrella is an image of sacrificed flesh and bone protecting other flesh. The wild man is the dog out for walk with his owner. This image is a perverse reminiscence of an impressionist painting of a lady walking a dog in a park, parasol angled against her shoulder.

The judge is a fascinating, multi-faceted character whom Harold Bloom considers to be the "most frightening figure in all of American literature" (475). The judge, however, is written to transcend mundane ideas of villainy. He is imbued with a divinity whose purpose is to mete out judgment on a cosmic scale. In line with this scale, Leo Daugherty constructs the judge as a demiurge in a gnostic tragedy in which he tries to consume the divine light—or "pneuma"—of humanity, leaving only the reeking corpses in the desert (160).

Fittingly for a gnostic archon who visits continual evil onto the world, the judge is perverse, violent, and murderous. However, he is also a charlatan of sorts who in his first scene of the novel convinces a party of strangers to kill a man based on lies that the judge presumably fabricated in the moment. The judge's action is gratuitous and provides no benefit to him. The judge behaves as a trickster god. And considering the comparison above concerning the "medicine show," we have the idea that the judge is capable of putting on a show—of charming and manipulating humans.

In addition, the judge is a scientist and philosopher. Amidst the bloody carnage created by his traveling band of scalpers, he collects relics from ancient native populations and records his findings in a notebook—like Charles Darwin recording the evolution of species. When the group exhausts its ammunition and is under threat of attack, the judge, like some combination of medieval alchemist and chemical engineer, makes gunpowder with minerals found in the hills and the men's urine. He also regales the men with stories in a way that reminds us of Jesus telling parables to his disciples. As one member of the gang recounts, "he commences to give us an address. It was like a sermon but it was no such sermon as any man of us had ever heard before . . . an oration to what end I know not, then or now . . . Then he turned and led the horse he had been ridin . . . and us behind him like the disciples of a new faith" (136). Thus, the judge is a complex character with many talents. He is a scientist, able to create the ammunition technology of his day. Yet he is also a teacher and religious leader.

The judge as showman is reminiscent of Nyarlathotep, who "gave exhibitions of power which sent his spectators away speechless, yet which swelled his fame to exceeding magnitude" (CF 1.203). We know that Nyarlathotep is a harbinger of doom for mankind, yet he is given to displays of power and speaks "much of the sciences—of electricity and psychology" (CF 1.203). Thus, similar to the judge, Nyarlathotep is a type of "itinerant showman" (Burleson 73) and professor.

Physically, the judge is described as a bald albino without body hair—inordinately tall and lean. This description recalls Nyarlathotep, who is described in "The Dreams in the Witch House" as "tall, lean . . . wholly devoid of either hair or beard, and wearing as his only garment a shapeless robe of some heavy black fabric" (CF 3.254). We can compare this to the description of the judge near the beginning of *Blood Meridian*: "An enormous man dressed in an oilcloth slicker had entered the tent and removed his hat. He was bald as a stone and he had no trace of beard and he had no brows to his eyes nor lashes to them" (6). Further, Nyarlathotep in the eponymous short story is described as the host of a traveling show of sorts. He confounds, entertains, and threatens—just as the judge does.

Thus, both authors choose to use a humanoid embodiment of their violent mythologies. They invest their respective creatures with features that render them alien yet persuasive as a demiurgical intermediate between the humans and the world beyond the sublunary. The care for these demiurges both authors provide in their loving descriptions shows their fascination with this kind of charming evil.

The reason for this interest in these particular characters could stem from their archetypical nature. Gavin Callaghan argues that Nyarlathotep follows a long tradition of sinister showmen who follow a Jungian "Old Man" or "Wizard" archetype (155). He shows that this character was a feature of the pulps in the first two decades of the twentieth century. The character functioned to bring revelation to the protagonist and to serve as an intermediary between "this world and that which lies beyond" (156).

The judge character, while not an old man, certainly could fit the description of a wizard, given the abilities displayed, much of which would have seemed magical to his less sophisticated fellow scalpers. On one occasion he even impresses his men with a show of prestidigitation—one of the few key scenes in which the novel unambiguously reveals itself as something more fantastical than historical fiction.

In his annotations to "Nyarlathotep" (1920), Leslie S. Klinger cites Will Murray to remind us that the works and life of Nicolai Tesla touched Lovecraft and that this connection was "sufficient to shape the description of Nyarlathotep" (32). Tesla was also a wizard of sorts and a scientific genius who traveled the world entertaining and frightening people with a show of electricity that might as well have been a magic show to the population at the time. In this comparison, we see Lovecraft's fear of scientific progress and what dangers advances in science may bring. This critique of scientific positivism is found in the judge, through whom "McCarthy expresses his own concerns about the dangers of science and the vigorous spread of knowledge" (Cusher 228). Further, Frye contends that "through the judge, McCarthy blends the evolutionary naturalism of the late nineteenth century, with its recognition of the violence in nature and the indifference to human suffering inherent in natural law" (*Understanding* 85). Here again we see a connection to the indifference of natural law—and by extension cosmic law. Thus, as humanity accumulates more knowledge of the natural world, we further elucidate a system that is fundamentally blind to us.

Conclusion

The Lovecraftian elements in *Blood Meridian* include vast panoramas of hostility. These vistas communicate an extension of the dangerous world of the naturalist writer of the late nineteenth century that Lovecraft expands to cosmicism. Although *Blood Meridian*'s purview does not include any glances into the larger cosmos,[2] the psychological impact of the geography of the novel communicates a similar type of cosmicism in which the human characters such as the kid face a hostile natural order as well as an unsympathetic intelligence such as the judge, who hunts in the desert along with them.

---

2. The epilogue is the exception to this, which is its own mystery beyond this paper's discussion.

By embedding their narrators into violent, uncaring worlds, both authors reveal a deep pessimism about the prospect of humanity's future. Desecrating Christianity attacks the institutions, symbols, and beliefs that would serve to mitigate this kind of pessimism. Both authors play a game of parody, which can threaten the seriousness of their content. By introducing elemental aspects of religion that, in the least, flirt with parody, the authors operate in an intersection of sacrilegious satire, literary realism, scientific positivism, and the mythopoeic—a difficult space to maintain without sliding into any one of them fully.

The grotesque in Lovecraft and *Blood Meridian* as treated in this paper has focused on metamorphosis, taking a gnostic epistemology that equates knowledge acquisition with bodily transformation. The violence that both authors show toward children and toward sexual function indicates a metaphorical challenge to the continuance of the human race itself.

Finally, a character such as the judge as compared to Nyarlathotep shows a common attraction to this archetypical demiurge who leads, charms, teaches, and destroys. An intermediary between the material world and whatever lies beyond our existence, this figure's presence gives human manifestation to the indifferent universe that these authors imagine. The authors want a human form into which they can pour their fear and skepticism of science, leadership, progress, and even learning. But more, the creation of these literary demiurges is a reach toward a Torah-style Jehovah, who is angry but travels in the deserts and wastes with us. It shows a possible weakness in the cosmicism and the divine pessimism of McCarthy and Lovecraft, which leads us to an interesting question: Why would an indifferent universe bother to create a human (or humanlike) intermediary in the first place?

Drawing these lines between these two sons of Providence born fifty years apart delineates the importance of the philosophical questions in their works. These connections show a commonality among serious artists who strive for a reconciliation of their art with their own philosophies. More specifically, we see two authors grappling with the advancements of human knowledge in science and technology, metaphysical questions about morality in the face of an amoral universe, and teleological questions about our purpose in this world.

Works Cited

Bloom, Harold. *The Bright Book of Life: Novels to Read and Reread*. New York: Alfred A. Knopf, 2020.

Burleson, Donald R. *H. P. Lovecraft: A Critical Study*. Westport, CT: Greenwood Press, 1983.

Callaghan, Gavin. "Sinister Showmen and H. P. Lovecraft." *Lovecraft Annual* No. 11 (2017): 153-78.

Cusher, Brent Edwin. "Cormac McCarthy's Definition of Evil: *Blood Meridian* and the Case of Judge Holden." *Perspectives on Political Science* 43 (2014): 223-30.

Daugherty, Leo. "Gravers False and True: *Blood Meridian* as Gnostic Tragedy." In Edwin T. Arnold and Dianne C. Luce, ed. *Perspectives on Cormac McCarthy*. Jackson: University Press of Mississippi, 1999. 159-74.

Frye, Steven. "*Blood Meridian* and the Poetics of Violence." In Steven Frye, ed. *The Cambridge Companion to Cormac McCarthy*. New York: Cambridge University Press, 2013. 107-20.

———. *Understanding Cormac McCarthy*. Columbia: University of South Carolina Press, 2009.

Henderson, Dylan. "Missing the Punchline: The Subversive Nature of H. P. Lovecraft's Occult Detective." *Lovecraft Annual* No. 14 (2020): 37-53.

Hopkins-Drewer, Cecelia. "Yuletide Horror: 'Festival' and 'The Messenger.'" *Lovecraft Annual* No. 14 (2020): 54-59.

Joshi, S. T. *H. P. Lovecraft: The Decline of the West*. 1990. Gillette, NJ: Wildside Press, 2000.

Klinger, Leslie S., ed. *The New Annotated H. P. Lovecraft*. New York: W. W. Norton, 2014.

Lévy, Maurice. *Lovecraft: A Study in the Fantastic*. Tr. S. T. Joshi. Detroit: Wayne State University Press, 1988.

Link, Eric Carl. "McCarthy and Literary Naturalism." In Steven Frye, ed. *The Cambridge Companion to Cormac McCarthy*. New York: Cambridge University Press, 2013. 149-61.

Mariconda, Steven J. "How to Read Lovecraft." *Lovecraft Annual* No. 14 (2020): 77-82.

McCarthy, Cormac. *Blood Meridian*. New York: First Vintage International, 1985.

Miller, Michael D. "Lovecraft's Open Boat." *Lovecraft Annual* No. 13 (2019): 145-52.

Neimann, Paul. "The Outsiders: Mapping Lovecraft's Loathing." In Dennis P. Quinn and Elena Tchougounova-Paulson, ed. *Lovecraftian Proceedings* 4. New York: Hippocampus Press, 2022. 84-99.

Nelson, Victoria. *The Secret Life of Puppets*. Cambridge, MA: Harvard University Press, 2001.

Sepich, John Emil. "'What Kind of Indians Was Them?': Some Historical Sources in Cormac McCarthy's *Blood Meridian*." In Edwin T. Arnold and Dianne C. Luce, ed. *Perspectives on Cormac McCarthy*. Jackson: University Press of Mississippi, 1999. 123-44.

Snyder, Phillip A., and Delys W. Snyder. "Modernism, Postmodernism, and Language." In Steven Frye, ed. *The Cambridge Companion to Cormac McCarthy*. New York: Cambridge University Press, 2013. 27-38.

Weise, René J. "Reordering the Universe: H. P. Lovecraft's Subversion of the Biblical Divine." In Dennis P. Quinn, ed. *Lovecraftian Proceedings* 2. New York: Hippocampus Press, 2017. 47-63.

Gnosticism, Epicureanism, and Deism in H. P. Lovecraft's Fictive Cosmology

Lorin Geitner
Independent Scholar

Can concepts of alternative theisms, derived from the field of religious studies, be applied and provide insight into the distinctive cosmology of Lovecraft's work and its ongoing appeal and relevance? In this essay I first set out the nature and extent of Lovecraft's personal theism. In light (and in spite) of his views, I set forth an argument for why concepts from the field of religious studies may be applicable and insightful when applied to his work, in spite of the specific theism (or lack thereof) that he personally espoused. I then set forth some of the more *recherché* concepts of theism from the world's religions and explain which of these are applicable in various stages of Lovecraft's career, citing examples from his fiction. Finally, I look at whether, and how, this might explain why, in his own time, his work was eclipsed in popularity and regard by his chief competitor at *Weird Tales*, Seabury Quinn, but also why this might explain why Lovecraft has now attained much higher literary and philosophical reputation, while the works of Seabury Quinn, as entertaining as they are, have fallen to the wayside.

When we consider Lovecraft's theism—his view of deity—it may seem counterintuitive to suggest that any of the varieties of theism identified in the field of religious studies would apply to the fictive universe portrayed in his writing. This is, after all, a person who identified as a "mechanistic materialist"—which is to say that he thought that all phenomena could be traced to physical causes, which operate in a manner akin to an automaton. Indeed, in an exchange with a devout epistolary friend, he went so far as to state:

> I have seen nothing which could possibly give me the notion that cosmic force is the manifestation of a mind and will like my own infinitely magnified; a potent and purposeful consciousness which deals individually and directly with the miserable denizens of a wretched little flyspeck on the back door of a micro-

scopic universe, and which singles this putrid excrescence out as the one spot whereto send an onlie-begotten Son, whose mission is to redeem those accursed flyspeck-inhabiting lice which we call human beings. (MWM 71)[1]

However, there are three arguments to be made for the notion that concepts borrowed from religious studies might be able to be applied profitably to understanding and appreciating Lovecraft's use of religious discourse for literary effect in his fictional cosmology and to draw a significant contrast with the most popular *Weird Tales* author at the time, now largely fallen into obscurity: Seabury Quinn:

First, there is precedent: In his book *Authentic Fakes,* David Chidester demonstrated the applicability of concepts from this field to phenomena as diverse as baseball, the human genome project, Coca-Cola, rock 'n' roll, the rhetoric of Ronald Reagan, the charisma of Jim Jones, Tupperware, and the free market, to name a few.[2] Surely, if such diverse an assortment of productions can benefit from the applications of concepts from religious studies, it is at least tenable that the works of Lovecraft might also reward examination from a similar approach.

Moreover, from an article by Dennis Quinn published on the Popmatters website, it seems that several new religious movements have actually been inspired, in whole or in part, by Lovecraft's fictive cosmology. This inspiration can be confirmed by looking up the organizations and persons named in this essay, such as the Church of Satan, Kenneth Grant, and Frater Tenebrous.

Finally, throughout the bulk of Lovecraft's stories such Great Old Ones as Cthulhu and Yog-Sothoth are often referred to as "gods." Now, admittedly, in some of the later stories, such as *At the Mountains of Madness,* they are recharacterized as extraterrestrials. However, this is a relatively late addition to the canon, and, in the spirit of Arthur C. Clarke's third law, which reads "Any sufficient advanced technology is indistinguishable from magic," let me suggest that the following derivative follows: "Any sufficiently powerful being is indistinguishable from a *god.*"[3]

---

1. See also *Against Religion: The Atheist Writings of H. P. Lovecraft.*

2. The list is borrowed from the back cover text on the book. David Chidester is a well-regarded scholar in religious studies, and this book has received many accolades.

3. If anyone cares to adopt this derivation, I refer to it as "Geitner's Addendum" to Clarke's law. This is, obviously, *not* arguing that HPL was anything but an atheist (which, ironically, is itself a specific form of "theism") but rather that we can employ some of the alternative theisms in the context of his fictional universe, and contrast them to the tacit

If we can, then, reasonably examine Lovecraft's fictive cosmology within the context of terminology developed in religious studies describing the various and sundry forms of theism found in the world religions, which one would be most applicable? The most common definition of theism is "a supremely good being, creator of but separate from and independent of the world, all-powerful (omnipotent), all-knowing (omniscient), eternal, and self-existent" (Rowe 6). Although this is a fairly accurate definition in the context of the religions of the Levant (Zoroastrianism, Judaism, Christianity, and Islam), it does raise several issues: the status of mysticism (Rowe 55–72; if someone can have a direct, unmediated experience of the divine, what need is there for an organized, institutional, or hierarchical religion to intervene?), and the problem of evil (Rowe 92–110; how can a genuinely all-loving, omnibenevolent, and all-powerful god allow evil or suffering to occur?), etc.[4]

Fortunately, the study of world religions provides us many alternatives to this understanding, ones that, moreover, have the advantage of greater internal consistency precisely because they do *not* posit that deity is simultaneously omnipotent, omniscient, and omnibenevolent. The following are some of the more common theisms in world religions, although I do not pretend that this list is exhaustive:

Polytheism is the notion that there are many gods, with roughly equivalent levels of power. This is found in the Greco-Roman religion, Norse mythology, and the more commonplace understanding of Hinduism. Closely related is the notion of "henotheism": there are many gods, but one is more powerful than the others. Thus, we find Zeus/Jove/Jupiter in the Greco-Roman pantheon eventually came to be understood as the father, and king, of the gods. Odin

---

theism in Seabury Quinn's work to gain insight as to why the former was, mostly, disregarded during his life but is now highly esteemed, and why the latter was highly esteemed in his life but has now largely fallen into obscurity.

4. Related questions are: whether there is an afterlife (Rowe 134–46; if there is, why isn't there better and more reliable documentation or substantiation of such?); whether there is divine foreknowledge/predestination (Rowe 147–60; if the future is already set in stone, what responsibility do we have for our—presumably foreordained—actions?; how can we be held culpable or responsible in that case?). Rowe strives mightily with all these issues, but whether he does so successfully is another question. His answers, though cogent, are also extensive and recondite, and often border upon the tortuous. Occam's razor would suggest that a more elegant solution would have been to jettison the original definition of "theism" for something that is more consistent with available knowledge, experience, and observation.

holds a similar place in Norse mythology.

Epicureans affirmed that there were gods but that they abided in such a state of perfect *ataraxia* (serene calmness) and *aponia* (lack of pain) that they seldom, if ever, intervened on their creation.[5] Deism developed out of the rediscovery and renewed appreciation of Epicureanism, but also held that God can best be known via the application of reason to its creation. They also denied authority of scripture, the existence of miracles, or divine intervention.[6]

Dystheism is the belief that a deity is not wholly beneficent and can even be considered evil. Closely related is maltheism, the notion that a deity exists but is actively malevolent. This notion is found within Gnosticism in general and Manichaeism in particular, which distinguish between an all-good ultimate deity, which, being all good, is beyond the need or use of a creation (this ultimate deity is known, in the *Apocryphon of John*, found in the Nag Hammadi library, as the "Monad") and a later, flawed, malevolent emanation from that ultimate deity, Yaldabaoth, which has created a flawed world and universe in its own image.[7] Maltheists effectively reason about the nature of the divine based on *inductive* reasoning: observing, in creation, the presence of evil, cruelty, and violence, they infer from its creation an inimical creator. By contrast, eutheists (those who believe in an entirely beneficent deity) operate *deductively*: proceeding from the assumption of an entirely beneficent creator god, they then must come to terms with accounting for the evil and violence that are all too evident in society and in the world.[8]

Very evidently, the Abrahamic/Levantine conception of the divine would *not* accord with Lovecraft, who identified as a "mechanistic materialist," since the putatively (semi-)divine entities in his fiction are not "supremely good, creator of but separate from and independent of the world, all-powerful (om-

---

5. See Greenblatt. This book provides an account of the rediscovery of the Epicurean poem *De Rerum Natura* ("On the Nature of Things") by the Epicurean poet Lucretius, and argues that this work helped jump-start the Renaissance.

6. For an interesting exposition of Deism and its impact on some of the more influential of the American founding fathers. See Stewart.

7. See Robinson et al. The Maltheist understanding is, thus, consistent with Shakespeare's observation: "As flies to wanton boys are we to the gods: They kill us for their sport." *King Lear* 4.1.36-37.

8. The various types of theism mentioned in this section are common knowledge in the field of religious studies. Anyone interested in learning more about these alternate theisms can make a good start by looking into Beyer and Cline.

nipotent), all-knowing (omniscient), eternal, and self-existent" (supra). But which of these alternative theisms would be most applicable to the cosmology he presents in his work?

In my reading, there are two discernible phases in Lovecraft's tacit theism in his stories. Some stories read as either Epicurean or dystheist—there are gods, but they either do not intervene or are, at best, not wholly beneficent. Thus, for example, we find in the story "Through the Gates of the Silver Key," Yog-Sothoth states to Randolph Carter:

> What you wish, I have found good; and I am ready to grant that which I have granted eleven times only to beings of your planet—five times only to those you call men, or those resembling them. I am ready to shew you the Ultimate Mystery, to look on which is to blast a feeble spirit. Yet before you gaze full at that last and first of secrets you may still wield a free choice, and return if you will through the two Gates with the Veil still unrent before your eyes. (CF 3.301-2)

A supreme being that usually does not intervene in human affairs is entirely consistent with Epicureanism. That said, the subsequent development that by granting this wish Carter ends up in a lamentable situation marks Yog-Sothoth as a "trickster god," and, thus more consistent with "dystheism."[9] Later stories in his oeuvre lean more into out-and-out maltheism: there are gods (or, at least, god*like* beings), but they are either indifferent to humankind or, indeed,

---

9. Although Yog-Sothoth also states all conscious beings are merely refractions of a greater being ("In the face of that awful wonder, the quasi-Carter forgot the horror of destroyed individuality. It was an All-in-One and One-in-All of limitless being and self—not merely a thing of one Space-Time continuum but allied to the ultimate animating essence of existence's whole unbounded sweep—the last, utter sweep which has no confines and which outreaches fancy and mathematics alike. It was perhaps that which certain secret cults of earth have whispered of as YOG-SOTHOTH, and which has been a deity under other names; that which the crustaceans of Yuggoth worship as the Beyond-One, and which the vaporous brains of the spiral nebulae know by an untranslatable Sign—yet in a flash the Carter-facet realised how slight and fractional all these conceptions are" CF 3.300). Shades of either pantheism or panentheism: the notion of deity as the consciousness or soul of the universe or, in the latter case, deity as being more than the universe in itself, but encompassing the universe within its being. There is some question as to whether this is a reflection of HPL's viewpoint, or perhaps an example of the moderating influence of his collaborator on this particular story, E. Hoffmann Price. The original sketch/outline/summary that Price submitted to HPL for his elaboration/expansion (held at the John Hay Library) would resolve this question.

entirely inimical: "The Call of Cthulhu," *The Case of Charles Dexter Ward*, "The Shadow over Innsmouth," etc.

Moreover, we can be confident that Lovecraft was aware of both Epicureanism and, at least, the one strain of Gnosticism: Manichaeism. In his correspondence he directly references the former:

> it is plain that [humanity's] only logical goal [. . .] is simply the achievement of a reasonable equilibrium which shall enhance his likelihood of experiencing the sort of reactions he wishes, & which shall help along his natural impulse[. . . .] Here, then, is a practical and imperative system of ethics, resting on the firmest possible foundation and being essentially that taught by Epicurus & Lucretius. (*Letters to Robert Bloch* 209–10)

Sarane Alexandrian, in his book *Histoire de la philosophie occulte* (*History of Occult Philosophy*), states: "A book on twentieth-century gnosis should also include the fantasy novelist H. P. Lovecraft, who was inspired by the Syriac text by Teodor bar Konaï on Manicheism" (70).[10] Lovecraft does allude to the (so-called) "devil-worshipping Yazidis" in "The Horror of Red Hook" and he did live near Red Hook for a time. The Yazidis are a syncretic ethno-religious group which absorbed Manichaean/Gnostic influences, including the notion that this world is ruled over by a later and lesser emanation of the divine, consistent with Manichaean Gnosticism. Lovecraft's epithet for them is consistent with that understanding. We can reasonably infer a direct or indirect Manichaean influence in the Mythos via the narrative of the Old Ones being exiled from our planet/dimension in a conflict with the Elder Gods in a remote era. The notion of this plane being a battlefield between forces of absolute evil and absolute good is a common, often tacit, trope in horror literature.

How might this account for why the works of Lovecraft's chief competitor at *Weird Tales*, Seabury Quinn, were so much more popular in the day, and for why Quinn's works have largely fallen to the wayside, while Lovecraft's have come to be re-evaluated and appreciated as serious literature? Despite their shared publishing venue, the two writers differed in almost every other conceivable way: Lovecraft's fictive universe was dystheist/maltheist, his stories usually have unhappy or ambivalent resolutions, and they are not moralistic. By contrast, Quinn's stories are even more eutheist than you would expect for a

---

10. The notion that at least some human beings are, in essence, energy beings, temporarily trapped in matter during our lives, found in HPL's story "Beyond the Wall of Sleep," is entirely consistent with the Manichean understanding of the human condition.

writer in this period. His stories have mostly happy endings, and it seems that there is hardly anyone who cannot be redeemed for violating even extreme taboos, if they only get to Quinn's occult detective character, Jules de Grandin, in a timely manner:

- In "Pledged to the Dead," an engaged man unwittingly makes a marriage pledge to a ghost, at the risk of his life. All parties—including no fewer than two ghosts—are redeemed.

- In "Incense of Abomination," a man is haunted by the ghost of a girl who died during a satanic ritual he had participated in. This ghost can drive people to suicide. Two have died already but, with the exception of the two victims who did not get to Jules de Grandin in time, everyone is redeemed in the end, including the ghost.

- In "The Jest of Warburg Tantavul," a young couple who had been tricked into committing incest are redeemed and their incestuous liaison is affirmed by Grandin (although, for once, the ghost of the deceased relative who manipulated them into this situation and torments them from beyond the grave is not redeemed, but, merely, driven away).

These stories are ultimately very moralistic and, ultimately, confirm conventional morality, with Jules de Grandin using his fund of knowledge and connections in the occult world and with the church to intervene and redeem almost anyone, no matter what terrible things they may have done in the past, so long as they have to humility to come to him and request his assistance. (I am indebted to Stephanie Claudio, whose master's thesis confirmed the impressions I had formed of Quinn's usual themes and narrative approach after reading a sampling of his short stories.)

So why was Quinn so much more popular than Lovecraft at the time? For one thing, per Claudio, he was a resolutely *commercial* writer, writing for the market of his time and, having found a winning formula for his tales, was content to stick with it, not only in his Grandin stories but also in other series he wrote for other magazines of the time. He was writing for money, to supplement his income from being an attorney working in mortuary law, in the depths of the Great Depression, and if that meant, for example, the any women in his stories must be described in abundant and sensual detail, and often held in bondage—all the better to lend his stories to a cover by Margaret

Brundage—so much the better. Quinn was a commercial writer and, as such, his focus was on *entertaining* his readers—to give them a bit of a *frisson* by portraying a violation of one or another taboo, but also providing them with a resolution that would reaffirm the status quo and their received, conventional mores and provide a happy ending. By contrast, it is well known that Lovecraft considered himself more of an *artiste*: he worked out a thoughtful thesis upon the nature and purpose of weird fiction (in his "Supernatural Horror in Literature") and identified as an atheistic "mechanistic materialist" at a time when such a worldview would, in the context of conventional wisdom and morality, have been regarded as profoundly transgressive. Lovecraft focused more on providing his readers with a *challenge*, and a shock, to their usual understanding.[11]

How have things changed since that time that might account for Lovecraft's ascendency, and Quinn's fall into relative obscurity? There are many changes and subsequent developments that would have surprised both of them and might account for this. For one thing, at the time they were both writing, the First World War was often referred to as the "war to end all wars" and was regarded as a brief paroxysm of violence before the re-establishment of an enduring and stable international order. Neither of them could have anticipated the coming of World War II, with all its attendant evils: massive fatalities in battles fought between the most culturally and technologically sophisticated nations of the day, ultimately leading to the discovery and realization of the atrocity of organized and systematic genocide in Fascist-controlled territories. The notion of a "serial killer" would not even be coined until 1974. Our current plague of semi-regular mass-shootings was outside of either man's frame of reference.

Moreover, Quinn's appeal can be traced to his tacit, if formulaic, endorsement of a monolithic, received "conventional morality" of the day (if, however, positing a divine force that was, comfortingly, *more* eutheistic than what we find in traditional, orthodox modes of Christianity). But in the wake of the events mentioned above the massive increase in ethnographic diversity in our country, far beyond the level of their time (of which Lovecraft would

---

11. This is not to say that there weren't other cultural factors that shaped this difference in popularity over time, but the difference in tacit worldviews, including tacit differing theisms, in relation to the received underlying understanding of the time was probably, at the very least, a contributory factor.

have disapproved!),[12] which undercuts the complacent assumption of a nearly universal and monolithic "conventional morality," and the decline in the preeminence of Christianity in our culture.[13] it seems, for good or ill, that Lovecraft's maltheistic cosmology and worldview are more compatible with our current times and understanding than Quinn's eutheistic worldview.[14]

Quinn was popular and successful in his time because he wrote to his own time, affirming most people's received understanding, morality, and worldview. Lovecraft has supplanted him because, whether it was by dint of his idiosyncratic good fortune, or vision, or genius, he anticipated the world in which we now live.

Works Cited

Alexandrian, Sarane. *Histoire de la philosophie occulte*. Paris: Editions Seghers, 1983.

Beyer, Catherine. "Types of Theism." *Learn Religions* (27 August 2020). www.learnreligions.com/types-of-theism-95709

Chidester, David. *Authentic Fakes*. Berkeley: University of California Press, 2005.

Claudio, Stephanie. "Seabury Quinn: A *Weird Tales* View of Gender and Sexuality." M.A. thesis: California State University–San Marcos, 2015. hdl.handle.net/ 10211.3/138865

Cline, Austin. "One or Many Gods: The Varieties of Theism." *Learn Religions* (16 February 2021) www.learnreligions.com/theisms-monotheism-polytheism-deism-and-more-250956

Greenblatt, Stephen. *The Swerve: How the World Became Modern*. New York: W. W. Norton, 2011.

Lovecraft, H. P. *Against Religion: The Atheist Writings of H. P. Lovecraft*. Ed. S. T. Joshi. [New York]: Sporting Gentlemen, 2010.

———. *Letters to Robert Bloch and Others*. Ed. David E. Schultz and S. T. Joshi. New York: Hippocampus Press, 2015.

---

12. See "The Horror of Red Hook."

13. The Pew Forum projects that Christianity will be a minority religion by 2070. See www.pewresearch.org/religion/2022/09/13/modeling-the-future-of-religion-in-america/ Accessed 26 February 2023).

14. For all that, his tales, in my experience, are still engaging, entertaining, and diverting.

Pew Forum. www.pewresearch.org/religion/2022/09/13/modeling-the-future-of-religion-in-america/ Accessed 16 February 2023.

Quinn, Dennis (as "Popmatters Staff"). "Cults of an Unwitting Oracle: The (Unintended) Religious Legacy of H. P. Lovecraft." *Popmatters* (19 August 2010). www.popmatters.com/cults-of-an-unwitting-oracle-the-unintended-religious-legacy-of-h-p-lovecraft-2496158350.html

Quinn, Seabury. "Incense of Abomination." *Weird Tales* 31, No. 3 (March 1938): 259-78

———. "The Jest of Warburg Tantavul." *Weird Tales* 24, No. 3 (September 1934): 296-16.

———. "Pledged to the Dead." *Weird Tales* 30, No. 4 (October 1937): 397-416.

Robinson, James M., and Richard Smith, ed. *The Nag Hammadi Library in English*. New York: HarperCollins, 1990.

Rowe, William L. *Philosophy of Religion: An Introduction*. 3rd ed. Belmont, CA: Wadsworth-Thomson, 2007.

Stewart, Matthew. *Nature's God: The Heretical Origins of the American Republic*. New York: W. W. Norton, 2015.

Naked Sailors in a Swamp: Sea Men and Homoerotic Initiations in Three Lovecraft Tales

Peter Muise
Independent Scholar

A few years ago I was reading "The Call of Cthulhu" and was struck by how frequently Lovecraft uses the word queer in it. So many queer things in one story! As a gay man, and therefore part of the queer community, I decided to play a mental game. I thought, "What happens if I read this story with the assumption Lovecraft was using queer in its modern sense, meaning something outside heterosexuality, rather than its older definition of something weird?" Reading the story with that filter was quite illuminating. While in many instances "queer" was clearly being used to simply mean "weird," in other instances its usage was ambiguous, and the modern definition made equal if not more sense. Reading it with that filter also showed me how central homoeroticism and queer pleasure is to the story's plot.

The homoeroticism is focused on sailors, and as I went on to re-read other Lovecraft stories I noticed that homoerotic sailors appear in two other tales. Interestingly, the sailors in all three stories play similar roles. They are emissaries of a god associated with the ocean and dreams, and they initiate other men into the mysteries of that deity, whether by revealing secret knowledge or physically introducing them to the god. In essence, these stories are all tales of queer initiation. These homoerotic sailors also disrupt heterosexual families and are portrayed as having dark complexions. All three stories also feature a sunken city.

Two other stories with these components and initiatory theme are "The Temple" and "The Strange High House in the Mist." These stories are written in a variety of styles, from classic horror to cosmic horror to wistful fantasy, but underneath the stylistic differences they all contain the same basic components. I am going to discuss the stories in the order they were written to show how Lovecraft used these components to express the theme of queer initiation differently in each one.

"The Temple": Young, Rather Dark, and Very Handsome

"The Temple" (1920), first published in *Weird Tales* in 1925, is in many ways a relatively straightforward tale of ghostly revenge. During World War I, the crew of a German submarine finds the body of a dead sailor clinging to their vessel. He is apparently a drowned crewman from a British freighter they torpedoed. They discover a small ivory sculpture on the dead man's body: an image of a youth's head crowned with laurels. One of the German officers takes the sculpture before the crew pushes the body back into the water. This, of course, is a terrible idea. The submarine's crew is subsequently plagued with nightmares and madness, and most are killed by mechanical failures and during a mutiny. Others just mysteriously disappear.

A school of strange dolphins arrives and follows the submarine, which completely malfunctions and sinks to the bottom of the ocean. It finally comes to rest in a sunken city that may be Atlantis. The last surviving crew member, the vessel's commander, leaves the submarine and walks toward a giant temple that is carved with images identical to that on the stolen sculpture. He sees that an eerie light like a sacrificial flame burns within the building.

"The Temple" is a criticism of German militarism and a classic ghost story that warns against violating the dead, but it is also about men encountering a god and being led to that god by another man: the drowned sailor. The drowned sailor is presented as an object of homoerotic attraction. The story is narrated in the first person by Karl Heinrich, the submarine's commander, and he describes the sailor in the following way: "The poor fellow was young, rather dark, and very handsome; probably an Italian or Greek." (CF 1.157). Rather than focus on the horror or ugliness of a drowned corpse, Heinrich focuses on the youth and attractiveness of the dead man. He is not merely handsome; he is "very handsome." And despite the increasingly nightmarish conditions on the submarine, Heinrich consistently describes the dead sailor as youthful: "the youth from the sea" (169), "the living mocking face of the youth" (168), and the "dark dead youth" (160) Heinrich sees the handsome young sailor in his dreams, and he is the center of Heinrich's fears: "And over all rose thoughts and fears which centred in the youth from the sea and the ivory image" (169).

The commander is not alone in his obsession with the handsome young sailor; the other men on the submarine are haunted by him as well. Lieutenant Klenze, the crew member who stole the ivory sculpture, says: "*He* is calling! *He* is calling! I hear him! We must go!" (162). Like the sirens luring Odysseus, the handsome young sailor calls to the crew to join him outside the safety of their submarine. This image, of a handsome, young man enchanting other men who are obsessed with him, is distinctly homoerotic.

Both Heinrich and Klenze have families, and Heinrich specifically mentions that he has children. These are salient facts that emphasize not only the all-male environment of the submarine but the homoerotic nature of its crew's plight. They are being lured irrevocably and irresistibly away from their heterosexual families by a handsome young man.

He is luring them to the temple of an ancient god. The temple's god is never named, but the stolen sculpture portrays him as a "youth's head crowned with laurel" (157). He seems to be some type of classical Greco-Roman deity, or perhaps an early precursor to one, given that the architecture of the sunken city is "the remotest rather than the immediate ancestor of Greek art" (CF 1.165). The god's identification with the classical or proto-classical world is also emphasized by the physical appearance of the youth who carries his image. The god and the person who carries his image are both young men and possibly Greek or Italian, and the boundaries between them are unclear. The handsome young sailor may just be the god's ghostly emissary, or may be an aspect of the god himself. Who will greet Heinrich when he enters the sunken temple: the handsome sailor, an ancient god, or both? Or perhaps the god and the sailor are the same being?

Lovecraft hints that the god may be Dionysus, or some archaic form of that god of madness and ecstasy. When Heinrich explores the sunken city, he sees on the temple's façade "exquisite carvings like Bacchanals in relief," carved in a style that is "largely Hellenic in idea" (165). The term "bacchanal" refers to celebrations in honor of Bacchus, the Roman version of Dionysus.

Another clue to the god's Dionysian identity are the mysterious dolphins that follow the submarine on its slow descent to the sunken city. In *H. P. Lovecraft's Dark Arcadia*, Gavin Callaghan points out the similarities between "The Temple" and myth of Dionysus and the Tyrrhenian pirates. In that myth, Dionysus, in the shape of young beautiful man, is kidnapped by the crew of a Tyrrhenian pirate ship. To punish them, Dionysus transforms the pirates into dolphins, who leap from the ship into the ocean. In Callaghan's interpretation, the handsome young sailor in "The Temple" plays the role of Dionysus, while the German crewmen are the Tyrrhenians who are transformed into dolphins (694). Lovecraft's story and the ancient myth are not identical, but they both share the same broad theme of a god punishing a ship's crew that has mistreated them. This resemblance between the story and the myth further strengthens the likelihood that the god in "The Temple" is Dionysus, and that the very handsome young sailor is an aspect of him.

In some versions of the Tyrrhenian myth, the pirates are inflamed by Dionysus's beauty and intend to violate him sexually. For example, the mythologist Hyginus notes bluntly: "They took him on board and planned to gang up and rape him because of his beauty" (144). Although the homoeroticism in "The Temple" is much less explicit, it is definitely highlighted by the story's similarity to this Dionysian myth.

To sum up, "The Temple" includes the following components. It features a dark-skinned homoerotic sailor: the very handsome drowned Mediterranean sailor the crew is obsessed with. He initiates them into the mysteries of a god by leading the submarine to the titular temple. The god dwells in a city that may be Atlantis and is associated with dolphins, both of which firmly connect the deity with the ocean, and also haunts their dreams. Lastly, the submarine crew's families are ruptured in this process.

"The Call of Cthulhu": Naked Sailors in a Swamp

All these components—homoerotic sailors, sunken cities, dreams, etc.—reappear in "The Call of Cthulhu," written in the summer of 1926 and one of Lovecraft's most famous stories. In it, Lovecraft revisits the themes and images from "The Temple," presenting them more bluntly and horrifically than he did in the earlier tale. S. T. Joshi notes that "Dagon," with its sunken island and giant aquatic monster, may be a precursor to "The Call of Cthulhu" (Lovecraft, *Call of Cthulhu* 393), and I would argue that "The Temple" is a precursor as well.

"The Temple" ends with Commander Heinrich on the brink of discovering the beautiful god's secret in the sunken Atlantean city, but the god is never revealed. In "Cthulhu," classically proportioned Atlantis is transformed into the nightmarishly angled R'lyeh, which rises above the waves. The god emerges from his resting place, but instead of a beautiful Dionysus he is the hideous and terrifying Cthulhu. The things that were hidden beneath the ocean in "The Temple" are displayed openly in "Cthulhu," including the homoeroticism.

The plot of "Cthulhu" is much harder to summarize than the "The Temple's" because it consists of multiple nested narratives. The story is presented as the writings of the late Francis Wayland Thurston, who was reviewing the papers of his deceased grand-uncle George Gammell Angell, who collected newspaper clippings and interviewed various people about strange phenomena, including New Orleans police inspector Legrasse, who arrested and collected confessions from some naked sailors in a swamp. The journey in "The Temple" is straightforward, as the submarine and its crew are led to the sunken city. The journey in "The Call of Cthulhu" is more circuitous, as the reader and the story's various narrators are ultimately led to R'lyeh and the revelation of its god through reams of accumulated evidence.

The narrative structure is complex, but it is again a sailor, or more properly multiple sailors, who initiate the reader and narrators into Cthulhu's mysteries. Like the handsome young sailor in "The Temple," Cthulhu's nautical emissaries are also presented homoerotically and disrupt the heterosexual family. They are vividly described in "II. The Tale of Inspector Legrasse," where the inspector and twenty police officers try to find some missing squatters who live in the swamps outside New Orleans. The only squatters who have disappeared are women and children—the adult men in their families have been left unharmed.

Inspector Legrasse and his men trace the missing women and children to a ritual being held by Cthulhu's followers on an island in a swamp. The word ritual may conjure images of robes, incense, and candles, but that is not the case here. Lovecraft instead describes the ritual as an orgy: "The present voodoo orgy was, indeed, on the merest fringe of this abhorred area" (CF 2.35), and "two were shaken into a frantic cry which the mad cacophony of the orgy fortunately deadened" (36).

The word orgy can mean several things, some non-sexual, but Lovecraft describes this orgy with language that is clearly sexual: "animal fury and orgiastic licence," "howls and squawking ecstasies" (35), and most tellingly, "Void of clothing, this hybrid spawn were braying, bellowing, and writhing about a monstrous ring-shaped bonfire" (36). Several paragraphs later, after the police arrest the Cthulhu cultists, Lovecraft explains that the participants in this orgy are all men, mostly sailors: "the prisoners all proved to be men of a very low, mixed-blooded, and mentally aberrant type. Most were seamen" (37). In short, the Cthulhu ritual is a homosexual orgy attended by naked male sailors. Many of them are also dark-skinned: "a sprinkling of negroes and mulattoes, largely West Indians or Brava Portuguese from the Cape Verde Islands, gave a colouring of voodooism to the heterogeneous cult" (37).

The homoeroticism in "The Call of Cthulhu" is much more explicit than that in "The Temple." The handsome young dark-skinned sailor leading the submarine crew to their doom in a sunken city is replaced by "mentally aberrant" dark-skinned naked sailors holding a homosexual orgy in a swamp. Their disruption of the heterosexual family is also more explicit. Rather than just leading men away from their wives and children, Cthulhu's cultists are holding their orgy surrounded by scaffolds which hold the "oddly marred bodies of the helpless squatters who disappeared" (36). These squatters were all women and children, so the sailors are having a homosexual orgy surrounded by the corpses of women and children. It is a vivid image of the heterosexual family being destroyed. The sailors claim the squatters were killed by Black Winged Ones, bat-winged creatures that emerge from the earth, but even if they are not the killers, the sailors still hold their queer sexual revel surrounded by the corpses.

It may seem strange that his followers would honor Cthulhu with a gay orgy, but an elderly cultist named Castro explains to Inspector Legrasse that pleasure is a central tenet of their cult. When Cthulhu and the Old Ones return, there will be shouting and killing, but also "revelling in joy" (40), and the Old Ones will teach mankind, among other less savory lessons, "new ways to . . . revel and enjoy themselves, and all the earth would flame with a holocaust of ecstasy and freedom" (41). It seems that the Cthulhu cult teaches liberation from traditional heterosexual mores. Later, when Cthulhu is accidentally freed from his crypt by another group of sailors, he emerges "ravening for delight" (53). After millennia of undead slumber, the ancient god is not hungry for murder or destruction, but is hungry for pleasure. Both the god and his followers want to enjoy themselves.

This is one of the secrets Castro passes to Legrasse, in essence initiating him into Cthulhu's mysteries. As in "The Temple," the centerpiece of the story focuses on a queer initiation into the mysteries of the god, on men being led to the god by other men. But unlike that story, Legrasse does not seem to be obsessed with Castro and the other queer sailors. They are presented as insane and bestial, rather than alluring and beautiful. What was hidden and mysterious in the earlier story is here revealed as grotesque and frightening.

The naked, orgiastic sailors are Cthulhu's mostly blatantly homoerotic emissaries, but there is another who is more discretely homoerotic. He is, however, quite explicitly called queer. That emissary is Henry Anthony Wilcox, a young Providence artist who comes to Professor Angell for help. Like the handsome sailor in "The Temple," Wilcox is described as young and dark, and is also associated with a sculpture of a deity, although Wilcox has carved his bas-relief of Cthulhu himself. Wilcox is described as speaking in "dreamy and stilted manner, which suggested pose and alienated sympathy" (25) and moving languidly (42). He associates primarily with other "aesthetes" (25) from towns beyond Providence. The reader might interpret these habits and mannerisms as clues that Wilcox is gay, and they would not be alone in this. Lovecraft tells us that people in Providence feel the same way about Wilcox: "He [Wilcox] called himself 'psychically hypersensitive,' but the staid folk of the ancient commercial city described him as merely 'queer'" (CF 2.25).

"Queer" in that sentence feels deflating, a way for the Providence establishment to put the poseur Wilcox back in his place. It also feels vaguely insulting, like a slur. But exactly what type of slur is it? Are the upstanding citizens of Providence (and Lovecraft) calling Wilcox weird (an older definition of queer), or are they implying he's homosexual (a slightly newer one)? Lovecraft uses the word "queer" nine times in "Cthulhu" to describe various things: architecture, art, dreams, rituals, reticence, and the way a door in R'lyeh opens. In those instances, "queer" probably does mean "weird," but when it is used to describe Wilcox, it could plausibly mean homosexual, particularly since the story includes a homosexual sailor orgy. People in Providence might be saying that Wilcox is not "psychically hypersensitive," he's just gay.

According to the OED, the word "queer" was originally used to mean strange, odd, or peculiar. The first recorded usage of the word in this way dates to 1513, and this is how Lovecraft uses "queer" when he describes, for example, "the queer dark courts on the precipitous hillside" (CF 2.22) near Providence Harbor, or the "queer recession of the monstrously carven portal" (52) that opens into Cthulhu's crypt.

By the late 1800s, "queer" was also used to mean a homosexual of any gender, but most particularly a homosexual man. The OED cites an 1894 letter from John Sholto Douglas, the Marquess of Queensberry, as the first documented use of the word in this way: "I write to tell you that it is a judgement on the whole lot of you. Montgomerys, The Snob Queers like Roseberry, & certainly Christian hypocrite Gladstone." Douglas believed that the Earl of Roseberry was having a homosexual relationship with his son, Francis Douglas. Douglas's other son, Alfred Douglas, was the lover of Oscar Wilde, the famous poet and leading figure of the Aesthetic Movement (Bloch 61).

"Queer" was also used to mean "homosexual" in the United States, with the OED citing a 1914 example as the first documented use in this country. While often used as a slur, George Chauncey shows in *Gay New York: Gender,*

Urban Culture, and the Making of the Gay Male World, 1890–1940, that many homosexual men also described themselves as "queer" or "queers" in the first four decades of the twentieth century. They used the word to refer to homosexual men who presented themselves in a traditionally masculine way, as opposed to "fairy," which meant a homosexual man who presented himself in a more feminine way. "Queer" was not just confined to subcultural use in the early twentieth century, however, but was widely used in the general American population. The folklorist Gershon Legman, who compiled a dictionary of homosexual slang in 1941, claimed that "queer" and "fairy" were the terms most frequently used by both heterosexuals and homosexuals to refer to homosexual men in the years before World War II (Chauncey 14).

"Queer" started to fall out of fashion with homosexual men in the late 1930s, when a younger generation of men started to describe themselves as "gay" instead, believing the newer descriptor carried less stigma than "queer" and was less derogatory. Its usage grew within the subculture and eventually spread into general American usage in the 1960s and 1970s, as the gay liberation movement became prominent (Chauncey 20–21). The word "queer" began to have a resurgence in popularity in the 1980s and 1990s, as demonstrated by the 1990 founding of the activist group Queer Nation, which rejected what it saw as assimilationist tendencies in the gay movement. Queer is now often used as an umbrella term to describe anyone (gay, lesbian, bisexual, transgender, etc.) who does not identify as straight (Clark).

So how should we interpret Lovecraft telling us that citizens of Providence considered Henry Wilcox queer? Are they, and Lovecraft, simply telling us that Wilcox was strange, or are they, and Lovecraft, telling us that Wilcox was homosexual? Although Lovecraft often adopted the persona of an old-fashioned gentleman and often wrote in an archaic style, he did live and write in Providence and New York, both large, urban, industrialized American cities. It is likely he was aware of the modern definition of the word 'queer,' and the languid and dreamy aesthete Wilcox certainly seems to fit certain stereotypes associated with queer men. The fact that Wilcox primarily associates with other "aesthetes" can even be read as a reference to Oscar Wilde, the most famous of aesthetes, and also one of the most famous queer men.

Lovecraft's use of the term "queer" to describe Wilcox is playfully ambiguous and subtly foreshadows the queer sailor orgy that comes later. Significantly, the only other characters described as queer are a group of dark-skinned Cthulhu-worshipping sailors encountered in the Pacific Ocean, described in a newspaper article as "a queer and evil-looking crew of Kanakas and half-castes" (CF 2.46). Are we to understand this to mean that the crew looks both weird (queer) and evil, or that they are homosexual (queer) and evil-looking? The word's use here again is ambiguous, but given the orgy described earlier in the story, its more modern definition may be apt.

Cthulhu himself certainly can be described as queer, although perhaps only in the older sense of the word, given that he is a gigantic, slobbering, gelatinous, lumbering amalgamation of octopus, human, and dragon. His sexual orientation (if he has one) is not disclosed. But despite his frightening appearance, he still has many similarities to the beautiful god of "The Temple." Both are associated with the ocean, indicated in Cthulhu's case by his octopoid head and the sailors who worship him, and with sunken cities (R'lyeh and Atlantis). Like the god of "The Temple," Cthulhu also calls to people (as the title of the story itself indicates), and he communicates through dreams. The beautiful Atlantis-dwelling god haunted the submarine crew's dreams, while Cthulhu speaks to his followers in dreams and causes "queer dreams" (24) and nightmares across the world. His initiated followers find these dreams inspiring, while others find them terrifying. One person's queer dream is another's nightmare. Cthulhu also inspires Wilcox to sculpt his image through dreams.

There are other similarities between the two deities. Sculptures of Cthulhu appear multiple times in the story. One is made by Wilcox, one appears at the orgy, and one is seen in Greenland, where it is used as part of "queer hereditary rituals" (32). The god of "The Temple" also is portrayed in sculptures: one carried by the handsome young sailor, and several on the temple's façade.

The god in the earlier story had many Dionysian qualities. Cthulhu has many as well, although his appearance is unlikely to inspire lust in Tyrrhenian pirates. The Cthulhu cult's emphasis on ecstasy, pleasure, and freedom are similar to how modern Westerners view the ancient Dionysian cults, and also Friedrich Nietzsche's concept of the Dionysian impulse. According to S. T. Joshi, Lovecraft is explicitly referencing Nietzsche's philosophy when he has Castro tell Inspector Legrasse that the Old Ones will return when mankind is "beyond good and evil" (Lovecraft, *Call of Cthulhu* 397), although it is not clear if Lovecraft read Nietzsche's work on the Dionysian impulse, *The Birth of Tragedy*.

Lovecraft describes the sailors' orgy as a "bacchanal," another clear reference to Dionysus. Even the word "orgy" itself has Dionysian connotations. According to the *OED*, the word comes from the Greek word *orgia*, meaning ecstatic religious rituals. The most famous ancient *orgia* were those associated with the cult of Dionysus. The gods in "The Call of Cthulhu" and "The Temple" are identical in many ways, despite their different physical appearances, and the stories themselves feature many of the same themes and motifs.

Both stories include dark-skinned homoerotic sailors who initiate other men into the mysteries of a god. The gods in both are associated with dreams, the ocean, and sunken cities. Heterosexual families are disrupted in both tales, quite violently in "The Call of Cthulhu." Lovecraft rearranges these components to different effect in the two stories, but the basic elements are the same.

"The Strange High House in the Mist": Joys Beyond Earth's Joys

A maritime god, a dark-skinned sailor, homoeroticism, and many other elements from the two stories reappear again in "The Strange High House in the Mist," which Lovecraft wrote on 9 November 1926, only a few months after completing "The Call of Cthulhu." It seems he was still working on the same themes that appear in that earlier and more famous story. "The Strange High House in the Mist" is much less Dionysian and much more wistful. In it, a college professor from Rhode Island named Thomas Olney and his family take a vacation in the seaside Massachusetts town of Kingsport. While there, Olney becomes intrigued by an old house that sits high on a cliff. The locals fear the house and claim its occupant is centuries old, but despite these warnings Olney climbs to the house. He is warmly greeted by its reclusive occupant, who regales Olney with tales and legends about the ocean. As night falls, the two men are visited by the god Nodens and other sea deities, who bring them on a journey into the mists that surround the house. Olney returns to his family the next day and they go back to Rhode Island. Olney's spirit, however, remains in the strange house, where the people of Kingsport hear him singing and laughing with its occupant.

The plot is quite different than either "The Temple" or "The Call of Cthulhu," but many of the same components recur. Again we have a dark-skinned sailor who reveals mysteries to the uninitiated. In this case, it is the man who lives in the strange high house, Lovecraft noting his "brown hand" and "great black-bearded face" (CF 2.92). His ethnicity is not specified, but he has a dark complexion. He also appears to be young (93) and has a gentle voice (92). Lovecraft does not specifically say the occupant is a sailor, but notes that he "was clad in very ancient garments, and had about him an unplaceable nimbus of sea-lore and dreams of tall galleons" (92). If he is not an actual sailor, he is still somehow strongly associated with the sea.

As in the other two stories, this dark-skinned nautical man initiates another man into the mysteries of a god. The man is Professor Olney and the god in this case is Nodens, Lord of the Great Abyss, who arrives at the house after its occupant lights candles and makes "enigmatical gestures of prayer" (94). The attributes of the historical Celtic deity Nodens are somewhat murky, but in Lovecraft's tale he is clearly a sea-god, arriving on a giant shell pulled by dolphins and accompanied by the god Neptune, along with tritons and nereids. The dolphins are reminiscent of "The Temple," but unlike the god in that story and unlike Cthulhu, Nodens does not seem particularly Dionysian. Still, Lovecraft situates him firmly in Dionysus's pantheon by filling Nodens's retinue with classical sea deities.

Nodens is connected to dreams, much like the deities in the other two stories. The strange high house is surrounded by mist, and that mist is "full of dreams of dank pastures and caves of leviathan" (87). When Nodens arrives at the house, it becomes filled with all the "dreams and memories of earth's sunken Mighty Ones" (94), and the house's occupant, Nodens's emissary, tells Olney stories about places in Lovecraft's Dreamlands, including Hatheg-Kla, Ulthar, and the river Skai (93).

Significantly, *The Dream-Quest of Unknown Kadath* is the only other Lovecraft story where Nodens appears. In it, he is the lord of the night-gaunts, black bat-winged creatures that are very similar to the bat-winged creatures who murder the squatters in "The Call of Cthulhu." Lovecraft began writing *Dream-Quest* in October 1926 (Lovecraft, *Dreams in the Witch House* 422), one month before he wrote "The Strange High House in the Mist" and a few months after completing "The Call of Cthulhu." Nodens's affiliation with the night-gaunts firmly connects him to Cthulhu, who is served by similar creatures. Dreams, oceans, dolphins, night-gaunts—the attributes and identities of Nodens, Cthulhu, and the unnamed temple's god overlap and blur. Are they even really different gods? Lovecraft may just be writing about one god in three different ways in these stories.

Lovecraft is shuffling and rearranging similar elements in these three stories, changing which ones receive the primary focus each time. Although "The Strange High House in the Mist" is set in contemporary New England, even a sunken city is mentioned, although not prominently. The house's occupant tells Olney many tales, including stories about "how the Kings of Atlantis fought with slippery blasphemies that wriggled out of rifts in ocean's floor" and how sailors lost at sea still see the ruins of its last temple (93). These references to Atlantis and "slippery blasphemies" echo themes in the earlier two stories.

Homoeroticism is also prominently featured and is presented almost romantically. "The Strange High House in the Mist" could easily be read as a gay coming-out story. Professor Olney leaves his family behind in Kingsport when he ascends the cliff to the strange house, and although his body returns to them, his soul remains with the house's young, gentle-voiced occupant. I suppose you cannot really blame him. Olney's wife and children are described simply and unflatteringly as "stout" and "romping" (89), while it takes just one night with the sailor-like occupant of the house for Olney quite literally to see God (or a god) and journey into the dream-filled aether. The next morning, Olney's spirit takes up permanent residence in the strange high house with its occupant. Their laughter tells of "joys beyond earth's joys" (96), and Olney's presence seems to strengthen the house's supernatural powers, causing the Aurora Borealis to appear above the house and thickening the mists that surround it. It all reads like a metaphor for someone finding true love and fulfilling sex for the first time in their life.

Thomas Olney's spirit leaves his wife and children to find happiness living with another man. Meanwhile, his soulless body returns to Rhode Island and lives out a traditional heterosexual married life, "through dull dragging years of greyness and weariness" (95). It is not surprising that the Terrible Old Man, Kingsport's resident warlock, mumbles "queer things" (95) after learning that Olney's spirit is now living in the strange high house. The situation is queer in every sense of the word.

Although the story seems to have a happily-ever-after ending for Olney, the elders of Kingsport are concerned that the young men in town will follow in his footsteps and their spirits will join him and the mysterious sailor in the strange high house. Hearing the music and laughter now emanating from the house, the young men have lost the fear of it that their elders instilled in them. If their spirits join Olney and the dark-haired sailor, the laughter and voices emanating from the house will grow "stronger and wilder" (96), until they summon back the old gods themselves. A joyous society of men outside heterosexual society summoning ancient gods is reminiscent of the Cthulhu cult. "The Strange High House in the Mist" is much more whimsical and wistful than "The Call of Cthulhu," but the same fears and concerns appear in both stories. For Lovecraft, there is a sinister side to queer pleasure.

Why So Many Homoerotic Sailors?

Lovecraft's fiction is densely written and complex, and in my experience always rewards re-reading with new insights. Its complexity also supports multiple interpretations, as all good fiction does. On one level, "The Call of Cthulhu" is simply a horror story about a giant tentacle-headed monster and his followers, but it can also be read as warning about the risks of humankind's rapidly expanding scientific knowledge. It can also be read as warning against the perils of Nietzschean morality. And, given what I have discussed above, it is also a warning about the threat that male homosexuality poses to the nuclear family.

Do the motifs discussed here, particularly the homoerotic sailors, say anything about Lovecraft's other fiction, or even his personal life? Perhaps these three stories simply appear homoerotic because Lovecraft wrote so few female characters. The stories could simply be homosocial, not homosexual, because they take place in the predominantly masculine world of Lovecraft's fiction. If they had been written by other pulp writers who included more female characters, the alluring and horrifically sexual sailors might have been portrayed as seductive female sirens or aggressive witch-like hags. Since Lovecraft wrote primarily male characters, those sirens and hags are instead men. And as sailors, they are obvious representatives of the ocean, a long-standing and potent symbol for the unconscious and the occasionally terrifying dreams that hide in it. They all have dark complexions because Lovecraft often conceptualized his supernatural threats as emanating from outside the charmed circle of middle-class white Anglo-American society.

But that does not quite explain why the sailors are presented erotically. There are many other ways Lovecraft could have portrayed these characters that would make them non-erotic, but he chose not to. In terms of his fiction, the queer eroticism in "The Temple," "The Call of Cthulhu," and "The Strange High House in the Mist" is not dissimilar to other motifs and themes present in Lovecraft's work. Male couples that can be interpreted as queer are featured in several of his stories, including the two thrill-seeking aesthetes in "The Hound," the unnamed sculptor and the beautiful man he meets at a train station in "Hypnos," and Herbert West and the hapless narrator of "Herbert West—Reanimator." These male couples live apart from society without female companionship for long periods of time. Herbert West and his companion live together for seventeen years and spend their time searching for other men with healthy physiques for their experiments (Sumrall). The sculptor in "Hypnos" meets and brings home a handsome man he meets at a train station: "I think he was then approaching forty years of age, for there were deep lines in the face, wan and hollow-cheeked, but oval and actually *beautiful* . . . I said to myself, with all the ardour of a sculptor, that this man was a faun's statue out of antique Hellas, dug from a temple's ruins" (CF 1.326). The two men end up living together and exploring strange realms of reality. It is not much of an interpretative stretch to imagine that the male couples in these stories are in sexual or romantic relationships with each other. As for the two aesthetes in "The Hound," their quest for "unnatural personal experiences and adventures" and their "diabolical penetrations" (340) can easily be interpreted as sexual as well as morbidly artistic.

Homoerotic themes also appear in several other works by Lovecraft. The narrator of "The Lurking Fear" travels to the abandoned Martense mansion with "two faithful and muscular men" whom he brings with him because of their "peculiar fitness" (CF 1.349). It is unclear if he wants the two men for protection or for a more erotic reason, because upon reaching the mansion the three men climb into a bed together. Sadly, the musclemen's purpose remains ambiguous, as they are both abducted by monsters and disappear from the story, leaving the reader (and perhaps the narrator) frustrated at their disappearance. Arthur Feldon, another muscular but more villainous man, appears in "The Electric Executioner," Lovecraft's revision of Adolphe de Castro's story "The Automatic Executioner." Lovecraft retained de Castro's basic plot—the large and handsome Feldon attempts to kill the smaller, frailer narrator on a train shortly before the narrator's wedding day—but added Feldon ritually chanting the names of the names of beautiful, male Greek gods and heroes such as Atys (the lover of the hermaphroditic deity Agdistis), Hylas (one of Hercules' male lovers), and, once again, Dionysus (CF 4.145). And in "The Thing on the Doorstep," Edward Derby learns that his new wife's body is possessed by the spirit of her deceased father, a powerful warlock, who plans to control Derby's body next. The relationship between Derby and his possessed wife can be described as both heterosexual and homosexual, and queer desires and gender identity are dominant themes in the story.

These homoerotic elements are clearly present in some of Lovecraft's fiction, but it is difficult to determine why Lovecraft incorporated them and how they reflect his own personal feelings and desires. Was he terrified of those naked sailors in the swamp, or did he want to join their celebration? There has long been speculation about Lovecraft's sexuality, much of it based on his apparent lack of interest in heterosexual sex. Famously, Lovecraft's wife Sonia Greene told August Derleth that she always had to initiate sex, and that "Howard was entirely adequate sexually, but he always approached sex as if he did not quite like it" (de Camp 194). This has led to speculation that Lovecraft may have been gay and closeted. Other factors contributing to this theory are the relative lack of female characters in his stories, the various homoerotic themes in his work, and Lovecraft's very close friendships with gay men such as Samuel Loveman and R. H. Barlow. L. Sprague de Camp's *Lovecraft: A Biography* (1975) and Bobby Derie's *Sex and the Cthulhu Mythos* (2014) both address this issue and argue that Lovecraft was not actively gay, but more likely had a low sex drive (or was perhaps asexual, to use a more contemporary term). Whatever Lovecraft's sexual orientation was, there is simply no evidence that he had sexual relationships with other men.

Lovecraft claimed he did not learn about homosexuality until he was more than thirty years old, and he expressed negative opinions of homosexuality and queer men several times. In various letters he denounced it as "naturally (physically & instinctively, not merely 'morally' or aesthetically) repugnant" (quoted in Derie 41), and wondered after meeting the gay composer Gordon Hatfield whether he should "kiss it or kill it!" (Derie 41), "it" referring to Hatfield. But even that choice between kissing and killing, between pleasure and death, displays a certain ambiguity about homosexuality. Kissing would not even be an option if Lovecraft were completely disgusted by homosexuality.

The "kiss it or kill it" line was probably just intended as a homophobic joke by Lovecraft, but the phrase's ambiguity is reflected in his fiction. The homoerotic sailors discussed in this paper are figures of both pleasure and terror. The handsome young sailor in "The Temple" is a representative of the homoerotic masculine beauty of the classical world, and also an implacable agent of divine vengeance. The naked orgiastic sailors in "The Call of Cthulhu" enjoy an enviable moral and sexual freedom, yet that freedom involves sacrifices to a terrifying god and a promised future violent apocalypse. Even the cozy and romantic male domesticity of "The Strange High House in the Mist" carries the risk of bringing the ancient gods back to Earth. In all these stories, men are initiated into a great mystery that may be pleasurable, or deadly, or both.

A reader can have multiple reactions to these sailors, including fear, attraction, and even identifying with them. A reader might have all these reactions at once, and perhaps Lovecraft did as well. It is not clear what these sailors meant to him. The whole of Lovecraft's fiction is queer and ambiguous, "full of sights or sounds which paralysed my heroes' faculties and left them without courage, words, or associations to tell what they had experienced" (CF 2.397). Like the unimaginable horrors and indescribable monsters that reduce his narrators to madness, Lovecraft's queer sailors are difficult to characterize. We can glimpse their forms and find hints of their purpose, but their final meaning remains just beyond reach, like so much in Lovecraft's queer fictional universe.

Works Cited

Apollodorus and Hyginus. *Apollodorus' Library and Hyginus' Fabulae: Two Handbooks of Greek Mythology*. Tr. R. Scott Smith and Stephen M. Trzaskoma. Indianapolis: Hackett, 2007.

Bloch, Michael. *Closet Queens: Some 20th Century British Politicians*. London: Little Brown, 2015.

Callaghan, Gavin. *H. P. Lovecraft's Dark Arcadia: The Satire, Symbology and Contradiction*. Jefferson, NC: McFarland, 2013.

Chauncey, George. *Gay New York. Gender, Urban Culture, and the Making of the Gay Male World, 1890–1940*. New York: Basic Books, 1994.

Clark, Mollie. "'Queer' History: A History of Queer" (9 February 2021). *The National Archives Blog* (UK). blog.nationalarchives.gov.uk/queer-history-a-history-of-queer/

Danziger, Gustav Adolf. *In the Confessional and The Following*. New York: Western Authors' Publishing Association, 1893.

de Camp, L. Sprague. *Lovecraft: A Biography*. Garden City, NY: Doubleday, 1975.

Derie, Bobby. *Sex and the Cthulhu Mythos*. New York: Hippocampus Press, 2014.

Lovecraft, H. P. *The Call of Cthulhu and Other Weird Stories*. Ed. S. T. Joshi. New York: Penguin, 1999.

———. *The Dreams in the Witch House and Other Weird Stories*. Ed. S. T. Joshi. New York: Penguin, 2004.

Sumrall, Erica. "'His Active and Enthralled Assistant': Homoromanticism in the Works of H. P. Lovecraft." Presentation at NecronomiCon 2019, 23 August 2019, Providence, RI.

Appendix: Abstracts from The Fifth Biennial Dr. Henry Armitage Memorial Scholarship Symposium of New Weird Fiction and Lovecraft-Related Research Providence, RI, 19–21 August 2022

Dennis P. Quinn, Chair
Elena Tchougounova-Paulson,
Co-Editors of Lovecraftian Proceedings

David E. Ballew
Associate Professor of History Chowan University
"H. P. Lovecraft: Subversive Cults and Conspiracy in Weird Fiction"

In the postwar Red Scare from 1918 to 1920, Americans were obsessed with the subversive activities of leftist foreigners. Xenophobia blended with conservatism to heighten this concern. H. P. Lovecraft shared much of this conservative worldview and frequently expressed nativist and antiradical sentiments in his personal correspondence and in stories such as "The Street" and "The Terrible Old Man," as well as later, more mature writings.

A reading of these sources demonstrates the shift in Lovecraft's fiction toward the prominent use of subversive cults and conspiracy narratives, especially following his exposure to Margaret Murray's controversial *The Witch-Cult in Western Europe*, which appealed strongly to his interest in New England history and the Salem witch trials. His subsequent use of fictional cults dedicated to the revival of the "Old Ones" and global apocalypse provided Lovecraft with a creative way to emphasize the weird elements he hoped to achieve with his writing. Beginning with "The Horror at Red Hook" and "The Call of Cthulhu" the idea of secret cults intent on subverting the civilized order became a staple of "Lovecraftian" and weird fiction.

Lovecraft's treatment of subversive themes was rooted in his conservative worldview and too often found expression in ugly stereotypes of immigrants and racial minorities.

However, such elements are not inherently racist or even conservative. Modern weird and horror writers such as Ira Levin have used conspiracy and cult narratives creatively to explore cultural change and engage in valuable social criticism.

Michał Choiński
Associate Professor of American Studies at the Jagiellonian University
"Beyond Heaven and Hell: On H. P. Lovecraft's Grotesques"

The aim of the paper is to explore various images of the grotesque in H. P. Lovecraft's fiction and poetry. Drawing on the contrastive aesthetics of the grotesque proposed by Mikhail Bakhtin (the carnivalesque grotesque of merging bodies) and by Wolfgang Kayser (the grotesque as the alien, parasitic presence of the Other), I intend to demonstrate how Lovecraft employs the figures of the carnal interior and exterior to deconstruct the bodily decorum and to generate different effect of the uncanny in his representations of horror. Close readings of three examples of descriptions extracted from Lovecraft's fiction will allow the hearers to better understand the effects his words had on his readers, and to have a better insight into what t Philip John Thomson described as the "aggressive weapon" of the uncanny aesthetics.

Ian Fetters
Robert E. Kennedy Library, San Luis Obispo
"Undying Earth: Extinction Romances in the Age of Anthropocene"

As science advanced newly theorized relations of humanity to the nonhuman world at the *fin-de-siècle* and onward, successive generations of horror and science fiction writers have capitalized on the conundrum of human subjectivity arrayed against the vastness of deep time's glacial advance, their work often highlighting perceptions of humanity's physical and existential "stranding" in a system of inevitable and gradual decline. These texts belong to the genre tradition of *dying earth narratives*—fictionalized imaginings of humanity's place in a far future Earth environment, a world of upheaval where the sun has blinked out of existence and the wasted planet is populated by a range of hybridized beings, hypernatural phenomena, and occultic powers from some inexplicable beyond.

The extinction romance, an offshoot of the dying earth narrative, capitalizes on this horror in upheaval by pitting a lone protagonist against weird darkness of a world without humans in a futile effort to rescue the beloved. But the "apocalyptic quest" of the extinction romance is always-already doomed because the human species itself is doomed to annihilation. This type of tale, then, allows for readers to think the unthinkable: the eventual demise of culture, civilization, and the human species. By reading extinction romances, like William Hope Hodgson's 1912 epic *The Night Land* and a more contemporary example in Hideo Kojima's 2019 video game *Death Stranding*, in the context of the Anthropocene age, the geologic era of human influence on earth systems, the vast deep time chasm between the here and now and the millions of years off horrific futures envisioned in these tales closes considerably, bringing that existential horror into the present. In many ways, as demonstrated in close readings of the texts and real-world examples of the horror of the Anthropocene (nuclear waste, global pandemics, civilizational collapse, etc.), the end is already here; and like our far future compatriots in the fictional romances of human extinction, we are helpless to avert catastrophe—stranded, as we are, on an undying planet.

Sophie Violet Gilmore
Ph.D. candidate in Film and Visual Studies at Harvard University, and lecturer in the Harvard Extension School
"Faint Drumming on the Distant Hills: Lovecraft, Aotearoa New Zealand, and the Postcolonial Politics of 'The Call of Cthulhu'"

> "In less than a month I was in Dunedin; where, however, I found that little was known of the strange cult-members who had lingered in the old sea-taverns. Waterfront scum was far too common for special mention; though there was vague talk about one inland trip these mongrels had made, during which faint drumming and red flame were noted on the distant hills."
> —H. P. Lovecraft, "The Call of Cthulhu"

In this paper, I explore the implications of H. P. Lovecraft's use of Dunedin, New Zealand (Aotearoa) as the setting of the story's climactic encounter with the titular eldritch monstrosity, exploring how Cthulhu's association with the South Pacific can be interpreted in postcolonial terms. Dunedin (Ōtepoti) is my hometown, and because it was a quiet rural settlement in the year of the story's publication, located a staggering 9,000 miles away from Providence, Lovecraft's decision to locate the fictive lost city of R'lyeh of the coast of this remote southern enclave has persisted for me as one of the most perplexing mysteries of his fiction.

In the first part of my paper, I briefly address the question of how Lovecraft initially heard about Dunedin, arguing that details from the story demonstrate some specific familiarity with the location. I will submit the archivally drawn hypothesis that Lovecraft may have become familiar with the area through his long correspondence with the New Zealand short story writer Katherine Mansfield.

The second part of the paper draws the question of Lovecraft's association with Aotearoa into dialog with recent scholarly debate about Lovecraft's attitudes towards race, indigeneity, and cultural difference. At one level, it is possible to offer a straightforward interpretation of Lovecraft's imagining of Southern New Zealand as an apocalyptic space host to horrifying cult practitioners as further evidence of his supposedly white-supremacist leanings. However, I will argue that such a reading of "The Call of Cthulhu" demands refinement through by a closer (and more culturally specific) inspection of thematic and descriptive elements of the story. Far from being merely an incidental choice of setting, I will argue that the spatial association Lovecraft forges between Cthulhu and Aotearoa prompts us to discern compelling allusions to Pacific culture at work in the story, more specifically to Māori mythology and customs (*tikanga*). Cthulhu himself bears striking resemblance to the mythological figure of the *Taniwha*, a tentacular, water-dwelling deity often depicted as predatory towards humans. In a similar way, the conceptualization of R'lyeh as an ancient city submerged beneath the Pacific Ocean bears some similarities to the central Māori legend that New Zealand's islands were fished out of the ocean by Maui. Depictions of these mythological traditions in Māori *tikanga* include the artform of carved sculpture (*toi whakairo*) and percussive musical performance (*kapa haka*), echoes of which can be detected in the rituals of the fictive Cthulhu cult.

My intention in the paper isn't to resolve the fraught status of "The Call of Cthulhu" as a text with colonialist leanings, nor is it to argue that Lovecraft intentionally reproduced Māori mythology in a disparaging way his work. Rather, through an examination of the extratextual circumstances and formal details of one part of the story, I hope to offer a more nuanced postcolonial interpretation that suggests another layer of cultural association at play in one of the most nebulous works of Lovecraft's mythos.

Edward Guimont
Assistant Professor of World History at
Bristol Community College in Fall River, Massachusetts
"The Colonialism of Cthulhu"

H. P. Lovecraft's life spanned an important period in European colonization, being born five years after the Berlin Conference inaugurated the Scramble for Africa, and dying at the start of the Italian occupation of Ethiopia which served as the height of European control of that continent. Lovecraft himself claimed that the question, "What of unknown Africa?," helped convince him to reject suicide in 1904.

Explicit depictions of European imperialism in Africa are rare in Lovecraft's work, most apparent through the role of the Congo in "The Picture in the House" and "Arthur Jermyn,'" Zimbabwe in "Medusa's Coil" and "The Outpost,'" and a variety of East African colonies in "Winged Death." But while outright appearances of the European colonial system are rare in Lovecraft's works, it does not mean its influence is absent. Indeed, the colonization of Earth by alien entities seeking resources (Mi-go), refuge (the Great Race), religious converts (Cthulhu), and settler territory (Elder Things), the core justifications used by Europeans in Africa, can be found across Lovecraft's work.

The way in which Lovecraft's aliens influenced the neocolonialist 'ancient alien' trope has been well documented, particularly by Jason Colavito. But there are subtler ways in which Lovecraft's worldview, both fictional and in his letters, was influenced by European colonization of Africa. This presentation will explore the ways in which settler colonial mythologies of African history influenced Lovecraft's extraterrestrial mythologies; how racial categorizations developed by the European colonial project influenced not only Lovecraft's notions of miscegenation, but his views on the relative habitability of different planets for their respective denizens; and the trope of exploration, particularly with scientific justification, resulted in Miskatonic University symbolizing an imperial metropole and its faculty as metaphors for colonialists engaged in civilizing missions and territorial conquests.

Ray Huling
Ph.D. candidate in the Department of Communication at the University of Massachusetts–Amherst
"Lovecraftian Ecology: Ernst Haeckel's Jellyfish Brides and Lovecraft's Alienworld Homesteads"

In *The Anthropocene as a Geological Time Unit* (2019), members of the Anthropocene Working Group, all serious scientists devoting themselves to the most consequential problems, make a point of rejecting the "Cthulhucene" as a name for the troubled age in which we find ourselves. The conclusion of *The Empty Sea*, a 2021 report to the Club of Rome, one of the most influential sustainability organizations, is titled "The Horror that Came to Sarnath." What is going on here? In a way, nothing new: Lovecraft's work has always had to do with ecology, not only because it communicates the experience of reckoning with how science brings us close to what is alien, but because Lovecraft was deeply influenced by the art and science of Ernst Haeckel, who coined the word "ecology". In another way, it is exciting and important that Lovecraftian thought has newly entered the ecological parlance of our times. This paper has two goals: first, to build upon scholarly work on the influence of Haeckel on Lovecraft, of which there are recent developments; second, to present a Haeckelized Lovecraftian ecology as useful for current debates in sustainability. Both Haeckel and Lovecraft crossed the proper boundaries of ecological thought: Haeckel, a widower, mystically communed with his dead wife through jellyfish; Lovecraft, a white supremacist, carried his horror for alien life into his feelings for people; and both Haeckel and Lovecraft perverted their ecology with racism. These excesses show important boundaries for ecological consciousness. By sketching the shape of Haeckel's and Lovecraft's ecological experiences, I offer a viewpoint that ecologically-minded scholars, scientists, and activists might consider in their pursuit of sustainability, one that reckons with the emotional depth and unequal consequences of a threatening and threatened human ecology.

Joshua D. King, M.D.
Assistant Professor of Medicine and Pharmacy
Medical Director, Maryland Poison Center
"Poisoning and Weird Fiction: Evolution from Before Lovecraft through the Modern Era"

Poisoning is a commonly used device in literature, both in the overt and metaphorical sense. In mystery or crime fiction, poisoning is a frequent means of murder; in other forms of fiction, however, the concept of spiritual or mental poisonings takes on added significance as agents of irreversible change. Lovecraftian and other forms of weird fiction periodically exhibit poisons with overlapping significance; the most notable example in Lovecraft's own work is the poisoning of the landscape, then the bodies, and finally the humanity of the Gardner family in "The Colour out of Space." It should come as no surprise that poisoning outside of the realm of fiction is generally quite different from poisoning in actuality. Historically, the concept of poisoning in the medical context has evolved substantially over time; conditions we now recognize as infectious diseases were encompassed within the category of poisons. Similarly, death by poisoning and public concerns over toxicity have evolved substantially. In Lovecraft's day, deaths due to strychnine and other dangerous medical "tonics" were not uncommon, while today we are plagued with deaths from opioids, concerned with toxicity from environmental chemicals, and have fundamental differences in the evaluation of drugs and toxins in human life. These shifts in our relationship with poisoning have fundamentally altered its role in weird fiction. This session aims to explore the similarities and differences between poisons in weird fiction and poisoning, and to elaborate on the changing role of poisoning in fiction from early examples through the modern era. The presenter aims to use the lens of experience gained by evaluation and treatment of poisoned patients to inform the session.

Alexander Lee
Independent Researcher
"Fate Is Cruel and Mankind Pitiable: Metaphysical Pessimism
and the Architecture of Weird Worlds"

Though often overlooked today, the works of Arthur Schopenhauer are important for introducing both metaphysical pessimism and, more generally, serious readings of Eastern thought to the Western philosophical canon. This study seeks to show how these insights—along with many others—can be applied to world building in weird fiction. In particular, the inherently evil character of Schopenhauer's Universal Will and his conception of the natural world as inherently carnivorous are studied next to his influence on modern Western understandings of paganism and Eastern religion. This, held up against the examination of his influence on contemporaries like Goethe, Hoffman and Eichendorff, and application of his philosophical system to the cosmologies of later writers like H. P. Lovecraft, Ramsey Campbell, and Laird Barron, will show how Schopenhauerian thought can be used as an incredibly sharp tool for both critics and creators of the weird alike.

Fred S. Lubnow, Ph.D.
Senior Technical Director of Ecological Services at Princeton Hydro, LLC
Illustrations Provided by Steve Maschuck
"Kenneth Sterling and Beyond the Walls of Eryx"

While Kenneth Sterling wrote several weird tales, he is best known for collaborating with H. P. Lovecraft on the story "In the Walls of Eryx." Even before the Sterling family moved from New York to Providence, Kenneth had a strong interest in both science and weird fiction. Sterling had several conversations with Lovecraft and was particularly interested in interplanetary travel. As a mentor to Sterling, Lovecraft had a positive influence on young Sterling and told him he had a future in biological research. Lovecraft was indeed correct; Sterling would go on to become one of the top physicians and medical researchers in the field of endocrinology. In fact, Sterling was one of the first scientists to use radioactive iodine to treat thyroid diseases. This presentation will discuss the relative contributions Lovecraft and Serling made on the development of "In the Walls of Eryx," the conservations the two had and Sterling's thoughts on Lovecraft, and a review of Sterling's life and career as a doctor and medical researcher.

Byron Nakamura
Department of History, Southern Connecticut State University
"The Classical Stain: Lovecraft's Racism and Greco-Roman Antiquity"

Scholars have documented and examined H. P. Lovecraft's racial views expressed throughout his published work, literary ephemera, and vast correspondence. What has been overlooked is the direct influence of the Classics on Lovecraft's racism and xenophobia. We know that Greco-Roman culture and history held sway over him from an early age and continued to be important to him throughout his adult life. Through an analysis of Lovecraft's personal letters, this essay will argue that from early on classical literature proved seminal in establishing Lovecraft's concepts of race and racial hierarchies. For Lovecraft, the ancient past provided trenchant object lessons that aligned with his own xenophobic fears and ideas of miscegenation. Lovecraft's often references, for instance, the work of the Roman poet Juvenal, who writes of how the city of Rome had been defiled by the influx of foreigners from Asia Minor, Egypt, and realms beyond the Tigris. This mirrored Lovecraft's own attitudes towards the large immigrant population he encountered while living in New York City. Also, the decline of the Roman Empire looms large as a resonant theme in Lovecraft's correspondence, and paralleled the writer's own concerns about the decline of western civilization due to race-mixing of "good Anglo stock" with dilute eastern blood. And finally, Lovecraft's racial ideal takes the form of an imagined ancestor, a Romano-Celt, "where the two great streams— Roman & British—actually and concretely met & became one for a time" (*Letters to Elizabeth Toldridge and Anne Tillery Renshaw*, p. 31).

Troy Rondinone
Professor of History at Southern Connecticut State University
"What Lies Beneath:
Creature from the Black Lagoon and Lovecraftian Horror"

In 1954, movie audiences witnessed a new face in horror—the Gill Man. In *Creature of the Black Lagoon*, a beast from the remote reaches of the Amazon River surfaces to terrify a beautiful woman and an accompanying crew of scientists. The movie was a landmark, featuring cutting-edge underwater photography and great creature effects. It was later recognized to be the only classic Universal monster designed by a woman (Milicent Patrick). In this paper, I will use the Creature as a touchpoint for exploring deeper themes of Lovecraftian watery horror, in both film and fiction. I will include a discussion of sea monsters, hybrid humanity, monstrous gender, and "deviant" sexuality. The *Creature* series, "The Shadow over Innsmouth," "The Call of Cthulhu," and other horrors will be analyzed.

Christian Roy
Independent Scholar, Montreal
"A Single Tale of Two Cyclopean Cities?: Reading Lovecraft's Intertwined Narratives of Quebec City and Antarctica as a Polar Shift in Outlook"

Writing a draft of a guidebook matching excerpts of Lovecraft's *Description of the Town of Quebeck* to photographs of corresponding locations, I became aware of intimate ties between his longest piece of writing, and his longest, best fiction work, *At the Mountains of Madness*, conceived and executed simultaneously in 1930-31. The latter explicitly connects Antarctica's "great ice barrier" to "the rocky cliffs of Quebec," a geopolitical fault line in the North American colonial world central to Lovecraft's self-understanding, which he probed and explored with extravagant studiousness, echoed in the reconstruction of an ancient alien civilization from markings on the walls of another labyrinthine, Cyclopean city. The tourist trip and the imaginative journey both bear witness to an enlargement of the heart to encompass definitions of humanity straddling friend/enemy distinctions, extending sympathy past familiar comfort zones to the rival other as keeper of equally valid heritage. Resenting the French-Canadian presence in New England, Lovecraft came to respect the hereditary enemy in the old capital of New France as part of his own dreamlands, tinged with "cosmic fear." "After all, they were not evil things of their kind. They were the men of another age and another order of being." surviving against all odds in a "polar waste." Like Antarctica's "poor Old Ones," "they had not been savages": "what had they done that we would not have done in their place? God, what intelligence and persistence! . . . whatever they had been, they were men!" Sympathy for the "devil" overcame Lovecraft in Quebec, as a harbinger of the revised, appreciative views of alien and social others gradually to appear in his later writings. He already acquired there the "adventurousness to wonder about the unknown realm beyond those mysterious mountains," glimpsed in "the purple, mystical Laurentians" looming on Quebec's horizon like "an unknown planet['s]" rise.

Joseph Sherren
Independent Scholar,
University Administrator from the mid-Atlantic region
"Art and Horror: Art to Elicit Fear and Disgust from 'Pickman's Model'"

The dual effect of awe or fear is a powerful tool in an artist's kit. To some, the viewer is treated to an awesome vista in which they are situated on top of a roaring waterfall and that conveys the terrifying and overwhelming power of Nature. To others, as noted in "Pickman's Model," fear comes through depictions of gruesome realism. That realism can be based in history, can be connected to fervent religious belief, or, as Lovecraft has shown through his literary works, can be a blur between fiction and reality. Lovecraft, in expected fashion, toes the line between fiction and realism in drawing together well-known artists, some of his acquaintances, and his avatar in Pickman to depict and comment on the complex emotions of fear, awe, and disgust through visual arts. This is a brief and selective survey of art that establishes the vernacular of fear and disgust established within the Western canon the artist Pickman, as Lovecraft's avatar, refers back to and draws partial inspiration from. Elements of realism and an art model drawn from life inform Pickman's depiction as was common practice for many artists. For Goya, it was drawing from contemporaneous events to tie together complex emotions such as fear. Others literally drew from life and drew from death to depict their atmosphere and emotions. Lovecraft's writing of Pickman, using an established vocabulary of fear and disgust from the Western canon of art, relied on that semiotic structure and his own vernacular to create a horrifying depiction in "Pickman's Model."

Justin Sledge
Ph.D. in Philosophy and a DRS in Religious Studies
"Lovecraft's Occult Literary Landscape:
Mentioned Historical Works and the Grimoire Revival"

A ubiquitous trope in the writings of H. P. Lovecraft is the foreboding tome of horrible, lost wisdom. Of course, the dread *Necronomicon* comes immediately to mind, but other volumes, both imagined and real, populate Lovecraftian literature. In this presentation I explore (1) some of the real, historical volumes mentioned by Lovecraft and (2) try to reconstruct what Lovecraft might have known about historical volumes of sorcery. Does his name-dropping indicate actual familiarity with the volumes in question or are their ominous Latin titles invoked merely for their sinister, antiquarian flair? Further, Lovecraft lived during the great explosion of the occult-revival in which historical texts of sorcery were widely printed. Is there any evidence of his familiarity with the then recently published *Books of Abramelin* or the *Keys of Solomon?* In a way, this presentation will try to triangulate Lovecraft's tales within the world of historical occult literature.

Michael A. Torregrossa
Independent Scholar
"Cthulhu and the Comics?: Accessing Representations of
Lovecraft's Mythos in Comics and Comic Art"

According to a recent "Everything" search of the *Grand Comics Database*, there are nearly 900 comics and graphic novels, produced (in fifteen countries) from the 1940s to the present, inspired by or adapted from the works of H. P. Lovecraft. This is an immense corpus that remains largely unexplored by scholarship. My purpose in this presentation is twofold with both goals designed towards helping enthusiasts gain better access to these comics. Building upon Chris Murray and Kevin Corstorphine's previous survey of Lovecraftian comics, "Co(s)mic Horror" (2013), I will highlight some of the various approaches (including retellings, linked texts, recastings, and biographies) that creators of comics have used in adapting and appropriating the stories, characters and creatures, and themes of Lovecraft's stories as well as Lovecraft himself. As part of this larger discussion (and as a supplement to be provided to attendees), I also want to sketch out some of critical trends in studies of Lovecraft-themed comics to expand the listings in the *Bonn Online Bibliography of Comics Research*. Drawing upon this material will offer a second means of access to the corpus and address the ways scholars have connected to these comics and offered useful means to describe and discuss them.

Elena Tchougounova-Paulson
Independent Scholar, Cambridge
"The Mystery of the Threshold as a Parable of Horror in
Works of Leonid Andreyev and H. P. Lovecraft"

On 30 October 2013, the online version of the *Weird Fiction Review*, an annual periodical devoted to the study of weird and supernatural fiction (edited by S. T. Joshi at that time), published the first ever English translation of Leonid Andreyev's novella "He: An Unknown's Story" («Он: Рассказ неизвестного»), made by Vlad Zhenevsky. One of the weirdest stories of the Russian *fin de siècle* era had finally found its Western readers in the magazine, one of the main online outlets of modern Lovecraftiana. In some sense, two authors—Russian Modernist writer Leonid Andreyev and horror writer H. P. Lovecraft—met on the pages of the *Weird Fiction Review*.

But it was not the very first time this happened: it is a well-known fact that a copy of Andreyev's works, *The Seven That Were Hanged* and *The Red Laugh*, was found in HPL's library after his death and then listed as an item in the "Lovecraft's Library" catalogue by S. T. Joshi.

Leonid Andreyev came into the spotlight as an author of short stories with twisted endings and, later, plays: quite quickly it became apparent that his experimental fiction contained strong supernatural elements.

Both stories, featured in a book that belonged to Lovecraft, are considered to be Modernist masterpieces, structured as Symbolist novellas with a classical horror narrative; "He: An Unknown's Story" also matches this description. In our talk, we want to analyse and to deconstruct the possible intertextual connections ("mystery of hidden structures") between Andreyev's stories and H. P. Lovecraft's works, such as "The Lurking Fear," "The Dunwich Horror," and *The Lurker at the Threshold*, where "the threshold" has become a symbol of mysterious frontiers between worlds and a portal to the unknown.

Contributors

Robert Landau Ames is an independent scholar of Persian literature, Iranian history, and continental philosophy. He received his Ph.D. from Harvard's Department of Near Eastern Languages and Civilizations in May 2018 and has taught in that same department as well as NYU's Global Liberal Studies Program and at St. Francis College in Brooklyn. Rob published his first book, *The Many Faces of Iranian Modernity*, with Gorgias Press in 2021, and has published articles in Equinox's *Comparative Islamic Studies*, Brill's *Journal of Sufi Studies*, and elsewhere.

Benjamin Breyer received his Ph.D. from Columbia University in English and Comparative Literature. His research focuses on pulp-era science fiction and horror literature, and modern graphic novels. Currently he is working on a book-length study of noted artist Richard Corben's graphic novel adaptations of the works of H. P. Lovecraft, Clark Ashton Smith, and William Hope Hodgson. He is a lecturer at Barnard College in New York City, where he teaches courses in first-year composition, world literature, and comics and graphic novels.

Riley Chirrick is an independent scholar in the fields of queer theory, games, and Lovecraft studies. They hold a B.A. and MFA each in Creative Writing, and were awarded Brown University's S. T. Joshi Endowed Research Fellowship in 2020. They write science fiction and fantasy under the nom de plume of Rory August.

George Colclough, independent researcher, is a writer and a technical consultant on matters of East Asian small arms and military procurement. His research interests include the current affairs and history of East Asia, small arms and light weapons, and aerospace. He has produced original research for organisations such as Armament Research Services (ARES) and for publications such as *Aeroplane*. He is a qualified firearms instructor.

Kyle Gamache earned his Ph.D. in Education from the University of Rhode Island. He also holds a master's degree in Forensic Psychology from Roger Williams University and a graduate certificate in counseling from Rhode Island College. He is a lecturing professor of psychology at the Roger Williams University, where he teaches courses on general psychology, risk assessment, psychotherapy, and psychopathology. He is a Licensed Mental Health Counselor and psychotherapist, specializing clinical risk assessment. Dr. Gamache conducts research on mental health and forensic psychology, presenting his studies at national and international research conferences and publishing in academic journals, recently in the journal of *Applied Psychology in Criminal Justice*. His essay "The Ebb of Sanity: 'The Night Ocean' and Bipolar Disorder" appeared in *Lovecraftian Proceedings* 4. Gamache is from Rhode Island and has been interested in weird fiction since childhood, voraciously engaging with Lovecraft's works and home city ever since.

Lorin Geitner, B.A., M.L.I.S., M.Rel., J.D., Esq., is a scholar, professor, writer, and public speaker who focuses on interdisciplinary work involving his various fields of study, mostly addressing world religions through concepts and practices drawn from the law, and/or examining legal issues, practices, and cases that involve the practices of religion. Geitner lives in a century-old house, reputed to be haunted, along with his wife, Terri Kennedy, a proprietor of a gothic/industrial lifestyle store. They both enjoy horror fiction, including Lovecraft's, and have independently studied occult philosophy, rituals, and practices, on a scholarly (and/or *practical*) basis. Like Lovecraft, they share a fondness for cats but have never, to date, raised an eldritch abomination from beyond the stars (that they *know* of!).

Matthew Holder teaches composition and literature for St. John Vianney High School and Saint Louis University's Prison Program. He holds a Ph.D. in Literature from Saint Louis University. His academic essays appear in *ImageTexT: Interdisciplinary Comics Studies* and *Disability Studies Quarterly*, while his contemporary reviews can be found at *Strange Horizons*. His fiction appears in *Old Moon Quarterly*, and he published the novella *Hurled Headlong Flaming; or, The Bishop's Tale* through Spiral Tower Press. Holder lives in Fenton, Missouri, with his wife, Maggie, and their dog, Lily.

Daniel J. Holmes is a writer and educator based in Rhode Island. He is a graduate of Villanova and Salve Regina University, and currently teaches at the New England Institute of Technology. Holmes has coordinated the Digital Humanities Research Initiative since introducing it in the university's 2022 Research and Innovation Showcase. He has presented on the subject of Gothic and weird fiction at conferences of the Modern Language Association, International Gothic Association, and the Horror Writers Association. In addition to his academic work, Holmes writes for a number of periodicals (and has received awards for feature writing and foreign language journalism) and has recently taken to writing for the stage for a few local theatre companies.

N. R. Jenzen-Jones is an arms and munitions intelligence specialist, historian, and publisher. He is the editor of *Armax: The Journal of Contemporary Arms*, the director of Armament Research Services (ARES), and the founder of Helios House Press, publishers of the *Miskatonic Missives* series of Lovecraftian epistolary readers and the *Miskatonic Literary Society* series of gothic horror tales. He is the creative director for *Miskatonic Missives* and the editor of the forthcoming *Christmas with H. P. Lovecraft* anthology. Jenzen-Jones holds a Visiting Fellowship in the School of Law, Policing & Forensics at the University of Staffordshire and was awarded the Buffalo Bill Center of the West's 2022–23 Resident Fellowship. He is a fellow of the Royal Asiatic Society, a life member of the Ordnance Society and the H. P. Lovecraft Historical Society, and a member of numerous other learned societies and associations.

Peter Muise received a B.A. in anthropology from Bates College in 1989, and a Master's in the same field from Brandeis in 1995. He is the author of *Legends and Lore of the North Shore* (History Press, 2014) and *Witches and Warlocks of Massachusetts* (Globe Pequot, 2021). He blogs about New England folklore at newenglandfolklore.blogspot.com.

Professionally, **Heather Miller** is a medical writer for the National Institutes of Health in Washington, D.C., where she works in oncology. In the world of Lovecraft, her book *Ripples from Carcosa: H. P. Lovecraft, Haunted Landscapes, and* True Detective was published by Hippocampus Press in 2024. She has a master's degree from the University of Southern Mississippi, is A.B.D. in technical communications at Louisiana State University, and has been a regular Armitage Symposium presenter since 2015. In addition, she is a tabletop role-playing game player, writer, and editor, having played in several actual-play games on YouTube for Into the Darkness and Miskatonic Playhouse. She is a wine enthusiast, holding a Level 2 Award with Merit through the Wine and Spirits Education Trust, and is a trustee for the Mensa International Charitable Foundation.

Zac Rutledge explores connections between disparate authors and topics. He enjoys tracing the ways in which themes and creative approaches travel through time and place from one text and author to the next. For this purpose, he considers a variety of genres including Victorian literature and twentieth-century works of weird fiction, gothic, and American realistic fiction. Some of the topics that interest him are psychogeography, the occult, and the influence of science and mathematics on literature. He is currently focused on a project that identifies common threads between psychogeographic authors and other writers not traditionally considered of that genre. He has an MFA from Goddard College and teaches at Peninsula College in Port Angeles, Washington.

Michelle Ann Saavedra is a lecturer, researcher, and esteemed Suffolk County Community College faculty member of English and the Educational Opportunity Program. Her ENG 102 Introduction to Literature course holds the motif of horror and features works of H. P. Lovecraft. She graduated with her B.A. in English, Speech Communication, and Journalism New Media Studies from St. Joseph's University in 2015 and her M.A. in English from Long Island University in 2017. Saavedra has committed to serving on an Embedded Support Committee. She has participated in lectures on supernatural horror literature, weird fiction, and cosmic horror, presenting extensively on "The Call of Cthulhu." Continuing her passions regarding "The Call of Cthulhu," her research explores connections to rhetorical theory.

Joshua Shockley IV is a Master's student and adjunct instructor at Old Dominion University in Norfolk, Virginia, teaching both English and Game Studies. His graduate work involves how early twentieth-century writers, such as Lovecraft and Robert E. Howard, are being reinterpreted in current entertainment media (such as movies, shows, video games). His side research includes the nineteenth-century occult revival, late nineteenth- and early twentieth-century esotericism, and how both of these have influenced modern occult culture. He hopes someday to be regarded as that strange scholar whose knowledge will become vital in Act 3.

Hans-Christian Vortisch is an independent German researcher specializing in firearms and their use in the interwar period, firearms used by criminals, and tracking official inventories. He holds a Master's degree in English and Scandinavian Studies from the Freie Universität in Berlin. Vortisch has written a number of articles and books for the tabletop role-playing game *Call of Cthulhu*, including three volumes in the *Investigator Weapons* series by Sixtystone Press. He is currently working to trace all submachine gun use by American criminals in the years between 1921 and 1939.

Nathaniel R. Wallace is an independent scholar and resident of Athens, Ohio, where he lives with his wife and son. He holds a Master's degree in Political Science with a focus on International Relations and a Ph.D. in Interdisciplinary Arts with a focus on the visual arts and film, both of which he attained from Ohio University. His dissertation "H. P. Lovecraft's Literary 'Supernatural Horror' in Visual Culture," available on OHIOLink, focuses on formal elements of visual and cinematic adaptations of the weird author's work such as perspective, sequencing, visual storytelling, polyocularity and anti-human architecture. Wallace has been a presenter at the Armitage Symposium for the past four events and has made significant scholarly contributions to the field through essays published in *Lovecraftian Proceedings* 2, 3, and 4, as well as in *The Medial Afterlives of H. P. Lovecraft: Comic, Film, Podcast, TV, Games*. His current research on weird fiction has centered on intellectual property, sound adaptations and self-radicalizing texts.

Nicolette A. Williams is completing her final year as a Ph.D. candidate in Gothic Literature at the University of Stirling. She holds an Associate in Arts from Northern Essex Community College, a B.A. in English Literature from Westfield State College, and a Master of Letters in The Gothic Imagination from the University of Stirling. Williams's current research investigates the cultural and thanatological implications of depictions of death and necrophilic desecrations of the corpse within twentieth-century American Gothic literature, focusing on works by Lovecraft, Ray Bradbury, Harlan Ellison, and Stephen King, among others. Her research interests also include the grotesque, necromancy, cannibalism, the undead (especially ghouls!), dark tourism, the history of burial practices, folklore and fairy tales, Disney, and fanfiction.

Index

Adler, Clement 152n3
Aggrawal, Anil 62
Ahmed, Sara 203n8
Alexandrian, Sarane 271
Alien Phenomenology (Bogost) 86, 89
All the Colors of the Dark (film) 157
Allgood, William 122
Alone in the Dark (video game) 173-74, 179
Amazing Stories 22
American Rifleman 136
American Songwriter 220
Ames, Robert Landau 16
Amnesia: The Dark Descent (video game) 177-78
Amulet of Pascal, The (Lélut) 234
Andreyev, Leonid 304-5
Anthropocene as a Geological Time Unit, The (Anthropocene Working Group) 298
Apocryphon of John 269
Appleton, Jay 175-76
Aquino, Michael 9
Aristotle 228-29
Arnold, H. F. 151
Asexual Visibility and Education Network (AVEN) 205, 207, 212
Ashley, Mike 43, 48n11
"At Providence in 1918" (Kleiner) 15n5
At the Mountains of Madness 14n2, 16, 21-35, 36, 172, 255, 257, 267, 302
Atlantis 277
Authentic Fakes (Chidester) 267
"Automatic Executioner, The" (de Castro) 289
Automatic Pistols (Pollard) 128

Bad Religion 220
Bakhtin, Mikhail 294
Bannon, Steve 97
Barlow, R. H. 124, 127, 204n10, 213
Bataille, Georges 98, 106-7, 113
Bateson, Gregory 47
Battle, Mike 156
Baudelaire, Charles 63
Bazerman, Charles 29, 31, 32, 33
"Beast in the Cave, The" 128, 129
Ballew, David E. 293-94
Bergson, Henri 98
Betting, Fred 150-51
"Beyond the Wall of Sleep" 271n10
Bienvenido, Héctor 181-82
Bierce, Ambrose 17, 146, 149, 152-54, 155, 156
"Big Two-Hearted River" (Hemingway) 38-40
BioShock Infinite (video game) 196-97
Birth of Tragedy, The (Nietzsche) 107, 284
Bitcoin 109-11
Bitzer, Lloyd 94
"Black Cat, The" (Poe) 232
Black Flag 216n1, 219n4, 220
Blackwood, Algernon 16, 17, 36-55, 151
Blavatsky, Helena P. 73, 105
Blish, James 151
Blood Meridian (McCarthy) 17, 247-65
Bloom, Harold 260
Blumlein, Alan 152n3
Bogost, Ian 86-87, 89-90
Books of Abramelin 303
Bradway, Tyler 202, 203
Breyer, Benjamin 16
Brown, Bill 171

313

314   Index

Brown University 14, 15, 237
Brundage, Margaret 272-73
Burke, Edmund 76, 148-49
Burleson, Donald R. 251, 256, 259
Burroughs, William 102-5
Burton, Robert 230
Byrd, Richard E. 132
Byron, George Gordon, Lord 231-32
Byzantine Generals Problem 109, 111

Call of Cthulhu (role-playing game) 17, 78, 170, 187, 190
Call of Cthulhu (video game) 177, 187, 188, 189, 190, 193-96, 198-99
"Call of Cthulhu, The" 10, 14, 16, 18, 71-95, 101-2, 105, 106, 107, 111, 113, 127, 170, 175, 182, 237, 241-42, 253, 276, 279-85, 286, 287, 288, 295-96, 301
Callaghan, Gavin 63, 261-62, 278
Camara, Anthony 51-52
Can Such Things Be? (Bierce) 152
Case of Charles Dexter Ward, The 127, 128, 135, 139, 170
Catren, Gabriel 101
"Celephaïs" 154
Chaplin, Charlie 220n6
"Charles Ashmore's Trail" (Bierce) 152n3
Chauncey, George 282-83
Chidester, David 267
Childe Harold's Pilgrimage (Byron) 231
Chirrick, Riley 17
Choiński, Michał 294
Clarke, Arthur C. 267
Claudio, Stephanie 272
Colavito, Jason 297
Colclough, George 16
Cole, David R. 98
Collapse 100
"Colour out of Space, The" 16, 36, 38, 40-42, 43, 45, 60-61, 256, 299
Combs, Jeffrey 61
Conley, Greg 53
Conway, Steven 171
Corstophine, Kevin 304

Crane, Stephen 249, 250
Creature from the Black Lagoon (film) 301
"Crypto-Current" (Land) 108-10, 112, 113
Cthulhu 74-77, 79, 81, 82-84, 86, 89-94, 102, 106, 241-42, 280-81, 284, 286, 290, 293, 295-96
Cthulhu Mythos 9, 10, 15, 95, 76, 78-79, 165, 167, 168, 170, 172, 174, 178-79, 183, 190, 193, 194-95, 199, 238
Cultural Politics of Emotion, The (Ahmed) 203n8
Curse of the Crimson Altar (film) 157
"Curse of Yig, The" (Lovecraft-Bishop) 127, 132
Cybernetic Culture Research Unit (CCRU) 96-99, 100-106, 113

"Dagon" 169, 194, 279
Dagon (video game) 175-77
Danse Macabre (King) 243
Dark Enlightenment, The (Land) 97
Darwin, Charles 260
Darwin, George 26
Daugherty, Leo 248, 260
Davis, Sonia 203n7. *See also* Greene, Sonia H.
de Camp, L. Sprague 206
de Castro, Adolphe 289
De Rerum Natura (Lucretius) 269n5
De Vermis Mysteriis (Prinn) 174
Dean, Aria 97
Death Stranding (video game) 295
del Toro, Guillermo 181, 209
Deleuze, Gilles 97, 98, 100
Demon of Socrates, The (Lélut) 234
Derie, Bobby 201, 290
Derleth, August 204n10, 290
Description of the Town of Quebeck, A 301-2
Dickens, Charles 172
Digital Humanities Research Initiative (DHRI) 166, 183
Dinerstein, Ana Cecilia 99
Dionysus 278, 284-85, 286

"Disinterment, The" (Lovecraft-Rimel) 129
Dixon, Don 156
Don Juan (Byron) 231
Douglas, Lord Alfred 282
Downing, Lisa 67
Doyle, Peter 154
Dream-Quest of Unknown Kadath, The 11, 66, 286
"Dreams in the Witch House, The" 251, 256, 261
Duff, William 230
Dunsany, Lord 154, 236
"Dunwich Horror, The" 14, 128, 129, 132, 133, 135, 139, 140, 145, 170, 210, 254, 259, 305
Dunwich Horror, The (film) 157

Ecological Thought, The (Morton) 48
Eddy, C. M., Jr. 56
Edmondson, Bill 155-56
1844; or, The Power of the "S.F." (English) 233
Eisend, Martin 159
Elagabalus (Emperor of Rome) 63
"Electric Executioner, The" (Lovecraft-de Castro) 129, 130, 289
"Eleonora" (Poe) 233
Emrys, Ruthanna 211
Empty House and Other Ghost Stories, The (Blackwood) 43
Empty Sea, The 298
"Endless Bacchanal" (Quinn) 10
English, Thomas Dunn 233
Epicureanism 269, 270-71
Escher, MC 181
Eternal Darkness: Sanity's Return (video game) 170-71
Eugene Onegin (Pushkin) 231
Everett, Anna 189
Everts, R. Alain 202n7, 207
Experimental Phenomenology (Ihde) 82
Eye of Kadath (video game) 172-73

"Facts concerning the Late Arthur Jermyn and His Family" 191, 209, 297

Fairbairn, William 136-37
"Fall of the House of Usher, The" (Poe) 150-51
"Familiar, The" (Le Fanu) 147
Farrow, Edward 138
Faulkner, William 56
"Festival" 257
Fetters, Ian 294-95
Ficino, Marsilio 229
Finbow, Steve 62
Fisher, Osmond 26
Fleurs du mal, Les (Baudelaire) 63
Frankel, Henry 27
Frankenstein (Shelley) 177, 231
Freud, Sigmund 235
"From Beyond" 129, 140, 223
Frye, Steven 258-59, 262

Gale, David 61
Gamache, Kyle 17
Gay New York (Chauncey) 282-83
Geitner, Lorin 17
Gernsback, Hugo 22
"Gesang der Jünglinge" (Stockhausen) 156
"Ghost-Eater, The" (Lovecraft-Eddy) 128-29, 131, 135, 137
"Ghost Lemurs of Madagascar, The" (Burroughs) 102, 103-5
Ghost of a Chance, The (CCRU) 104
Gibbs, Tony 153, 159
Gildea, Florence 100
Gilmore, Sophie Violet 295-96
Gnosticism 269, 271
Golden Dawn, Hermetic Order of the 47n8
Goodman, Steve 156
Gordon, Stuart 61
Goya y Lucientes, Francisco 238, 303
Graffin, Greg 220
Graham, S. Scott 87, 89
"Great God Pan, The" (Machen) 36, 151
Greenblatt, Stephen 269n5
Greene, Shane 217

316 Index

Greene, Sonia H. 205-7, 213, 290. See also Davis, Sonia
Griswold, Rufus Wilmot 233
Gross, Alan 32
Guattari, Félix 98
Guimont, Edward 24, 297
Gunn, Joshua 71-73, 74-75, 76, 78-79

H. P. Lovecraft: The Decline of the West (Joshi) 248, 278
H. P. Lovecraft Centennial Conference 15, 206
Haeckel, Ernst 298
Hamlet (Shakespeare) 218-19
Harman, Graham 75, 81, 88-89, 100
Harmon, Joseph 32
Hatfield, Gordon 290
"Haunter of the Dark, The" 238, 250, 258
Hawranke, Thomas 166-67
Hayim, Etz 154
He, Craig 160
"He: An Unknown Story" (Andreyev) 304
Heidegger, Martin 81, 82, 84, 88-89
Hemingway, Ernest 38-40, 45-46
Henderson, Dylan 249
"Herbert West—Reanimator" 16, 56, 57, 58-65, 66, 67-68, 129-30, 137, 138-39, 140, 177, 288
Heston, Charlton 197
Histoire de la philosophie occulte (Alexandrian) 271
"History of the 'Necronomicon'" 170
Hobbs, Niels 18
Hodgson, William Hope 295
Holder, Matthew 16
Holmes, Daniel J. 17
Homer 150
Hopkins-Drewer, Cecelia 257
Horace (Q. Horatius Flaccus) 229
"Horror at Red Hook, The" 191, 210-11, 271, 293
"Horror in the Museum, The" (Lovecraft-Heald) 128, 140

"Hound, The" 16, 56, 62, 65-69, 129, 238, 288, 289
Howarth, Alan 160
Huling, Ray 298
Husserl, Edmund 83, 84
Hussey, Derrick 7, 11, 18
"Hypnos" 239, 288-89

Idhe, Don 82
In Our Time (Hemingway) 40
"In the Walls of Eryx" (Lovecraft-Sterling) 127, 300
"Incense of Abomination" (Quinn) 272
Inflammable Material (Stiff Little Fingers) 220
International Situationists 217
Inventing the Future (Srnicek-Williams) 99-100

Jameson, Frederic 37n2
Jenzen-Jones, N. R. 16
"Jest of Warburg Tantavul, The" (Quinn) 272
Joly, John 23, 25, 26-28, 30, 33
Joshi, S. T. 10, 15, 18, 21, 23, 46-47, 64, 68, 118, 123, 138, 188, 196, 212, 217, 248, 279, 284, 304
Juvenal (D. Junius Juvenalis) 301

Kant, Immanuel 98, 100, 109-10
Kayser, Wolfgang 294
Keys of Solomon 303
King, Joshua D. 298-99
King, Stephen 181, 243
Kircher, Athanasius 148
Klinger, Leslie S. 262
Kojima, Hideo 181, 295
Kokot, Joanna 50n13, 51
Kolozova, Katerine 98
Krauss, Lawrence 157
Ku Klux Klan 194
Kuttner, Henry 149n2

Laderman, Gary 57-58
Lakish, Resh 154n5
Land, Nick 16, 96-115
Langer, Lawrence L. 59

"Last Test, The" (Lovecraft-de Castro) 127, 128, 129
Latour, Bruno 37n2, 52-53, 81, 86
LaVey, Anton 9
LaVine, Morgana 202n5
Lawrence, T. E. 132
Le Fanu, J. Sheridan 147
Led Zeppelin 156, 160
Lee, Alexander 299-300
Legend of Zelda, The 170
Legman, Gershon 283
Leiber, Fritz 21, 219n3
Lélut, Louis-Francisque 234
"Lemurian Time War" (CCRU) 101, 102-4
Lévi, Eliphas 72
Levin, Ira 294
Lévy, Maurice 257, 259
Lewis, C. S. 172
Listener and Other Stories, The (Blackwood) 43
"Literary Copernicus, A" (Leiber) 21
"Literary Nightmare, A" (Twain) 149n2
"Little Girl Lost" (Matheson) 154-60
Livy (T. Livius) 10
Lombroso, Cesare 234
Long, Frank Belknap 30, 78, 206
Lovecraft, H. P.: and colonialism, 295-97; and comic books, 303-4; and continental drift theory, 21-28, 30; and cosmic horror, 37, 40-42, 249-51; and death, 56-69; and ecology, 298, 300-301; and firearms, 116-41; and ghouls, 66-67; and madness, 218-19, 227, 235-43; and occultism, 71-80, 303; and phenomenology, 82-84, 89-94; and Providence, R.I., 14-16; and punk rock, 216-25; and religion, 257-59, 266-67, 270-71; and science, 28-34; and sexuality, 201-14, 276-91; and video games, 165-83, 187-99; xenophobia of, 187-99, 293-94
Lovecraft, Sarah Susan Phillips 236
Lovecraft, Winfield Scott 236

Lovecraft Annual 10
Lovecraft Studies 14-15
"Loved Dead, The" (Lovecraft-Eddy) 56, 60
Loveman, Samuel 203n7, 204n10
Lubnow, Fred S. 300
Luckhurst, Roger 100
Lucretius (T. Lucretius Carus) 269n5
Lurker at the Threshold, The (Derleth) 305
"Lurking Fear, The" 128, 131-32, 135, 139, 140, 192, 289, 305

McCallum, E. L. 202, 203
McCarthy, Cormac 17, 247-65
MacCreagh, Gordon 132
McGee, American 180-81, 183
Machen, Arthur 36, 43, 151
Mafe, Diana 196-97
Man of Genius, The (Lombroso) 234
"Man Whom the Trees Loved, The" (Blackwood) 51n15
Mandal, Anthony 60
Manichaeism 269, 271
Mansfield, Katherine 296
Mariconda, Steven J. 259
Marx, Karl 108
Marxism 221
Matheson, Richard 154-55
Maudsley, Harold 344
"Medusa's Coil" (Lovecraft-Bishop) 131, 137, 140, 297
Menegaldo, Gilles 173
Menegus, Brian 179n5
Metamorphoses (Ovid) 150, 161
Miller, Heather 17
Miller, John MacNeill 45, 50
Miller, Michael D. 249
Milton, Franklin 155-56
Milton, John 172
Moby-Dick (Melville) 231
Moldbug, Mencius 97
Modern Occult Rhetoric (Gunn) 71-73
Moore, Alan 210n18
"More Light" (Blish) 151

Morton, Timothy 45n6, 46n7, 47, 48, 53
"Mound, The" (Lovecraft–Bishop) 129, 130, 135, 139, 212
Muise, Peter 18
Murray, Chris 304
Murray, Margaret A. 293
Murray, Will 262
"Music of Erich Zann, The" 239–40

Nagel, Thomas 84–86
Nakamura, Bryan 300–301
"Nameless City, The" 154, 170
Narrative of Arthur Gordon Pym, The (Poe) 34
Necronomicon (Alhazred) 14, 78, 79, 174, 303
Neimann, Paul 254
Nelson, Victoria 248, 254, 255
New York Times 24
Newell, Jonathan 36n1
Newman, Robert P. 27
Nguyen, Doyen 61
Nietzsche, Friedrich 98, 106, 107, 284
Night Land, The (Hodgson) 295
"Night Wire, The" (Arnold) 151
Nodens 286
Norris, Duncan 66
"Notes on Writing Weird Fiction" 127, 139
"Nothing But Gingerbread Left" (Kuttner) 149n2
Noys, Benjamin 99
"Nyarlathotep" (prose poem) 261, 262

Oakes, David A. 28, 29
Object Oriented Rhetoric 79–80, 81–82, 87
"Occurrence at Owl Creek Bridge, An" (Bierce) 149
O'Connell, Kevin 160
Odyssey (Homer) 150, 235
Ojeda, Alan 101
"Open Boat, The" (Crane) 249
Oreskes, Naomi 30–31
Origin of Continents and Oceans, The (Wegener) 23–25, 30, 32, 33, 34

"Origins of the Cthulhu Club" (CCRU) 96, 101-2
Orton, Vrest 133
O'Sullivan, Simon 99
Outer Limits, The (TV show) 146, 159–60
"Outpost, The" 297
"Outsider, The" 66, 209
Ovid (P. Ovidius Naso) 150, 161

P. T. (video game) 181–83
Partridge, Christopher 79
Pemmaraju, Gautam 154
Perton, Bernard 174
Petersen, Sandy 78
Phillips, Whipple Van Buren 118, 237
Phonosophia Anacamptica (Kircher) 148
"Pickman's Model" 66, 129, 137, 138, 139, 140, 223, 240, 302–3
"Picture in the House, The" 238–39, 297
Pillsworth, Anne M. 211
Pitts, Frederick Harry 99
Planet of the Apes (film) 197–98
Plant, Sadie 97
Plato 228
"Pledged to the Dead" (Quinn) 272
Pleromática (Catren) 101
Poe, Edgar Allan 17, 34, 94, 149, 150, 232–33, 236, 237, 241, 243
Pollard, Hugh 128
Poltergeist (film) 160
Price, E. Hoffmann 270n9
Price, Robert M. 204n11
Prince, John Dyneley 42
Providence (Moore) 210n18
Providence, R.I. 15–16
Providence Detective Agency 119
Przybylo, Ela 205, 207

Quake (video game) 179–81
Queensbury, Marquess of 282
Queer Child, The (Stockton) 202
Quinn, Dennis P. 18, 267
Quinn, Seabury 266, 267, 268n3, 271–74

Rais, Gilles de 107-8, 113
"Rats in the Walls, The" 170
Raynal, Frederick 174
Re-Animator (film) 61
Red Laugh, The (Andreyev) 304
Reddell, Trace 145-46, 159
"Reflections of Ghosts, The" (Thomas) 222-25
Reidy, Michael 32
Reiss, Benjamin 344
Resident Evil (video game) 173
Resnick, Phillip J. 62
Reznor, Trent 179
Rhetoric, Through Everyday Things (Graham) 87
Rhetorical Ontologies 82, 84, 86, 87, 92, 93-94
Rhode Island Journal of Astronomy 120, 125
Rise of the Planet of the Apes (film) 197, 198
R'lyeh 76-77, 91, 92-93, 296
Rollins, Henry 220
Romero, John 179
Rondinone, Troy 301
"Rose for Emily, A" (Faulkner) 56
Roseberry, Earl of 282
Rosman, Jonathan P. 62
Roy, Christian 301-2
Rudiger, Daniel von 153
Ruiz, Marta 181-82
Rutledge, Zachary 17

Saavedra, Michelle 16
Sade, Marquis de 106
San Francisco Examiner 152
Satanic Rituals, The (LaVey) 9
Schafer, R. Murray 146, 148, 149-50, 153, 160, 161
Schlesinger, Judith 242
Schmidt, Susanne 159
Schopenhauer, Arthur 299-300
Schultz, David E. 11, 18, 23, 209n16
Secret Life of Puppets, The (Nelson) 248
Sedgwick, Eve Kosofsky 201n1
Sefel, John Michael 10-11

Sellar, Sam 98
Seneca the Younger (L. Annaeus Seneca) 228
Serling, Rod 154-55
Seven That Were Hanged, The (Andreyev) 304
Sex and the Cthulhu Mythos (Derie) 290
"Shadow out of Time, The" 14, 111, 250-51
"Shadow over Innsmouth, The" 128, 131, 135, 193, 194, 209n17, 252, 253, 256, 257-58, 259, 301
Shakespeare, William 269n7
Shelley, Mary 111
Shelley, Percy Bysshe 231, 232
Sherren, Joseph 302-3
Shockley, Joshua E. 17
"Shunned House, The" 135-36
Silent Hill (video game) 173, 181, 182
Silent Hills (video game) 181
Sinking City, The (video game) 17, 187, 188-89, 190-99
Sledge, Justin 303
Snyder, Delys W. 256
Snyder, Philip A. 256
Soundscape, The (Schafer) 146
Spider-Man: No Way Home (film) 160
Spielberg, Stephen 160
Srnicek, Nick 99-100
"Statement of Randolph Carter, The" 174-75, 180, 208n15, 290
Sterling, Kenneth 300
Stewart, Matthew 269n6
Stewart, Paul 155n7
Stiff Little Fingers 220
Stockhausen, Karlheinz 156
Stockton, Kathryn Bond 202
"Strange High House in the Mist, The" 276, 285-87, 288
Stranger Things (TV show) 160
Stratford, Tracy 155n6
"Street, The" 135, 293
"Supernatural Horror in Literature" 37, 235-36, 237, 273
Surface History of the Earth, The (Taylor) 27

Taylor, Frank Bursley 23, 25, 26–28, 30, 33
Tchougounova-Paulson, Elena 11, 304–5
"Tell-Tale Heart, The" (Poe) 149, 232
"Temple, The" 127, 128, 131, 276, 277–80, 281, 284, 285, 286, 288, 290
Terman, Lewis 234–35
"Terrible Old Man, The" 293
Tesla, Nicolai 262
Theberge, Paul 155
Theosophy 73, 105–6
"Thing on the Doorstep, The" 137, 140, 237, 241, 289
Thinking Sideways (McCallum-Bradway) 202
Thirst for Annihilation, The (Land) 106, 113
Thomas, Jeffrey 222–25
Thomson, Philip John 294
"Through the Gates of the Silver Key" (Lovecraft–Price) 270
Tides and Other Phenomena in the Solar System, The (Darwin) 26
Tolkien, J. R. R. 165n2, 199
Tomb and Other Tales, The 9
Toop, David 149
Torregrossa, Michael A. 303–4
Troy, Andy 60–61
Trump, Donald 97
Twain, Mark 149n2
Twilight Zone, The (TV show) 17, 146, 155

Van Gogh, Vincent 242
Verma, Neil 147
"Victim of Higher Space, A" (Blackwood) 151
Vortisch, Hans-Christian 16

Waddington, Keir 60
Wallace, Nathaniel R. 17
Wang, Yufeng 40

Wark, McKenzie 97
Watkins, Charlie 156
Watkins, S. 189
Wegener, Alfred 16, 22, 23–28, 30, 32, 33–34
Weird Fiction Review 304
Weird Realism (Harman) 75
Weird Tales 94, 151, 266, 267, 271, 277
Weise, René J. 257
Wells, H. G. 43
"Wendigo, The" (Blackwood) 43
"What Is It Like to Be a Bat?" (Nagel) 84, 86
"Whisperer in Darkness, The" 14, 127, 129, 132, 133, 138, 139, 140
"Whither?" (Bierce) 146, 152–54, 156
Whittington, William 157
"Whole Lotta Love" (Led Zeppelin) 156, 160
Wilde, Oscar 231, 236, 282, 283
Williams, Alex 99–100
Williams, Nicolette A. 16
Williams, Roda 155n6
"Willows, The" (Blackwood) 16, 36–55, 47n9
Wilson, Wilfred 47n9
"Winged Death" (Lovecraft–Heald) 297
Witch-Cult in Western Europe, The (Murray) 293
Wolanin, Tyler 112
Wolfe, Peter 155n7
Woodard, Ben 100
World Fantasy Convention 188
Worley, Matthew 217, 220

Yamaoka, Akira 181
Yeats, W. B. 43, 47n9
Yezidis 271
Yog-Sothoth 270

Zhenevsky, Vlad 304

www.ingramcontent.com/pod-product-compliance
Lightning Source LLC
Chambersburg PA
CBHW051037160426
43193CB00010B/979